PRA
BLOO
W9-CYU-408

"A terrific thriller in which Vaughn's personal and professional lives deftly intertwine . . . *Bloodstone* is a terrific, taut, thought-provoking thriller." —*Genre Go Round Reviews*

"The suspense never flags, resulting in rapid page-turning, and the author skillfully weaves together the multiple story threads into a satisfying whole." —*Bitten by Books*

"Fans of Holzner's other Deadtown novels will enjoy this solid yarn." —*Publishers Weekly*

"*Bloodstone* is the best Deadtown novel yet. Vicky's life and trials have been fascinating to date, but in this newest book, author Nancy Holzner takes it to a new level."
—*Romance Reviews Today*

"The latest and in my opinion the greatest Deadtown novel . . . If you haven't started this series, then you are missing out on one of the most original urban fantasy settings to date."
—*Bite Club*

"Make sure you reserve a place for Holzner's novels on your bookshelf." —*RT Book Reviews*

HELLFORGED

"*Deadtown* was good, but *Hellforged* is even better . . . The writing is airtight; her characters have been honed to an edge. There is comedy, drama, romance, and a whole lot of ass kicking. *Hellforged* is the total package." —*Fantasy Literature*

"The thrills are nonstop in Holzner's latest Deadtown novel as the action races from continent to continent and into the reaches of Hell itself. Even better than the first book; this series is becoming highly addictive!" —*RT Book Reviews*

continued . . .

"Gripping the reader from its highly entertaining opening scene, the terrific *Hellforged*, the second installment in the Deadtown series, maintains that hold until the very end . . . Holzner's expertise as a mystery author shines brightly throughout the narrative as she flawlessly connects threads of both the tale told in *Hellforged* and the overall story arc of the Deadtown series. This fabulous novel skillfully combines several distinct elements into a highly satisfying whole: action, adventure, suspense, Welsh mythology, humor, and pitch-perfect characters that live and breathe on the page . . . This excellent series belongs in the collections of all urban fantasy fans."

—*Bitten by Books*

"The demons Vicky chases in *Hellforged* are bigger, badder, and so much more fun. I love the unexpected twists and turns . . . I cannot wait to see what is in store for my new favorite demon hunter!"

—*Intense Whisper* . . .

"The second Deadtown novel is jam-packed with action. A quick and satisfying read, *Hellforged* will have readers on the edge of their seats for more. Vicky is a very likable and headstrong lead . . . A fun yet serious novel; fans of Laurell K. Hamilton, Rachel Caine, Kim Harrison, and Karen Chance are likely to enjoy this series."

—*Night Owl Reviews*

"Vicky is the kind of kick-butt heroine fantasy lovers can get behind—rough and tough, afraid to jump into the fight but too stubborn to stay out of it . . . Aided by a whole cast of interesting characters, including her aunt, Mab, who is a perfect mix of hard taskmaster and sweet and comforting aunt, Vicky and crew are ones you can't help but root for in the battle of good versus evil . . . *Hellforged* is a novel lovers of fantasy, urban fantasy, and paranormal fiction in general won't want to miss."

—*Romance Reviews Today*

DEADTOWN

"Fresh and funny, with a great new take on zombies."

—Karen Chance, *New York Times* bestselling author of *Hunt the Moon*

DARKLANDS

NANCY HOLZNER

ACE BOOKS, NEW YORK

THE BERKLEY PUBLISHING GROUP
Published by the Penguin Group
Penguin Group (USA) Inc.
375 Hudson Street, New York, New York 10014, USA

Penguin Group (Canada), 90 Eglinton Avenue East, Suite 700, Toronto, Ontario M4P 2Y3, Canada (a division of Pearson Penguin Canada Inc.) • Penguin Books Ltd., 80 Strand, London WC2R 0RL, England • Penguin Group Ireland, 25 St. Stephen's Green, Dublin 2, Ireland (a division of Penguin Books Ltd.) • Penguin Group (Australia), 250 Camberwell Road, Camberwell, Victoria 3124, Australia (a division of Pearson Australia Group Pty. Ltd.) • Penguin Books India Pvt. Ltd., 11 Community Centre, Panchsheel Park, New Delhi—110 017, India • Penguin Group (NZ), 67 Apollo Drive, Rosedale, Auckland 0632, New Zealand (a division of Pearson New Zealand Ltd.) • Penguin Books (South Africa) (Pty.) Ltd., 24 Sturdee Avenue, Rosebank, Johannesburg 2196, South Africa

Penguin Books Ltd., Registered Offices: 80 Strand, London WC2R 0RL, England

This is a work of fiction. Names, characters, places, and incidents either are the product of the author's imagination or are used fictitiously, and any resemblance to actual persons, living or dead, business establishments, events, or locales is entirely coincidental. The publisher does not have any control over and does not assume any responsibility for author or third-party websites or their content.

DARKLANDS

An Ace Book / published by arrangement with the author

PUBLISHING HISTORY
Ace mass-market edition / August 2012

Copyright © 2012 by Nancy Holzner.
Cover art by Don Sipley.

ISBN: 978-1-937007-70-6

ACE
Ace Books are published by The Berkley Publishing Group, a division of Penguin Group (USA) Inc., 375 Hudson Street, New York, New York 10014. ACE and the "A" design are trademarks of Penguin Group (USA) Inc.

PRINTED IN THE UNITED STATES OF AMERICA

10 9 8 7 6 5 4 3 2 1

ALWAYS LEARNING   **PEARSON**

To my friend Kathy Giacoletto and her daughter,
the one-and-only Maria

ACKNOWLEDGMENTS

My biggest thanks go to everyone who reads this series. Thank you so much for spending time in Vicky's world. I hope you're enjoying the ride!

Thanks, as always, to Cam Dufty for pulling my manuscript from the slush pile and giving me a chance. As long as Vicky keeps having adventures, I'll keep saying thank you.

My editor, Kat Sherbo, read the manuscript with conscientious care and attention. Kat has a keen sense of story and asks all the right questions. Her guidance greatly improved this book.

Many thanks to the professionals who helped to produce this book, including my agent, Gina Panettieri; cover artist Don Sipley; publicist Brady McReynolds; cover designer Edwin Tse; text designer Tiffany Estreicher; production editor Michelle Kasper; assistant production editor Andromeda Macri; copy editor Jessica McDonnell; and proofreader Dan Kaufman.

Writer friends are the best. Among the writers whose company I've enjoyed as I worked on this book are Jeanne Mackin (writers' happy hour was the greatest idea ever!), Nicola Morris (thanks for sharing my books), P. M. Carlson, Janis Kelly, Chris Moriarty, K. A. Laity (and her various alter egos), Deborah Blake, Keith Pyeatt, Christina Henry, Sean Cummings, Erin

Kellison, Wayne Simmons, Ann Rought, Emily Johnson, and Linda Welch.

Book bloggers work tirelessly to share their love of books with readers. Bloggers to whom I'm especially grateful include Roxanne Rhoads, Amber Chalmers, Carol Malcolm, Robin Kae, Larissa Benoliel, Pam (SpazP), Jen (Twimom), Sara M., and Sharon Stogner. You all rock!

I've got some wonderful friends, both online and off, and I want to express my appreciation to them. So thanks to Michelle Brandwein, Sydney Chase (who never fails to help me think more positively), Margaret Strother, Kathy Giacoletto, Carlos Thomas, Kaysi Peister (artist extraordinaire and mom to the adorable Cricket), Scott DeLugan, Jane Rogers, and Beq Vyper.

My family is wonderfully supportive and deserves mention: my daughter (and biggest cheerleader), Tamsen Conner; my parents, Harold and Lois Brown; my sisters, Laurel Nolet and Paula Kennedy (along with their terrific husbands); my nieces, Jessi Meagher (and family) and Patricia Kennedy; my nephew, Nate Nolet, and his wife, Julie. Also, my mother-in-law, who, I know, wishes I'd write a more peaceful and consensus-seeking heroine—maybe for the next series, Anne!

Finally, humongous thanks to my husband, Steven Holzner. You've helped my dreams come true in so many ways. Thank you for your unfailing love and support.

1

IF THERE'S ONE THING I HATE, IT'S SPEAKING IN FRONT OF A group. That's why my job is so perfect for me. No reports to give, no presentations to make. I go in, I kill the demons, and I get out. Simple.

So I wished somebody would explain to me what the hell I was doing sitting on a folding metal chair, facing a room of teenage zombies, their greenish faces attentive, as I wiped my sweaty palms on my jeans and waited for my turn to speak. When Tina, the zombie who'd briefly been my apprentice a few months back, asked me to speak to her class for Career Night, the answer had been easy.

"No."

"Why not?" she'd demanded, her bottom lip jutting out.

"You're not my apprentice anymore. You quit, remember? What would be the point of me talking to your classmates about a career that none of them will ever pursue? It would be a huge waste of everyone's time."

"But you *have* to."

I looked at her, trying to pick one of the several dozen reasons I *didn't* have to, just to get started.

"We've been working on our career projects all year," she

said. "When I dropped out of school to sing backup for Monster Paul, I was like, 'Yeah, whatever.' I mean, who thinks about some dumb school project on the road to fame? Then when I went back to classes, it was too late to start over with a new project. My portfolio, my poster, my final paper—it's all about demon slaying. If you don't come in and talk to my class, I'll fail the whole project."

I doubted that. What teacher would fail a student for being unable to cajole an adult into talking to the class? Yet Tina looked at me earnestly, her bloodred eyes wide. After Monster Paul's band broke up, she hadn't shown the slightest inclination to return to school until several encounters with my aunt, Mab, had changed her mind. Mab would be disappointed if Tina dropped out again. I could almost hear her now: "Surely, child, there must have been something you could have done to keep that young lady in school."

So here I sat, sweaty palms and all, waiting for my turn to speak. It was a typical school classroom: dingy walls, tile floor, a blackboard in the front. A bulletin board held a display about *Frankenstein*, which the class was reading for English, while career-related posters were taped to the walls and even to the big window at the back of the room. Tina's poster featured a hand-drawn depiction of a blonde zombie, dressed in black jeans and a pink jacket with sequins glued on, using a flaming sword to battle a skyscraper-sized demon. The ten students, all zombies, were squeezed into chair-desk combos, while their zombie teacher sat behind a big oak desk near the door.

Each speaker got ten minutes, including a few minutes for Q&A. Somehow I'd been appointed to go last. Lucky me. I tried to look like I was paying attention, although anxiety made it hard to focus on others' words. Even in my leather jacket I was shivering. I didn't know whether that was from nerves or from the fact that zombies don't feel the cold, so they don't bother to heat their buildings. Either way, I was giving new meaning to the phrase "cold sweat." Again, lucky me.

The first three zombie speakers were all manual laborers: one worked in construction, the other two hauled around boxes in a warehouse. Because of their super strength, zombies are in demand for that kind of work, and it's what most of the students in this classroom would eventually do for their jobs. All three speakers had brought props: a hard hat, a hand truck, pictures of a forklift. I, on the other hand, was completely propless, utterly bereft of the tools of my trade. I work with weapons, and the school board has a zero-tolerance policy on those. Tina had argued with me, but I'd be the one who had to explain to the Goon Squad why I'd shown up for Career Night armed to the teeth. No, thanks.

The current speaker—I didn't catch his first name, but I thought his last name was Blegen—was the short-order cook at Munchies, a popular snack shop that serves every kind of junk food a zombie could ever dream of. And that's *a lot* of junk food. Zombies are nonstop eating machines; Munchies's menu is the size of a small city's phone book. Blegen was discussing the challenges of his job.

"You know what's hardest?" he was saying. "Onion rings. Mmm, that smell. There's something about the combination of hot grease and onions . . ." He gazed skyward, his gray-green lips stretched taut in a grimacing smile, as though he were seeing a vision of onion rings at the pearly gates. "When I cook a batch of onion rings . . . man, it is just so easy to forget that I work in a restaurant and the food is for the *customers*. As soon as those rings come out of the deep fryer, I want to grab them by the handful and stuff the whole basket in my face."

He could do it, too. Zombies didn't feel heat, either. A little grease burn wouldn't bother one at all.

The class sat riveted, devouring his words like . . . well, like onion rings. My nerves kicked up a notch. Damn it, this guy should've gone last. The Munchies cook was going to be an impossible act to follow.

A tall, skinny boy with curly red hair raised his hand. "What about pizza?" he asked. "Have you ever made a pizza and then eaten it before the server could take it to a table?"

"Every night." An excited murmur ran around the room. "For some orders, like double sausage with green peppers and onions and extra cheese—that's my favorite—I've learned to make two pizzas at a time. That way, the waitress has a chance to grab the second while I'm scarfing down the first."

"Brilliant!" exclaimed the teacher. Mrs. McIntyre, a frizzy-haired zombie with wire-rimmed glasses, wiped her mouth with the back of her hand. She looked like she was considering a career change herself.

Blegen answered a few more questions, then passed out

buy-one-get-one-free coupons to the class. "I tried to bring our Munchies super-deluxe chip-and-dip platter to share with you guys, but I got hungry on the way over." The sigh of disappointment ran so deep that he handed out another round of coupons. Mrs. McIntyre got a couple extra.

The teacher clutched the coupons to her chest, then she looked at the clock and gasped. "Goodness, I'm afraid I let Mr. Blegen go over his allotted time by a few minutes," she said. I glanced at the clock, above the bulletin board to my right. Only five minutes left. Good. I'd get this over with and then get out of here. I wanted to hear the end-of-day bell every bit as much as I did back when I was in high school. "I do apologize, Ms. Vaughn," she went on. "Why don't we skip Tina's introduction and go straight into the details of . . . er, what is it that you do?"

"No fair!" Tina shouted before I could answer. She stood up. The rhinestones on her T-shirt, which outlined the Playboy bunny, sparkled under the classroom's fluorescent lights. "Everybody else got to introduce the speaker they invited. I made notes and everything!" She waved a sheet of paper at her teacher.

"We're running short on time now." The note of strained patience in Mrs. McIntyre's voice showed she'd had many dealings with Tina. "Sit down, please. You can hand in your notes to get credit for your introduction."

"This sucks," Tina muttered. But she plopped back into her seat.

And then it was my turn. I stood, not surprised that my knees felt a little shaky.

"Hi," I said. My voice was shaky, too. I cleared my throat, paused, then cleared it a second time. "Hi," I tried again. Better. "My name is Vicky Vaughn, and my job is a little different from the others you've been hearing about tonight. I'm Boston's only professional demon exterminator."

"Slayer!" Tina slapped both hands on her desk. "*Slay-er.* See, that's why I wanted to introduce you. When you say 'exterminator,' it sounds like you kill bugs and stuff. That's just gross. If you want to sound cool, you've got to call yourself a demon *slayer.*"

"Now, now," Mrs. McIntyre interrupted. "Let Ms. Vaughn talk about her job in her own way."

"Her own *lame* way."

"Tina!"

Their back-and-forth had taken up another minute. Just three minutes left before school ended for the night. Almost there.

"So. What my job is . . . I exterminate—or 'slay,' if you prefer—other people's personal demons. That's what I do for a living. There are many kinds of personal demons, but for the most part I deal with three main types. There are dream-demons, called Drudes, which invade people's dreams to cause nightmares. Drudes feed on fear; that's why they like to scare people." I twisted my mouth into a weak smile. "Fear, to a Drude, is kind of like onion rings to Mr. Blegen."

That got a laugh. Maybe I wasn't so bad at this.

"How do you kill a nightmare?" the red-haired boy asked.

"I don't kill the nightmare; I kill the Drudes that cause it. Once the Drudes are gone, the nightmares go away."

Tina bounced in her seat. "She's got this awesome machine that gets her inside people's dreams," she said. "I followed her into a guy's dreamscape once. It was *freaky*."

Right. She'd followed me, blasted a dream-image of the client's mother into oblivion, and then set his dreamscape on fire. "Freaky" didn't begin to cover it. But now wasn't the time to remind Tina of the havoc she'd caused. I still had two demons left to describe.

"The second kind of personal demon is called an Eidolon," I said. "A guilt-demon."

"So that kind feeds on guilt?" asked a girl in the second row.

"Exactly. When a person can't resolve guilty feelings, an Eidolon may appear to make things worse. When you've got an Eidolon, it feels like a giant maggot gnawing at your guts."

"Eww." The girl wrinkled her nose. "Tina, I thought you said she *didn't* kill bugs."

Tina rolled her eyes and sank in her chair. She looked like she wanted my presentation to be over almost as much as I did.

Only one minute left before the bell. I pressed on, speaking fast. "Harpies are the third kind of demon. Those are revenge-demons. Unlike Drudes and Eidolons, which are attracted by a person's emotions, Harpies must be conjured by a sorcerer. If you've got an enemy with some spare cash—well, a lot of spare cash—your enemy might pay a sorcerer to send some Harpies against you."

"What do they look like?"

Before I could answer, the bell rang. Students gathered up their books. It was over. I breathed a sigh of relief.

Bang! Glass shattered as something crashed through the window.

Kids screamed and crouched in their seats, covering their heads as the glass sprayed everywhere.

A large, feathered body hurtled into the classroom, clawed feet first. Huge talons, sharp as spikes, reached for me, aiming for my chest.

I dropped and rolled, and the Harpy hit the wall. It bounced off the blackboard and landed hard on the floor.

"Awesome!" Tina shouted. "You *did* bring a prop!" She ran to the front of the room.

"No, I . . ." My voice trailed off as I concentrated on the invader.

The Harpy shook itself and stood. I reached into my boot for a dagger. Nothing. That stupid zero-tolerance policy meant score zero for the demon slayer.

"Okay." Tina's voice took on a lecturing tone. "So, as you can see, a Harpy has the body of a large bird. Like a vulture—at least, it sort of reminds me of the vultures you see in cartoons."

The Harpy sprang back into the air to take another dive at me. On my knees now, I grabbed my folding metal chair and swung. That knocked the demon back, but it locked its talons around the chair and yanked it from my hands. Before I could react, it crumpled the chair into a ball of twisted metal and tossed it aside. The Harpy landed and, almost too fast to see, ran at me.

I shoved it hard in the chest. The Harpy whipped its head to the side, and its beak gouged a bite from my right arm. I pulled away before one of the snakes that hissed out from its scalp could latch on to my flesh. I sat, drew back both legs, and kicked. The Harpy took to the air, hovering near the ceiling and shrieking.

Tina raised her voice over the din. "As you can see, Harpies have Medusa heads, with snakes for hair and everything, except instead of mouths they have beaks." She paused. "Oh, crap. I shouldn't have said, 'As you can see.' Don't look at its face. Just like Medusa, it'll paralyze you with fear. If one of those snakes bites you, that paralyzes you, too. Oh." Another pause. "I guess I should've mentioned that part about not looking earlier." Her voice brightened. "Except this way I guess everyone will stay until the end of Vicky's demonstration. Sweet."

A quick glance around the classroom showed Tina's warning had come a bit late. All the students, plus the teacher, plus the career-day guests, were as immobile as lumps of rock. Except for mine and Tina's, everyone's eyes were fixed on the demon's head. Mrs. McIntyre stood beside her desk, her hands clutching her skirt, a statue of an anxious high school teacher.

I stood and grabbed her vacated chair and hoisted it. I poked at the air, keeping the chair between me and the Harpy like a lion tamer. I watched the Harpy's body, its great flapping wings, but avoided looking at its face.

"Harpies usually attack in threes," Tina was saying, "but I guess Vicky figured that would be overkill for a classroom demonstration. Also, it's really awesome that we can see this Harpy. I mean, okay, it's not all that awesome for those of you who are paralyzed right now. But Harpies usually stay in the demon plane, becoming visible only to the victim. When one's fully materialized like this, it means—" She turned to me. "Um, Vicky, how come we can all see it?"

The Harpy shrieked out its battle cry and dived at my head.

"Because it's trying to kill me!" I shouted, batting at the Harpy like it was an ugly, oversized piñata. The chair made contact, slamming the demon to the back of the room and out through the broken window. Its howls grew distant.

I stood, panting, still holding the chair.

"Yeah, that's what I thought," Tina said. "Just like when that crazy sorcerer dude sent all those Harpies to attack the Halloween parade. Everyone could see them because they were told to kill." She turned toward the broken window. "So is that it? The Harpy's gone? How come nobody's moving yet?"

Before I could answer, the Harpy blasted back into the classroom. Tina ducked, but it flashed past her. Once a Harpy locks on to its victim, it ignores everything else. And this one was sure as hell locked onto me.

I swung the chair again, but the demon swerved at the last minute and went around behind me. It landed on my shoulders. I wriggled them, trying to keep its talons from digging into my jacket. I dropped the chair and put both arms over my face, shielding it from the snakes' fangs. Then I reached back and got my right hand around one of its legs. I pulled hard and flung the demon away from me. It flew back up toward the ceiling.

Tina pinched her nose. "Oh, and in case you're wondering what that smell is," she said, "that's the Harpy. They stink like garbage and rotten eggs and I don't even know what else. That's why Vicky puts eucalyptus oil in her nostrils before she fights a Harpy, to cover up the smell." She turned to me. "You know, you could've warned us you'd be bringing a real Harpy for show-and-tell," she scolded. "It's not as much fun when I feel like puking."

"I—"

The Harpy dived again. I somersaulted, and it crashed to the floor. It leapt into the air, jumping over me and landing on my left ankle. Talons dug through my jeans and into the thick leather of my boot. They didn't penetrate to my skin, but this time the Harpy had a strong grip on me. I kicked. The demon spread its wings for balance; its beak tore into my leg. Cloth ripped, and pain slashed through my thigh. A moment later, I felt the sting of a snake bite. My leg went numb.

"To fight a Harpy," Tina was saying, "it's best to use bronze bullets. You want to kill the demon before it can get close to you. As Vicky is demonstrating for us, once a Harpy gets its claws into you, you've got a real problem."

No kidding. My left leg, useless as a fallen log, now merely served as a perch for the Harpy. I kicked at the demon with my right leg, trying to knock it off while avoiding its beak. I smashed the sole of my boot into its beak and chest, but its grip only tightened. Its beak slashed my right calf, and I pulled my leg back to keep it out of range of the snakes.

The Harpy hopped up my paralyzed leg, digging its talons in above and below my knee. It was trying to make its way to my torso, where it would rip into my abdomen to feed on my guts. I kept kicking. I was not going to be disemboweled as the finale to Career Night.

Still kicking with my good leg, I worked my arms out of my jacket. If I could wrap the thick leather around the Harpy, I might be able to trap it long enough to wrestle it into a locker. With the demon encased in metal, a quick containment charm would hold it in place while I figured out how to finish it off.

I shrugged off the jacket as the Harpy inched up my leg. I was running out of time. Keeping my gaze slightly to the right of the Medusa head, I waited for it to strike. Tina's voice droned on. I wasn't listening to her, I was listening for the soft, guttural clucking that a Harpy makes when it's about to feed.

There.

The Harpy lunged forward to strike, and I threw my jacket over its head. It shrieked with fury as I wrapped it up in the jacket. Keeping the head covered, I clasped the demon in a bear hug, pushing with my good leg so I rolled over on top of it. It bucked and writhed, but I held it.

Now to stuff it into a locker. Not so easy to do with only one working leg.

"Tina," I said. "I need your help. We have to—"

"I thought you'd never ask," she said. "We were only supposed to get ten minutes, you know." But she didn't come over. She kept talking to the class. "Now, if you don't have bronze bullets, you need a bronze blade of some sort. Bronze is like poison to demons. So—"

The Harpy heaved, almost bucking me off.

"Tina!" I shouted. "We've got to imprison this Harpy. I don't have a bronze blade."

"But I do," she said. She pulled a six-inch bronze dagger from her backpack. "You told me you wouldn't bring a weapon into school, so I did."

Bless the girl. And zero tolerance be damned.

"Toss it to me." I tried to hold out a hand so she could throw me the knife, but the Harpy's frenzied movements were too wild. I had to grab the demon again before it threw me off.

Tina sauntered over. The Playboy bunny on her shirt winked as she bent to examine the situation.

"I'm going to pull back the edge of the jacket," I said. "Just a little. When I do, stab the exposed part—"

Before I could finish, a taloned foot worked its way out from under the jacket. The bronze blade flashed as Tina stabbed upward, under the jacket, spearing the Harpy in its leg.

It let out a furious shriek, loud enough to make all the demons of Hell cover their ears.

"Good!" I shouted. "Move the blade around. Maximize contact with the bronze."

Tina made a face. "It's getting, like, all mushy." She pinched her nose again. "And it smells even worse."

"That's exactly what we want." The Harpy's struggles were getting weaker. "Give me the dagger. I'll finish it off."

Tina pulled the dagger from the Harpy's body. Black slime dripped from the blade in long, gooey strings. The smell was eau de sulfur, accented with notes of rotting garbage, decaying flesh, and vomit. Tina handed me the dagger, then covered her nose with both hands and backed away.

Keeping the Harpy's head firmly wrapped in my jacket, I exposed its body. Its wings flapped weakly, without the strength to lift it into the air. I raised the dagger high and drove it straight down into the demon. And then again. And again. With each blow, the Harpy got smaller. Its cries grew fainter, its movements more feeble. In a minute, all that remained was a still, deflated body in a stinking puddle of demon guts.

As soon as the Harpy was dead, the class came back to life. Zombies blinked and coughed. They stretched and looked around. "Dude," someone muttered. "I feel like I've been reanimated all over again."

Feeling was creeping back into my leg, but I couldn't yet get it under me to stand. Tina came forward and put out a hand. I reached out so she could help me up, but instead she plucked her dagger from my hand. She faced the class and brandished it.

"And that," she declared, "is how you slay a demon."

2

"WHERE," I ASKED TINA AS I RUBBED ANTISEPTIC CREAM INTO my leg, "did you get the money to pay a sorcerer?" We stood at a row of sinks in the girls' bathroom. I'd finished washing out the cuts and gouges left by the Harpy; Tina held the first-aid kit Mrs. McIntyre had given us. I peered at the cut I was treating. In a couple of days I'd be good as new. At least I wasn't human. Any norm who tangled with that Harpy would land in the hospital for a week. The Cerddorion, my race of shapeshifters, don't heal as fast as vampires and werewolves, but we do okay.

"What sorcerer?" Tina set the first-aid kit on the edge of a sink and leaned over to inspect her makeup in the mirror. She turned on the faucet, wet her finger, and rubbed at a smudge of mascara. "I didn't pay anybody anything."

Oh, no. "Don't tell me you conjured that Harpy yourself." *Please* don't tell me that. "Sorcery is nothing to mess around with, Tina. You can't just bring in a demon for show-and-tell. Someone could have been hurt, even killed." Like me. I rubbed the spot, now slowly tingling back to life, where the snake had bitten my leg.

"What are you talking about?" She paused in reapplying her baby-pink lip gloss. "I thought you conjured that Harpy. You know, for a prop."

"You mean the Harpy that was doing its best to kill me? Some prop."

"It was an *awesome* prop—almost as good as those coupons for Munchies. I thought you did it to surprise me." She smacked her lips at the mirror, then turned to me, frowning. "But you told Mrs. McIntyre that you didn't."

The teacher, as red-faced as it's possible for a zombie to get, had stammered, "Did you bring that . . . that *creature* into this classroom?" while I sat on the floor, trying to get my paralyzed leg under me. The idea of conjuring a Harpy against myself—and in a room full of innocent bystanders, no less—knocked me flat. I'd stared at her and shook my head.

"You're lucky your own 'prop' didn't get you kicked out of school," I said to Tina.

She shrugged. "Whatever." Why do teenagers *do* that—go all surly right at the moment they might actually learn something? Had I been like that? My aunt, Mab, never would have put up with it. Okay, maybe once or twice I muttered something under my breath during the years I was her demon-fighting apprentice, but Tina made surliness an art form.

"No, not 'whatever.' So you don't care about school. Fine. But what if Mrs. McIntyre had followed procedure and called the Goon Squad?"

The Goon Squad, officially known as the Joint Human-Paranormal Task Force, was tasked with keeping law and order in Deadtown. Because those of us who live here have few legal rights, the Goons have almost unlimited powers to detain whoever they feel like detaining. And some of those detainees never come back.

Tina's reply was another shrug.

"You were lucky, Tina." Zero tolerance was supposed to mean exactly that. No exceptions, no excuses. And that's what it did mean in Boston's other schools. But Deadtown's one and only school operated under the radar, apparently. Most zombies are adults; the virus that had turned two thousand Bostonians into zombies swept through Downtown Crossing in the middle of a school day (guess who'd cut classes to go shopping). Soon after, the former quarantine zone became Deadtown. But it had taken more than two years for the kids who lived here to get their own school. It served all grades, with a student body made up of a few werewolves but mostly zombies—kids, like Tina, who'd gotten caught in the path of the plague. The school was understaffed and underfunded. The school board didn't even bother to supply the standardized tests that all students were supposed to take.

Tonight, Mrs. McIntyre had snatched the dagger from Tina's hand. I was sure she'd march Tina to the principal's office to wait for the Goons. But she didn't. She inspected the dagger, then handed it back. And why not? It wasn't made of silver, so it was no threat to werewolves, and a dagger of any sort was about as dangerous to a zombie as the pencils the teacher kept in a mug on her desk. "Remove this from the building, and don't bring it again," she'd said in a tight voice. "Weapons are not allowed in school." By that time, I'd made it to my feet. Mrs. McIntyre looked at my torn, bloody jeans and rummaged around in her desk until she found the first-aid kit.

For whatever reason—maybe she didn't feel a need to enforce the policies of a school board that pretended her school didn't exist—Mrs. McIntyre had given Tina a second chance.

"Lucky?" Tina snorted. She peeled open a Band-Aid and handed it to me. "That's the first time anyone's called me that since I got zombified." The tip of her tongue poked out of the corner of her mouth as she opened another Band-Aid. She focused on the task, not meeting my eyes. "So, um, what are you going to tell your aunt?"

For some reason, when Mab had visited Boston from her home in north Wales, she and Tina had really hit it off. If Mab sat at Mrs. McIntyre's desk, Tina would be a front-and-center, straight-A student.

Holding the edges of a cut together, I stuck on a bandage. "I'll tell her that I was attacked by a Harpy." I looked at Tina, narrowing my eyes. "Origin unknown, right?"

She nodded, red eyes wide, the picture of zombified innocence. I decided to believe her.

"And that you helped me kill it," I finished.

A grin stretched her face. A smiling zombie isn't what you'd call pretty, but Tina looked pleased with herself. "What about my report, all that stuff I told the class about Harpies?"

"Tina, I was wrestling with a demon that was dead-set on killing me. You have to admit that's a little distracting."

"Oh. Yeah, I guess you're right." She chewed her lip, then nodded. "That's okay. Your aunt went over Harpies with me while she was here. I did good—she'll remember that."

Tina lifted my arm and draped it around her shoulders, letting me lean on her as I limped out of the girls' room and down the hallway. As we went along, she chattered about the Harpy and how it compared to what she'd read in books. Maybe Tina wasn't as indifferent to learning as I'd thought.

Good for her. But there was one thing I really wanted to learn: If Tina didn't conjure that Harpy, who did?

NIGHTTIME IS DEADTOWN'S BUSIEST TIME. VAMPIRES AND zombies prefer to avoid direct sunlight (a zombie sunburn results in pitted, orange skin that doesn't heal), so they're out and about from dusk until dawn. Tina's school "day" went from eight P.M. to two thirty A.M. By the time I was patched up and back on the street, it was nearly three in the morning.

The mid-April night was chilly. Boston had been having a cool spring, but you wouldn't know it to look at the zombies who thronged the streets. Because they don't feel heat or cold, they wear whatever they want, whatever the weather. Most zombies cling to their legal status as previously deceased humans, or PDHs—they're definitely not norms, but they're still human, and they want to look the part to whatever extent they can. Tonight I saw the full range of zombie fashion: most wore jeans and T-shirts, but there were business suits, uniforms, dresses, khakis, shorts and flipflops—you name it. And then, of course, there was Tina. When it came to zombie fashion, she was in a class by herself.

When I limped through the front door of my apartment, my roommate was watching TV. Juliet sat in the dark and stared at the giant flatscreen that took up an entire wall, its flickering light tingeing her pale skin with blue. I turned on the overhead light. She blinked rapidly, like someone coming out of a trance, and refocused on me.

At six hundred fifty (give or take a couple of decades), Juliet still looked like the twenty-two-year-old who was turned by an unscrupulous vampire posing as a friar. Her long raven hair, wide brown eyes, and shapely curves had been popping eyes and turning heads for more than six centuries.

I was glad to see it. A month ago, Juliet had nearly died in an attack by the Old Ones, shadowy, ancient super-vampires who wanted to move beyond undeath and into eternal life. The Old

Ones were responsible for the zombie virus, which they'd unleashed on Boston as an experiment. That experiment had sent its human victims through death and back into life, but the Old Ones didn't want to become zombies; they wanted to be gods. They kept working on their magically enhanced virus, using Juliet and other vampires as their lab rats. The other vampires had died, dissolving into piles of dust. Juliet had survived thanks to Aunt Mab, who'd used her personal talisman to restore Juliet's life force. When Juliet's comatose body started to disintegrate, Mab performed a life-giving ritual that didn't just save Juliet; it restored her. She said she felt better than she had in centuries.

Mab's bloodstone was her personal object of power. She didn't know what its long-term effects might be on Juliet. But so far, so good.

Juliet cocked an eyebrow at me, taking in my torn, bloody clothes. "Rough night?"

"You might say that." I hobbled over to the closet. When I tried to put my jacket on a hanger, I realized the garment hung in ribbons. Guess I wouldn't be wearing that jacket again. I pulled it off the hanger and dumped it in the trash.

"I warned you." She shook a deep-red-nailed finger at me. "High school students are more dangerous than any demon. I've had a few scrapes over the centuries, but I'd rather be chased off a cliff by an angry mob than set one foot across the threshold of an American high school. Those places are *scary.*"

"It wasn't the students, it was . . ." I sighed. "I'll tell you later. I need to clean up." Feeling like an old lady, I shuffled down the hall to the bathroom. My injured leg was taking my weight okay, but as feeling came back, so did the pain. Each step felt like that damn Harpy was gouging out another chunk of flesh.

I showered, washing off blood and sweat and the stink of Harpy, then rebandaged my various cuts and gashes. Gingerly raising my sore leg, I pulled on a pair of yoga pants.

The pants and a sweatshirt made me feel as comfy as I was going to get tonight. I went back to the living room, where Juliet had stretched out on the sofa. I slumped into an armchair, taking the weight off my aching leg.

"Do you think we need one of those?" Juliet asked, nodding at the screen. A smiling woman was applying some kind of torture device to a poor, innocent egg. "It scrambles the egg *inside* the shell, then cracks it open automatically. No mess."

"You don't eat eggs." And scrambled eggs were beyond my cooking skills. Even with a contraption that prescrambles them for you.

"I'm just hungry," she pouted. "They're late delivering my dinner again."

Normally, Juliet would be hunting at this time of night, or hanging out at Creature Comforts, flirting with norms who'd ventured into a monster bar in search of a little supernatural excitement. But not tonight. And not any night for the past week. Whenever I saw Juliet, it was always the same: She sat on the sofa, one leg tucked under her, the other leg sporting a clunky electronic anklet.

My roommate was under house arrest.

For nearly two months, she'd been wanted in connection with the murder of a Supreme Court justice in Washington, D.C., a murder for which Alexander Kane—prominent paranormal rights attorney, werewolf, and my boyfriend—was briefly the main suspect. The Old Ones had murdered the judge, and at the time Juliet had been in their thrall. She'd managed to break away, going on the run from both the Old Ones and the cops.

A week ago, she'd located Colwyn, the Old Ones' power-mad leader. She made the feds an offer: She'd lead them to Colwyn if they gave her amnesty in the murder case. They agreed, making house arrest a condition. There were other charges pending against her, including escaping from Goon Squad custody. If Colwyn could answer questions about the zombie plague and the justice's murder, the cops would drop all charges against her.

The truth was that the cops needed Juliet. The Old Ones communicated telepathically, and Juliet could listen in on their thoughts, making her a valuable asset. But that didn't mean the police trusted her. Until they had a clearer picture of what the Old Ones were and how she fit in, they weren't letting her beyond the walls of our two-bedroom apartment.

She was bored out of her mind. Lately, that boredom had led to an obsession with infomercials.

Juliet sat up straight and inspected me. "You look terrible," she announced. "So what did happen to you in that adolescent chamber of horrors? I'm betting zombie mean-girl bullying. With Tina as the ringleader. Am I right?"

"Nothing like that. I got attacked by a Harpy."

Juliet's eyes widened. She covered her mouth with both hands.

She was the picture of shocked sympathy—until the laughter she was holding back erupted full force. She collapsed in a fit of very unvampirelike giggles. I waited, fingers tapping the arm of my chair, for her to catch her breath.

"So let me get this straight." She gasped as she struggled to sit up again. "You're there to tell a bunch of zombie brats how to kill demons, and a demon shows up to kill *you*." When I nodded, she hiccupped with laughter. "When do I get to see the video?"

"No video." Thank goodness. Everyone in the room had been paralyzed before they had a chance to get out their cellphone cameras.

"No film at eleven? Pity. That's the most amusing thing I've heard all week. What did Tina do?"

"She ran to the front of the classroom and started lecturing everyone on the behavior and habits of Harpies."

"Are you sure no one recorded it? Your chance to be an Internet sensation, and you missed it."

"Not my ambition. So sorry to disappoint you."

An ad for a steakhouse came on the TV, showing a thick slab of bloody meat sizzling on a grill. Juliet's mouth fell open, her fangs extended to their full length. A moan escaped from her before she closed her mouth and wiped her chin with the back of her hand. "By all that's unholy, where *are* they?" she muttered.

One of the conditions of Juliet's cooperation with the police was that, since she couldn't go out hunting, they'd bring her dinner each night. And none of that refrigerated, watered-down blood in a bottle. To keep up her strength, she'd argued, she needed fresh blood still hot with the donor's life force. So each night, two Goons arrived, escorting a human volunteer, so Juliet could feed. That is, when they remembered to show up.

When a gleaming steak knife sliced into a filet mignon on the TV, she'd had enough food porn. She picked up the remote, hit the Mute button, and flipped through some channels.

A familiar face flashed across the screen. "Wait!" I said. "Go back."

A couple of clicks and there he was: Kane, in all his silver-haired glory, flashing the smile that had won many a court case. I felt a little cross-eyed; it's disconcerting to see your boyfriend's face expanded to movie-screen size. Then the camera pulled back and showed him sitting next to Simone Landry, the were-wolf member of Deadtown's Council of Three. I remembered now—he'd told me he was going to be on Channel 10's *Paranormal Perspectives*.

"Do you want me to turn it up?" Juliet held the remote poised.

"No, I know what this interview is about. Kane taped it a couple of days ago. He's helping Simone Landry launch her reelection bid."

The Council of Three was the bone that the government threw us monsters so we could pretend Deadtown had some kind of self-regulation. Made up of a vampire, a werewolf, and a zombie, it was a trio of figureheads with no real power. But that didn't mean no one wanted the job. It came with certain perks, including connections in city and state governments. At least five were-wolves were trying to unseat Simone—werewolves love to challenge each other—and Kane had agreed to manage her campaign. That's why they were appearing on *Paranormal Perspectives*.

Olympia Misko, the show's human host, asked a question. Both Kane and Simone started to answer at the same time, then laughed. Simone motioned to Kane to go ahead. Olympia tilted her head and nodded at whatever he was saying.

"She wants him," Juliet said.

"Who, Olympia? What are you talking about?" Olympia Misko's highest-rated show last year had been when she married her long-time girlfriend, a vampire, on the air.

"Not her. Simone. She just deferred to him. And watch how she looks at him." Juliet leaned forward, squinting at the screen. "There—did you see that? How her nostrils flared and her upper lip twitched, like she wants to take a bite out of him? Classic werewolf mating behavior." She sat back. "Councilor Landry is ready to start her own pack. And she's looking at your boyfriend as her potential mate."

"You're crazy. All werewolves do that stuff. It doesn't mean anything." But now that I was paying attention to Simone, I didn't like what I saw. Simone was slim and attractive, with sleek chest-nut hair. Usually she wore it up in a twist, but tonight it tumbled down her back in glossy waves. A close-up showed eyes a star-tling shade of emerald green. She sat too close to Kane, leaning in closer whenever he spoke. Every minute or two, she touched him—on his arm, his shoulder, even his leg. For the most part,

Kane ignored her. When Simone let her hand linger on his thigh, though, he picked up the hand and deposited it on the arm of her chair, all the while keeping his focus on the host.

"She wants him," Juliet repeated. "Watch out for that one."

Simone bent toward Kane, her nostrils flaring again as she picked a piece of lint from his lapel. Jealousy simmered in my gut. I wanted to reach through the screen and slap her hand away. "Well, who cares what she wants?" I said. "Kane's a lone wolf. He has no desire to change that. He's too busy with his work." Even to my own ears, it sounded like denial.

"He wasn't too busy with work to manage her campaign." Her fangs glinted as she grinned wickedly. "I wonder who'll be managing whom."

The simmering rose to a slow boil. "I really don't think that—"

The phone rang. Juliet grabbed it. "Yes? Hello, Clyde." Clyde was the zombie who worked as our building's doorman. She listened for a moment. *"Finally,"* she said and hung up. "Dinner's on the way."

Paranormal Perspectives had gone to a commercial, but the image of Simone brushing Kane's lapel was burned into my brain. Who did that werewolf think she was, pawing him like that? He'd probably told her to back off. But why hadn't he mentioned it to me? He'd told me about the interview—but not a word about Simone's behavior. And as far as I knew he was still advising her campaign.

Maybe we needed to have a talk about whether that was a good idea.

The doorbell rang, and I stood. "I'll get it." I wasn't going to sit around and watch Juliet eat. It was already bad enough that the two Goons who acted as chaperones didn't leave the room while she fed. Anyway, I was feeling hungry myself—rather ferociously so, all of a sudden—and the idea of a vampire sucking on some norm's neck threatened to quash my appetite. While Juliet was busy, I'd rummage around in the kitchen for a more palatable snack.

I opened the door to see two Goons—a zombie and his human partner—flanking a short, scrawny, nervous-looking guy. Juliet's dinner pushed up his wire-rimmed glasses and squinted at me. "Are you the vampire?"

I shook my head and stepped aside.

"Oh, Hades," Juliet said when she saw him. "*That's* what you bring me? He doesn't look like he's got a full pint in him. Where do you find these norms?"

The grim-faced Goons stepped into the apartment.

The guy's eyeballs bulged when he saw Juliet reclining on the sofa. His Adam's apple bobbed. "*You're* the vampire? Wow." He rushed inside, already unbuttoning his shirt. Then he paused. "Um, I'm sorry, but you're wrong."

Juliet looked at him like he was a bug she'd enjoy squashing under her stiletto.

The Goons flanked the door, arms folded, and stared straight ahead.

"My name," the scrawny guy said, baring a chest that made me think of those novelty rubber chickens. "It's not Norm. It's Marvin." He rotated his hips in a circle, then winked. "At your service, baby."

Juliet rolled her eyes, but her fangs extended.

I fled into the kitchen. Before the door swung shut behind me, chicken-chested Marvin gurgled out an ecstatic moan. *Eww.* Maybe I wasn't so hungry after all.

3

A BOOK LAY ON THE KITCHEN TABLE, EXACTLY WHERE I'D LEFT
it hours ago. Its pale leather cover looked cadaverous under the
fluorescent lights. No wonder—the book was bound in human
skin. I walked by, trying to ignore the waves of malevolence that
radiated from it, and went to the freezer. Nothing like a pint of
chocolate ice cream to help you cope with a demonic book written in the language of Hell.

I got a spoon and sat down at the table. I pried the lid off the
pint and dug in. Rich, sweet chocolate melted on my tongue as
I eyed the book. I didn't want to open it. But I wanted even less
to keep picturing Simone Landry sniffing around Kane. Juliet
was right, damn it—Simone was after my boyfriend. I needed
to see him, talk to him. Until I could do that, anything was better
than thinking about Simone. Even trying to read this damned
book.

The Book of Utter Darkness and I had a long and unpleasant
history. Its pages contained both the history of the demon races
and prophecies about how the centuries-long conflict between
demons and humans would end. My race, the Cerddorion, was
presented as the main obstacle that stood between demons and
their goal of taking over the Ordinary, the humans' world. Mab

had stolen the book from the demons. During the years I was her apprentice, she'd forbidden me to even look at it. Ten years ago, when I was eighteen and near the end of my training—and thought I knew everything—I'd broken the rule and taken the book from its shelf in Mab's library. The result: I'd accidentally conjured a Hellion. Difethwr, the Destroyer. The demon that killed my father.

On that terrible night, the Destroyer had marked me, creating a bond between us. For years, the demon mark on my right forearm had subjected me to intense rages that I struggled to control. Two months ago, I'd killed the Destroyer. Although my arm still bore the mark—a bright-red scar two inches long that resembled a burn—the rages had died with the Destroyer. For the first time in more than ten years, I finally felt like myself.

After my father died, I'd vowed never to touch the book again. But the book wasn't done with me. When a demonic force started feeding on Deadtown's zombies, reducing them to puddles of black goo, Mab summoned me to her home in Wales, saying it was time to continue my training. What I hadn't counted on was that my training would involve studying this book—or trying to. *The Book of Utter Darkness* was written in an ancient, demonic language I didn't understand. As if that wasn't bad enough, the book tried to trick anyone who attempted to read it. It was almost like a living being—one that hated me and would do everything in its power to defeat me.

At Mab's insistence, I'd brought the book back from Wales. I would love to burn the thing, but Mab wouldn't let me. "There's much the book has not yet revealed, child," she'd said. "You must keep going."

So every once in a while, I forced myself to do what I was doing now. Taking another spoonful of cold, creamy chocolate for courage, I opened the book to a random page. It didn't matter where I started. The book would share its contents with me only when it decided to do so. And anyway, the contents moved around inside its pages. A page showing an illustration today could be a solid block of text tomorrow, or vice versa.

Just thinking about *The Book of Utter Darkness* made my head ache. Trying to read it was infinitely worse.

I stared at the page, a jumble of unfamiliar characters, waiting to see if its meaning appeared in my head. The letters blurred.

Nothing. The pages went double as my eyes crossed. I blinked and scooped out more ice cream.

As I lifted the spoon to my mouth, a glob of ice cream fell and splatted on the page. *Crap.* I jumped up to grab a paper towel. Mab would be beyond annoyed if she knew I was dropping dairy products on her ancient, unique manuscript.

I dabbed at the blob. A surge of power shot from the book and up my arm, buzzing through my demon mark and hitting my brain like a bolt of lightning. A white flash exploded behind my eyes, and scenes sped through my mind like a movie played on a super-fast projector.

First, a man's face in close-up: pale skin; a long, straight nose; and black lashes framing eyes so dark they seemed to dim the light. Pryce, my demi-demon "cousin" who wanted to lead demons from their realm to overrun the human plane. His mouth moved, but he made no sound—my ears were filled with a roaring like hurricane-strength winds. Pryce sneered at someone. The scene shifted and I saw that "someone" was me. We stood in a cemetery. I recognized the place—it was in Boston, on the night of last February's Paranormal Appreciation Day concert. The night Pryce had tried to release the demonic essence that would make demons too strong for humans to withstand.

Then Pryce's eyes closed, and he collapsed on the ground. The vision switched to me, driving my flaming sword over and over into the body of a huge, writhing demon. God, I was bloody. I was killing Cysgod, Pryce's shadow demon. Without his demon half, Pryce became nothing more than a living shell.

Another scene, another face. This man looked like Pryce, but he was older, bearded, with a crazy gleam in his eye. He smiled, revealing rotted teeth, and a high-pitched giggle cut through the background roar. This was Myrddin, Pryce's father. The Old Ones had released him from centuries-long imprisonment to make a deal—he'd help them gain eternal life, and they'd help him resuscitate Pryce. The vision showed Myrddin stooping over a freshly murdered human, capturing the departing life force in a jar. Suddenly, Myrddin was in some sort of lab, transferring the life force to the comatose Pryce.

It had taken the life forces of five people to revive Pryce. The last had been Myrddin himself. I could see the moment now— me, bloody again, this time killing Myrddin's shadow demon, as his mortal half gave his own life force to his son. Pryce sitting up, disoriented, then cocking his head as though listening to an inner voice. He ran away before I could stop him.

The vision ended as abruptly as it began. I blinked, trying to figure out where I was. Kitchen. There was the table—I was looking up at it. I sprawled on the cold floor, clutching a chocolate-smeared paper towel. I got to my feet, stiff and sore all over, and looked at the open book. Not a speck of ice cream on it.

I closed the cover. I tossed the paper towel in the trash. Then I put the lid back on the ice cream container and returned it to the freezer. Why is it that ice cream starts off looking like the solution to a problem and ends up feeling like nothing more than a big, queasy lump in your stomach?

The book hadn't shown me anything I didn't already know. I'd killed Pryce's shadow demon, rendering Pryce catatonic until Myrddin stole four people's life forces—then added his own—to bring him back. Pryce was walking and talking, out there somewhere, but without his shadow demon. Why couldn't the book show me something useful, like where he was now or what he was planning?

I picked up the book and dropped it in the trash. I stood over it for a full minute, admiring the way it looked there—so natural, so *right*. Then, with a sigh, I took it out again. The book seemed to quiver with indignation as I lifted it from the trash can and stashed it at the back of a cupboard. Mab said it was important for me to keep working with the book, so I would. But otherwise, I didn't have to look at it. As I shut the cupboard door, the kitchen light brightened.

I'd report my experience to Mab the next time we spoke. (Well, maybe I'd leave out the part about spilling chocolate ice cream on the book. No harm done, no need to tell her, right?) But this was the third time in a week the book had rehashed recent events—although the most dramatic in its presentation. The previous two times, Mab had simply said, "Keep trying, child." I was sure she'd say it this time, too. In fact, she wouldn't be happy that I'd hidden the book away. I sighed again as I retrieved the book from the cupboard and returned it to the table. Face down. I knew I'd have to go back to it, but I was done with the book for tonight.

Now what? I cracked open the kitchen door. Voices came

from the living room, a trill of Juliet's laughter. Huh. Maybe she and Marvin were hitting it off. Not that I wanted to join their party. I got myself a glass of water and wandered back to the kitchen table. Still not ready to think about Simone. Instead, I flipped the pages of a two-day-old copy of *News of the Dead*, Deadtown's cheesy tabloid. Even the monsters need a good gossip rag.

Not thinking about Simone. *Flip.* How dare she put her hand on Kane's leg? *Flip.* And on television, for all of Boston to see. *Flip.* It was like she was staking her claim to him. *Flip.* Not thinking about Simone. *Flip.* Was I remembering wrong, or had he caught her eye and smiled once? The page ripped in my hand.

I stared at the torn piece, part of a full-page ad for designer coffins for any décor. I didn't remember seeing it, didn't remember seeing any of the previous pages. My eyes had skimmed over half the paper without taking in a word. I pushed *News of the Dead* aside.

No use making myself crazy over Simone. Just because she wanted Kane didn't mean *he* wanted *her*. We were all adults. I'd reserve judgment until I could talk to him. And then I'd yank a big handful of that gleaming chestnut hair right out of Simone's scalp.

Now, there was a picture I could get behind.

I sipped some water and turned my thoughts to tonight's Harpy attack. Harpies don't attack at random. They're conjured to go after a specific target—usually to torment, but this one was going for the kill. Who'd sent it after me?

Simone? Would she pay a sorcerer to get rid of the competition? I didn't think so. Most werewolves preferred a more direct approach. They relished confrontation. Sneaking around and dealing with sorcerers wouldn't occur to a werewolf. Okay, so I had Simone on the brain. And I was looking for the slightest excuse to make that hair-ripping picture a reality. But I didn't believe she'd sent the Harpy.

No, if I were betting on who was behind the attack, I'd put all my cash on Pryce.

Pryce had lost his shadow demon, but he knew how to conjure Harpies better than any sorcerer. And he'd already tried so many times to kill me that he could list "attempted murder" under Hobbies on his résumé.

In the weeks since Myrddin revived him, Pryce had been

quiet, in hiding. But maybe he was active again. Maybe that's why the book kept showing me recent events. Not for my benefit, of course, but to taunt me, to remind me that my nemesis—the would-be king of the demons—was still out there.

And probably trying to kill me.

I could be jumping to conclusions, but I didn't think so. In February, I'd ruined his attempt to take over the Ordinary. If he was getting ready to try again, he'd want me out of the way.

A hand pushed the door partway open and Juliet's voice came through. "Bye now," she was saying. "Parting is such sweet sorrow." (Juliet loves to quote Shakespeare—she can hold entire conversations stringing together the Bard's immortal words.) The front door opened and closed. A moment later, Juliet strolled into the kitchen. She looked better—her eyes were bright and a pink flush colored her cheeks—except for the scowl that twisted her features. Her expression didn't match the flirtatious, musical quality of her farewells. "I'm still hungry," she said. She yanked open the refrigerator and pulled out a bottle of blood. After dumping the contents into a mug, she put it in the microwave and jabbed some buttons. "See what I'm reduced to?" she demanded, as the microwave hummed. "I have an appetite for steak, and they bring me a celery stick."

"I thought you liked Marvin."

Her mouth dropped open. "Why ever would you think that?"

" 'Parting is such sweet sorrow'? Aren't those words for a Romeo?"

"Please. First of all, Romeo did not make my Top Ten Lovers list, not even for his century. Second, I was not talking to that Marvin worm." Her eyes glazed as she licked her lips. "I was talking to Brad."

"Brad?" I thought about who else had been in the room. "Don't tell me you have a crush on one of those Goons."

"Crush—such a brutal word. I prefer to say I have a . . . thirst for him." Her small, private smile revealed the tips of her fangs.

"So which Goon is Brad, the norm or the zombie?" Both were big and muscular, the way Juliet liked her men.

She rolled her eyes at my question. Vampires don't drink zombie blood—or whatever it is that flows through those reanimated veins. If she was thirsting, it was for hot human blood.

The microwave dinged. Juliet removed the mug and carried it to the table, where she sat down across from me. She took a sip and made a face. "I don't know which is worse, stale blood or an anemic norm." She downed the rest of the blood, then wiped her mouth with the back of her hand. "So, what are you going to do about Simone Landry?"

Damn. Just when I'd actually managed to stop thinking about Simone for five whole minutes. In a row.

"How about I invite her over here on some pretense and you can help me beat her up?"

"Yes!" Juliet's eyes glowed. "You could tell her we're having a party and Kane is coming. Then when she gets here—" She smiled evilly. But both smile and glow faded when she caught my expression. "Oh. I take it you were kidding."

"I'm not going to beat up a city councilor." Juliet might be thirsting for Brad, but I didn't want a visit from the Goons.

"But you *must*. She's a werewolf. If you don't slap her down, she'll think you're weak. She'll think she can push you around."

"Let her try. Anyway, I trust Kane."

Juliet opened her mouth, but I didn't want to hear whatever it was she was going to say. Enough about Simone. I kept talking. "That Old One you've been interrogating, Colwyn. Has he said anything else about Pryce?" The Old Ones had hidden Pryce during the time Myrddin worked to revive him. Juliet's Old One was the best lead for finding him now.

She shook her head. "Only what I told you before. The Old Ones are looking for him, too."

"Do you think they're working together?"

Juliet considered. "I doubt it. When Pryce's name came up, Colwyn's thoughts flared crimson. Lots of anger on that topic." She stared into her empty mug. "I think Colwyn has realized I can eavesdrop on his thoughts. He tries to shield them. But sometimes things slip through. I'm not certain, but I think Pryce has something the Old Ones want."

"What?"

"I don't know. That's what Colwyn is shielding. But the thought of it makes him livid."

"Do you think Pryce has his precious secret to eternal life?"

Juliet shrugged. "Personally? I don't think any such thing exists. But that doesn't mean Colwyn has given up his illusions. All I know is that Pryce has something Colwyn believes is his." She stood and stretched, yawning. "Dawn's on its way. I'm going to resume the shroud." She carried her mug to the dishwasher and placed it in the top rack. "But speaking of people who want something someone else has—keep an eye on that Simone. If you're not going to beat her up, at least 'watch her like Argus,' as the Bard might say. That werewolf thinks Kane is already hers."

JULIET MAY HAVE BEEN TUCKED SNUGLY INTO HER COFFIN, but I wasn't ready for bed. Not with her warning about Simone still ringing in my ears. I *did* trust Kane. He'd traveled across an ocean to tell me I was important to him. More than once, he'd stepped up to face danger beside me. He'd risked his own life to rescue me. Those things mattered. Emerald eyes and glossy chestnut hair weren't enough to turn his head.

Or they wouldn't be, if Kane were human. But he was a werewolf. What if the pull of raw instinct was strong enough to stir a need in the lone wolf to start a pack of his own? Although he hadn't said anything, the signs were there that he wanted to take our relationship to the next level. Signs my own commitment-shy brain had chosen to ignore. He'd given me a key to his apartment. My bathrobe hung beside his on the bathroom door. Last fall, he'd asked me to come with him on his full-moon retreat. As a shapeshifter, I could take on a wolf's form if I chose. But I'm Cerddorion, not a werewolf, and the whole idea had made me uncomfortable. If I pretended to be a wolf, I wouldn't fit in with the real ones. Worse, I wouldn't be true to myself. When I explained all that, he dropped the matter.

Kane knew what I was. He knew I'd never be an ersatz wolf. And he also knew I'd never be a mother. Among my kind, only females can shift—and they lose the ability if they give birth. I'd decided long ago that my path was to carry on the Cerddorion tradition of protecting the world against demons. If Kane wanted to start his own pack, it wouldn't be with me.

Did he want to start his own pack? Kane had always been so immersed in his work—his goal was to establish paranormal rights at the federal level—that other concerns got pushed aside. Work came first, just as it did for me. It was one of the reasons we got along so well. Or so I thought.

If instinct was tugging at Kane, Simone knew how to manipulate its pull. I didn't have a clue. But I didn't want to manipulate him. I wanted to talk to him. If he wanted more than I could offer, it was something we both needed to know.

I checked the kitchen clock. Six thirty. As a lawyer, Kane kept norm hours, so he was usually up by seven. I'd surprise him with breakfast in bed, and we could talk.

I pictured him, lying between the sheets, his silver hair rumpled, his gray eyes hooded with sleep and desire. *Mmm*. First bed, then breakfast, then talk.

IN GENERAL, DEADTOWN ISN'T BIG ON BREAKFAST. THE norms' morning is Deadtown's bedtime. When the sun comes up, most residents are home snoozing behind their blackout shades, as Juliet was now. But for werewolves it's a different story. Most werewolves hold professional jobs in the human-controlled part of town: they're bankers, lawyers, accountants, architects, engineers. They earn salaries and have expense accounts and go to work in clothes that need dry cleaning. Each month, for the three days and nights of the full moon, state law requires them to be in residence at one of the state's three secure werewolf retreats. But state law also requires that employers make accommodations for werewolves to go on retreat. Werewolves tend to be such valuable workers that employers are happy to comply. As long as the guy who manages your investment portfolio or the woman who arranges your business loans stays out of sight while becoming a huge, slavering, bloodthirsty wolf, it all works out fine.

I stopped at a place I knew would be open, a cafe that was a popular spot for werewolves to grab coffee and a bite to eat on their way to work. Inside, the air was fragrant with scents of coffee and frying bacon and sausage. (Werewolves need their protein in the morning.) The cafe was decorated in cheerful shades of yellow and green, and ferns hung in the big front window. Werewolves lined up at the takeout counter; others sat at tables or the booths that lined two walls. I threaded my way through the tables to join the line.

I was halfway to the counter when a familiar voice called my name. I turned, scanning the room, to see Kane sliding out of a booth near the back.

His smile cast a warm glow over the bustling cafe. His silver hair gleamed, and his suit—black with a subtle pinstripe—looked like it had just waltzed out of a Milan menswear show. The cut emphasized his broad shoulders and slim hips. Nice. Too bad I hadn't made it to his place before he'd put it on.

He wrapped me in a warm hug. His scent, which always made me think of a moonlit forest at midnight, sent shivers through me. His lips brushed the top of my head.

"Sit with me for a minute," he said, pulling me beside him into the booth. His arm felt good around my shoulders.

"You're out early," I said.

"Breakfast meeting." He gestured at his open laptop on the table. "I was going over my notes before the others arrive. But I'm surprised to see you here. I thought you'd be asleep by now."

"I was going to do that at your place." Heat flushed my cheeks as that image of him between the sheets flashed into my mind. "After I woke you up with breakfast in bed."

His gray eyes shone. "I wish you'd been an hour earlier. I gladly would've blown off this meeting for the chance to . . ." He leaned in close, his lips brushing my ear as he whispered, "To have you for breakfast."

"I do have the time right, don't I?" A woman's voice cut through the moment like a hatchet. "We did say seven o'clock."

Simone Landry stood over our table. In person, she looked even lovelier than she did on TV. That damn chestnut hair framed her face in silken waves. Skillfully applied makeup highlighted her green eyes, and her suit, a matching shade of green, was tailored to show off her curves. In my sweats, I suddenly felt less comfy and more like a bag lady.

"Simone," Kane said, keeping his arm around me. "Have you met my girlfriend, Vicky?"

Her smile didn't waver as her eyes shifted to me. "I can't say I've had the pleasure."

Kane made the introductions, and Simone extended her hand. I didn't like squinting up at her, so I stood to shake it. Her palm was cool, her handshake firm and confident. She looked like any successful norm businesswoman, except for the way her nostrils flared and twitched as she sized me up by scent. Her eyes gave nothing away.

"I almost feel like I know you," she said. "Kane has told me so much about you."

"He has?" I mentally kicked myself for sounding surprised.

"Of course." Kane had gotten out of the booth to stand beside me. His arms circled my waist.

Simone didn't back off; her smile broadened. "He's very proud of you. Just the other day, when we had drinks after taping our *Paranormal Perspectives* interview, he made it sound as though you'd single-handedly driven all the demons out of Boston." She chuckled, and the tone of her laugh revealed the malice that her face held in check.

That laugh declared war.

You want to challenge me, Councilor Landry? Bring it on.

Before I could say anything, a werewolf and a human came over, both junior partners in Kane's law firm. As they greeted me, Simone had to step back. Good. Let her learn who's part of Kane's inner circle—and who's not.

"I'll let you have your meeting," I said. Touching Kane's cheek with one hand, I buried the other in his hair and pulled him to me. I kissed him the way I'd planned to wake him up— deep and slow and sensual. "See you tonight."

Kane caught his breath, his smile full of promise. "Can't wait."

He sat down again, sliding over in the booth. "I'm glad we met," I said to Simone, stretching my lips back in a grin that I hoped would look territorial to a werewolf. I stood in front of her, smiling and blocking her way, until one of the junior partners sat beside Kane.

Simone glanced at the booth, whose sole empty seat was now the one farthest from Kane. When she returned her gaze to me, she dropped the mask, and I could see everything in her eyes: her desire for Kane, her confidence, her utter contempt for me. I'd been wrong about Simone. There was no challenge there. She was certain she'd win.

4

IN THE LOBBY OF MY BUILDING, I WAVED TO CLYDE, WHO stashed a bag of chips in his doorman's desk. He swallowed and patted his mouth with a handkerchief. Nobody cares that zombies eat on the job, but Clyde's big on propriety. I pretended not to notice his snacking.

"I'm glad to see you're walking better," he called.

Mid-stride, I realized my injured leg no longer hurt at all. I *was* walking better. Good. At least I hadn't been limping in front of Simone. She'd interpret any sign of weakness as vulnerability—and I was not going to let that bitch-in-heat perceive me as vulnerable. My memory burned with the image of her smug face, those green eyes already lit up with triumph.

I was going to wipe that expression right off her perfectly made-up face.

Upstairs in my apartment, I picked up the phone to check for messages. The voice mail's robot voice told me I had four new ones. The first was from my mother in Florida, just to say hi. A wave of guilt hit me as I listened to her describe a dinner-theater play she'd seen with friends. Mom's tone was cheerful and chatty—nothing to suggest I'd done anything wrong—but mostly

I heard, "You should call more often," even though she didn't say the words.

She was right; I should. I pressed the button to get out of voice mail and dialed Mom's number. Her machine answered. I'd bet anything she was out having breakfast. Mom loved going out for breakfast. When I was in high school, once a week I'd grab some toast and pack my own lunch so my parents could have their breakfast date. Mom always said she'd rather go out at the beginning of the day, when she felt fresh and awake, than eat a heavy restaurant dinner at the end of a long, tiring day.

I left her a chatty message saying I was sorry I'd missed her call and telling her I'd spent the night at the local high school lecturing a classroom of zombies on demon extermin—er, slaying. I left out the part about being attacked by a Harpy—no point in worrying her. I ended with a quick "Love you" and hung up with the hollow feeling that I hadn't said enough.

I went back into the voice mail menu and listened to the remaining messages, one after another. All three were cancellations.

"You won't believe it!" raved one client. "For three nights in a row, not a single nightmare. The first night, I thought it was a fluke. After the second, I thought maybe I was getting lucky. But after three nights of deep, wonderful sleep, I know they're gone. *Gone!*" His voice rose to a giddy pitch. "Sorry to cancel at the last minute and all, but I no longer need your services. So, um, give me a call when you get this so we can discuss refunding my deposit. Thanks."

I'd give the guy a call, all right. He obviously needed a reminder of my no-refund policy.

I checked my calendar. It showed one Drude extermination still on for tonight. Otherwise, my schedule for the next week had been wiped clean. I didn't get it. What was happening to all the demons? If not for last night's Harpy attack, I'd almost think Boston had become a demon-free zone.

Not what you'd call great PR when Boston's demon exterminator is the only person in the entire city being attacked by demons.

I was debating whether to call the ex-client back and argue about his deposit when the phone rang in my hand. Oh, no, I thought as I pushed the button to answer. Please don't let this be another cancellation. The few dollars left in my bank account were getting lonely.

But it wasn't a client. It was my sister, Gwen.

"Will you please talk to your niece?" Gwen's voice sounded like she'd reached the end of her rope and kept on going. "Maria is refusing to go to school."

"Sure, put her on."

"No, I mean come out here and talk to her. She's barricaded herself in her room and won't answer no matter how hard I pound on the door. I bet she's got her iPod turned up full blast. She's probably giving herself permanent hearing damage as we speak." I wondered if Gwen knew how much she sounded like our own mother twenty years ago, except instead of an iPod, Gwen would have been blasting her boom box for the whole neighborhood to hear.

"What makes you think she'll open the door for me?"

"Of course she will. You're the great and powerful Aunt Vicky who can do no wrong." The bitterness in her voice made me think that driving out to Gwen's suburban home and getting in the middle of a mother-daughter dispute might not be the best way to round out my morning. But then she softened. "Please, Vicky. Right now, Maria doesn't want to hear a word I have to say, but I know she'll listen to you."

"I'm on my way."

TEN MINUTES LATER I WAS IN MY JAG, PAST THE CHECKPOINTS out of Deadtown, and driving through the human-controlled world. Navigating rush-hour traffic is never fun in Boston, but at least I was driving out of the city when everyone else was heading in. Inbound traffic on the Mass Pike was bumper-to-bumper, but the westbound side wasn't so bad once I reached Newton.

During the half-hour drive out to Needham, I wondered what was going on with my niece. At eleven, Maria was reaching the age where shapeshifting tendencies start to manifest. Gwen had married a human—Nick was a great guy, but at least part of the reason Gwen had picked him was a hope that her kids would be norms, not monsters like her own family. Like me.

Since Cerddorion females lose the ability to shapeshift when they give birth, Gwen had chosen to be as human as it was possible for her to be when she became a mom at twenty-two. I don't know if it was her *very* worst fear that her daughter would become a shapeshifter, but that one was pretty high on the list. And it was happening. Maria was showing all the early signs of being a full-blooded Cerddorion female: shapeshifting dreams, a talent for controlling her dreamscape, an ability to communicate with others of our race while sleeping.

I wondered what had happened to make Maria so upset she wouldn't go to school. Probably a dream had turned into a nightmare that she couldn't control. I'd gone through the same thing at her age, and I remembered how scary it could be. It had to be even worse if you couldn't go to your mother for comfort. Gwen didn't mean to let her fears about Maria's Cerddorion nature show—I was sure of that. Yet the kid couldn't help but pick up on those fears. They'd surrounded her from the day she was born.

I STOOD IN THE UPSTAIRS HALLWAY OF GWEN'S COLONIAL-style home, knocking on a door decorated with a hand-drawn sign that proclaimed NO BROTHERS ALLOWED. When I'd arrived, Gwen was in the kitchen picking up Cheerios that Justin, her two-year-old, kept dropping on the floor from his high chair. She hadn't said much, just that Maria was still in her room.

"Maria?" I knocked again. "Maria, it's Aunt Vicky. Can I come in?"

I heard a thump on the other side of the door, but it stayed closed. "What are you doing here?" Maria's muffled voice asked. "I thought you go to bed in the morning."

"Usually I do. Not always. Your mom said you weren't feeling so great and thought maybe I could help."

"I told her not to call you." A pause. "Nobody can help."

"Let's talk about it and see. It'll be easier, though, if you open the door. Now that I've driven all the way out here, I'd hate to go back home without seeing my favorite niece."

"You want to see me? *Fine.*" The lock clicked and the door flew open as though an explosion had blasted it off its hinges. Maria stood there, one hand on the door, her chin jutting out defiantly. "Okay, now you can see me. Happy?"

"Yeah, I am. Although I'd rather see a smile on that pretty face."

Maria's eyes were red and puffy. Her lips quivered as she

drew in a shaky breath. "Don't tease me, Aunt Vicky. I can't take it right now."

Gently, I put a hand on her hair. She flinched but didn't pull away. I stroked her hair, then put a finger under her chin and tilted her head upward. "Tell me what's going on. Why do you think I'm teasing you?"

"Look at my face!" Her voice caught on a sob. "Will it stay like this?"

"Well, it's a little blotchy from crying. Otherwise, you're as gorgeous as always."

"Really? I don't look different to you? But—" She frowned and touched her cheek.

I was pretty sure now I knew what was going on. "When you woke up this morning, I bet you felt strange, not like yourself." She nodded. "Tell me what you saw when you looked in the mirror."

"This!"

"Tell me."

"A cat's face. But not like a real cat. It was me, with my hair and eyes. But I had pointy ears and my nose and mouth were like a cat's. And gray fur. And whiskers." She ran over to the full-length mirror that hung on the wall. "It's still there! Why did you tell me it was gone?"

I leaned against the doorframe and watched her. "It's an illusion."

She peered into the mirror, her hands moving over her face. Then she shook her head. "It's not! It's real. I can feel it."

"I'll show you. Do you have a camera?"

She picked up her phone from the nightstand and handed it to me. I used its camera to snap a picture, then handed her the result. She stared at the image, mouth open. Along her cheeks, her fingers traced whiskers that weren't there.

"See?" I said. "The same Maria we all know and love."

"But I can *feel* the whiskers," she said. She looked in the mirror, frowned, and looked at the photo again.

"Like I said, it's an illusion, one you can see and feel. But only you can. It's called a false face. It'll pass, and you'll feel normal again. And the next time it happens, you'll know what's going on."

Maria held up the phone and took another picture of herself.

She studied it, then looked up. "Why didn't anyone tell me I'd get a false face?"

Good question. I'd promised Gwen that I'd help Maria make the transition to shapeshifting, but walking the line between helping and taking over was tricky. I didn't want to muscle in on Gwen's parenting, but at the same time Maria had a right to know what was going to happen to her.

"We should have told you. I guess neither your mom nor I expected you to start experiencing false faces yet. They usually show up six, maybe eight months after the first shapeshifting dreams, and those only started a month ago, right?"

"Yeah."

"So you're ahead of schedule. We would have told you if we'd known it would happen so fast—honest."

"I was scared." Tears welled but didn't spill over. "I thought I was going to stay like that, like some kind of freak. You know, because mom's Ker . . . Kerth . . . like you are."

"Cerddorion."

"Right, Ker-THOR-ee-on." She pronounced the word slowly, drawing out each syllable, like she was tasting it as she spoke. "Cerddorion," she said again. "And Dad's human. What if I get stuck in between?"

"First of all, that won't happen. The Cerddorion have married humans before. Some of their kids have been human, and some have been shapeshifters. But nobody's ever been a hybrid of the two. So you don't need to worry about that, all right?"

"Okay." Her voice brimmed with doubt. "I guess."

"You're Cerddorion, Maria. There's no question about that any more. So you will be going through some changes. The good news is that your mom and I have both been through those same changes, so we can tell you what to expect. There won't be any surprises."

"Today was a surprise," she accused. "A bad one."

"You're right. We should have prepared you for it."

"What else do I have to be prepared for?"

"You'll get some weird feelings in your body, mostly in your arms and legs. Like growing pains. They'll pass. And here's something cool—you'll get stronger and faster than other kids. Better coordination, too. You'll be the best soccer player on your team."

"Really?" She brightened at the thought. "What about dancing?"

That's right. Gwen had mentioned Maria's favorite activity was dance class. "Strength, stamina, coordination—those things are all important for dancers, right? If you keep practicing, they'll definitely help."

Maria struck a couple of ballet poses in front of the mirror. Then the frown returned. "What if I shapeshift in front of everyone? Mom did."

So Gwen had told her daughter the story of how stage fright had caused her to shift into a mouse during the class play. No wonder the poor kid was worried she'd look like a freak.

"We'll make sure that sort of thing doesn't happen. I'll teach you how to stay in charge. Remember I showed you how to control your dreamscape?"

Maria nodded, a smile playing at her lips. "I like doing that."

"Shapeshifters can control their form, as well."

"Then how come Mom turned into a mouse?"

Gwen really shouldn't have told her that, not before Maria had experienced shapeshifting a few times. "It's true that a very, very strong emotion can cause us to change shape. But there are tricks you can learn to keep that from happening. I'll teach them to you."

Maria's forehead wrinkled. "But even you . . . Remember? I saw you turn into . . . into that *thing*. Up in New Hampshire."

Oh, that. Yeah, it was true. When a crazy scientist had kidnapped Maria to use her in shapeshifter experiments, sheer rage had turned me into a Harpy—snakes-for-hair, ear-splitting screeching, garbage-truck stench, and all. Witnessing that shift had to be a million times scarier than any story Gwen could tell.

"Seeing me change like that must have freaked you out, huh?"

"A little." She wouldn't meet my eye, which showed me how much "a little" meant "a lot." I'd rescued her as soon as I could—even in Harpy form, I'd managed to bring her home—but we'd only talked about the experience a couple of times. I'd have to sit her down, soon, for a heart-to-heart, make sure she was doing okay. With so much happening so fast in Maria's life, there was a lot we needed to discuss. But for now, I'd stick to the matter at hand. "A shift like that is really unusual. A Harpy is one of the fiercest creatures there is. I turned into one so I could get you out of that creepy place and bring you home." I sat down on the bed and patted the mattress. Maria sat beside me, and I put an arm around her. "I won't lie to you. The next months are going to bring lots of changes. But they'll follow a predictable pattern. Even if things happen faster than we expect, we know what's coming next, and you can get ready for it. Okay?"

"Okay." She sighed. "I don't know why I'm saying that. It's not like I have a choice."

"That's true. Not right now, anyway. But you will have control, once you learn how to use it. You might love shapeshifting. But if you hate it, you don't have to do it—you can stay in human form all the time. It will be up to you."

Maria leaned against me, and we sat like that for a couple of minutes, neither of us saying anything. Then she straightened suddenly, touching her face. She jumped up and ran to the mirror. "It's gone—the cat face. I don't feel weird anymore." She turned to me, relief brightening her expression. "So what do I do the next time that happens?"

"False faces are like those shapeshifting dreams you've been having. Both are ways for your body and mind to adjust to the idea of changing. Sort of like practice before you start doing it for real. You practice dancing before you go on stage, right?"

She nodded.

"Same thing. It's just practice. So the thing to do is remember it's not real. No more than a dream is real."

"But . . ."

I picked up the phone she'd left on the bed and tossed it to her. "You can trust this. If you start feeling funny or think you look strange, take a picture. The camera will show you the truth. Before long, you'll realize that false faces are just that—false. And you'll know that you're still yourself."

Maria clutched the phone to her chest, nodding. "You promise I won't change into a mouse or something at school?"

"Nothing like that will happen today, or any time soon. It could be a year or more before you start shapeshifting. And before you reach that point, we'll make sure you're ready. I promise." I held out my hand, the little finger straight up. "Want me to pinky swear?"

Maria rolled her eyes. "Please, Aunt Vicky. That's for little kids. I'll . . ." She searched for a suitably grown-up phrase. "I'll take your word for it."

DOWNSTAIRS, GWEN HAD FREED JUSTIN FROM THE HIGH chair. He ran over to me and raised his hands. I picked him up and got a banana-smeared kiss.

"Justin, come here, honey," Gwen said, lifting him out of my arms. "Let Mommy wash your face." Balancing Justin on her hip, she tore off a paper towel, wet it under the faucet, and handed it to me so I could wipe banana off my face. She wet another and passed it over his face, then his hands. Newly clean, Justin squirmed to get down. He toddled over to a basket in the corner, pulled out a plastic firetruck, and began pushing it across the floor.

Gwen watched him, silent.

"Maria's taking a shower," I said. "I think she'll be okay to catch the rest of the school day." Gwen nodded once but didn't look at me. "It was just a false face episode. She looked in the mirror and saw a cat-human mix. I did the camera trick, and that calmed her down." I leaned against the counter. "Thank goodness for digital cameras. Remember the first time it happened to me? I hid under the covers, thinking I'd suddenly grown a dog's head, while you ran to the one-hour photo center at the corner drug store with a roll of film."

I smiled at the memory, but my sister remained stone-faced, her eyes averted.

"What is it, Gwen?"

She looked at me then, her face taut with emotion. "I could have done the camera trick. But Maria wouldn't talk to me, wouldn't open the door. It had to be Aunt Vicky."

"She said she didn't want you to call me."

"Of course she didn't, because I suggested it and whatever Mom says *must* be wrong. But she knew I'd call you. What other option did I have?"

Justin's head snapped up at her tone. He picked up his firetruck and held it out to Gwen like an offering. "Play?" he asked.

The anger melted from Gwen's face. "Thank you," she said, taking the truck. She sank into a chair. Justin patted her leg, then went back to his basket of toys.

Gwen set the truck on the table. "I'm sorry, Vicky. I ask you to help with Maria, and you do a great job, and then I act like a resentful bit—" She glanced at Justin. "A resentful witch. I don't mean to. Things are hard right now."

I sat down across from her. "Puberty is a rough time, even when there's no shapeshifting involved."

"I suppose that's true. Lucky me—I get twice the fun." She rolled Justin's truck back and forth. "I suppose it's my own fault. I was so worried that Maria would develop shapeshifting abilities, I know my anxiety has rubbed off on her. I just want my baby to have a normal life."

I wanted to ask Gwen what she thought "normal" meant. For a Cerddorion girl, Maria was doing fine. In fact, she was way above average. If only Gwen could accept her own heritage, she'd be bursting with pride.

But I didn't have to ask Gwen that question, because Maria appeared in the doorway and asked it for both of us. " 'Normal'? What's 'normal,' Mom? Because if you want me to be like Kelsey or Megan, it's already too late for that." Kelsey and Megan were Maria's best friends—and one hundred percent human.

"Maria—"

My niece held up a hand to show she didn't want to hear whatever her mother had to say. Gwen bristled, then sagged.

"Aunt Vicky," Maria said, "can you give me a ride to school?"

"Um, sure. If it's all right with your mom."

Maria didn't wait for Gwen's answer. She swept past her and through the door to the garage. Gwen jumped at the slam.

"Go ahead, take her to school. Wait, though." She opened a drawer under the tabletop, took out a pad of paper, and scribbled something on it. "She'll need to give this note to the office. And here's some lunch money." She almost knocked over her chair as she got up and went to the counter. She reached into a canister and then handed me some crumpled dollar bills. "If you hurry, she'll be in time for third period."

I took the note and the money, not knowing what to say. Gwen was a great mom. She and Maria would work things out. But it wouldn't help for me to say so right now. I gave my sister a hug and headed for the door.

"Vicky?" I stopped with my hand on the knob. Gwen's voice sounded thick. When I looked back, her eyes were shiny with held-back tears. "Can you come over some day next week? School's out for April vacation, and I think it would help if you and Maria spent some time together."

"Of course. I'll give you a call tomorrow to work out a time."

"Thanks. I'll talk to you then." She turned away, loading breakfast dishes into the dishwasher.

5

YOU KNOW HOW AFTER A NICE, LONG, RESTFUL SLEEP, YOU wake up to find that things don't seem so bad after all?

Me neither.

While I slept, I'd tried to contact Mab using the dream phone, a special Cerddorion method of communication that operates through the psychic passageways that open in sleep. Mab doesn't own a real phone, the kind that goes *ring ring* and you pick it up and say "hello." At three hundred years old, she's not impressed by modern technology, even something as basic as a telephone. And she's skilled enough to answer a dream-phone call at any time of day. But today she hadn't answered.

There could be a million reasons why Mab didn't answer. It was afternoon in Wales when I'd tried to call. My aunt has a life; she doesn't sit around waiting to hear from me. And the call wasn't really urgent; I'd survived the Harpy attack, and the book hadn't told me anything new. Still, her silence concerned me. Mab had been badly weakened in our battle with Myrddin, and although she'd recovered, I worried about her sometimes. So I'd gotten up, gone into the kitchen, and called the pub in the village near Mab's home. Mr. Cadogan, the publican, told me Mab was fine as far as he knew; he'd spoken with her at the post office that morning. He took my message that I was trying to get in touch with her and promised he'd send someone out to deliver it right away. When I crawled back into bed, I fell into a deep, exhausted sleep.

All too soon I opened my eyes, and the problems of the past days elbowed their way back into my consciousness. My business was still crumbling. Maria and Gwen were still fighting. Simone Landry was still after Kane. And Pryce was still out there somewhere, probably getting ready to attack me again.

Welcome to another day in the life.

I checked my bedside clock and found it was only four thirty in the afternoon. I turned over, thinking I could catch another hour's worth of z's. But it was no good. All the things that were on my mind might as well be lined up by my bed, poking me with sticks. Sleep wasn't an option. I threw back the sheets and got up. I started some coffee, and took a shower while it brewed.

As I toweled off, I inspected my wounds from last night's Harpy attack. Everything was healing nicely. The edges of the wound where the Harpy had gouged my leg had knit together and scabbed over. There'd be a scar, but I couldn't do anything about that.

Dressed in jeans and a blue cotton sweater, I sipped a mug of strong black coffee. I turned on the phone's ringer and checked for messages. Just one—the exact number of clients I had left. I crossed my fingers. *Please don't let it be a job cancellation.*

It wasn't. The number was Kane's. "Hi, it's me," he said. His warm, deep voice sent tingles shivering through me. "I've been thinking all day how great it would've been to have breakfast in bed with you. Couldn't get the idea out of my mind." He chuckled, and the tingles reached my toes. "Especially because I have to work tonight. Simone is giving a talk at a meeting of the Human-Paranormal Women's Business Association, with some potentially big donors in attendance, and I need to be there." *Oh.* Funny how fast tingles can evaporate. "It wasn't on my calendar—I guess her assistant forgot to notify my assistant or something. Simone told me about it this morning, right after you left."

I'd bet she did. She was probably batting her eyelashes and telling him how much she needed him there before the door had closed behind me.

"I know you're working tonight, too," Kane went on, "so

maybe I'll see you tomorrow? Oh, not for breakfast, though. I've got another meeting with Simone in the morning. Always the way, isn't it? And this month's retreat is almost here. I hope we can get together before then. If not, I guess it'll have to be some time next week. Call me when you can."

Always the way—well, yes and no. In some ways, it was a typical message from Kane. Our work schedules didn't have a lot of overlap, and one or the other of us was always canceling plans. But what wasn't typical was hearing another woman's name woven through his message. *Simone, Simone, Simone.* I knew what she was trying to do—push herself between us until the werewolf retreat, when she'd have him all to herself.

Why was he managing her campaign, anyway? Kane had never been interested in Deadtown politics before. He was all about getting the norms to recognize paranormal rights, preferably in Washington. How had she talked him into this?

Those triumphant green eyes. That smug assurance that she'd win.

I needed to talk to Kane. And not on the phone. It wasn't yet five in the evening, and he never left the office until six. If I went there now, maybe—just maybe—he could pencil me in for an appointment between Simone and Simone and goddamn Simone.

THE NORMS' RUSH HOUR WAS RUSHING FULL FORCE AS I walked along Tremont Street toward Kane's office near Government Center. Sidewalks and streets were choked with people, all in a hurry and yet not getting anywhere very fast. As I approached Kane's building, workers poured out the front door. Among them was a woman in an emerald green blazer. A woman with long, wavy chestnut hair.

She turned right, walking away from me. But there was no mistaking Simone Landry.

That damn shampoo-commercial-gorgeous hair of hers was so unfair. I ran a hand through my own hair—whatever I tried to do to it, after a shift it always returned to the same straight, short, strawberry-blonde style. How come werewolves lucked out with their luxurious hair?

Inside, I crossed the lobby and took the elevator to Kane's floor. Iris, the blonde human receptionist who kept things running while the firm's werewolf staff was on retreat, was leaving. She smiled when she saw me.

"Is Kane still here?"

"Do you have to ask? He always beats me to work, and he's always here when I go home. Sometimes I wonder if he lives in his office."

"Me, too."

"Your timing is good. He just got out of a meeting."

"With Simone Landry?" God, my voice sounded tight. I coughed some of the tension out of it.

"Yes. She left a minute or two ago. I was waiting for her to leave so I could lock up." She held the door open for me.

"Thanks." I passed into the reception area.

"Must have been a good meeting," Iris remarked. "Simone was grinning like she won the lottery when she came out." She closed the glass door and turned the key. Then she waved and headed for the elevators.

I unclenched my fists and inspected the half-moon fingernail marks in my palms. Okay. Simone was hanging on Kane like a monkey on a banana tree. But she wasn't here now. I'd finally have him all to myself.

Kane's outer office looked like the offices of any other top-tier law firm in the city: elegant and understated. The reception area held black leather chairs and sofas, with accent lighting showing the tasteful artwork to its best advantage. Simone, in her tailored suits, would look right at home here. I glanced down at my jeans, wishing for a moment I'd dressed up. But that was silly. I shook my head and walked down the hallway. Kane's door was last on the right, the corner office.

I tapped on the door, cracked it open, and peered inside. Kane sat at his desk, his suit jacket draped over the back of the chair, his shirtsleeves rolled up. When he saw me, his don't-interrupt-me scowl morphed into a grin. Tingle alert. He pushed back his chair and came around the desk, then opened the door wide and drew me inside. His arms were strong and solid around me as he greeted me with a deep kiss.

Simone who?

Yet there was a lingering scent of perfume in the office, sweetly floral with spicy notes and a musky undertone. If I could detect Simone's perfume, to a werewolf's sensitive nose it was probably as though she were still standing right here. Which, no doubt, was her intention. She was making sure that she'd register in some part of Kane's brain, even while his mind focused on other things.

I frowned and pulled away, wishing the big plate glass windows were the kind that open. The room needed air.

Kane curled his fingers around mine with one hand and smoothed his tie with the other. We sat in the visitors' chairs that faced his desk. "This is a nice surprise," he said. "Did you get my message?"

"I did. But I wanted to see you, not play our usual game of phone tag for the next couple of days."

"I'm glad." He held my hand in both of his and gazed at me. I saw no trace of guilt in his eyes, nothing but pleasure that I was here.

And yet Simone's scent floated between us like a ghost.

"I was finishing up a couple of things here, and then I was going to grab a burger before Simone's event. Do you want to get something to eat? It'll be quick, but—"

"Why are you managing Simone Landry's campaign?" Okay, so I'd blurted, but at least I'd asked the question. I watched his face, but all I saw there was surprise.

"You mean why am I wasting my time managing a bid for a figurehead position that has no real power?" He chuckled. "Good question. Well, Simone's a friend, and she asked me to. But . . ." He stopped and remained quiet for a moment. I leaned forward, my heart beating way harder than I wanted to admit, waiting to hear what came next. "But you're thinking there's more, and you're right. I've been wanting to discuss this with you, but work's been so busy I've hardly seen you."

No, my heart thumped. *No, no, no. Don't break up with me. Not over her.*

If Kane saw what I was feeling, he didn't show it. He kept talking. "Simone's campaign is a practice run. I want to see from the inside how a political campaign works, because I'm thinking of running for Congress next year."

Congress. A werewolf could be elected to Congress about as easily as I could take a running jump and land on the moon, but so what? If anyone could pull it off, it was Kane. And I liked the sound of "I'm running for Congress" way better than "I'm starting a pack with Simone." I sat back, my heart no longer threatening to leap out of my chest.

His eyes shone, staring into some far-off place, perhaps the marble halls of the Capitol. "What better way to change the system than from the inside? I'm tired of standing on the outside, banging on the door and begging to be thrown a few scraps of justice." He refocused on me. "But that's a long way off. Right now, I'm just exploring the possibility. And as I said, my main reason for helping Simone is that she's a friend. Our families go way back."

My head was buzzing—it was too much to take in. "Does Simone know?"

"About—? Oh, you mean that I'm considering a run for Congress? Yes, I've mentioned it. Why?"

Simone didn't care about being reelected to the Council of Three. She was campaigning for a different job: politician's wife. I mean, who would look better standing beside Kane at political events—a successful politician with model looks and a tailored wardrobe, or a demon exterminator whose only dress was crumpled in a ball at the back of her closet? There was no contest, and Simone knew it.

Now, she was showing him what an asset she'd be to his political aspirations. And soon, at the werewolf retreat, she'd do whatever it is she-wolves do when they're after a mate. Kane didn't stand a chance.

I didn't stand a chance.

"Don't look so stunned," Kane said, squeezing my hand. "I know running for office would be a big step. But like I said, I haven't decided yet, and we can discuss it after I get back from Princeton." Princeton was the location of the werewolf retreat closest to Boston, the one Kane—and, I had no doubt, Simone—attended each full moon.

I searched his eyes again. Why was I even looking for guilt? I had no special hold on this man—and after all, that was how I'd always said I wanted it. I wasn't cut out for the wife-and-mother routine. If he wanted to start his own pack, he'd find a suitable mate, and we both knew it wouldn't be me. I had no right to hold him back.

So why did I suddenly feel like I was choking on the cloying scent of that damn perfume?

"Vicky." Kane's hand traced light circles on the back of mine. "Was there something you wanted to tell me?"

I blinked. "What do you mean?"

"Well, most of the time I practically have to make an appointment to see you. Today you appear unexpectedly both before and after work. Don't get me wrong—I like it." His smile was warm. "I like it a lot. But you have to admit it's unusual."

The warmth of that smile. I didn't want Simone basking in it. I didn't want it shining on anyone but me.

"I . . . well, I was thinking that maybe I'd go to Princeton with you." The words were out of my mouth before I knew I'd say them.

Now it was Kane's turn to look stunned. His smile froze. His hand stopped moving on mine. "To the retreat?"

"Oh, well, if you don't want me to go . . ." If I backpedaled any faster, I'd be halfway across Boston in a minute.

"Want you to go? Of course I do. That invitation is always open. Always. And you know how long I've been hoping you'd say yes. But I didn't want to push you. No pressure." The surprise left his eyes as his smile went supernova. "So, when were you thinking of coming? Some time in the summer?"

"This month."

"But . . . have you looked at a calendar? This month's retreat is less than two days away."

"Maybe I don't want to lose my nerve." My attempt at a light-hearted laugh sounded idiotic. "Maybe I want to, you know, close my eyes and jump in at the deep end."

"Vicky, if you're worried about losing your nerve, perhaps you should wait." When I started to object, he held up his hand. "I don't want you to close your eyes and jump. I want you to be sure. You know, I'd accepted that it wasn't going to happen. But now you're sitting here telling me not only do you want to come, you want to come this month—that means the day after tomorrow. It's sudden."

"So you're saying you don't want me to come." I spoke slowly, as though that would keep my voice from shaking. It didn't.

"That's not what I'm saying at all. I want you there with me. Of course I do. But not on a whim."

"It's not a whim," I lied. "I've been thinking about it for a while. My schedule opened up—more clients canceled." Well, at least that much was true. I tried to decipher the concern on his face. Was it for me, or for a missed opportunity with Simone? "But if you'd rather wait until the summer . . ."

"The hell with summer." He pulled me from my chair onto

his lap. He nuzzled my neck, and I gasped at the touch of his lips. "If I could, I'd be running through the woods with you right this minute. Vicky, I have wanted this for so damn long. I can't even tell you how happy you've made me."

"I'm happy, too." At least, I thought I was. It felt so right to be close to Kane, surrounded by his strength, his warmth. Feeling his lips brush my skin, then press harder. Breathing his scent that always sent a shiver through me. Feelings I loved, that I never wanted to end.

But somewhere inside all that, a tiny voice whispered, "What have you done?" I wasn't a werewolf. I didn't want to pretend to be one.

I shook off my doubts and reached for him.

For the first time since I'd known him, Kane said his work could wait. We went out for a celebratory burger. Well, he had a burger; I had coffee. It was too early in my day for a heavy meal. The whole time, he talked about what to expect at Princeton. Picking me up and traveling there together. Checking in. How the day cabins were arranged. How packs were based around family units, and who belonged to which pack.

"What about Simone Landry?" I asked, trying to sound disinterested. "Does she have her own pack?"

Kane shook his head. "Simone is still part of the Landry pack, her family of origin. The oldest daughter. She hasn't gone solitary, and she hasn't mated. I guess she's content where she is."

I wanted to ask what happened when a werewolf chose a mate, but I couldn't think of a way to phrase the question without sounding like either (a) I was paranoid about Simone, or (b) I was dropping hints about our own relationship. So I let Kane talk.

Finally he checked his watch. "I've got to get over to the Back Bay for Simone's talk. Where's your job tonight?"

"Cambridge, near Porter Square. I'm getting rid of a little old lady's nightmares for her."

"It's a pity we didn't have time to celebrate properly tonight. What about tomorrow? How about we get together at Creature Comforts and pop open a bottle of Axel's finest champagne?" He grinned.

"Champagne?" I made a face.

"Okay, then, we'll unscrew the cap of your favorite lite beer.

Whatever you want. Simone has another fund-raiser, but she can manage without me. It'll be our night."

Our night, with no Simone to be seen? "Sounds perfect."

We arranged to meet at ten the next night. At the door, Kane swept me up in an embrace that turned heads throughout the room. He was whistling—actually whistling—as he walked along the sidewalk toward the parking garage.

I watched him recede into the night. Half of me felt like I'd scored a major triumph. The other half felt like I was standing on the high dive, eyes closed, toes curled around the edge, taking a last breath before I plunged into the deep end.

6

I NEEDED TO STOP BY THE APARTMENT TO PICK UP MY equipment for tonight's job. When I walked in, the television was on, but the volume was below its normal ear-shattering level. Juliet was just hanging up the phone. *Oh no, don't tell me my one remaining client has canceled.*

"That wasn't for me, was it?"

"Feeling a little self-centered tonight, are we? Why would it be for you?"

"Clients have been canceling right and left, and I'm about to leave for a job."

"Oh. Well, in that case, don't worry. Your little old lady—what was her name?" She hunted through scraps of paper strewn across the coffee table.

"Phyllis."

"That's right, Phyllis. You'll be happy to know that Phyllis is still tormented by nightmares. She called to confirm that you're coming tonight."

"You told her yes?"

"Do I look like a secretary? I told her you'd call her back."

I put out my hand, and Juliet tossed me the phone. I wasn't exactly *happy* that the poor old thing was having nightmares, I thought as I dialed; I was just relieved to have a job. Phyllis sounded thrilled to hear from me, and I reassured her I'd be on my way within half an hour.

"Ooh, give me the phone—quick!" Juliet, her eyes fixed on the TV, was almost shouting as I hung up.

"Why, what's so urgent?"

"If I call *right now*, I'll get a free apple corer in addition to the food chopper and extra bonus knives!" On the screen, a smiling woman mercilessly sliced the heart out of a juicy-looking apple. A toll-free phone number scrolled across the bottom of the screen.

"Um, Juliet, when was the last time in your six-hundred-fifty years of existence that you needed to core an apple?"

She sent me a withering look. "If I *had* needed to core one, I'd have been completely unprepared—'as one that unaware / Hath dropp'd a precious jewel in the flood.'"

Shakespeare again. She regarded me as though she expected me to respond in kind. *No, uh-uh.* No Shakespeare game for me tonight. Juliet always won, anyway. I knew maybe half a dozen lines of the guy's work, the same ones everybody knew, like "To be or not to be" and "Romeo, Romeo, wherefore art thou, Romeo?" I hadn't had several centuries to memorize every word he ever wrote. And if I'd been around as long as Juliet had, I like to think I'd have found other things to do. I ignored the quotation and offered her the phone. She took it but set it on the coffee table without dialing.

"So that's what you were doing when I came in—adding more stuff to your 'as seen on TV' collection? What did you buy tonight?"

"Not much. Well, I did get one of those little gizmos that scramble an egg inside the shell. Don't look at me like that, it's clever. I want to see how it works. And I ordered a dozen micro-fiber dust cloths in assorted colors and sizes."

"Dust cloths? You don't dust."

"I don't cook meatloaf, either. But if I want to get two self-draining meatloaf pans, complete with recipes *and* a guide knife for cutting perfectly uniform slices, for only nineteen-ninety-nine plus shipping and handling, that's my business. I can afford it. I—Oh, wait. I forgot to tell you the best thing I bought. A pair of slippers, fuzzy blue ones, with working flashlights built into the front. So you can see where you're going without turning on the lights! Isn't that brilliant? I'd have bought a pair for you, too, but I wasn't sure of your size."

"That's okay." I grinned as a relevant line from Shakespeare popped into my head. "Romeo would love it: 'But soft, what light through yonder window breaks?'"

"'It is the east, and Juliet's fuzzy blue slippers are the sun!'" She collapsed in a fit of laughter. When she sat up, wiping tears from her eyes, she said, "Don't you think if Shakespeare were alive today he'd be writing infomercials?"

"I think I need to get our cable company to block any and all shopping channels. And I also think you need to get out more."

"That won't be a problem tonight, thank Hades. I'm working. My Goons will be here shortly to escort me to Colwyn's prison cell."

"Let me know if anything related to Pryce comes up."

She nodded. "I will. Anyway, after we're done questioning that old fossil, I plan to eat out. I just have to convince Brad and his partner to stop at Creature Comforts on the way home." She smiled, showing her fangs. "So don't wait up."

PHYLLIS'S SMALL, TWO-STORY HOUSE STOOD IN A NEIGHBOR-hood of triple-deckers on a side street north of Porter Square. The house looked modest, with gray shingles and white trim behind a chain-link fence, but given the explosion in Cambridge real-estate prices, it was probably worth more money than I'd see in the next nine or ten years.

Carrying the duffel bag that held my demon-fighting gear, I let myself in through the gate, went up the short walk, and rang the doorbell. The door was opened by a tiny woman wearing a pink terry cloth bathrobe. Her white hair was rolled in curlers, and she held the biggest cat I'd ever seen. With long gray fur and a lazy expression, he was nearly half the size of the small woman who held him. The animal was so large I could almost imagine Phyllis saddling him up and going for a ride—not that any cat that ever lived would suffer such an indignity.

"Come in, dear, come in," Phyllis said. "Close the storm door quickly. I don't want Pookie to get out."

Pookie. Okay. Currently Pookie was lounging in Phyllis's skinny arms with half-closed eyes, looking like a nap was way higher up on his feline to-do list than an adventure in the streets of Cambridge. But I stepped inside, pulling the door shut behind me.

Phyllis poured Pookie from her arms. He lay at her feet where he'd landed, adjusting his position a little, then started snoring. She watched the cat with the fond expression of a mother watching her sleeping child. Then she looked up at me, her eyes large behind her glasses.

"Well, dear," she said, "let's go slaughter some demons."

UPSTAIRS, PHYLLIS SAT IN HER BED, PROPPED UP AGAINST SEVeral pillows and tucked under a frilly pink coverlet. Her bathrobe hung on the door, and her fuzzy pink slippers (no flashlights in the toes) waited beside the bed. She watched me through her glasses as I plugged in the dream portal generator and flipped it on. "Oh, my," she murmured when a beam of multicolored, sparkling light lit up the room.

"This is how I'll enter your dreamscape," I explained. "It opens a doorway between this plane of existence and the one where dreams occur. It's password protected, which means I have to say the password to step through the portal. That way, no demons can sneak out of your dreams to bother you while you're awake, okay?"

She nodded, her eyes wide.

"The colors you see are like coordinates; they automatically key themselves to this location. Put your palm here, on this plate." She did, and I fiddled with the dials until the machine beeped. "Right now, I'm calibrating the machine to your vibration. Every human has a unique vibrational signature, like a fingerprint. The calibration makes sure I go straight into your dreamscape and no one else's. The colors make sure I come back here. Okay, I've got it."

Phyllis pulled back her hand and looked at it like she'd never seen it before. "So you have to be with the sleeping person for it to work?"

"No, but it's easier that way." I turned off the machine. The colors hung in the air for a moment, then blinked out. "Mostly I work out of clients' homes so we can get the paperwork out of the way." I nodded to a stack of standard forms that Phyllis had signed. "And, more important, so I can get a sense of the dreams that have been troubling you." Fear crossed Phyllis's face, and I patted her hand. "Don't worry—the nightmares will be gone after tonight. But tell me about them so I'll know what I'm looking for."

"Oh, dear." She clutched my hand. "The dreams make me so *tired*. That's the worst part. Every morning I wake up exhausted, as if I hadn't slept at all."

"That's a common trick of Drudes, the nightmare demons. It keeps the victim's resistance low. Is there one dominant dream, or are the nightmares always different? Tell me what you can recall."

"Oh, it's one dream. Night after night after night—it's always the same." She closed her eyes and took a deep breath. "I'm standing in a long hallway that stretches endlessly before me. And I do mean endlessly, dear, it goes on and on forever. The hallway is empty, but all down the length of it, on both sides, are doors. The doors are evenly spaced, every three or four feet. And they're all closed."

"How do you feel when you look down that hallway?"

"Frightened." She opened her eyes, and I could see the fear there. "I know there's one door I *must* open, that something important is behind it."

"Do you know what?"

She shook her head. "I haven't a clue, I'm afraid. But I *do* know that if I pick the wrong door, something terrible will happen." Her frail shoulders shrugged helplessly. "I don't know what that is, either. Just that I must avoid it—whatever it is—at all costs."

"So what do you do?"

"Nothing. Absolutely nothing. I stand there like a statue, sick with indecision and fear. There's so much riding on me, and I can't act. The impulse to pick a door gets stronger and stronger. The pressure becomes horrible, unbearable. I wake up screaming." She covered her face with both hands. "It's so distressing," she said softly through her fingers. "Poor Pookie refuses to sleep with me anymore."

Gently, I pried her hands from her face. "Well, tonight you won't have to do a thing. It's not up to you to pick a door. That's my job."

Relief flashed across her face, followed immediately by worry. "But what if you open the wrong one?"

"I won't. The worst thing behind any of those doors is a demon. And I'm going in equipped to kill demons." I showed her my pistol. "Bronze bullets," I said, loading the magazine. "Kills 'em dead." I shoved a spare magazine into the front pocket of my jeans.

She stared at the gun, then nodded once. "Good."

"Here's how this job will go. I'll enter your dreamscape through the portal I showed you. Since you've been having a recurring dream, I'll land in the hallway you described. This"—I showed her my InDetect—"is like a Geiger counter for demons. It helps me flush out the Drudes hiding in your dreamscape. I'll move down the hallway, pointing the InDetect at each door. If it doesn't click, there's no demon there and I move on to the next door."

"And if it does?"

"If the InDetect clicks, it means there's a demon behind the door, hoping you'll turn the knob so it can jump out and yell, 'Boo!'" Phyllis flinched. "No worries. When I open the door, the demon will be the one who's in for a surprise." I brandished the pistol again.

Phyllis's expression turned puzzled. "But if you only open the doors that have demons behind them, how will you find the right one?"

"What do you mean?"

"The right door. The door I'm supposed to open. The one with something important behind it."

"Phyllis, that's nothing but manipulation by the Drudes causing your nightmare. There isn't anything important behind a door—only demons. They feed off your fear and indecision. They want you to open a door, any door. If there's a Drude behind it, they get a rush out of scaring you. If there's nothing behind it, they feed on your fear that you've chosen the wrong door. You can't win." I smiled reassuringly. "But I can win for you. I can kill the demons."

"I certainly hope so, dear." Phyllis looked doubtful. I couldn't blame her, since she'd never actually seen any demons in her dreams. But she swallowed her doubts, along with the magically enhanced sleeping pill I gave her, and lay on her back. A few minutes later, soft snores filled the room. She sounded exactly like Pookie.

I double-checked my gun. Then I powered up the portal generator and stepped into Phyllis's dream.

I STOOD IN A LONG, BRIGHTLY LIT HALLWAY. JUST AS PHYLLIS had described, it stretched ahead of me as far as I could see. I turned around. There was nothing behind me but dense, gray fog. Ahead, the white floor and walls glared relentlessly under harsh fluorescent lighting. Doors lined up along both sides. They were the rusty brown color of dried blood.

Open a door. The thought tickled the back of my mind. *But, for heaven's sake, don't open the wrong one!*

I pushed the nightmare whispers aside and switched on the InDetect. With my left hand, I pointed it toward the first door. My right hand held the pistol ready.

Not a click. The InDetect remained silent. I moved on to the next door.

For door after door, the InDetect found nothing. I shook it, trying to remember the last time I'd recharged the battery. I turned it off, waited ten seconds, then turned it on again. The unit hummed to life, its green light blinking. *Click click click,* it calibrated itself. No technical malfunction, and the battery was fine. There simply weren't any demons behind those doors.

I squinted down the hallway. The harsh light made my head ache. The hall stretched on forever, just as before, even though I'd checked dozens of doors. The fog was still at my back, the dream portal beam still beside me. Either they'd moved with me, swallowing up Phyllis's dreamscape as I went forward, or I was somehow back where I started. Either was possible in dreams.

I sighed. Nothing to do but keep going. I pointed the silent InDetect at another door, then another. And still another.

Inside Phyllis's dreamscape, time lost meaning. It felt like I'd spent decades, centuries, in here. Like I'd been checking doors since dinosaurs roamed the earth—there was probably a Tyrannosaurus rex behind this one. I sneaked a peek at my watch, which kept real-world time, and saw that ten whole minutes had passed outside. I sighed again. It was going to be a long night.

I'd checked several more doors—it could've been three or three hundred, no way to tell—when a scream ripped the air. I tensed. Far down the hallway, a door banged open and out hurtled a demon. It was too far away for the InDetect to pick up, but there was no mistaking the creature, even at this distance. It was a textbook illustration of a demon: huge, pointed horns; massive bat wings; and long, razor-sharp tail. Phyllis's Drude must have gotten tired of waiting for her to open its door.

As I raised my pistol to fire, a second figure bolted into the hallway. The demon shrieked and ran down the hall. This second figure wasn't a demon—or if it was a demon, it was hiding its true form. It had the silhouette of a man. He chased the demon. In a moment, he'd tackled it. The demon shrieked and thrashed as they struggled.

I moved forward, quickly but cautiously, pistol ready.

The man stood. The demon remained on the floor.

My InDetect was silent. Still too far to pick up any demon vibes. The man could be a demon in disguise, or he could be a beloved dream figure—Phyllis's husband or son or high school sweetheart. I didn't dare shoot him.

The man pointed at the demon, and it levitated. As it floated above the floor, he gestured around it with his hands. The demon started to shrink. Rapidly, it grew smaller and smaller. The man pulled a sack from his pocket. He plucked the infant-sized demon from the air and dropped it inside. Then he tied the sack shut at the neck. Even from here, I could see the sack bouncing around as the captured demon struggled. Its howls, full of rage and pain and fear, echoed down the hallway.

Shrinking demons and trapping them in a sack. I had a feeling I'd just met my competition—the one who'd been clearing out Boston's demons and making all my clients cancel.

"Hey!" I yelled.

The man didn't even look my way. In two seconds, he'd opened the nearest door, run through, and slammed it shut behind him.

What the hell?

Keeping my eye on the door, I sprinted down the hallway. My boots pounded the tiles, my breath rasped in my ears. By the time I reached the place where he'd disappeared, I wasn't sure which door he'd gone through. The damn doors all looked the same.

There should be residual traces of the captured demon here. My chest heaving, I picked a door and pointed the InDetect at it. No clicks. The InDetect didn't register any demonic presence at the next one, either. But at the third, a faint, rapid clicking started up. I pressed the device closer, and the clicks got louder. Bingo.

I turned the knob, pistol ready. Keeping to one side, I pushed the door open.

I braced my gun with both hands and spun into the doorway. Another long, white, empty corridor led toward infinity. No closed doors. Instead, the hallway branched into a seemingly endless number of other hallways. I ran forward, pointing the InDetect down each branch, listening for the clicks that would indicate demons lurked that way. When the InDetect told me to, I veered off to the left or right, trying to catch up with the shadowy figure.

Following the clicks, I raced through the impossible architecture of a complex dreamscape—up and down staircases, along ledges, through hallways that led to other hallways, rooms that morphed into different rooms. It was a building designed by M. C. Escher's insane brother. My InDetect got louder as I caught up, telling me I was getting closer. The clicking was almost deafening as I pointed the device at a black-painted door.

I tucked the InDetect inside my sweater. Holding my pistol ready, I ran over and pushed open the door.

On the other side was nothing but blue sky.

I teetered on the threshold, then threw myself back a step. My heart pounded as I realized how close I'd come to running through that doorway into empty air.

In dreams, the dreamer can't die. But I sure as hell could. When I entered a dreamscape, I was there physically. A demon, a gunshot, an explosion, a zillion-story fall from a crazy building—anything like that could kill me for real.

I panted, hands on my knees, trying to catch my breath and calm my hyperactive pulse.

Then something slammed into me from behind, and I plummeted into the void.

7

SHAPESHIFT! MY TERRIFIED BRAIN SCREAMED.

The gun flew from my hand. My pinwheeling arms began to elongate and sprout feathers. Energy built up around me.

No. The thought pushed its way through my panic. *Not in a dream.* I forced my arms to keep their shape. Don't change shape in someone else's dream—it was the first thing Mab taught me about fighting dream-demons. The consequences could be disastrous. I could end up trapped in here forever, my physical body slowly absorbed into Phyllis's dreamscape. And that would be worse than dying.

Wind blasted my face as I hurtled through the air. I wiped the water from my eyes and squinted. No ground rushed up to meet me. I was falling, but I fell through endless space.

My stomach was in my throat. My fingers and toes twitched for something to grab hold of. But at least I wasn't about to slam into some solid surface at a hundred miles an hour.

Think, Vicky. My body still wanted to become a bird and use the air to hold itself up. But that wouldn't work, I reminded myself; not in a dream. During a shift, the animal brain takes over, and the shift can last for hours. Even if I could find the dream portal and remember what it was, I couldn't speak the password that would let me through. If Phyllis woke up while I was in bird form, the portal would close and I'd dissolve into her dreams. No, the way to get out of here wasn't by changing myself. I'd have to manipulate Phyllis's dreamscape.

Not that I had a lot to work with. To my left, the building I'd been pushed from flashed by. All its doors were closed. There were no knobs, nothing to grab and stop my fall. Reaching forward, I changed my position and dived straight for one. I braced for impact but bounced off it like it was made of rubber. I tried again. This time I shouted, "Open!" right before I hit. No luck. I bounced back into the sky, still falling.

I glanced downward. Still no sign of the ground.

Okay, there were other opening spells and commands. I'd try "open sesame" next.

I angled myself to take another dive when a shadow fell over me. Something grabbed my waist.

Oof! The air whooshed out of my lungs as my fall suddenly stopped.

Inside my sweater, the InDetect clicked to life. The arms that held my waist were scaly and slimy. I cocked my head upward and saw leathery wings and a hideous, fanged face.

I'd come here to catch Phyllis's demons. Now, one of them had caught me.

The demon clutched me to its chest. When it saw me looking, it snarled and dug in its talons. It flapped its wings, and we moved upward in a wide, slow spiral.

High above us, the black-painted door hung open. We seemed to be heading for it. Probably the Drude wanted solid ground under its feet before it tore off my head and drank my blood.

My pistol was gone, but I still had several knives strapped to my body. I reached toward the sheath I wore on my hip. As soon as this demon landed, I'd bury eight inches of bronze in its gut.

The demon sensed my movement. With a nasty laugh, it pinned my arms against my sides. Holding me with its left arm, it frisked me with its right hand. One by one, it plucked my daggers from their sheaths and threw them into the void.

So much for that idea.

I tried wishing for a weapon—sometimes that works in dreams—but nothing materialized. And we were almost up to the black door.

I had one last, desperate idea. My weapons were gone, but I still had some bronze.

My right hand was pressed against the front pocket of my jeans, the pocket that held my spare clip of bronze bullets. The way my hand covered the magazine, the demon had missed it while frisking me.

Moving as unobtrusively as possible, I worked the magazine from my pocket. My fingers found the groove at its top, and I thumbed out the first bullet of the clip. Clutching it with three fingers, I removed another, then let the magazine drop. I passed a bullet into my left hand and clenched the two bullets tightly, one in each fist.

We'd ascended higher than the open door. I could see it below us, about fifty yards away. The demon dived toward it, folding its wings at the last moment to get through the doorway.

As soon as we touched the floor, I was ready. I wrenched out of the Drude's grasp, spun around, and shoved both bullets up its nose.

The demon's yellow eyes squinted in puzzlement, then opened wide. The skin of its face bubbled. It clawed at its nostrils as its nose collapsed and the bullets went deeper into its head. Sulfurous smoke billowed as it staggered backward toward the open door. I slammed both hands into its chest, pushing it through. I managed to shut the door seconds before the demon's head exploded with a thunderous boom. Chunks of flesh and bone slapped against the door.

My legs were shaky on the solid floor. My knees buckled, and I sat down hard. I stayed that way for a couple of minutes, enjoying the feeling of blessed stillness, as my heartbeat slowed to normal. No falling. No flying. Just sitting.

But I couldn't sit here forever. My watch told me that more than five hours had passed since I entered Phyllis's dreamscape. Time passes differently in dreams, so it wasn't surprising that the first ten minutes had dragged on like centuries, then the next several hours zipped by in mere minutes. I was running short on time. I needed to find my way back to the dream portal and return to the real world.

As soon as I thought about the portal, I saw it in front of me. I love when that happens in dreams. Its beam sparkled like an oasis after a long crawl across the desert. Beside it, the fog that had followed me through the building billowed and swirled.

I stood—my legs felt more steady now—and went over to the portal. I was more than ready to leave this dreamscape. Speaking the password, I stepped into the beam.

Nothing happened.

I tried again, pronouncing each syllable precisely. Colored lights shimmered around me, but I didn't get that fizzy feeling of dissolving into them.

I stepped back and examined the beam. Something was wrong. The colors were off. This wasn't the portal I'd used to step into Phyllis's dreamscape from her bedroom. It was probably a simple dream image created by her subconscious.

I hate when that happens in dreams.

But could it be a real portal? It seemed likely that the guy who'd stuffed that demon into his sack was the same person who was making Boston's demons disappear. To get into people's dreams, he must have his own dream portal generator. So who was he? And why on earth was he collecting other people's personal demons?

Before I could pursue that line of thought, the portal started buzzing. It brightened, its colors vibrated faster. A silhouette appeared in the beam. Someone was entering Phyllis's dream. Someone tall—and carrying a very big gun.

I was unarmed, and that gun didn't exactly look friendly. I turned my head, trying to find an exit, but the room had changed. The hallway that had brought me here was gone. Except for the black-painted door that led to the outside, all the walls were blank. There was no place to hide. I was trapped.

The silhouette grew more solid.

I stepped back. Fog swirled up around me. I moved deeper into the fog, until I could no longer see the portal. Whoever was entering, if I couldn't see him, he couldn't see me. Or so I hoped.

The fog was so thick I literally couldn't see my own hand when I held it an inch in front of my face. It cloyed like cotton in my nose and lungs, making breathing difficult. I couldn't walk forward to face whoever had come through that portal, but I couldn't stay here and suffocate, either.

The fog had followed me all through the building. Maybe I could step out of it and be back where I started. I pictured my entry point: the white tile floor, the harsh lighting, the red-brown doors. Most of all, the sparkling beam of the dream portal, its colors keyed to Phyllis's bedroom. In my mind's eye, the beam was to my right, as though I'd stepped through it only a moment ago, its colors moving in a kaleidoscope of shifting patterns. I imagined myself in that hallway, making the image real. When I moved out of the fog, I told myself, I'd be there.

I strode forward, my boots clicking on the tile floor, not letting myself think about the second portal and its threatening silhouette. The fog thinned, caressing my hair and skin with wispy fingers as I departed its grasp. I was back where I'd started, in an endless hallway lined with red-brown doors. To my right, the dream portal shimmered and glowed. There was no silhouette, and the colors looked right this time. I allowed myself a moment to sag against the wall. But the fog swirled behind me, and who knew what might emerge from it, as I had a minute ago?

Speaking the password, I stepped through the beam and back into the real world.

PHYLLIS'S KITCHEN WAS THE SORT OF GRANDMOTHERLY place that should always smell like gingerbread. Red-and-white-checked curtains framed the window over the sink. Between the tall wooden cabinets hung plaques with sayings like BLESS THIS KITCHEN and RECIPE FOR FRIENDSHIP. An oval braided rug in shades of blue and brown warmed the yellow linoleum floor. There was even a teddy bear–shaped cookie jar sitting chubbily on the counter.

I sat at the kitchen table, a glass of cool tap water in my hand, my third since I'd exited Phyllis's dreamscape. My throat was dry, and I was still coughing up cottony puffs of fog. Pookie rubbed against my legs, his purr rumbling like a diesel engine. Phyllis was asleep upstairs. After exiting her dreamscape, I'd checked her vital signs and they were fine—better than mine, probably. Now I was waiting for her to wake up.

I reached down and absently stroked Pookie's gray fur. This job had been a disaster. I'd killed exactly one Drude. The interloper with the sack had snatched at least one other, but I hadn't been able to make sure Phyllis's dreamscape was totally clear. I'd have to come back another night and do a sweep for any lingering Drudes. That is, if Phyllis would allow me back. That black door I'd opened—it was obviously the forbidden door, the one behind which terror lurked. Not only had I opened it; I'd gone through, plummeting headfirst into her fear of falling.

Falling and heights, two of her biggest fears. She'd checked those boxes on her pre-extermination information sheet.

A noise in the hall made me look up. Phyllis stood in the doorway, wearing her pink robe and slippers. Pookie ran over to her. She picked up the cat and offered me a tentative smile.

"How are you feeling?" I asked, jumping up to pull out a chair for her.

"Hungry," she said, waving me off. She set Pookie back on the floor and went to the refrigerator; its light reflected from her glasses as she peered inside. She removed a carton of milk and a slice of cake. "Would you like something?" she asked as she poured the milk into a glass. More milk went into a saucer for the cat.

"No, thanks. Do you feel ready to talk about what happened tonight?"

"Give me a moment, dear." She returned the milk carton to the fridge and set the saucer on the floor. Then she carried her glass and cake over to the table. She settled into her chair with a sigh, took a long swallow of milk, then smiled at me. "Well, that certainly was exciting, wasn't it?"

"I hope you weren't frightened."

"Frightened? Whatever for? Why, I haven't had a dream like that since I was . . . well, since I was much younger." A blush colored her powdery cheeks. "And much more romantic."

Romantic? That was a funny word for a dream about endless corridors, falling through space, exploding demons, and shadowy figures with automatic weapons. She must have had a follow-up dream after I left. If it wasn't a nightmare, that was a good sign.

"But where is he?" Phyllis leaned sideways and craned her neck as though trying to see behind me.

"Who?"

"Your helper." She twisted around in her chair, then bent over and looked under the table before returning to me. "And why didn't you introduce him to me before I went to sleep? I would have slept better knowing *he'd* be in my dreams." Her blush deepened.

I sat up straighter. "Did this helper carry a sack?"

"Yes. For removing demons." She frowned. "Nasty, scaly things they were. I'm glad I never opened a door if that's what waited on the other side."

"Tell me about him. What did he look like? What did he actually do in your dream?"

"He came into the dream the same way you did, stepping out of a beam of light. I saw you both do that. But I watched him because . . ." Girlish dimples framed her smile. "Well, because he was so attractive. The very picture of tall, dark, and handsome." The dimples faded as she concentrated. "Well, not dark. I wouldn't describe his complexion that way; in fact, his skin was perhaps too pale. But his hair was the blackest I've seen. Black as . . . black as crows' wings. And his eyes were lovely and dark. Like a midnight lake. Eyes you could dive into and swim around in forever."

The room suddenly felt twenty degrees colder. Strip out the poetry, and Phyllis had just described Pryce.

I hadn't seen the face of the man who'd invaded Phyllis's dreamscape. But his height, his build, the way he moved—yes, it could have been Pryce. What the hell was he up to?

"This, um, helper. Did he kill any demons?"

"No, he made them small and put them into his sack. I thought maybe he was collecting them so you could shoot them all at once with that gun you showed me." She frowned. "Why didn't you? I was rather looking forward to watching them die. Instead . . . oh, my, now I recall. Instead you opened the forbidden door, and your helper pushed you through it." Her frown deepened. "That wasn't very helpful of him, was it?"

No, it wasn't. Not helpful at all. "What did you see after he pushed me?"

"Well, I wasn't going to follow you through *that* door. Besides, I liked watching that young man." She drank some milk, then wiped her mouth thoughtfully. "In the dream, everything he did seemed natural. But now that I look back . . . why *did* he push you through that door?"

"Let's put it this way: He's not my helper."

"I was beginning to wonder about that. Well, he did get those nasty demons out of my dream. Most of them, anyway."

"Most of them?"

"Right after he pushed you, he reached into the sack and pulled out a demon. Hauled it out by its ear. The demon grew bigger and bigger, until it was taller than he was. Even so, it cringed before him and I thought, 'Oh, good. Now he'll kill it.' But he didn't. He spoke to it, and it flew out the door, the one you went through. Then the young man tied the sack shut again and tossed it into one of those light beams." That meant Pryce had transferred the demons he'd captured to the human world. Why? I wondered. "Then he stepped into the light, too. I waved good-bye and blew him a kiss, but I don't believe he saw me." She sighed and rested her chin in her hand.

"Did you hear what he said to the demon?"

"'Bring her to me, and I'll free you.' That's why it seemed all right, I suppose, that he'd pushed you, because he sent someone to rescue you." Her mouth curved in a prim smile. "It's funny with dreams, isn't it? Things make perfect sense at the time, but then you wake up and those very same things have you scratching your head. Why was that young man collecting demons, not killing them? Why did he push you? Why did he send a demon to bring you back?"

All questions I'd like the answers to, myself.

"And for that matter," she continued, "why did you kill the demon that helped you? You did kill it, didn't you?"

"That's what you hired me to do, remember? Believe me, that demon had no intention of helping me. And if I hadn't killed it, it would have kept giving you nightmares."

"Do you think so? After you disappeared into the fog, your helper came back. He didn't have his sack with him, but he had a gun—much bigger than yours, some kind of machine gun. 'Finally,' I thought, 'it's demon-shooting time.' But he didn't use it. He looked around the room and took half a step into that fog. Then he seemed to change his mind. He stepped into the beam and went away again."

Pryce hadn't returned with a gun to shoot demons. He planned to use it on me. The Harpy attack had failed; this time, he wanted to make sure I was dead.

"After that, I had a lovely dream about being in a garden. Not a wall or a door in sight. Quite refreshing." Phyllis got up and went over to the cookie jar. The teddy bear's head sat on the counter, its button eyes staring vacantly over its smile, while she rummaged around inside its body. I thought she was going to offer me a cookie, but she pulled out a wad of bills.

"Now, dear, how much do I owe you?" she asked, licking her thumb and peeling off twenties.

"Nothing." It pained me to say it, but I hadn't finished the job. "I'll have to come back and make sure your dreamscape is clear of Drudes." She'd already paid half up front. It was my policy not to collect the full fee until the job was done.

"Nonsense. I'm certain the demons are gone. I could feel the difference as I was sitting in that beautiful garden; it was like a fresh wind blowing across a rain-swept landscape." Phyllis was definitely a poet at heart. "If the nightmare comes back, I'll call you." She held out a thick stack of bills. "Take the money, dear. You've earned it." When I hesitated, she picked up my hand from the table and closed my fingers around the cash.

"Thanks." I stuffed the money into my pocket. "But if you find yourself in that hallway again, promise you'll call right away."

She nodded. "You could send that nice young man. Oh, but you said he wasn't your helper." Her eyes went all dreamy. "Well, if you do happen to see him, tell him he may visit my dreams whenever he likes."

8

PRYCE WAS PLANNING SOMETHING, AND HE WANTED ME OUT
of his way. Two murder attempts in two days. When he wasn't
trying to kill me, he was running around Boston, snatching personal demons. What was he up to?

I was back in my apartment, getting ready for bed. It was
early, still several hours before dawn, but I wasn't going to sleep,
anyway. Not yet. Juliet was still out with her Goon Squad guards. I
hoped she was having fun at Creature Comforts, not stuck in
some extra-long interrogation session. Maybe a night out would
quench her desire to buy every product advertised on TV.

I closed my bedroom door. I was going to try something, and
I didn't want to be interrupted when Juliet returned.

"Forewarned is forearmed." It was one of Mab's favorite sayings. I must have heard my aunt say that a thousand times during
the years I trained as her apprentice. Know your enemy. Understand how that enemy thinks. Learn what you can of the other
side's plans before you rush in to fight.

Before I came face-to-face with Pryce again, I needed to learn
as much as I could about what he was scheming. Nothing good,
I was sure of that. But "nothing good" wasn't much of a starting
point. Pryce's demon-napping must be causing a stir in the demon

plane. What did the demons know that I didn't? What rumors were buzzing around there that hadn't reached my ears?

There was one way to find out: Conjure a demon and question it.

I lay in my bed, covers tossed to the side. The bedroom was cold and I shivered, but that was okay. What I was about to do would work better if I was uncomfortable.

I'd decided to summon an Eidolon, a guilt-demon. Unless you've lived the life of a saint, Eidolons are the easiest kind of demon to conjure. All you have to do is focus on regrets and remorse, things you wish you could do over or take back. Eidolons respond to all kinds of anxiety, but guilt is their favorite. They love guilt like flies love honey.

Reaching over to my nightstand, I checked that the bronze-bladed dagger I'd hidden behind my alarm clock was close by. A similar dagger was tucked under my pillow. I needed to be ready to send the Eidolon back into the ether as soon as I'd finished questioning it. Guilt is tough to get rid of once you've stirred it up. Whenever I exterminate a guilt-demon for a client, I always recommend follow-up sessions with a therapist. Unless you deal with the root causes of the infestation, the demon will regenerate.

I was playing with fire, and I knew it. But I needed answers. I closed my eyes and searched my feelings for twinges of regret.

I didn't have to look far. Immediately, Maria sprang to mind. The poor kid had been so scared by waking up to experience a false face—and there was no reason for her to suffer that fear. I'd thought we'd have more time before she moved into that phase of her development, but that was no excuse. Maria deserved to understand what was happening to her. I should have laid everything out for her as soon as it became clear that she had the shapeshifter gene. But I'd held back, mostly because I was trying to stay out of Gwen's way. Yet in doing so, I let my sister down, too. Gwen had turned to me for help in guiding Maria through the transition to shapeshifting; she knew she couldn't handle it alone. And I'd agreed to help. So how come I was doing such a lousy job? Without trying, I'd somehow managed to wedge myself between my sister and her daughter. I wasn't doing either of them any good.

Explanations, justifications, plans to handle things better—they all arose in my mind. I pushed them down. I did want to solve this problem, but now wasn't the time. Now, my focus was on stirring up guilt. To judge by the uncomfortable feeling in my gut, like I'd swallowed a baseball-sized lump of lead, I was off to a good start.

I moved on to Mom. She was right; I didn't call often enough. I pictured her in her condo in Florida—or tried to. As I reminded myself harshly, I'd never visited her there. Still, I imagined her in the evening, sitting at a generic kitchen table and paging through an old photo album, looking at childhood pictures of Gwen and me. She gazes fondly at Gwen. Gwen is the good daughter, the one who turned out right. She has a delightful family. She gave Mom the grandbabies she longed for. She calls often, and visits when she can. Of course, she always brings the whole family.

In my imagination, Mom turns to a photo of me, a chubby-cheeked toddler of two or three, sitting on Dad's shoulders, grabbing his hair in both fists. The picture makes Mom smile, but it's a sad smile. Her second daughter was never much for snuggling or hugs. And I'd been Daddy's girl from the moment I was born. Even as a baby, Mom had once told me, I'd always smile when Dad walked into the room. My first word was *Dada*. I'd howl when he left for work in the morning, and drop whatever I was doing to run to him when he came home. Although Mom never said so, my obvious preference for my father must have hurt her.

She probably thought that was why I was so bad about calling. I meant to call—really, I did—but the weird hours I kept made it hard to stay in touch. *No—no excuses.* In my mind, I focused on the image of my mother with her photo album, remembering the girls she once had. Sitting by the phone in hopes one of us would call, knowing it wouldn't be me.

The lead ball in my gut grew warmer, heavier. It spiked outward, expanding into multiple sharp aches. A sensation like nausea but deeper—and with knives—roiled through my abdomen. I didn't feel like I was going to vomit, but I almost wished I did. It would be a relief to eject the feeling from my body.

Instead, I went deeper. A surge of dread swept through me, knowing what was coming, but I ignored it. To conjure an Eidolon, I had no choice; I had to reach down into my deepest, most heart-wrenching guilt. So I did. I turned my thoughts to my father.

It was my fault he'd died. The moment I allowed that thought into my consciousness, the pain cut through me like a laser. But it was true. I grabbed the thought and held on to it, examined it, made myself see all the ways in which I'd let my father down—leading to his death.

It was nothing more than stubbornness. At eighteen, I thought I knew it all. I thought the rules didn't apply to me. Back when I started my apprenticeship at age eleven, Dad said, "Listen to Aunt Mab. She may seem tough, but she loves you and she knows what she's doing. She'll never steer you wrong."

Why didn't I listen?

Seven years after my father spoke those words, I broke my aunt's one unbreakable rule: I opened that damn book, the one she'd told me not to touch.

Even as I lifted the book down from its shelf, I knew I shouldn't do it. I knew it would cause trouble. But I *wanted* trouble. I thought I could handle it. I thought my father would see my amazing prowess as a demon fighter, and he would be proud.

Instead of proud, he ended up dead.

The pain in my gut surged. I rolled onto my side and curled into the fetal position. But instead of pushing away the memories, I probed them further.

I writhed on my bed, remembering the horrible moment the Destroyer appeared in Mab's library. The huge demon hunched over, cramped, too tall for the high-ceilinged room. Its warty blue skin dripped with slime. Flames shot from its eyes and mouth, flames that burn to utter annihilation. Flames that headed toward me.

Helpless. I'd been helpless against it. Unable to run, even to move, I watched in horror as the Destroyer advanced. Its flames crept closer, closer. They touched my arm. The pain, searing, was indescribable. I screamed and screamed. I was dying—I knew it.

My father saved me. He appeared in the doorway and challenged the Destroyer, turned the Hellion's wrath away from me. Dad was no fighter. He was a teacher, a scholar who lived in a world of books. Yet this gentle man stood his ground, glasses glinting in the flames, against the worst demon ever to pass through the fiery gates of Hell.

He should have won. If life were fair, he would have won. He would have saved his younger daughter, and I'd have thrown my arms around his neck, weeping with gratitude. But life isn't fair. Because my father fell.

My heart pounded erratically, and my mind struggled to shove away the memory of that night. But I couldn't. I forced myself to remember, to experience again what I'd seen and felt on the worst night of my life.

My father on the floor, twisting and screaming as hell-flames consumed his body. The Destroyer, pinning him in place with twin jets of flame. My utter inability to move. Staring at my father in his torment, knowing there was nothing I could do.

Dad's eyes were clenched against the pain. As the flames diminished, his body stilled. A greenish flicker played over him. He shuddered, and his eyes flew open. They locked onto mine. I saw love there, and regret, but not an iota of blame.

A new emotion appeared in those eyes, pushing out everything else. Terror. Terror claimed my father. Not just fear—what I saw there was an unholy combination of horror and panic and utter despair. It consumed the man I knew and loved, and I saw my father fall away from me, the spark of his soul fading like a lit candle falling into the blackness of a deep well.

My father died in pain and hopelessness. He died in terror.

So what if he didn't blame me? I blamed me.

Pain seized my gut with the gnawing of hundreds of needle-sharp teeth. I rolled from side to side, clutching my stomach, doubled up with agony. I couldn't bear it. My father's terror-filled eyes wouldn't leave me. *Dad, no—don't die. I'm sorry. I'm so sorry.* I waved a hand in front of my face, fruitlessly trying to wave the vision away.

In my mind's eye, my father's expression changed. The despair and terror left his face, replaced by an urging. There was something he wanted me to do. It was the way he looked at me when he was cheering me on in some difficult task. *You can do this, Vic. I know you can.* Dad was the only person in the world who got away with calling me "Vic."

His expression was the reminder I needed to return to the present. The Eidolon was here. There was no question about that. Guilt, remorse, regret—they all chewed on my guts with a steady, unstoppable gnawing. Now, I had to stare that guilt in the eye and question the Eidolon.

I took a deep breath. "Materialize!" I commanded.

The gnawing slowed.

"You heard me, demon," I said. "Materialize so I can see you."

"Nooooo." The word drifted through the room like a feather on a breeze.

"I conjured you." I made my voice stern. "Do as I say. Now."

"No," came another whisper. "No, don't. I'll go."

I said nothing. I bent my whole will toward forcing the demon to take shape.

The gnawing ceased, and I felt a presence rise up through me. It passed through my skin as a misty, yellowish cloud, stinking of sulfur and offal. The cloud spread across my torso, gaining density as the Eidolon took on its physical form. Within a minute a fat, quivering maggot the size of a German shepherd squatted on my chest and stomach. The maggot body had a demon's head, with a hooked nose, too many teeth, and a forked tongue. It flicked its tongue at me, spraying slime.

Gross. But this demon could tell me what I needed to know.

"Why did you summon me?" the Eidolon sniveled in a surprisingly high-pitched voice, like a mosquito whining in my ear. "Don't you know you're putting me in danger?"

Seeing how I planned to pop this maggot like an overinflated balloon when I was finished with it, I wasn't too concerned about its welfare.

"There I was," it continued, "minding my own business, and you pull me out of the demon plane and make me manifest here. What did I ever do to you?"

"Shredded my guts with agony, for starters. Now, I—"

"That's because you summoned me!" The whine turned indignant. "What was I supposed to do once all that delicious-smelling guilt started floating my way? Demons gotta eat, too, you know."

"Shut up, and I'll tell you why I conjured you." I needed to stay in control here. Of all demons, Eidolons are the most treacherous and manipulative. "It wasn't to give you a meal. I need you to answer some questions."

"Oh, charming. So you tempt me with the promise of food and then threaten my poor demon ass. Typical." Its face turned crafty. "Isn't that what your sister has always said about you?" The whine changed into Gwen's voice. "'You are *such* a bully, Vicky. Don't you care about anything besides fighting?'"

"Gwen never—" Well, okay, she *did* say that once, when we were teenagers arguing over something stupid. I knew she didn't mean it, but the memory sometimes stung, even now. In fact—

"Hey!" I said. "Cut that out. Your meal is over, done, finished—no second course, no dessert. I command you to be silent unless you're answering my questions."

The Eidolon pouted, drawing its wiry eyebrows together in a scowl, but it didn't reply. I'd conjured the demon, and it was bound to obey me until I released it from its material form.

Okay. Now we could get down to business.

"Why have personal demons been disappearing from Boston?"

"Because we're afraid." The whine was back. "We'd rather stay safe at home in the demon plane, unless some *bully* forces us to come forth." The demon glared at me. "Or unless hunger drives us—poor, weak spirits that we've become—out into the Ordinary in search of food." The Ordinary is what demons call the human world.

"Will you stop with the food already?"

"No. That was a question, by the way, so I'll elaborate. Every creature needs to eat. You blame us because our feeding habits happen to torment humans. But do you ever stop to consider your own eating habits? Do you? Of course, you don't. That frozen chicken Parmesan you microwaved for dinner yesterday—did you ever stop to think that the hunk of chicken in it was once a living creature? That it started off life as a cute, fuzzy, yellow baby chick going *peep peep peep*?"

An image of a fluffy chick hopped into my mind, peeping adorably. Pain shot through my gut as the Eidolon used its second mouth, located in its belly, to chew on my feelings. "Stop it!" I forced my thoughts away from baby chicks. "This isn't about what I ate for dinner. Now tell me, what are the demons afraid of?"

"Peep peep peep."

Time to fight dirty. I rummaged around for a happy memory, something that made me feel good. I'd dived so deep into guilt that it took a minute, but then I had it. On a recent walk through the New Combat Zone, the block between Deadtown and human-controlled Boston, I'd noticed some daffodils and tulips blooming in a half-barrel planter. In that gray, gritty neighborhood, someone had cared enough about beauty to create a miniature garden.

"Owww!" the Eidolon wailed. "Quit it—that pinches!"

I smiled. Yellow and red and white. The flowers were so pretty, like a promise of hope . . .

"All *right*. Jeez, there's no need to torture me. I'll tell you what we're afraid of." I let the flowers fade from my mind, and the Eidolon huffed an overly dramatic sigh. "There's a wizard. He looks like a demi-demon I used to know, but he has no shadow demon."

Pryce wasn't a wizard, but his father, Myrddin, had been. At his resuscitation, Pryce had absorbed Myrddin's life force, along with much of his knowledge. "Is this wizard named Pryce?"

The maggotlike demon made a gesture I interpreted as a shrug. "I have no knowledge of Ordinary names. His shadow demon was Cysgod." It squinted at me accusingly. "You killed Cysgod."

"Damn right, I did." Getting rid of Pryce's shadow demon had put an end to his plans to throw open the gates of Hell. Or so I'd thought. "Why are you afraid of this wizard?"

"I'm not afraid of him when I can stay at home all snug in the demon plane. He has no shadow demon; he can't enter there. It's only when someone lures me into the Ordinary that I'm in danger."

"You didn't answer my question." I started to picture spring flowers again.

"The wizard is grabbing demons," the Eidolon said in a hurry.

"I've seen that. Why?"

"How should I know? All I know is I want to stay far, far away from him. He has this . . . this big kettle thing. A cauldron—that's what you call it. He collects demons in a sack and then imprisons them inside the cauldron. There must be *thousands* crammed into that thing." The demon glanced around the bedroom, real fear widening its eyes. "I'd rather you eviscerate me with one of your hidden bronze daggers than let him do that to me. I've heard about the cauldron. They say you can hear the demons who are trapped in it screaming. Screaming for miles around." The Eidolon shifted on my chest and narrowed its eyes. Its belly-mouth licked its lips. "That's what you're planning to do, isn't it? Force me to answer your questions and then kill me with one of those daggers. I'm not surprised. Mrs. Kinicki wouldn't be surprised, either. She never gave you a Satisfactory on your report card for 'plays well with others,' did she?"

Mrs. Kinicki was my second-grade teacher. Her nephew, Timmy, thought he was a tough guy and tried to beat me up on the playground, so I fought back. I didn't pick those fights. My social skills were perfectly satisfactory. I'd deserved that S, damn it. Okay, so maybe I did go a little too far that one time when Timmy ended up in the emergency room. Fifteen stitches is kind of a lot. I still felt bad about that . . .

I shook my head, blinking. "I told you to stop that."

"What? I was just answering your question. I'm supposed to sit here and spout off answers, knowing you plan to murder me in cold sludge?" The demon's face contorted in indignation.

I ignored its question. "Where's Pryce keeping this cauldron? In the demon plane?"

"I *told* you. He can't enter the demon plane, not without his shadow demon. Without Cysgod, he's as weak as any human. The cauldron is not in the demon plane. It's in the Ordinary, but it's hidden. The guy's a wizard; he's using magic to cloak it."

"Where in the Ordinary—do you know?"

"If I tell you, will you spare me?"

"If you don't tell me, I'll wrap you up in a pretty pink bow and hand you over to Pryce myself."

"Pink is *not* my color. Of course, you wouldn't notice that. It's not like a single thought for anyone else ever crosses your mind. When's the last time you bothered to pick up a phone and call your mother?" The demon uttered a sigh that sounded a lot like Mom. "'I wish Vicky would call. I wish she were a *good* daughter, like Gwen,'" it said in her voice.

"Overkill. My mother wouldn't compare Gwen and me like that." Although that was exactly what I'd imagined her doing. Of course, the Eidolon had eavesdropped on my thoughts.

"How do you know what she says all alone, late at night? Just because you've never heard her say the words—"

"You know, the other day I saw the cutest puppy."

"No! Not a puppy!"

"Big brown eyes. Floppy ears. And—"

"Stop! Puppies give me indigestion." The demon let out a huge, sulfurous burp to prove it.

I turned my head away. "Then knock it off with the guilt trips."

"I can't help it." I'd tangled with more than a few Eidolons, but never had I met such a whiny demon. "What do you expect, anyway? I'm a guilt-demon—I'm only doing what comes naturally."

"Just answer my question," I said through gritted teeth. "Do you know where Pryce is hiding the cauldron?"

"Humans call the place the Devil's Coffin."

I'd never heard of it. "Where's that?"

"No clue. All I know is it's a gateway between your world and the realm of the dead. Not a place I'd hang out—demons aren't exactly welcome in the Darklands."

That was true. In Cerddorion mythology, demons and departed souls don't mix. The dead pass through Annwn, the Darklands, on their way to wherever they were going. Demons live in their own realm, Uffern. According to legend, although Uffern and the Darklands share a border, an impassable range of steep, rocky mountains protected by sentries prevents demons from crossing into the realm of the dead.

"Why would Pryce want to smuggle a cauldron full of demons into the Darklands?"

"You keep asking me questions I can't answer. I'm not exactly hoping to play confidant to some crazy wizard who'd snatch me and stuff me into that thing. But I can tell you this: The cauldron is nearly full. In Uffern, the word is that after the full of the moon, we'll be safe. Whatever this wizard, this Pryce is planning, everyone believes it will happen then."

"What's so special about the full moon?"

"That's when a mortal wizard can open the door."

"Okay." Pryce. Cauldron of demons. Devil's Coffin. Full moon. I had the dots, even if I didn't know yet how they connected. "Can you tell me anything else?"

"Yeah, this: I've given you good information, and I don't deserve to die. Just release me and I'll be on my way."

"Sorry." I slid my hand under my pillow, feeling for the dagger there. "You, demon. Me, demon exterminator. It's what I do."

"And feeding on guilt is what *I* do. So how come I'm all wrong and you're okay? What kind of ethics is that?"

"My kind." My fingers curled around the dagger's grip.

"I didn't attack you. You conjured me." The Eidolon talked faster. "I answered all your questions. Let me go back to the demon plane. If you don't call me out again, I'll stay there."

"I don't believe you."

"I could be useful to you!" The whine rose to a frightened squeal. "I'll ask around. Maybe I can find out more about the wizard's plans." The demon's eyes opened wide, pleading, as its voice dropped to a whisper. "Don't kill me. *Please* don't."

Do you know how hard it is to kill a creature who looks you in the eye and says, "Please don't"? In movies, the bad guys do it all the time. So do the very toughest of the super-tough good guys, but only when the pleading villain is way too evil to live. In my life, I was used to blowing away the nasties that jumped out at me, intent on harm, in kill-or-be-killed situations. I wasn't used to "please."

I knew how to deal with guilt-demons. Even if you kill one, sooner or later another will take its place. The only way to *really* get rid of an Eidolon is to cut off its food supply. If I didn't wallow in guilt and worry, the demon would leave me alone. Besides, maybe it *could* bring me more information about what Pryce was up to. It might be useful to have a spy in the demon plane.

The Eidolon watched me, its eyes hopeful in its hideous face.

"I cast you back into Uffern," I said, knowing already I'd regret this. "And I bind you not to return to me unless I summon you. If you try to infest me, I'll kill you without hesitation."

"Yippie!" Immediately the pressure on my chest eased. "Er, I mean, as you command." The Eidolon shimmered and grew transparent. It shrunk in size as it sank back into my body. There was no gnawing in my guts. The Eidolon passed through me and back to where it came from.

I lay in my still, silent bedroom, trying to shake the feeling that I'd just become the biggest sucker in the history of demon fighting.

9

THERE'S NOTHING LIKE A LONG CONVERSATION WITH AN
Eidolon to make sleep impossible. Residual guilt slithered
through me, searching for thoughts to attach itself to. Free-
floating guilt is a horrible feeling. It's different from the gnawing
of a feeding Eidolon, more like a tide of poisonous sludge that
seeps through you, stinging and burning body and mind. To push
it away, I distracted myself by thinking about what the guilt-
demon had told me.

I knew it had told me the truth. One thing about Eidolons:
They don't lie. They can twist and distort and exaggerate, but
everything they say is true at its core. Has to be. Otherwise, it
would be easy to ignore them. The more an Eidolon victim rec-
ognizes the essential truth of what the demon insinuates, the
more firmly the Eidolon attaches to that person's conscience.
Damn parasites. So maybe I *had* punched Timmy Kinicki a little
harder and a little longer than was necessary to teach him a lesson, that didn't mean—

Was that me or the demon, stirring up those old feelings? Just
in case, I spoke out loud. "If that's you, demon, cut it out. I
warned you: I'll conjure your ass back into the human plane and
pop you like a slimy soap bubble."

A different feeling flared up—doubt. I should've killed that demon while I had the chance. Yet banishing it had felt like the better choice. The ethical choice. Maybe my ethics weren't as black-and-white as I thought. It was confusing. But the guilt-nausea settled down, and I left both ethical debate and the second-grade playground behind.

So Pryce was terrorizing the denizens of the demon plane by grabbing demons and imprisoning them in a cauldron. He was hiding the demon-packed cauldron near a door to the Darklands that would open at the full of the moon. What could he gain by smuggling demons into the realm of the dead? Had he decided to shift his quest for power from the world of people to the world of shades? Did he want to become the new lord of the dead? I wanted to call Mab on the dream phone and discuss these questions with her, but I couldn't. Every time I tried to relax enough to place the call, that tide of leftover guilt rose again.

Try sleeping when guilt keeps poking you in the ribs. Especially when you know an Eidolon might construe each poke as an invitation to a midnight snack.

I got up. Can't push away guilt? Distraction is the next best thing. Something nagged at the back of my mind, something I thought I'd seen when I sat at the kitchen table, paging through the newspaper while Juliet fed. I padded down the hall to the kitchen.

The Book of Utter Darkness sat on the table, but I didn't have the energy or the patience to deal with it now. If it told me anything at all, it would be to confuse me further.

I found *News of the Dead* in the recycling bin. I checked to make sure it was the right issue, then sat down with it and flipped through, scanning each page.

There it was. The headline read, "Museum Theft Stumps Police." Under the headline was a photograph of a cauldron. I remembered glancing at the photo before. Now, I read the story.

CAMBRIDGE—Police have not been able to determine how a large, heavy cauldron was removed from an exhibition of Bronze Age artifacts at Harvard's Peabody Museum. The cauldron, on loan from the National Museum of Wales, disappeared overnight between April 13 and April 14, while the museum was closed. No alarm sounded during the break-in, and there was no sign of forced entry. The cauldron's size—three feet high, nearly two feet in diameter, and weighing approximately two hundred pounds—would make it difficult to transport.

Traces of magic were found at the site, police said, but the fragmentary magical signatures were inconclusive. Police are appealing for witnesses who may have seen unusual activity, whether natural or supernatural, near the museum on the night in question.

Wow, that was one big cauldron. Not exactly something you could stick in your pocket and sneak out past the guards. If Pryce had tapped into Myrddin's magic to break into the museum and spirit the cauldron away, it wasn't surprising police didn't recognize the magical signature. Myrddin had spent centuries imprisoned in a yew tree, so of course the Boston PD wouldn't have his magical signature on file.

I scrutinized the photo of the stolen bronze cauldron. It wasn't a work of art or a thing of beauty. The cauldron balanced on three legs, leaning drunkenly to the right as though one of the legs had been damaged. Two thick bronze rings served as handles. The surface was pockmarked with dents. It looked like what it was: a big, old, beat-up pot that had been buried in the mud for a couple of thousand years.

But Pryce didn't need something pretty. He needed something that would hold trapped, struggling demons. A big bronze cauldron, dented or not, was the perfect vessel.

The article said that the cauldron was from Wales. I searched my mind for what I knew about cauldrons from Welsh mythology. There was the cauldron of Ceridwen, which had granted shapeshifting abilities to her descendents, but that cauldron had shattered. I knew there were other magic cauldrons—one, I seemed to recall, was associated with the Darklands. Maybe that would provide a clue to what Pryce was doing.

I dropped *News of the Dead* back into the recycling bin and went to the living room, to the corner desk where Juliet keeps her computer. I started the machine and, when it came to life, opened a search engine. I typed *cauldron* into the search field. Great. Twelve million results—hopefully I wouldn't have to scroll through them all to find what I was looking for. The first couple of pages were packed with places to buy cauldrons: ritual cauldrons for witches, cast-iron cauldrons for cooking, plastic cauldrons for Halloween parties, cauldron planters for the garden . . . Somehow I didn't see Pryce cramming demons into a cauldron in the hope they'd emerge as petunias.

I looked at a few websites discussing the mythology and symbolism of cauldrons, quickly finding the one associated with the Darklands. In the medieval poem "The Spoils of Annwn," King Arthur leads a raiding party into the Darklands to steal a magnificent cauldron. The poem, obscure and hard to understand even in translation, seemed to discuss two different cauldrons. One cauldron—Ceridwen's shattered one?—gave the poem's author literary skill. The other cauldron belonged to the lord of Annwn. Presumably this was the cauldron stolen from the Darklands by Arthur's men. It had a dark ridge around its rim, it was encrusted with pearls, and it wouldn't cook the food of a coward.

I went to the *News of the Dead* website and found the story I'd read. The stolen cauldron may have had a dark ridge around the rim; it was hard to tell from the photo. But there were no decorative gems of any kind. No word either about how a coward would have to find a different cooking pot.

I suppose the ability to tell a brave man from a coward came in handy in King Arthur's day, but I didn't think Pryce was getting ready to cook up a big batch of demon stew. He wanted to rule demons, not eat them.

I found several other references to magical cauldrons in Welsh folklore. The most interesting was the cauldron of rebirth, which could restore dead warriors to life. But that didn't seem to fit Pryce's activities, either. He wasn't killing demons, just imprisoning them. Nothing I could find online gave me any hints about why.

I was feeling better, and almost sleepy enough to place my dream-phone call. But before I called Mab, I wanted to check one more thing. I typed "Devil's Coffin" in the search field. I considered. The place couldn't be too far from Boston, not if Pryce was collecting his demons here. I added "Boston" to my keywords and hit Enter.

At the top of the results was a link to a page about a state park called Purgatory Chasm—promising name. I clicked the link and read. The park, about fifty miles west of Boston in a town called Sutton, centers around a granite chasm formed by glaciers thousands of years ago. The chasm is noted for its caves, tunnels, and rock formations, with names like Lovers' Leap, Fat Man's Misery—and the Devil's Coffin. Bingo.

I squinted at some photos of the Devil's Coffin rock formation. It looked like a large slab of rock lying on the floor of a shallow cave. Could there be a doorway to the Darklands here? A place to hide a stolen cauldron? Impossible to tell from looking at photos on a computer screen. I'd have to check out the place in person. I printed directions to get to Purgatory Chasm from Boston.

Doing some research had banished the last, lingering traces of guilty feelings after my encounter with the Eidolon. I could fall sleep now, I thought, without inviting the Eidolon back for more munchies. And sleeping meant I could contact Mab.

IN SLEEP, I LET MYSELF DRIFT FOR A WHILE. I WANTED TO LET the information I'd gathered spend some time in my subconscious, that part of the mind that holds all of the memories, thoughts, and emotions that we accumulate over a lifetime. The subconscious can discern patterns and make connections that the conscious mind misses. It could take days, weeks, or even longer for the subconscious to process everything I'd seen and learned recently. But I knew a way to speed things up.

In my dreamscape, I created a wooden floor with a trapdoor. Beneath the floor was my subconscious. I went over to the trapdoor and opened it. It was dark down there. Sounds arose— echoes of music, traffic, ocean waves, a child laughing, a woman crying. I used my thoughts to gently push them down, and the sounds faded. My subconscious waited, still and receptive.

Next, I imagined a printer, like the one attached to Juliet's computer, and it materialized, sitting on a desk. I pulled open the paper tray; it was full. Good. I'd use this printer to feed my subconscious the experiences and thoughts I wanted it to work on. Then, I'd share them with Mab.

I started with the Harpy attack at Tina's school, reliving those minutes in my mind, making them as real as I could. The garbage-and-vomit smell filled my nostrils, almost making me gag, and I could feel the steely talons digging into my leg. When I'd relived the attack up to the moment of the Harpy's death, I pressed a button on the printer. The machine whirred and clacked. A sheet of paper emerged; on it was printed an image of me, grappling with the Harpy.

I picked up the paper and examined it. Yeah, that was me, fighting the Harpy. All the details were there: the classroom's blackboard, the teacher frozen at her desk, Tina pointing as she lectured her peers on the finer points of Harpies. Perfect. This wasn't some generic Harpy battle; I must have dozens of those downstairs in my subconscious. This was specific to last night.

Now to feed the image to my subconscious. I opened the trapdoor and dropped the sheet through, peering after the paper as it fluttered into the darkness. A few feet down, the sheet paused in midair. It shuddered. An avatar of the Harpy rose from the page, taking on three dimensions as it flapped its wings. Another avatar, this one of me, somersaulted off the page and crouched in a fighting pose. The Harpy attacked her. Tina gestured and described its maneuver. The page, now blank, crumpled itself into a ball and continued falling. The avatars, still fighting, moved off into the darkness.

Good. The process was working.

Next came my most recent experience with *The Book of Utter Darkness*. Then, I printed off an image of a far-off figure capturing a demon in Phyllis's dream. Then another that showed me being pushed through that door, then snatched by a demon.

The printer whirred as I printed out everything I'd learned related to Pryce and what he might be up to: Purgatory Chasm. The Devil's Coffin. A three-thousand-year-old bronze cauldron. I visualized each one, pouring into the picture everything I knew about the subject. One by one, I dropped the printouts through the trapdoor, watching them fall, become real, and disappear into the murk.

I reached to close the door, then paused. I wasn't done yet, not completely. I shouldn't be letting all those images loose in my subconscious without specifying where some of them came from. I needed to add an avatar of the Eidolon.

Admittedly, it's not a great idea to purposely introduce a guilt-demon—even just the image of one—into your dreams. I might as well send that giant maggot an engraved invitation to come back for dinner tomorrow. Dropping a graphic reminder of guilty feelings into my subconscious would make it harder to deal with those feelings once I woke up. Waking or sleeping, the subconscious never rests. Still, if I was going to share this information with Mab, I needed to include everything.

I pictured the Eidolon that had risen from my guts and sat on my chest. Its quivering, slimy maggot's body. Its sneering demon face. Its whiny, insinuating voice. Those needle-sharp teeth of its second mouth chewing my insides. A tide of feelings, none of them good, surged in me like nausea. Guilt. Regret. Shame. Worry. Dread. When the feelings became almost too much to bear, I slammed the Print button. I shoved every speck of Eidolon out of my imagination and onto the page. Then I snatched the sheet from the printer and hurled it down the hole. I didn't wait to see the Eidolon shudder to life and slither off the page. I slammed the trapdoor shut.

Okay, so I'd just dropped a guilt-demon into my own subconscious. Not an actual demon, I reminded myself; an image of a demon. A picture. It was just a picture.

Even though the nauseous slop of feelings in my gut told me otherwise.

The trapdoor bounced and rattled, like something from below was trying to get out. I conjured a huge padlock, one as big as my head, and secured the hasp. *There*. That would keep any demons at bay.

With my subconscious locked up tight, I pushed all worry from my mind, willing myself to calm, to relax. The bad feelings subsided, and I let myself drift through my dreamscape. The floor with its trapdoor faded away as I floated through a dim, gray twilight. Whatever Pryce was doing, however all those pieces fit together, I let it all be. My subconscious would work on it.

Time passed as I slept without dreaming. After a while, I felt a little nudge, almost like the way Mom used to shake my shoulder gently to wake me up for school, except this nudge came from my subconscious. It was time to contact Mab. I hoped she'd answer tonight.

I roused myself and started to think about my aunt. To call someone on the dream phone, you picture that person and then call up their colors. All of the Cerddorion have a pair of colors, their shades and brightness unique to the individual. Bringing up a person's colors is sort of like dialing a phone; it lets that person know you want to communicate. To answer, they focus on your colors. Or they can ignore the call, and their colors fade from your dreamscape.

Now, I pictured my aunt as I always thought of her: sitting in a wing chair by the fireplace in her library, book in hand. I focused on her iron-gray hair, short like mine; on the reading glasses perched at the end of her nose. I saw her frowning in concentration at the book she held until she blinked and looked up, cocking her head as though she'd heard a sound in another room. That's when I brought up her colors, blue and silver, in a swirling mist that momentarily obscured my mental picture of her. *Please answer,* I thought as I watched the shimmering swirls of rich color.

She did. When the mist subsided, Mab was there. Not in her library, although she did hold an open book. She was outside on the terrace. She sat at a round wrought-iron table, a pot of tea in front of her. Yesterday's worry still with me, I scrutinized my aunt. She looked good. The April sun tinged her skin with gold. Although Mab's current lifetime stretched across three centuries, she could easily be a woman of forty-five. Other than a few fine lines sketched around her eyes, her face was smooth and soft-looking.

When I didn't say anything, Mab closed her book and set it on the table beside her cup. "You've been working with *The Book of Utter Darkness*?"

That was Mab. No chitchat. No wasting time on preliminaries like, "Hi, how are you?" She always cut straight to the chase.

Still, recent events had made me realize that, despite her longevity and her abilities, Mab wasn't eternal. That made the preliminaries seem more important. "How are you doing, Mab? You look wonderful."

"Fine, fine." My aunt waved her hand impatiently, but a gleam of pleasure lit her eyes, as though my compliment pleased her. "But surely you didn't contact me to ask about my health."

"I was worried about you. You didn't answer when I tried to call last night."

"Yes, I'm sorry I was indisposed. I was dealing with a committee of ladies from the village. The spring fête, you know." Each April, Mab opened the grounds of her manor house, Maen-llyd, for a garden party attended by the whole village. I could see why she wouldn't want to go into a trance to chat with me long-distance in front of the refreshments committee, or whoever was there. "I did try to return your call after they'd gone, but you must have been awake by then. And later, Mr. Cadogan sent out a message saying you'd try again today. I've been awaiting your call."

"So you're all right."

"As well as I've ever been. I assure you, child, there's no need to worry. My bloodstone has spent two full weeks underground, drawing power from the land. It's completely recharged." Mab's bloodstone was her object of power, chipped from an ancient altar and infused with the blood of several lifetimes. She reached inside the neck of her blouse and pulled out the bloodstone, which she wore as a pendant. It glowed with a silvery light. "In fact, I believe the stone is stronger than ever." She tucked the bloodstone back inside her shirt and sipped some tea. "And me with it."

"I'm glad to hear that," I said. And I was. In our struggles with Pryce and his father, Myrddin, I'd nearly lost Mab. I'd vowed that never again would I take my aunt for granted, never again would I assume she'd always be there, as eternal as the rocks of Mount Snowdon. So it was good to see her now, strong and vital. "But to answer your original question," I continued, "yes, I've been working with the book. It gave me another rehash of the past couple of months."

"The same as the previous two times?"

"More or less. Same information. More dramatic in its presentation." I told her about the vision I'd received from the book. "It knocked me out of my chair. When I came to, I was sitting on the kitchen floor."

"Hmm. Perhaps it's emphasizing that past events are coming to a head."

"Well, I wish it would turn the page, because we're starting a new chapter. Pryce is back."

Mab drew in a sharp breath. "You've seen him?"

"Yes, tonight. In a client's dreamscape."

"But surely that was an avatar."

"No, it was Pryce. There was a second dream portal. He was there physically, just like I was." I told her how Boston's personal demons had been disappearing. "But Pryce isn't out to ruin my business. He wants me dead."

Mab pounded the table, making the teapot lid rattle. "*Damn* the spring fête—I knew I should have answered your call." She shoved the tea things aside and leaned toward me. "Tell me what happened, child. Don't leave anything out."

"I can do better than that." I could show her. I made the trap-door reappear. Mab's eyes registered the knowledge of what I was about to do. "Ready?" I asked.

She nodded.

A huge key appeared in my hand. I opened the padlock and stepped back. The door exploded off its hinges like a bomb had gone off under it.

Then, nothing. No sound, no movement. We waited. The silence from below felt thick with menace.

I stared at the open doorway until my vision blurred. My breathing all but stopped.

Then, as casually as if he were walking up a staircase, Pryce climbed from my subconscious and stepped into my dreamscape. Mab tensed. I knew he was a dream avatar. Even so, a sword appeared in my hand.

The avatar Pryce didn't look at us. He raised his arms, and a Harpy rocketed out of the trapdoor. With a horrible shriek, it flew right at me.

I braced myself, holding the sword out in front of me. Given the demon's speed and angle of attack, it would skewer itself on the blade, making itself into a Harpy kebab.

But the Harpy didn't strike. Right before it hit my sword, it vanished. So did Pryce.

Mab exhaled loudly, like she'd been holding her breath, too. "He sent a Harpy to kill you?"

I nodded. "It found me at Tina's school. I was giving a Career Night presentation." I remembered my promise to Tina. "She helped me kill it."

Mab's lips moved in what might have been a tiny smile. "Don't underestimate that young lady," she said.

That almost sounded like praise. Tina would be thrilled to hear it.

A scream howled up from my subconscious. It was the same scream I'd heard in Phyllis's dream. A Drude leapt out from the trapdoor and sprinted across my dreamscape. Pryce was right behind it. He tackled the fleeing demon, knocking it flat. As the Drude struggled, yowling with fear and fury, he pinned it down. It was the same scene I'd witnessed in Phyllis's dream, but closer and from a different angle. The demon went rigid. It lay still, moaning, its yellow eyes glazed over. Pryce stood and began gesturing. Although I could see his lips move, I couldn't tell what he was saying. I glanced over at Mab. Her eyes stayed riveted on the scene.

The demon floated upward and hovered in the air. Its moans intensified to shrieks again as its body started to shrink. Pryce gestured faster. His hands became a blur as the demon shrank to the size of a child's doll. With a shout of triumph, Pryce picked up the miniaturized demon and dropped it into his sack. The sack bulged and squirmed, as though it was already full of struggling demons.

Pryce tied the neck shut and slung the sack over his shoulder, then strode away from us. I turned to Mab, wanting to discuss what we'd just seen, but she pressed a finger to her lips. She pointed back to Pryce.

As he walked, carrying his bag, a landscape formed around him. He made his way along the floor of a narrow, rocky chasm, granite walls stretching fifty feet or more above him on both sides. At the mouth of a cave, he stopped. A cauldron squatted crookedly on a horizontal slab of rock. The Devil's Coffin; I recognized it from the images I'd seen online. Pryce untied the sack and upended it. Miniature demons—about two dozen of them—tumbled out and landed in the cauldron. Some leapt up, trying to escape. Pryce pushed them back inside. His hands made a flat, smoothing motion over the rim. A glow surrounded the cauldron. Pryce stepped back, his narrowed eyes staring at the vessel. The glow sat on top of the cauldron like a lid. He threw his head back and laughed, looking way too much like the movie version of an evil genius. The image grew transparent. The whole thing—Pryce, rocky chasm, and cauldron—sank through the floor of my dreamscape, back into the basement of my subconscious.

Mab started to say something, but the show still wasn't over. A book with a pale leather cover rose through the door. As *The Book of Utter Darkness* entered my dreamscape, it grew. It loomed over us, blocking everything else, until it was the size of a house. Slowly, its cover swung open.

When I saw the moving picture that stretched across two pages, I cried out. I couldn't help it. I'd never imagined such complete devastation.

We gazed at some sort of urban battleground. A huge,

bombed-out building poured out smoke from the fires raging inside. Bodies lay everywhere, whole or in pieces. Several hung from streetlights, twisting and swaying. A woman lay half on a bench, her head and shoulders on the ground, bloody glass shards glinting from her shredded business suit. Unrecognizable lumps of twisted metal littered the area. Blood and ash covered everything.

Wait. I knew this place. Absurdly intact in the middle of all that destruction were yard-high bronze sculptures of a tortoise and a hare, installed to mark the finish line of the Boston Marathon. I was looking at Copley Square. The smoking ruin was Trinity Church, or what was left of it. The central tower with its red roof was gone, the walls collapsed into piles of rubble. Beside it, the Hancock building was an empty frame, its mirrorlike windows all shattered. A crater gaped where the Boston Public Library had stood.

A man stumbled out of the smoke, coughing. Immediately, a robed, hooded figure appeared and lifted the man from his feet. The hood fell back, revealing a yellow, skull-like face with huge fangs. An Old One. The ancient vampire bent his head to the struggling man's throat. A half-scream, wracked by coughs, rose and then was cut off. The man's body went limp. In moments it was a mere husk, drained of all its blood. The Old One flung the body aside and disappeared again in the smoke.

The sound of tiny sobs brought my attention back to the tortoise and hare sculptures. A small girl, no older than three, clung to the tortoise's neck. She hugged the statue with her chubby arms, pressing her face against it as though it could save her, as though it could carry her away from this terrible place.

The ground shook as something dropped from the sky and landed behind her. A huge demon, fifteen feet tall, cast a shadow over the girl. She screamed and tried to scramble beneath the sculpture. The demon encircled her waist with one scaly hand and tugged. Her screams grew frantic as she lost her grip on the tortoise. She kicked and flailed as she was pulled away. The demon kicked the sculpture and didn't even seem to feel the bronze. The tortoise flew into the air and landed upside down, rocking back and forth on its shell.

The demon shook the child, and her screams stopped. She hung like a rag doll from its hand as it flapped its wings. As the demon rose into the air, the picture's perspective changed and widened. We saw Copley Square from above, then all of Boston. The city was in flames. The South Shore, the North Shore—they burned as well. The entire eastern seaboard was an inferno, the Atlantic red with blood.

The book snapped shut with a blast of wind that blew ashes into my eyes and filled my nostrils with smells of smoke and death. It shrank back to book size, then fell into my sub-conscious.

Enough. Whatever else might be lurking down there, I didn't want to see it. My hands shaking, I picked up the trapdoor and fitted it back on its frame. I locked it again. Then I conjured three more padlocks, one for each side, and locked those, too. Finally, when I thought maybe I could speak without screaming, I turned to Mab. She was standing, her hands clenched into fists, her gaze fixed on the trapdoor.

"I hate that book," I said. I didn't have to ask for her inter-pretation of what we'd seen. It was obvious. If Pryce succeeded in whatever he was trying to do with his captured demons and the cauldron, the result would be a war unlike any in history. Demons and the Old Ones would attack. And humanity would fall.

10

"HOW CAN WE STOP PRYCE?" I ASKED MAB. WHAT I REALLY wanted to know was how we could stop that vision of utter devastation from becoming real.

"One step at a time, child." She sat down heavily and fingered her bloodstone pendant. "Let's start at the beginning. You said Pryce has tried twice in as many days to kill you. One attack was by Harpy. I didn't see the other."

"I'm not opening that door again."

"No need, child." I could have been wrong, but I thought I saw a slight shudder pass over Mab. "Tell me what happened."

"It was in my client's dreamscape." I described the black door that opened to empty air, and how I'd been pushed through it, only to be hauled back inside by a demon. "When I found the second dream portal, Pryce started to come through it—with a rifle. I got out of there."

"As well you should have." She tapped her chin, thinking. "So," she said, "Pryce wants you not merely out of the way, but dead. Interesting."

Of all the words to describe that situation—alarming, scary, terrifying, disturbing—"interesting" wasn't even near the top of my list.

"Pryce is collecting demons and trapping them in that cauldron," she continued. "But how on earth did he get hold of it? I thought it was in Cardiff."

"The cauldron?" I shook my head. "It was in Boston. Well, in Cambridge. The Peabody Museum—it's part of Harvard—had it on loan from the Welsh National Museum as part of an exhibit of Celtic artifacts from the Bronze Age. It was stolen over a week ago."

"Presumably at the same time your clients began canceling their engagements."

"Yes, that's right." I'd made the same connection. After Pryce had nabbed the cauldron, he'd wasted no time filling it with demons.

"What do you recall," Mab asked, "of the poem 'The Spoils of Annwn'?"

Usually Mab's pop quizzes caught me off guard, and this one would have, too, if I hadn't just reread the poem online. "King Arthur led a raid on the Darklands and stole some sort of magic cauldron. The poem says the cauldron wouldn't cook a coward's food."

Mab looked pleased. "It's an odd, obscure poem," she said. "And of course poetry always dresses things up. The part about a coward's food is nonsense, of course. A tale made up to inspire men to acts of bravery during brutal times." I could see that: *Hey, look, the cauldron cooked my food! I must be a hero!* Mab continued: "Outside the Darklands, the cauldron is merely an ordinary vessel. In its proper place, though, it is the cauldron of transformation."

"What's that?" I'd never heard of the cauldron of transformation.

"The Darklands are home to three magical cauldrons: the cauldron of rebirth, the cauldron of regeneration, and the cauldron of transformation. The first, rebirth, returns the shades who inhabit the Darklands to new lives in this world. The second, regeneration, renews the shades who dwell permanently in the Darklands. The third—when it is where it belongs—changes one thing into another."

"And that's the one Pryce is cramming full of demons." He was grabbing all the demons he could get his hands on and imprisoning them in the cauldron in hopes of transforming them . . . into what? I asked Mab what she thought.

"The cauldron cannot transform anything while it remains in our world," she answered. "Perhaps he has some reason for trapping demons and needed a bronze vessel to contain them." She didn't look like she believed that for a second.

"But you saw the place where he dumped the demons into the cauldron, right?" She nodded. "It's the site of a doorway into the Darklands. I think Pryce plans to open it at the full moon."

"How do you know this? Have you visited this place?"

I shook my head. "Not yet. I only learned about it tonight. I know where it is, though. A . . . um, demon told me."

Mab pursed her lips. Silence stretched between us.

"After what I saw in my client's dreamscape"—I gestured toward in the direction of the reenactment we'd witnessed—"I figured there had to be rumors buzzing around the demon plane. So I conjured a demon and questioned it."

"What kind of demon?"

"Well, Eidolons are easiest—"

"Oh, child, surely you know better than to summon a guilt-demon on purpose." Mab radiated disapproval.

"Usually, yes." Didn't she see I'd had no choice? "I didn't call it for fun. How else was I going to get information about what's happening in the demon plane? An Eidolon was the best choice. It wouldn't lie to me, not directly. It confirmed the figure I saw was Pryce. It told me that a lot of demons were staying in Uffern because they were afraid of him. And it also told me about the cauldron and the portal. We'd be totally in the dark if I hadn't talked to it."

Lips still pursed, Mab gave a long, slow nod. "Well, at least you killed the Eidolon after you were finished with it." Suddenly, I had an intense desire to inspect my fingernails. "You *did* kill it?"

Fascinating things, fingernails. They have this little pale moon at the base . . . I made myself look my aunt in the eye.

"No, I didn't." How could I explain why I let the demon go? Admit that it had manipulated me? Rationalize that I'd sent it back to the demon plane as a spy? I went for the truest reason. "I planned to kill it. I had my dagger in my hand. And then it said, 'Please don't.'"

Okay, so I couldn't explain. The whole thing sounded stupid now, the worst kind of beginner's mistake.

"Ah." Mab sighed, and I braced myself for a lecture. But her face softened. "Compassion is a fine and ennobling trait, child. Even when shown to an enemy. Perhaps especially then. Without compassion, we'd be . . . well, we'd be no better than the things we fight. But I do hope that in this instance, yours hasn't been misdirected."

"If it tries to feed on me again, I'll kill it without a second thought. I told it so when I banished it."

"Beware, child. Dangerous times are coming." She looked at the trapdoor, then back at me. I felt like she was trying to peer inside my head. "It's important that you're ready. Don't allow this Eidolon to manipulate and distract you." A crease appeared between her eyebrows. "I do hope I'm right about you," she murmured, almost too quietly for me to hear.

"Right about me? What do you mean?"

Mab shook her head. She filled her teacup, dismissing the issue.

"Mab," I began.

She shook her head again. "Not now, child. We must focus on the matter at hand."

I watched the steam spiral upward, wondering what she'd meant. Ready for what? Right about me how? But I knew it was useless to press her now. Anyway, she was right. We needed to focus.

Mab set down the teapot, lifted her cup, and blew on it. "Now, tell me what you learned about this portal. You say it's called the Devil's Coffin?"

"The Eidolon said a door opens there at the full moon. A door to the Darklands."

"There are such doors. Normally they open only for souls to pass through on their journey to the other side. But a wizard could indeed use the power of a full moon to open one. And because Pryce received Myrddin's life force, we must assume he also received at least some of his father's knowledge. We must assume that Pryce knows how to open the portal."

"So now we just have to figure out why Pryce wants to smuggle a cauldron full of demons into the Darklands."

"Not simply a cauldron, child. The cauldron of transformation. Think of that." Mab frowned. "What is Pryce missing? His shadow demon. Without it, he cannot realize his ambition to rule Uffern. And he cannot lead demons to war in the human realm." She paused, and I felt sure she was remembering that terrified, screaming toddler clinging to a sculpted tortoise. It was the same image that haunted me. "Pryce wants his shadow demon back. I believe that he'll attempt to transform all those lesser demons into a single entity, which he will then bind to himself."

It took me a minute to process that. "You mean he's going to try to make himself a new shadow demon." This was bad news. Pryce was aiming to turn himself back into a demi-demon. If he succeeded, he'd be more powerful than before.

"Without his demon half, Pryce is merely human. Mortal. Weak. He cannot enter the demon plane. So, yes. I think that he would do whatever is necessary to regain his full power." She sipped her tea. It seemed odd. Such a civilized act, after we'd both witnessed the end of the world.

"Friday is the first night of the full moon," I said. "I'll go to the Devil's Coffin as soon as it's light. Maybe I can find the cauldron and kill its stash of demons."

"Take care, child. Pryce has tried twice in as many days to kill you. He will almost certainly try again."

"I think he's learned by now that I'm not so easy to kill."

"And so he may try all the harder. Remember, he doesn't merely want to stop you; he wants you dead. And that's especially dangerous when you're looking for a doorway into the Dark-lands."

Good point.

"I think we've discussed enough for now, child. We both have much to think about. Let's talk again tomorrow."

"All right." My head was spinning as it was.

Mab's colors filled my dreamscape. I waved to her through the blue and silver strands, watching as her silhouette faded.

I do hope I'm right about you.

What had she meant? In all the years I'd known Mab, she'd never expressed any doubt about me. A wish that I'd work harder, sure. Disappointment, yes. But never doubt. I didn't like it.

We'd talk again tomorrow, after I'd checked out the Devil's Coffin. I'd ask her then. And I'd keep asking her until she explained. "Forewarned is forearmed"—it was her saying, after all.

For now, I had things to do. I'd just tidy up my dreamscape and get started on them. I turned to the trapdoor to make it disappear.

With a deafening crack, a padlock exploded. Then another.

Then the final two. The door blew twenty feet into the air. Through it sprang a massive wolf. I conjured a weapon and tensed, waiting for it to charge.

But it didn't. It stayed were it was and looked at me with accusing eyes.

With Kane's eyes.

Shit. The full-moon retreat. I couldn't be with Kane at his werewolf retreat because I had to stop Pryce.

The wolf stood statue-still, disappointment radiating from its eyes.

In another part of my mind, Copley Square burned. A little girl sobbed in fear.

I couldn't let that vision become reality.

Kane would understand. No pressure—that's what he'd said. Not on a whim. I'd simply tell him I needed more time. He'd be fine with that.

So would Simone. Simone Landry would be very, *very* fine with my absence.

But I had no choice. I'd deal with her later.

I dropped my weapon and put out my hand. Stepping closer to the wolf, I began to explain. "Kane, I—"

The wolf shuddered. Its skin split. A giant maggot bulged out. With lightning speed, it jumped on me, knocking me to the ground. The thing was as big as a Volkswagen, as mushy as a garbage bag filled with toxic sludge. It stank like death. Sharp teeth bit into my gut, an eager, sucking mouth fastened on the wound.

Thoughts of every bad or wrong thing I'd ever done flooded my mind. Every time I'd ever been nasty or hurtful. Every time I'd disappointed someone. Every time I was petty or didn't give a damn. Faces swirled around me like leaves in a whirlwind: Kane, Mom, Gwen, Maria. Even Mab. And Dad—especially Dad. His eyes were closed in death, but I knew he was staring at me.

I could never escape the fact of my father's death. He'd always be dead. And it would always be my fault.

I woke up yelling and thrashing, struggling to free myself from the Eidolon's oppressive weight.

11

MY HAND WENT TO THE DAGGER ON MY NIGHTSTAND. BUT
as soon as I pulled it out I realized there was nothing to strike
at. Nothing was attacking me. I crouched against the headboard,
heart galloping, adrenaline like lightning in my veins. But alone.
The Eidolon wasn't here.

I slid my legs forward so I was sitting up in bed, waiting for
my pulse to quit pounding. That maggot-shaped horror could
have been anything. Most likely, the image I'd dropped into my
subconscious had combined with Mab's warning to emphasize
the Eidolon's threat to me. But it also could have been a Drude,
whipping up my worry about the Eidolon into a banquet of fear
for it to feast on. I really hoped I wasn't dealing with two demon
infestations. I could handle a Drude if I had to—although I'm
skilled at controlling my dreams as they unfold, I do get occa-
sional nightmares. Any Drude that trespasses in my dreamscape
soon gets blasted back into the ether.

The worst possibility was that my new Eidolon BFF had managed to enter my dreamscape. But I didn't think that was the
case. Eidolons prefer their victims awake. Guilt tastes best, I
guess, when sleep doesn't dull its piquancy.

I replaced the dagger on my nightstand, glancing at my

bedside clock as I did: nearly four A.M. I might as well get up. Tina was coming by after school so I could quiz her on a chapter of *Russom's Demoniacal Taxonomy*, the demonology textbook I'd loaned her. I hadn't taken her back as my apprentice, but if the kid wanted to study demonology on her own time, I didn't mind helping her.

I climbed out of bed. It was too early to call Kane. More than anything, I wanted to go over to his place and slip under the covers. Kane always slept on his right side. I'd snuggle up against his muscled back, curving my body into his, breathing in his warm, sleepy scent. He'd wake up and reach for me and—

And hear that I wasn't going with him on retreat.

When would I break the news—before? After? Why not just blurt it out at the height of passion? My fantasy melted like a snowflake in a hot skillet.

I'd talk to Kane tonight, when I met him at Creature Comforts. We'd both be relaxed, and I could tell him face-to-face. I'd say that he was right, that I was rushing ahead too fast and summer would be a better time. Maybe even fall. He'd understand. He'd probably agree with me. We'd discuss the issue calmly and maturely, like adults. Everything would be fine.

Everything would be just peachy-keen-wonderful-fine—as long as Simone Landry stayed away. Yeah, like that would happen. I headed for the shower, wondering if there was a listing for "Kidnappers" in the Yellow Pages.

SPRAYED BY WATER AS HOT AS I COULD STAND IT, I SCRUBBED and scrubbed. My skin turned lobster red. And still I scrubbed, trying to remove all traces of clinging Eidolon slime. Guilt is like that. Once it comes to the surface, it sticks.

Juliet would probably have a Shakespeare quote for the occasion. Lady Macbeth and her damned spot or some such thing.

I turned off the water and stepped out of the shower stall. My big, fluffy towel chafed my raw skin. You can't wash off Eidolon slime—I knew that. It's a psychic substance, not a physical one. But that didn't stop me from feeling as ooze-covered as some slime monster in a horror film.

Perfectly normal after an encounter with an Eidolon. It didn't mean I was infested. Maybe the Eidolon would honor our agreement and stay away.

Uh-huh. And then it would spend the weekend in Acapulco sunning itself on the beach beside Simone Landry.

Mab said compassion is a good thing, and I was sure it was true. Be that as it may, I had to admit it: I'd let the demon manipulate my emotions. It was exactly what I'd advised dozens of clients *not* to do. There's only one way to deal with guilt. You've got to maintain a strictly logical mind-set. The moment feelings come into play—like going all soft because you hear the word "please"—guilt pounces. I knew that. But feelings are so damn tricky.

Compassion, hah, I thought as I went into my bedroom to get dressed. I should have killed that Eidolon the minute I'd finished questioning it. Because there's one essential thing to remember about guilt: Once you give in to it, it always comes back. Guilt had taken over my dream. It had left me terrified and sick upon awakening. And despite all my scrubbing, it still clung to my skin.

The bronze blade of my dagger glinted as I lifted it from the nightstand. The next time that Eidolon approached me, I'd be ready. The damn demon wouldn't fool me twice.

STANDING IN THE DOORWAY TO MY APARTMENT, I WATCHED the elevators down the hall. Clyde had called to let me know that Tina was on her way up. The bell dinged, the doors opened, and out came a walking pile of boxes.

"What's all this?" I asked, taking the top couple of boxes from the stack so Tina could see where she was going.

"They're for Juliet. Your doorman dude had them piled halfway to the ceiling on his desk. I said I'd bring them up. Where do you want them?"

"Over there, in the corner, I guess," I said, pointing to a spot near Juliet's desk where they'd be out of the way. Juliet was in her room with the door closed, and I didn't want to disturb her. My roommate had come home and, proclaiming she was more exhausted than she'd been in a century, headed straight for her coffin. She was smiling, though, so maybe she'd talked Brad and his partner into a night on the town.

Tina let the packages tumble from her arms. They landed in an untidy heap. "Is it Juliet's birthday or something?"

I shook my head. After so many centuries, I didn't think Juliet even recalled the date of her birth. "She wants to figure out how to scramble eggs inside their shells."

Tina gave me a look, then shrugged. She tugged at her tight-fitting T-shirt—it featured a zombified Betty Boop—but she didn't quite manage to close the gap between its hem and her low-slung jeans.

"Do you want something to eat?" I asked. Saying that to a zombie was kind of like asking a fish if it wanted water.

"Yeah." Tina glanced at the jumble of boxes. "But not eggs." She pushed past me and went into the kitchen. My hands felt dirty from carrying boxes, so I went over to the sink and rinsed them off. As I did, Tina rummaged through the cabinets. The kid knew my kitchen better than I did. "Got any popcorn? That's what I'm in the mood for. Oh, here's some." She pulled out a bag, stuck it in the microwave, and pressed some buttons.

"So, um, have you talked to your aunt lately?" Tina kept her voice nonchalant as she watched the microwave turntable.

"I did. Just a little while ago, in fact." I shook the water from my hands.

"Oh. That's nice. Did anything, you know, interesting come up?"

"You mean like you, for example?"

"Well, yeah. I was just wondering if you, like, happened to mention how I helped you kill that Harpy."

"The subject did come up."

"Really?" Tina straightened. "What did she say?"

"That I shouldn't underestimate you."

"She said that? Honest?" Tina bounced up and down on the balls of her feet. At the same time, popping erupted from the microwave. It was an odd effect, like she was full of exploding kernels.

More like bursting with pride. Praise from Mab could do that.

The microwave dinged. Tina yanked open the door and ripped open the bag. A geyser of steam jetted out as she grabbed a handful of popcorn. I winced as I watched her stuff the burning-hot kernels into her mouth, even though I knew the heat didn't bother her. Tina paused to put a second bag in the microwave, then scarfed another handful.

"You know," she said around the popcorn in her mouth, "what your aunt said, it's kind of like what Mrs. McIntyre said about my career report. Guess what grade I got." Her cheeks bulged as she chewed. "Go on, guess."

"D for disaster?"

"Nuh-uh. Quit trying to be funny. She gave me an A. She said our Career Night talk gave the clearest demonstration she's ever seen of what a job requires. She even said she hopes she never sees another presentation like it again. That's good, right?"

"I think she meant she doesn't want any more Harpies invading her classroom."

"Well, duh. Who would?" Tina carried her bag of popcorn to the kitchen table and set it down. She dug around in her backpack until she found *Russom's*. Handing the book to me, she said, "Do you think maybe your aunt would be interested to hear what I got on my report? I did a whole portfolio—a paper and a poster and an oral presentation and everything. Mrs. McIntyre said it was the best work I've done all year."

"If I get a chance, I'll tell her."

"Awesome." Tina stared at me, chewing her bottom lip, like she was trying to decide whether to say something else.

I regarded her levelly. I knew what she wanted to ask me, whether I'd take her back as my apprentice, and I had no intention of encouraging her. I wasn't trying to be mean. Tina was no longer my official apprentice because she'd quit, and fighting demons isn't something you can do only when you feel like it. Plus, when she had been my apprentice, she'd interfered with several jobs, insulted clients, and stolen my most valuable weapon. If Tina wanted to work her way through *Russom's*, I'd help her, but I wasn't bringing her along to wreak havoc at job sites. Not that I had any jobs lined up at the moment.

But I would tell Mab about the A.

The microwave dinged again. Tina went over and pulled out the second bag of popcorn. We sat down at the table.

"What are we going over today?" I asked.

"Chapter 37."

Oh, great. I didn't quite have *Russom's* memorized, but I knew what Chapter 37 covered. I turned to the opening page, and there it was in black and white: Eidolons. Below the chapter title was an illustration showing the demon's fat maggot body and snarling demon head. Next to it was a close-up illustration of a typical belly, with its second mouth full of jagged teeth. Nausea rose, and I shuddered.

"Gross, huh?" Tina said. "Imagine having one of those things gnawing on your guts."

Yeah, just imagine. Suddenly I felt all slime-covered again. I knew it wouldn't do any good, but I really, really needed to wash my hands. Just one more time. I got up and went back to the sink. "All right." I tried to keep my voice steady, even sounding slightly bored, as I lathered up. "Give me the basics."

"Eidolons are a kind of personal demon. Their species is *Inimicus anxietatum*. Anxiety, right?"

I nodded, pushing up my sleeves and washing my forearms to the elbows. There was nothing there—I knew that—but the soapy water felt good.

"Okay, so that's what they eat," Tina continued, "people's feelings of anxiety and worry. But they like guilt best. To an Eidolon, guilt is as yummy as . . ." She paused, searching for the right analogy as I dried my hands on a dishtowel and came back to the table. "As popcorn to a zombie." She grinned and tilted her head back, pouring the crumbs into her mouth.

As I sat down, she opened the second bag. "Want some?"

Nausea welled again. I shook my head and suppressed the urge to return to the sink.

"So," Tina said, "Eidolons get the munchies when a victim is almost asleep. The victim lies in bed, trying to relax, and these bad feelings—guilt and worry and stuff like that—start to rise up. The Eidolon feeds on those feelings. At the same time, it tries to make them worse, keeping the victim awake. It can, like, read the thoughts that are making the person feel bad. It's like it infects those thoughts, making them, you know, fester. Sucks for the victim."

That was for damn sure. "Habitat?" I asked.

"Most of the time they live in the demon plane and only cross over to our world when they get a whiff of somebody's guilt. But once the infestation, like, takes hold, the Eidolon can actually live inside the host. That *really* sucks for the victim, because it means the Eidolon can feed all the time, not just after dark when most demons come out to play."

The sick feeling in my stomach was growing by the minute. I never should have let that demon get away. "What's the best way to kill an Eidolon?"

"Wait, you didn't ask about symptoms. I know that part; we can't skip it."

Hearing my own symptoms recited to me was not a thrill I wanted to experience, but it wasn't Tina's fault that the timing of this lesson was so awful. "Okay, go ahead."

"First of all, the victim is, like, super-exhausted from lack of sleep." Tina looked at me for confirmation at the very moment I was stifling a yawn. I coughed into my hand.

"Are you getting a cold?" she asked. "Spring colds are the worst. I'm glad zombies don't get those."

"I'm fine." I'd gotten plenty of sleep yesterday. Running around Phyllis's dreamscape had taken a lot of energy, that's all. "What else?"

"Um, let me see." She looked at the ceiling as though the answer were written there. "Other telltale signs include lack of appetite and feeling dirty all the time. If someone keeps washing their hands . . ." She paused, and I shoved the dishtowel out of sight under the table. "Or takes, like, four or five showers a day, that's a major clue."

She ate another handful of popcorn, chewing slowly, a thoughtful expression on her face as she regarded me. Crap. She'd just listed the classic symptoms of an Eidolon infestation, and here I sat, the perfect textbook case for every single one, from the purple circles under my eyes to the near-crazy need to wash my hands yet again. *I'm not infested!* I wanted to shout. *I only summoned the demon to question it.*

The words were almost on my lips when Tina spoke. "Do you have any ice cream? I kinda hate to ask. It's not like I want to eat you out of house and home or anything, but I'm still hungry."

"Ice cream?" I almost laughed. She wasn't diagnosing me, just judging how many snacks I'd let her have. For a minute, I'd worried I was going to have to fend her off while she waved around a mail-order dagger, challenging my Eidolon to a duel. "Yeah, there's chocolate. There might be another kind, too. See what's in the freezer."

Tina grinned and went to the fridge. I sat on my hands to suppress the urge to wash them.

"Anyway," she said, pulling out a pint of cookie-dough flavor, "those are the symptoms. Did I miss any?"

"You hit all the important ones." I didn't want to go through a long list of minor symptoms and find myself twitching with every single one.

"Cool. *Now* we can move on to how to kill Eidolons." She

took a spoon from the silverware drawer and returned to the table. "The book says that a bronze dagger will do the trick, like with most demons. A couple of stabs, and *pop!* It explodes." She pried the lid off the container and dug in. "But you know," she added, speaking around a mouth full of ice cream, "that seems like it'd make a big mess. An Eidolon looks kinda like a maggot, right? Have you ever squished a maggot?"

Bile rose, and I swallowed hard a couple of times, shaking my head.

"Well, it's really gross. Who'd want that gunk all over their bed? I mean, if an Eidolon already makes you feel all slimy, popping one would *really*—"

"I get the idea, Tina. Move along."

She dug out another big scoop. "So I was thinking. The book says that if you kill an Eidolon, another one will follow unless you get rid of the feelings that attract the demons to you in the first place. That Russom dude recommends psycho-whatsis—"

"Psychoanalysis. R. G. Russom was a big fan of Sigmund Freud."

"Who's that—like, some actor?" Tina rolled her eyes. "I'm talking about demons here."

"Freud wasn't—" I sighed. "Never mind, go on."

"So anyway, Russom recommends using that psycho stuff to, like, pull out guilt and other negative emotions at the root. But here's what I thought: Why not *start* with that? No maggot-popping needed."

I closed my eyes for a moment against the image of a popped maggot—I'd killed enough Eidolons to know how accurate it was—and wiped my hands on the dishtowel under the table. "Psychoanalysis can take years, though," I said. "Killing the Eidolon gives the victim relief and some time to work on the psychological issues."

"No, that's not what I mean."

"Explain, then. Let's say you were faced with an Eidolon. Not a client's—one of your own. What would you do?" My voice sounded a little too eager.

"I'd embarrass the sucker to death."

I almost laughed. That was not an idea I'd expect from Tina, who thought weapons were the cool part of demon slaying. On the other hand, she *was* a teenage girl. I motioned for her to continue.

"See, I was thinking about personal demons and why they're so scary and all. And I realized that they're scary mostly because we're scared of them." She shook her head. "Wait, that sounds kind of obvious. What I mean is, the victim gives the demon the power to be frightening. If you give something, you can take it away, right?"

I leaned forward. "And how would you do that?"

"You know that trick to get rid of stage fright—the one where you imagine the audience in their underwear?"

"You think people should picture their demons wearing underwear?" This time I did laugh, as the image flashed through my mind of my scowling Eidolon with a matching bra-and-panties set stretched around its bloated, slimy body. Pink satin. With lace. And rosebuds.

Tina grinned, taking my laughter as encouragement. "Sure, why not? But it doesn't have to be underwear. When you're scared of something, make it seem all lame and ridiculous. If you've got an Eidolon, give it a nickname, like Snookums or Tinkerbell or Butterfly. I mean, who could be scared of a demon called Snookums?"

"So when you're lying in bed and your Eidolon shows up . . ."

"I'd say, 'Hi, Snookums. I hope you're not hungry, because I had the most awesome day.' I'd imagine Snookums wearing a silly-looking party hat and those glasses that have a big fake nose attached. I'd tell jokes and think about things that make me happy. You know, think about them on purpose. If old Snookums tried to make me feel bad, I'd push away that thought and find one that made me feel better. Even just a little bit better." Tina finished the last spoonful of ice cream and pushed the carton to one side. "Okay, so now you're going to tell me what's wrong with my idea."

"No, I'm not. It's a very solid idea." Parts of it were exactly what I'd done to keep the Eidolon I'd summoned under control, thinking about flowers and puppies. "You've put a twist on what I usually recommend to clients, which is to find a way to get rid of those feelings of guilt and worry. When you do that, you cut off the Eidolon's food supply."

"You mean *Snookums's* food supply. 'Eidolon' sounds too serious and scary. Anyway, that's what I was thinking, too. 'Cause if there's one thing zombies understand, it's food. When you're hungry and there's nothing to eat, you're not going to hang around. You're going to go somewhere else, some place where you have a chance to score some chow." She eyed the empty ice cream container a bit sorrowfully.

"It's a good method. Just remember that some clients find it hard to follow. Once anxiety takes hold, some people can't push it away, no matter how hard they try. In those cases, it may be necessary to kill the Eid—er, Snookums—first and *then* get psychological help. It doesn't have to be psychoanalysis; there are faster, more modern methods. I recommend meditation, hypnosis, counseling. It depends on the individual client."

"Speaking of chow," Tina said, "I'd better get home or I'll miss dinner. And that would be, you know, a disaster." She pulled a candy bar from her backpack and ate it in two bites as she put *Russom's* away. "So I did good today?"

"You did. I like that you're thinking outside the box. Fighting demons isn't always about weapons."

Tina beamed as she shrugged on her backpack. "Sometimes you have to think like that. Sometimes your teacher tells you not to bring your dagger to school anymore."

After Tina had gone, I found myself back at the sink, washing my hands again. This had to stop. I pictured the Eidolon that sprawled on my torso, its horrible larval body quivering as it fed. Not a Snookums. Not even a Tinkerbell. What was the other name Tina had tossed off? Butterfly.

Something in my gut cringed.

Butterfly. Yeah, I could see that. It already looked like a bug. I imagined the lump of a body sprouting wings, beautiful wings covered in delicate, colorful patterns. They fluttered gently above me.

The nausea I'd been feeling shrank to a pinpoint, then disappeared.

"That's right, Butterfly," I said out loud. "You stay in your chrysalis." Maybe Tina's trick would help me keep it there.

12

ACCORDING TO THE INFORMATION I'D SEEN ONLINE, PURGA-
tory Chasm State Reservation opened at 9:00 A.M. By the time
I exited the Mass Pike at Millbury to take Route 146 South, it
was already a few minutes past the hour. The morning was chilly
and overcast, one of those April days that make you wonder if
spring has decided to go back into hibernation. Since I'd be
traipsing through the woods, I'd worn a fleece jacket over a
T-shirt, along with comfy jeans, and traded my city boots for a
sturdy pair better suited to hiking. I had a flashlight in my pocket
and carried a couple of concealed daggers; I also wore my InDetect around my neck, tucked inside the jacket. There wouldn't
be any demons running around here in the daylight, but it might
pick up something from Pryce's hidden cauldron—assuming I
had the right Devil's Coffin.

The parking lot was empty except for one other car. It probably belonged to the ranger who was staffing the Visitors' Center.
Near that building was an outdoor information center displaying
a big map of the park. Hugging myself against the cool morning
air, I stopped to examine it. The entrance to the chasm was just
ahead: go up the road, pass a picnic shelter, and then turn left.
The Devil's Coffin was at the far end of the chasm, about a

quarter of a mile down the Chasm Loop Trail. A quarter of a mile—what was that, two or three city blocks? Not so bad.

The display held photocopied maps of the park. I grabbed one to take with me and headed toward the chasm. A stiff breeze nipped at my face, making my eyes water. Clouds tumbled across the sky, occasionally letting a sunbeam through. It was the kind of sky that might drizzle or clear up or even toss a few snowflakes at you. I wasn't surprised I was the only hiker here.

In a couple of minutes I stood at the entry to the Chasm Loop trail. I looked at the map in my hand. I looked back at the rough wooden sign that read TO CHASM. Yep, it definitely pointed this way. And then I looked at the jumble of boulders that littered the steep slope ahead. This was the trail? A trail is supposed to be wide path covered with pine needles and meandering through shady woods. This mess looked like the rubble left over after a boulder-hurling contest between giants.

Just a quarter of a mile, I reminded myself. No more than three blocks—if those blocks were an obstacle course going straight downhill. At least I'd worn decent hiking boots. I sighed and stepped onto the first boulder.

Blue stripes, spray-painted on the rocks, marked the so-called trail. But at this point, there was only one way to go: down. I jumped from one rock to the next, sometimes sitting and sliding to the one below. Steep cliffs rose on either side of the narrow chasm. In shaded places, some ice still clung to the rock walls. Halfway down, when I landed awkwardly and almost twisted my ankle, I began to have doubts. How the hell could Pryce lug a heavy bronze cauldron packed with demons over this terrain?

The same way he'd got it out of the museum, probably. Using his father's magic, some kind of levitation spell. Like the spell he'd used on Phyllis's Drude. I stumbled and whacked my hand on a rock. *Ow!* I wouldn't mind knowing a levitation spell myself right now.

I paused and leaned against a boulder, catching my breath and examining the scrape on my hand. Thinking about Myrddin's magic had opened the door to an unwelcome thought I'd been trying to avoid. It had taken the life forces of five people to resuscitate Pryce after I'd killed his demon half. I was supposed to have been one of them. Myrddin had tried to transfer my life force to his son. He'd failed, of course, but some part of my life force—some part of my soul, of what made me *me*—had gone into Pryce. I'd felt it being ripped, slowly, agonizingly, from my body. I didn't know how much of my life force Pryce received. Any was too much. What advantage did it give him? Was he aware of my movements? Could he hear echoes of my thoughts?

Pryce didn't have to know my location to send that Harpy after me. When you sic Harpies on someone, you focus on the person. The Harpies lock onto the victim, wherever he or she may be. Then, Pryce had raided the dreamscape of my last remaining client the night I was doing her job. That could have been a coincidence, but somehow I didn't think so. Pryce knew I'd be there and set me up for a fall. One hell of a long fall.

Clouds dimmed the light, and I shuddered. Did Pryce know I was here now? The chasm was deserted. No one descended the slope behind me. No one I could see, anyway. Those huge boulders offered way too many hiding places. A chill prickled the back of my neck. Was it the breeze, or was I being watched? I scanned my surroundings. A flash of movement caught my eye, and my heart leapt. My hand went to my dagger, then relaxed. A chipmunk. It was just a chipmunk, scurrying from the shelter of one rock to another.

Quit spooking yourself, Vicky. It was a good thing no one else was here. If I were any jumpier, I'd be a menace to other hikers. I shook off the creepy feeling and scrambled the rest of the way down the slope.

At the bottom of the gorge, the going became a little easier. Boulders littered the chasm floor, but a narrow path—one that actually looked like a trail—wound through them. The ground was spongy and wet, its puddles glassed with a thin layer of ice. In some places deep, gooey mud sucked at my boots and sent me back onto the rocks. I passed signs marking named formations: Lover's Leap, the Devil's Pulpit. They all looked like everything else down here—huge hunks of gray rock.

A low wooden bridge crossed a particularly swampy section of the chasm floor. Ahead, on the right, was the Devil's Coffin. A sign bolted to the chasm wall identified the spot. Beside the sign was a shallow boulder cave, like the pictures I'd seen online. A large rectangular rock rested on the cave floor, jutting out past the entrance. The rock tilted, making the head of the Coffin, the part inside the cave, higher than the foot. It was more the size and shape of a bed than a coffin, but I guess "the Devil's King-sized Mattress" doesn't sound quite so scary.

I hopped onto the Coffin and scrambled up it into the boulder cave. The cave was as shallow as it looked from the outside. There was barely enough room to stand behind the Coffin. The wall was solid; no narrow passages wound deeper into the cliff. I breathed a sigh of relief. No cave exploring for me today.

It took only a couple of minutes to inspect the place. The walls, covered with ghosts of graffiti that park workers hadn't managed to scrub away, crowded the slab on three sides. There was no sign of digging on the cavern floor. I got down on my hands and knees to peer beneath the Coffin, shining my flashlight into niches and cracks. Nothing there but rocks and dirt.

Rearing up, I pulled out my InDetect, lifting its cord over my head, and turned it on. The device buzzed to life, shooting out rapid-fire clicks as it warmed up. The clicking grew fainter, slowed, and then stopped. I stood on the Coffin and scanned the boulder cave with it, moving in a slow circle and sweeping the device up and down. Nothing. I let my arm drop, and the InDetect clicked a couple of times. I moved sideways, and scanned the center of the Coffin stone. It clicked again, but faintly, picking up residue of past demonic activity.

That could mean anything, I thought, turning off the device. A demon-haunted hiker carrying the effects of previous attacks. Some kids sneaking in at night to scare each other with a séance. It was also just possible the InDetect could be picking up a cauldron full of demons that had sat in the center of the Coffin. Yet there wasn't any cauldron here now.

I tapped on the stone, searching for a hollow spot, but I found nothing. Of course, Pryce could have cloaked the cauldron using magic. Wizards have ways to deflect people's perception, so that even though you'd swear you were moving in a straight line you'd actually go around the cloaked item. The cauldron could be right here in front of me, and I'd never see it. I waved my hand over the spot where the InDetect had made those faint clicks. Nothing but air. I tried again, keeping my arm straight, making straight lines in an X, feeling for anything out of the ordinary—a brush of bronze, a strange airflow pattern on my hand. Still nothing. I turned the InDetect back on and made another X. Again, just a few faint, irregular clicks. If the cauldron was here, it would stay hidden until Pryce was ready to use it.

That's why I'd be back at night. If Pryce showed up to dump another sackful of demons into the hidden cauldron, I'd be ready for him.

I went to loop the InDetect around my neck again. Clicks erupted like a sudden hailstorm on a tin roof. I looked at the device. It was pointing at my abdomen.

The Eidolon. My stomach roiled at the thought of that parasite attaching itself to my guts, gorging itself on my emotions. The discomfort grew, and the InDetect made even more of a racket.

I turned the device off, then hung it around my neck and tucked it back inside my jacket.

"Listen up, Butterfly," I said loudly, glad there was nobody around to hear me. "You disentangle yourself from my guts and flutter your ass back to Uffern, or I'll dress you up in frilly pink underwear and conjure a bunch of your demon buddies to come and laugh at you."

My stomach settled down immediately. The tingles of dread pulled back from my limbs.

What do you know? Tina was right. As much as the thought scared me in so many ways, maybe she might make a halfway-decent demon exterminator.

I spent the next couple of hours exploring the rest of the park, hiking its trails and looking for anything that might give me a clue about the cauldron. The park isn't very big. There are some picnic areas and playgrounds, but all its trails together add up to only three miles of hiking. Most of those trails are the kind of easy nature walks through the woods I'd pictured before I got here. But to get to the Devil's Coffin, no matter which way you approached, you had to climb down a boulder-strewn slope into the chasm.

FOR LUNCH I GRABBED A CHEESEBURGER AT A DINER IN MILL-bury. I sat at the counter, dunking my fries into a pool of ketchup, and thought about what I needed to do. I'd have to return to the Devil's Coffin to watch for Pryce. Maybe I could end this tonight and still go with Kane to his retreat this weekend.

Fat chance. I've never been that lucky.

Kane. Butterfly stirred in my gut as I wondered how the hell I was going to give him the news about canceling. *No . . . yes . . .*

no . . . well, maybe another time. Whatever my reasons, all the back-and-forth made me look like a flake.

That's because you're acting like a flake, a familiar, whiny voice buzzed in my mind. *You're going to hurt him. You'll lose him to that Simone—and it will be your own fault.*

"Shut up, Butterfly," I muttered.

"Did you want something else?" the waitress called from the other end of the counter.

"Just thinking out loud." I picked up the red plastic ketchup container and squeezed a big, gloppy puddle onto my plate, imagining I was squirting the stuff all over my Eidolon's ugly demon head. The voice went silent, and the guilty feelings withdrew, letting my stomach settle. Even so, I pushed away my half-eaten lunch.

"Could I get the check?"

Kane and I would work this out. And I only had to keep Butterfly at bay a little while longer. Tonight, after I'd staked out the Devil's Coffin, I'd force the demon to materialize. And then, please or no please, I'd take great pleasure in sending it back into the ether.

BACK ON THE MASS PIKE, I WAS COMING UP ON EXIT 14 WHEN I decided to swing by Gwen's house. Maria would be getting home from school, and I could check in with her, see how the kid was doing. I'd told Gwen I'd try to spend some time with Maria next week, but since I was so close, why not now?

Maybe I just didn't want to go home and try to nap with Butterfly hanging around, since dark was hours away and I couldn't force the demon to materialize before then. I didn't relish the idea of trying to sleep with an Eidolon lodged in my guts. But I pushed that thought from my mind and flipped on the turn signal to exit the turnpike.

I got on Route 128, heading toward Needham. Traffic on 128 is always heavy, but the road was even more choked up than usual for early afternoon. By the time I pulled into Gwen's driveway, I was thinking I should've driven straight home. Too late now. Maria came rocketing out of the garage on her bike, swerving away from the Jag's bumper as I came to a stop. She waved to me and yelled, "Don't leave!" Then she zipped out into the street and down the block. She didn't smile. Despite the wave, her face was grim. A scowl bunched her forehead, and her lips were compressed into a thin line.

Maybe this wasn't such a great time to drop by unannounced. I should've called. But that's harder than it sounds. I don't carry a cell phone (it got too expensive after the energy blasts from shapeshifting destroyed three in a month), and payphones are almost impossible to find these days. Still, it might have kept me from barging in on another family crisis. At least Gwen would have expected me.

She stepped forward now from the shadows of the garage, staring at the Jag as I got out. No, wait. That wasn't Gwen. This woman was a little taller, a little thinner than my sister. Her face was tanned, and her hair was white, not blonde.

"Mom?"

It couldn't be my mother; she was in Florida.

If you bothered to call once in a while, you'd know—

"Shut up, Butterfly." I mentally bonked the demon on the head with a beach ball, in keeping with the Florida theme.

"Vicky!" My mother opened her arms as Gwen came out of the house, with Justin on her hip, and stood beside her. I marveled at how much the two of them looked alike. Then I rushed forward and hugged my mother.

I didn't inhale the warm vanilla-and-Jean-Naté scent I remembered from my childhood. Mom wore a different perfume, one I didn't recognize, overlaid with the beachy smell of suntan lotion. I drew back and held her at arm's length. She was trim and toned, her hair cut in a bob like Gwen's, her face mapped with smile lines.

"You look great," I said.

She bit one side of her bottom lip as she studied me. "You look a little tired," she judged. "Have you been getting enough sleep?"

Such a mom. I hugged her again.

"Where's Maria?" Gwen's taut voice stretched those two words almost to the breaking point.

"She took off on her bike. That way." I pointed in the direction she'd gone. "I don't think she went far. She wanted me to wait for her."

"Hmph." Gwen walked to the end of the driveway and peered down the block.

My mother hooked her arm in mine. "It's good to see you," she said, drawing me toward the garage.

"I didn't know you were coming." She hadn't mentioned a trip north in her phone message. "When did you get here?"

"Gwen picked me up at the airport late this morning." Her soft Welsh accent wrapped around me like a warm blanket. "The trip was spur-of-the-moment. I got a good deal on a last-minute flight. Florida is lovely in winter, but I do miss New England in the spring." She glanced at the overcast sky and laughed. "Well, some days. Let's go inside, shall we? I was just sitting down to a cup of tea."

We went through the garage and into the kitchen. A teapot and mug waited on the table. "Would you like some?" Mom asked.

I shook my head. In a family of tea drinkers, I went for coffee. But I didn't want any now.

Mom picked up the mug and leaned against a counter.

"How's life in Florida?" I asked.

"Busy. I go for a swim each morning, play a lot of tennis. Golf sometimes." She grinned at me over her mug. "At the grand old age of sixty, I'm one of the youngsters in my retirement community. I've had to polish up my rusty demon-fighting skills; they come in handy when I have to fend off some of the horny old goats in that place."

My mother had put in several years as a professional demon fighter before she married my dad and they emigrated from Wales in the late seventies. She was five years older than my father, yet she'd been smitten with the handsome young man. Mom had experienced both my world and Gwen's, active shape-shifting and then motherhood. I realized with a start that she must have been my age—younger, even—when she'd chosen Dad over demons.

"You didn't come up here to see the tulips and daffodils bloom, right?" I asked. "Gwen asked you to help with Maria." It was a good idea. Gwen had turned away from demon slaying and shapeshifting when she was still in her teens, and those same things were my way of life. To Maria, we must seem like polar opposites. Mom had experienced both, first embracing shape-shifting and then giving it up because she fell in love and wanted a family. When I was growing up, Mom had stayed in the background, letting Dad and Mab guide me as I explored shapeshifting and trained to fight demons. But she'd always been supportive—of both me and my sister. She'd do the same for Maria.

"Poor Gwen." Mom sipped her tea. "She was in denial for so long about the possibility that her daughter would be a shifter. She's not ready for this. And poor Maria, too. She doesn't know whom to trust. Between puberty and her awakening abilities, her own body has become something alien."

"I remember that feeling. But I also remember I had a lot of help navigating the confusion. I'm glad you're here."

"I wish Maria felt the same way. She didn't seem at all happy to see me."

"What happened?"

Before she could answer, the door opened. Maria came inside, with Gwen gripping her shoulder. Justin squirmed, and Gwen set him down. He toddled over to his grandmother, stopping just out of reach, and stared at her, sucking his finger. Maria's head was tilted downward, her gaze fixed on the floor.

"Maria?" Gwen's voice still held that tautness.

"I'm sorry I took off like that, Grandma."

Mom's face was soft with love as she looked at her granddaughter. "How about a hug?"

Gwen released Maria's shoulder, and the girl walked over to Mom. She leaned in stiffly and allowed herself to be embraced for five whole seconds. Then she went to the back staircase and thumped loudly up the stairs. A minute later a door slammed.

Justin watched all of this with wide eyes. When Maria had gone, he looked back at his grandmother. He raised both arms. "Hug," he demanded.

Mom picked him up. His chubby arms circled her neck, and he planted a sloppy kiss on her cheek. "Now, that's a *real* hug," Mom said, putting him down. Justin giggled and went to his basket of toys in the corner.

Mom smiled, watching him dig through his toys. "Maria believes that her mother has brought me here as . . . what's the word? As a ringer, I suppose. Someone who'll unduly influence her toward Gwen's way of thinking."

"She's a smart kid," I said. "She'll figure out that's not true."

"Smart, yes, but as stubborn as . . ." Gwen searched for an apt comparison.

"As you were at that age," Mom finished for her.

One corner of Gwen's mouth twitched upward. "You think so? I don't remember it that way." She turned to me. "I've got to go pick up Zack from T-ball practice." Zack, Gwen's middle child, was a six-year-old future Red Sox pitcher. "How long are you stopping by?"

"I just intended to say hello and get back to town. I was checking out a, um, job site west of here. I have to go back there tonight, so I really need to go home and get some sleep."

Mom nodded her approval of that plan.

"I'd invite you to crash here, but this isn't the quietest house during the afternoon." Gwen nodded at Justin, who'd pulled a plastic hammer from the basket and was pounding the floor. Her eyes went to the ceiling as though she could see what Maria was doing upstairs. "Are you still planning to come out next week? I was thinking we could make Monday a family day. It's Patriots' Day, the first day of the kids' school vacation. We could have a nice meal, maybe go to the park if the weather is good. Let the kids burn off some energy."

"Park?" Justin paused in his banging.

"Later, honey," Gwen said. He dropped the hammer and went back to the toy basket.

I considered. Monday was a whole weekend away—a weekend when anything might happen. "I'd love to." *Assuming Pryce doesn't manage to kill me first.* "Around eleven okay?"

"Perfect." Gwen scooped up the hammer and set it on the table.

I turned to Mom. "How long are you staying?"

"That's open-ended right now." She glanced at Gwen. "We'll see how things go."

Gwen left to pick up Zack, and Mom got down on the floor to play with Justin. I climbed the stairs to say good-bye to Maria. When I knocked on her bedroom door, there was no answer.

After a couple more knocks, I tried the knob; the door was unlocked. I opened it far enough to stick my head inside. "Maria?" Still no answer. Her room was empty. I made a quick check of the other rooms but didn't find her.

Back downstairs, I told Mom I'd see her on Monday and accepted one of Justin's trademark soggy kisses. Outside, Maria leaned against my car. For a moment, I thought she was going to try to hitch a ride back to Deadtown. She'd already tried running away to Deadtown once, and that hadn't worked out so well.

I opened my mouth to remind her of that, but she spoke first. "How come you never answer when I try that dream-phone thing?"

"If I don't answer, it's because I'm not asleep. I'm usually at work while you're in bed." Mab could sense a dream-phone call when she was awake, but I didn't have that skill.

"There should be some kind of voice mail."

I smiled. "I was thinking the same thing not long ago. But there *is* regular voice mail. You can always leave me a message that way."

"Did Mom tell you about 'family day' on Monday?" Maria's voice oozed sarcasm on the words *family day.*

"I'm looking forward to it."

"Promise you'll come."

"I'll do my best. I have a job tomorrow night."

"No, you have to *promise.*" She gripped my arm with both her hands. "Aunt Vicky, you don't know what it's been like around here. I need somebody who's on my side."

"Maria, everyone is on your side. Me, Grandma, your mom—"

"*Promise.*"

"Okay. I promise." When I said the magic word, Maria threw her arms around me in a tight hug. I patted her shoulder. "But you have to promise me something, too." She pulled back, her eyes wary. "Promise me that between now and then you'll be nice to Grandma, and you'll at least try to get along with your mom. Can you do that?"

She bit her lip, then nodded. "I'm happy to see Grandma," she admitted. "But I don't want them to gang up on me."

"That's not why Grandma is here—you can trust me on that, okay?"

Another nod.

"Good. I've got to go home now, but you can start working on your side of the bargain. Something tells me you didn't get a chance to welcome Grandma, right?"

"I didn't know she was coming. When I saw her, I thought . . . I don't know what I thought. I ran outside and got on my bike because I needed to burn off some energy."

I tried not to smile at her repeat of her mother's phrase. It was one of Gwen's favorites. "Well, now's a good chance to start over."

"She's not mad?"

"No, she's not mad. Your grandmother understands a lot more than you think she does."

I gave Maria a kiss on the cheek, and she went into the garage. I heard her call, "Grandma?" as she opened the kitchen door. With any luck, the truce in my sister's household would hold for a couple of days.

As I drove back toward Boston, Butterfly stayed quiet in my gut. That was surprising, since I'd made my niece a promise I wasn't at all sure I could keep. Pryce was out there somewhere, with his kettle full of demons. He'd attacked me twice in two days and would probably try again before the door to the Darklands opened at the full moon.

"Family day" was only a few days away, but it might as well be at the far side of eternity.

13

GETTING A COUPLE OF HOURS OF SLEEP HERE, A FEW MORE
hours there is not an ideal way to let the body rest, but sometimes
it's the best I can do. After a mug of warm milk to help me
relax—the "magical sleeping potion" Mom used to give me as
a child—I set my alarm, crawled into bed, and did my best to
let my mind go blank. It was still afternoon, too early to do battle
with Butterfly, so I turned away from guilty or anxious thoughts.
I didn't have to worry, though. I was so tired I sank into imme-
diate, dreamless sleep. Nothing troubled me until the alarm
jolted me awake, way sooner than seemed possible.

I hit Snooze and turned over, pulling my comforter closer
around me, my body reaching for another few minutes of rest.
Just five minutes more . . .

Kane.

The thought zapped me like a Taser, jolting me awake. I had
to meet Kane and explain why I couldn't be with him this weekend. After that, I'd drive back to Purgatory Chasm and stake out
the Devil's Coffin. This was not going to be a fun night.

No "five minutes more" for me. I threw aside my warm covers
and felt around on the floor with my feet until I found my
slippers.

In the shower, I realized that I didn't feel all slime-covered, like I had earlier. Maybe Tina's technique was working. Or maybe old Butterfly had wised up and slithered back to the demon plane.

I toweled off and pulled on jeans and a sweater. Kane wouldn't expect me to dress up for our date, but I scraped the mud off my hiking boots as best I could, so I wouldn't look like I'd tramped through a swamp to get to Creature Comforts.

Juliet was at her usual station on the living room sofa, flipping through television channels with preternatural speed, making me feel a bit seasick. She turned off the TV and tossed the remote onto the coffee table. "I'm bored," she pouted.

I gestured toward the untouched stack of boxes heaped in the corner. "You could see how that magic egg-scrambler works."

"Please. I'm not that bored." She stretched, twisting left, then right. She picked up the remote, looked at it, and put it down again. "But I *am* bored."

"Must be nice," I countered. "I could stand a little boredom."

"That's because you're not cooped up in this apartment. It's beginning to feel a bit too much like the Capulet family tomb. That's one thing Shakespeare got right: 'Shall I not, then, be stifled in the vault, / to whose foul mouth no healthsome air breathes in / and there die strangled . . . ?'" She pressed a hand to her forehead and sighed as dramatically as any amateur actress playing her role in a community theater production.

"I take it you're not going out to interrogate Colwyn tonight?"

"No. Even worse, I've been assigned a new pair of Goons. My boys got in trouble because we didn't come straight back here last night. It wasn't *really* a detour; Creature Comforts is practically my second home. And I don't see why it's against the rules for me to take a tiny little sip of one of my keepers. He was willing; it's not like I ambushed him."

"You snacked on one of your Goon Squad guards?"

Juliet licked her lips and smiled.

"The human one, I hope."

"Brad." She sighed. "Such a tasty man. Military background, he told me. Did you notice how big and brawny he was? It's been far too long since I had a meal like that. Mmm. It was like a nice, juicy porterhouse, after all that limp bologna they've been delivering."

I didn't know how to answer that. It didn't matter, though,

because Juliet wasn't finished. "Is there a Craigslist category for Ugly? Because that's how I think they find my meals."

"Sorry you're bored," I said, "but I can't entertain you. I'm meeting Kane."

"What time is it?"

"Almost nine. I have to leave in a few minutes."

Juliet heaved another sigh. "Over an hour to go before they deliver dinner. And I'm *famished*." She slumped on the sofa. Then she brightened. "How about you bring me back some take-out?"

"Why do I think you're not talking about a bucket of fried chicken?"

"You're going to Creature Comforts. They know me there. I'm sure some little puppy would be happy to follow you home."

"I'm not coming home."

"Oh. So you get to spend the night having fun at Kane's place, and I sit here alone. And hungry. Well, that just sucks. Or doesn't—and that's the problem." She didn't even crack a smile at her joke, and that showed how unhappy she was. Maybe it was all that Shakespeare, but puns (especially bad ones) are Juliet's favorite form of humor.

"No fun for me tonight. I'm working."

"I thought all your clients have canceled."

"It's not a paying job. I got a tip on a place where Pryce might show up." I briefly explained about the Devil's Coffin. "Did Colwyn ever mention the place?"

She shook her head. "A portal to the Darklands, you say? Colwyn has spent centuries trying to stay *out* of the realm of the dead. If he knows about your Devil's Coffin, it's only to avoid it."

"Well, that's where I'll be tonight. I'm going to stake it out."

"I get it. You're a fighter, not a lover. You sound like Hotspur in *Henry the Fourth*: 'This is no world / to play with maumets and to tilt with lips. / We must have bloody noses and cracked crowns!'"

I wasn't sure what she was saying, but everything from "Hotspur" onward sounded dirty. The only dirty thing I'd be doing tonight would be lying in the mud, and I told her so.

Juliet leaned forward and snatched up the remote. She clicked on the TV and tuned in to the Weather Channel, where the local forecast was just coming on. It didn't sound good. *Cold . . .*

fog . . . steady drizzle . . . chance of precipitation is one hundred percent.

Juliet muted the sound. She was smiling. "Well, now I feel better. It's good to know there'll be one person in Massachusetts tonight who's more miserable than I am."

CREATURE COMFORTS WAS PACKED. ACTUALLY, "PACKED" WAS an apt description in more ways than one, because the place was brimming over with werewolves. They clustered around tables, sharing pitchers of beer, talking, and laughing. They kept Axel, the bartender, hopping. For years, I'd wondered what species Axel was. At seven feet tall, he had a hooked nose, beady eyes—and what I'd like to call a kind smile, but it was hard to tell behind that bushy beard. Axel, I'd recently learned, was a troll. Instead of a bridge, Creature Comforts was his territory—and nobody messed with Axel in his territory. Partly because he was so damn big and scary looking, and partly because they didn't want to get banned. Creature Comforts was the most popular bar in the New Combat Zone. Now, Axel moved as fast as I've ever seen him, supplying the werewolves with drinks.

For werewolves, the night before a full-moon retreat is like the beginning of a mini-vacation. Even though they're compelled to go—any werewolf caught outside a retreat during a full moon can legally be shot on sight—werewolves treat retreats like a holiday. And why not? In a way, that's exactly what they are. Three days away from jobs and societal responsibilities, when they can loose the inner beast—running through the woods, hunting deer, and howling their hearts out at the moon.

Right now, that sounded pretty damn good to me. And I couldn't go.

"Vicky!"

My name cut through the buzz of conversation.

Kane leaned out of a booth near the back of the room, waving and wearing a big grin. I waved back, thinking he wouldn't look so happy in about five minutes. My palms were sweating; I wiped them on my jeans and took a deep breath to steady my nerves. Kane was a grown-up. He could handle this. If he couldn't, then maybe our relationship wasn't what I thought it was.

I squared my shoulders, plastered a smile on my face, and made my way through the crowd toward the booth.

To find myself face-to-face with Simone Landry.

The smile dropped from my face like a boulder tumbling off a cliff.

Simone slid out from the seat opposite Kane, beaming as though running into me were the most wonderful thing to happen all day. *Hah.* I knew the reason behind her smile—she'd wanted me to see her with my boyfriend.

Kane stood and put his arms around me, brushing his lips against my cheek. I kept my gaze on Simone. *He's kissing me, not you. Got that?*

Simone said, "I guess I'll be going." When Kane pulled back from me and nodded, she reached out and grazed his arm with her fingers. Her touch was both light and brief, but it conveyed extraordinary intimacy. It wasn't a touch, it was a caress, damn it.

"I'll see you tomorrow." Her low, throaty voice thrummed with promise.

"You'll see both of us," Kane said. "Remember? I told you Vicky is coming with me."

Simone's glance flicked my way, frost chilling her smile. "How nice." The words held a subtext of challenge. Her face warmed as she turned back to Kane. "I'm looking forward to it." She sauntered away, hips swaying. Several male werewolves injured their necks whipping their heads around to watch her go.

Bitch.

Of course, that isn't exactly an insult to a female werewolf.

Kane wasn't one of the throng drooling over Simone. His eyes were on me, and they shone with pleasure. Damn, I wished I didn't have to disappoint him.

"Let's sit down," he said, scooting over to make room.

I sat across from him. It felt wrong to be getting all snuggly just before I broke the bad news that he'd be spending the weekend alone.

No, I reminded myself, seeing Simone's cold smile. No, he would most definitely not be alone.

Damn it all to hell.

Deep breath time. "Kane—" I began.

"No, wait." He reached across the table and took my hand in both of his. So warm. "I want to start things off right tonight."

"But—" As if by some signal, Axel appeared at our table, bearing a silver champagne bucket. He put it down, and then set two flutes on the table. Behind him were a couple of werewolves who worked with Kane. They carried trays and were handing out glasses of champagne to everyone in the room.

"Kane—" I tried again.

With a flourish, Axel popped the cork. Everyone cheered as bubbly fizzed from the bottle. Even Axel was smiling as champagne frothed into our glasses.

Kane stood. He pulled me up to stand beside him. One arm around my waist, he raised his glass. I wanted to sink through the floor.

"May I have everyone's attention?" His courtroom voice rang out.

"Stop," I hissed, jabbing his ribs with my elbow. He kissed the top of my head.

"Most of you know my girlfriend, Vicky. And everyone who knows her also knows how crazy I am about her."

Applause rippled around the room. Someone started clinking a champagne glass with their silverware, like we were at a wedding reception, and within seconds the whole room had joined in. Kane pulled me to him and gave me a deep, lingering kiss. The kind that would have melted me if it weren't happening in the middle of a disaster.

I pulled away. "Kane, don't."

Kane smiled and turned back to the crowd. "So I'm pleased—no, *thrilled*—to announce that Vicky has agreed to come with me to Princeton this weekend." Another round of applause. "Now, those of you who don't know Vicky may wonder how this is possible. She doesn't smell like a werewolf. And that's true." He pressed his face against my neck and inhaled deeply. "Although she does smell delicious, she's *not* a werewolf. She's a shapeshifter. She can become whatever animal she chooses. And this full moon, for my sake, she's choosing to be a wolf."

Why, oh why did Kane have to make such a production out of it? It was too late to put the brakes on this train wreck. I managed a feeble half-smile.

The werewolves cheered loudly, clapping and stamping their feet. Howls rose. Then, everyone quieted down as Kane lifted his glass.

"I just wanted to say how honored I am that the woman I love is coming with me on retreat. So please raise your glasses and join me in a toast to Vicky."

"To Vicky!" everyone shouted. But suddenly it felt like my ears were stuffed with cotton.

Love. The word echoed in my mind. All I could think of was that he'd said, "The woman I love"—*love*—and there were too many eyes on me for me to even begin processing how I felt about that. Couldn't he have said it in private first? Or was it just part of the show he was putting on?

Love. A small word, a tiny word. But one that was way too big for me to deal with right now.

Especially when I was about to blow him off.

Kane tossed back the contents of his glass and kissed me. He tasted like champagne. And guilt. A whole lot of guilt. No, the guilt was all mine. Butterfly would be feasting tonight.

"Oh, and one more thing." The crowed quieted as Kane's voice took on an edge. "This weekend, Vicky is under my protection. Anyone who messes with her, anyone at all, answers to me." He subjected the entire room to a hard stare, one table at a time. Some of the werewolves stared back at him, their features just this side of a scowl. But sooner or later, every single wolf dropped his or her gaze and looked away.

When he'd made his point, Kane treated the room to another of his million-dollar smiles. "Enjoy yourselves," he said. "The bar's open for the next hour. My treat."

The wolves cheered and crowded the bar. Axel, always up for a challenge, rubbed his thick-knuckled hands together and picked up the pace. This was going to cost Kane a fortune, and all for nothing.

Love. Why did he have to say "love"? If he'd said it in private, I'd be confused enough. But a public declaration . . . My brain refused to process what was happening.

Kane surveyed the room with satisfaction. I sat down again, on the same side of the booth where I'd been sitting before. Kane started to take his seat on the opposite side, then sat down next to me. I slid over, but I could feel his heat along the length of his thigh, pressing against mine.

Time to rain on Kane's parade. Rain, who was I kidding? We'd passed "rain" ten minutes ago. This was more like dropping a nuclear bomb smack on the marching band.

"You're not drinking your champagne," he said, pushing my untouched glass in front of me. "Do you want something else?" He turned toward the bar, his hand half-raised to signal Axel.

"No." I reached over and captured his hand, returning it to the table. I let my hand rest lightly on his. "Kane, I wish you hadn't done that."

His gray eyes darkened with concern. "What, the announcement? I'm sorry if I embarrassed you. That wasn't my intention. It's a werewolf thing. They're used to seeing me as a lone wolf. And any new wolf, male or female, gets a hard time the first time it shows up at a retreat. I had to make sure they understand you're mine." *You're mine.* A smile touched his lips as he said the words. "Now, they'll leave you alone."

Okay, so maybe "love" was part of some werewolf territorial declaration. I hoped so. It made what I was about to say a little easier.

"No, listen to me. I *really* wish you hadn't done that." I tried to swallow the lump in my throat. "I can't go with you."

He went utterly still, except for a narrowing of his eyes. I don't think he was even breathing. He didn't say a word. I hated that. Kane, who's always full of opinions and comments and theories on every topic under the sun, had absolutely nothing to say.

"It's not what you're thinking," I said.

"How could you possibly know what I'm thinking right now?" His lips barely moved as he spoke.

"You're right, I don't. But something has happened. Pryce is back."

He waited for me to continue.

"It, um, started two nights ago, when he sent a Harpy to kill me."

"Wait. Pryce tried to kill you, and you didn't even *mention* it to me?"

"I exterminated the Harpy. By the time I saw you, I had other things on my mind." Things like Simone.

"Other things. I see." His face was expressionless. "Go on."

I told him everything I'd learned—the captured demons, the missing cauldron, the door into the Darklands. "The door can be opened at the full moon, and Pryce knows how to open it. Mab and I think he's trying to reconstruct his shadow demon."

"And?"

"And—what do you mean 'and'? I've got to stop him."

"You do? Why? Pryce is wanted by the police for his attack on the Paranormal Appreciation Day concert. You know where he'll be tomorrow night. Tip off the police and let them do their job."

"I can't turn this over to the cops. Pryce has hundreds of demons packed into that cauldron. If he lets them loose, they'll massacre the police."

"So that's it, then." His face was a marble statue. "Pryce tried to kill you, and you tell me as an afterthought. You won't call in the cops. You're going to go after him alone, knowing he'll try his damnedest to kill you—and you expect me to be okay with that."

What could I say? The enmity between demonkind and the Cerddorion stretched back over centuries. That conflict was coming to a head, and I had a role to play. Mab's hints, *The Book of Utter Darkness*, Pryce's relentless quest for power, the reemergence of the Old Ones—all of it pointed to the ancient prophecies now being realized. I was part of those prophecies. I would not shirk my destiny.

If Kane had seen that vision—all that destruction, those bodies, that poor, hysterical child—he'd understand. But how could I begin to describe it? It was a vision inside a dream, shown to me by a treacherous book that tried to manipulate whoever read it. Kane would laugh.

"I'm sorry about missing the retreat," I said. "But I can't help the timing. The door can only be opened at the full moon."

"Do you think I give a damn about the retreat? If you never set foot in Princeton, that would be fine with me. But I would like some assurance that you'll be alive when I get back." He gripped my hand. Urgency sparked in his eyes. "Vicky, you take everything on your own shoulders, and you don't have to. *You. Don't. Have. To.* I've fought by your side before, and I'm always ready to do it again. Always. Don't go alone—wait until I can be with you. Maybe Pryce will fail. But even if he becomes a demi-demon again, so what? We beat him before. We can do it again. You and me. Together, we're unbeatable." His face shone with sincerity.

Reluctantly, I shook my head. "I have to stop him, Kane. Now, while he's weak. If Pryce gets his shadow demon back, he'll raise a demon army and invade our world. I don't know if anything could stop him then."

"Nothing I can say will change your mind, will it?" When I

didn't answer, the spark in his eyes darkened into something like sadness. He looked away. "Vicky, let me ask you one thing."

"Go ahead." I wanted to search his face for a clue about what he was going to say, but he kept it averted. A muscle twitched in his jaw.

When he turned back to me, his expression was wary. "For a long time, I've been wanting to take our relationship to the next level. If you don't . . . if you don't share that desire, I need to know."

"This isn't about you and me." God, that sounded harsh. I hadn't meant for it to sound harsh. I gentled my voice and squeezed his hand. "This is about Pryce."

"I see." Slowly, he pulled his hand away. "I wish you'd told me earlier."

"I—"

"You've known since last night, yes? A call would have been nice."

"I thought it would be better to tell you in person."

"All right." He rubbed his cheek and scanned the room again. This time, he didn't look so pleased as his gaze moved from one table to the next. "And now I've managed to humiliate myself in front of half of Boston's werewolves."

What do you say when there's really nothing *to* say? Kane was right; every single word he'd uttered was true. I couldn't argue with him. I couldn't soothe him. All I could do was sit there miserably and stare at the table.

"That's not your fault, Vicky. I shouldn't have created a spectacle. But I was so . . ." He made a fist and hit the table. Not hard. There was no bang. The glasses didn't shudder. But his restrained power and held-back emotion sent a shiver through me.

"I'd better go," he said. "Tomorrow's an early day for me. I've got some things I need to deal with at the office before we . . . before *I* leave for Princeton." He stood. I moved to follow, but he shook his head. "Don't worry about me, really." His look said he wished he could feel the same way about me. "I'll call you when I get back." And then he turned away. He took a step, then paused and spoke to me over his shoulder. "Be careful."

With his back straight, he strode across the room. As he passed, werewolves looked up, nostrils twitching. Conversations faded to a murmur, then died out. Without looking back, Kane pulled open the front door and walked out into the night. All the werewolves who'd watched him leave turned and gaped at me.

Never let a werewolf win a staring contest—I knew that. Still, I looked away.

Voices started up again, at first in hushed tones but soon growing louder. I slumped in the booth. On the table in front of me sat my untouched glass of champagne, fogged with condensation, golden bubbles skittering carelessly up its sides.

14

ON THE DRIVE TO PURGATORY CHASM, I PUT KANE AND THE
werewolf retreat out of my mind. Or tried to. I'd done more than
cancel a weekend date. I'd hurt him. It had showed in the set of
his shoulders as he left Creature Comforts. I'd hurt him and left
him wondering about our relationship. When he asked how I felt
about us, I hadn't even answered; I'd changed the subject to
Pryce.

Idiot.

How *did* I feel? When Kane and I first started dating, we kept
things casual, and I liked it that way. I was comfortable with
him. His career was central; he had big ambitions, and I respected
that. For both of us, it was work first, relationship second. And
that was fine. It was good, even.

*Yeah. Because you don't want to wonder whether you're miss-
ing out on the important things, whether your sister is the one
who made the right choice. So when your boyfriend started to
get serious, you didn't even notice.*

"Shut *up*, Butterfly!" I slammed on the brakes and swerved
into the breakdown lane. "I swear I'll make you materialize right
here. Killing you now would be worth whatever it costs to clean
the car."

That still, small voice went silent. No extra twinges troubled my stomach. I still felt miserable, but at least the Eidolon had retreated. Good. I didn't have time to conjure and kill it now, anyway.

Checking the rearview mirror, I pulled onto the highway. As soon as I was back on the road, I was thinking about Kane again.

Why did he want to change things? What did he mean by "take our relationship to the next level"?

I knew perfectly well what he meant. He hadn't said as much, but Kane was ready to choose a mate.

Bonding with a mate is a big deal among werewolves. It means two wolves have chosen each other as life partners and are ready to start a pack of their own.

I could never be Kane's mate.

I thought he knew that. I thought he understood that, to me, carrying on my race's commitment to fighting demons was every bit as important as his own political ambitions.

I thought that was why we had an unspoken agreement never to use the L-word.

If Kane wanted a mate, he didn't need someone who'd come home at three o'clock in the morning, clothes torn and spattered with dead demon, and put away her weapons before bed. He needed a politician's wife, someone who'd stand behind him and look pretty in designer dresses while he made speeches. Someone who'd give him lots of werewolf cubs.

Simone Landry would be the perfect mate for Kane. Better than I could ever hope to be.

I hated the thought. But I couldn't deny the truth of it.

WHEN I REACHED PURGATORY CHASM, I DIDN'T LEAVE MY CAR in the parking lot. The park closes at sunset, and a lone car in the lot late at night might stir the curiosity of a passing cop. I didn't want any cops jumping out during the little surprise party I'd planned for Pryce.

If Pryce showed up here tonight, I'd kill him. And cops tend to frown on that sort of thing.

Staying on Purgatory Road, I drove through the park and turned onto a side street. A bit farther, and I parked on the grassy verge. Outside it was cold, not quite wintry but not comfortable, either. I lifted out the duffel bag that held my weapons, then locked up the car. I hoped the Jag would be safe here. I looked up the street, then down. Dead-of-night stillness. Woods bordered the road on both sides. Somewhere in the darkness, peepers were calling. A breeze made the tree branches click against each other like bones. There were no other sounds. I opened my senses to the demon plane. All was quiet there, too. The dim, dirty twilight of Uffern suffused the woods. I heard a distant cackling, probably an echo of someone's nightmare. No demon sounds came from inside the park.

Butterfly slept inside my gut, heavy, like a stone. The Eidolon was there, but for now it was letting me be. Butterfly was terrified of Pryce—it wanted Pryce stopped almost as much as I did. Being this close to the Devil's Coffin must spook it.

I pulled back from the demon plane, and ordinary night settled around me again. I waited for my eyes to readjust to the dark. I put on a headlamp but left it unlit. Pryce probably wasn't here. Butterfly had spoken of the screams of trapped demons, and it was so quiet in the woods that, if I did have the right place, the cauldron must still be cloaked. Tomorrow was the first night of the full moon, but Pryce might deliver another load of demons to the cauldron tonight. If he was here, I didn't want to give myself away with a light. Of course, depending on how Pryce entered the park, he might see the Jag, which might as well be a neon sign flashing *Vicky's here! Vicky's here!* But there wasn't much I could do about that.

I hoisted my duffel bag over my shoulder and set off down the road toward a trail I'd explored in the afternoon. It was drizzling a little, and the air felt clammy on my face. Tendrils of fog, ghostly in the dark, rose from the damp ground. I paused and removed a black, waterproof jacket from my duffel bag. I put it on, pulling up the hood. Juliet might be bored, I thought, but at least she was warm and dry. Sighing, I continued along the road.

The trail I wanted didn't descend into the chasm but skirted it widely, meandering through the woods in a big, lopsided loop around the gorge. I found the path and followed it for a while, until I judged I was getting close to the Devil's Coffin. At that point, I turned north and cut through the woods. The rain had dampened the ground, and I moved quietly over the soft earth. There was mud, but it didn't suck at my boots like the stuff on the gorge's floor. After a few minutes I could see the chasm ahead. I prowled along its edge until I spotted the Devil's Coffin below me, in the opposite wall.

Crouching, I watched. Fog rose along the bottom of the gorge, but not enough to obscure my view. Rain dripped from branches. A night bird cried. There was no sign of Pryce. No sign of the cauldron in the human or the demon plane.

The night wasn't over yet, of course. Near the chasm's edge, I chose a bush that would provide some cover. No leaves—the buds had barely begun to swell—but the branches grew thickly enough that someone scanning the rim from below would be unlikely to see me. Lying on my stomach right at the edge, though, I'd have a good view of the Devil's Coffin.

I checked the weapons I already wore—knives in thigh and ankle sheaths, a pistol in a shoulder holster, another at my hip. All set. Good to be prepared, but I didn't expect to use any of those weapons here. I unzipped my duffel bag and took out a case. In it was tonight's real weapon: a sniper rifle. If things went according to plan, it was all I'd need. One bullet, one carefully aimed shot, and I'd be rid of Pryce forever.

Earlier, I'd hesitated before packing it. Without his shadow demon, Pryce was technically human, and that meant I was planning a murder. Was it right to set up an ambush and take him out the moment he walked into my sights? I considered the evil Pryce had done. He'd tried to kill Gwen when she was just a teenager. He'd set loose a demonic spirit to feed upon Deadtown's zombies. He'd almost taken down an airplane full of innocent people in one of his many attempts to kill me. Not three months ago, he'd injured Mab in the heart. I flashed back to my aunt lying on the ground, struggling to breathe, her lifeblood pumping over my hands as I tried to hold the wound shut.

And Pryce was barely getting started. The devastation I'd seen in that vision was his goal. He'd do everything he could to make it real.

Hell, yeah, it was right to kill him. Or if not, it was a wrong I could live with.

I took the sniper rifle from its case. I connected the barrel and housing, then attached the infrared night-vision scope. I folded down the barrel's biped mount. Lying on the muddy ground, propped up on my elbows, I squinted through the sight and located the Devil's Coffin. If Pryce stood in the middle of the coffin stone, on the spot where the InDetect had picked up that residual demon presence, I'd have a clean shot.

One bullet, one carefully aimed shot.

I settled in to wait, clearing my mind of everything except my focus on the Devil's Coffin.

WHEN DAWN BROUGHT ENOUGH LIGHT INTO THE WOODS that I could see my hand in front of my face, I sat up. I was stiff as a slab of concrete, every muscle sore. My eyes ached from staring at the same spot for hour after hour. Pryce hadn't set foot in the woods. I, on the other hand, felt like I was as much a part of Purgatory Chasm as its granite boulders.

I stood and stretched. I whirled my arms in big circles and twisted left and right, limbering up my spine. I jogged in place for a minute, my breath steaming the air, to warm my frozen limbs. As I disassembled the rifle and returned it to its case, all I wanted was a hot shower and a warm bed. And coffee. A mug of hot coffee would be the gateway to paradise right now.

Somehow my stiff legs kept trudging forward, one step at a time, until I made it back to the Jag. If anyone had been around to watch me from a distance, my lurching gait would have them calling 911 to send the zombie removal squad. The car was covered with condensation in the cold morning air. I dumped my duffel bag on the floor of the passenger's side, climbed in, and swiped the windshield wipers back and forth a couple of times. Then I cranked up the heat and hit the road.

But not for very long. A couple of miles up Route 146 was a motel. Two single-story wings of maybe a dozen rooms each stretched out on either side of a central office. Why drive all the way to Boston just to turn around and come back out here tonight? I pulled into the parking lot. Only three cars were in the front lot; one other sat out back. Plenty of vacancies, obviously. I'd stay here, rest up, and be back in place in my sniper spot before moonrise.

In fact, since the motel was so close to the park, I could leave the Jag here, parked out of sight, and hike in. Then I wouldn't have to worry about Pryce spotting my car.

It sounded like a plan.

I removed all my sheaths and holsters and put the weapons

away in their bag. A quick check in the mirror showed a smudge of dirt on my cheek; I licked two fingers and rubbed it off. I got out of the car and took off my muddy rain jacket, laying it on top of the duffel bag. Some mud streaked my jeans, but I was more or less presentable. I locked up the Jag and went into the office.

The clerk started to argue with me about checking in early, but since the motel wasn't exactly overflowing with guests he grudgingly gave me a room. I paid cash and showed him a forged, out-of-state license—one that didn't shout PARANORMAL in big red letters. It's a felony for paranormals to misrepresent themselves as human, but lots of us who can pass carry phony IDs. Mine was made by the best forger in Deadtown. Anyway, I was here to kill Pryce, and murder was a felony, too.

I snagged a foam cup of lukewarm, bitter coffee from the lobby, then retrieved my duffel bag from the Jag and lugged it into my room. The room wasn't anything special: a queen-sized bed with a pink-and-blue flowered coverlet, a dresser with a circa-1990 television on top, a couple of beat-up chairs, and a crookedly hung print of a spring garden. Good enough, though, for what I needed.

I got out a dagger and placed it under the pillow, then stashed my duffel bag under the bed. I pulled the window's heavy drapes closed. Deciding to skip the shower for now, I stripped down to my underwear and climbed into bed. Despite the coffee, I was asleep within moments. No guilty thoughts, no tormenting dreams. Just the rest I'd need to get up and try again.

WHEN I AWOKE AT A LITTLE PAST TWO IN THE AFTERNOON, the first thing I thought of was Kane. He was in Princeton by now, had been there for a couple of hours. The law requires werewolves to check into their retreats by noon on the first day of the full moon, so he would have set out from Boston by ten thirty or eleven this morning to get there on time.

I wondered what he was doing right now.

He'd described the retreat center to me. A pack is a family unit, and each pack has its own cottage. Some packs are big enough to need a small complex of several buildings. Lone wolves, like Kane, stay in a dormitory. From what he'd said, his room there was a lot like the motel room I was in now, minus the tacky décor: a bed, a few furnishings, a window, a private bath. His room had a desk so he could work while he was in human form during the day. He was probably sitting there now, shuffling papers and typing on his laptop, until it was time to get ready for the change.

And where was Simone? She was still part of her family's pack, Kane had told me, working her way up the hierarchy among siblings and cousins. That meant she'd stay in their family compound. Better than down the hall from him in the dorm, I guessed, but still too close. Especially when I was on this side of the silver-plated razor wire that surrounded the retreat.

Damn. I wanted to be there. The realization surprised me. For a long time, I'd believed that going on retreat with Kane would take something away from me, would force me to be something I wasn't. Then, when Simone started making her move, I'd rushed forward in a blind panic and insisted on going. What a mess I'd made. Kane must think I was playing some stupid game. But the truth was, if I could be anywhere right now, I'd want to be with him.

Well, why not? This motel was only about twenty-five miles from the retreat center—a short drive into Worcester and then a straight shot up I-190 to Princeton. I could shower, dress, hop in the Jag, and be there in less than an hour. That would give me plenty of time to talk my way in, find Kane, and be at his side when the moon's influence hit.

I could picture it now: me tapping on Kane's door and cracking it open. Him looking up and turning in his chair. His expression changing from annoyance to a huge grin when he saw it was me.

Or not.

I could just as easily picture his expression going from annoyed to angry. I couldn't assume he'd be pleased to see me there. I'd jerked him around enough to cause a serious case of whiplash. He had a right to be angry.

The image faded. There'd be no retreat for me this weekend.

Besides, I had a job to do.

During my long nap, I'd reported to Mab via dream phone. Not much to report. The cauldron, if it was there, was well cloaked. No sign of Pryce. When I told her I'd set up a sniper rifle, ready to kill him the moment he appeared, she nodded once and said, "Good."

"Good" was also her response when I told her about Tina's A on her career portfolio. I felt a twinge of jealousy—ridiculous, but there all the same. When I'd been Mab's apprentice, she seemed much more stingy with her praise. But that was a long time ago, and anyway, Tina wasn't her apprentice. Surely I'd outgrown the need for pats on the head from my aunt.

We agreed my best course was to return to the Devil's Coffin in time for tonight's moonrise. Then we ended the call so I could rest. Talking on the dream phone lets the body rest but keeps the mind active. And tonight, I'd need body and mind to work together.

I got up and showered. I dressed. Flakes of dried mud fell from my jeans, and I brushed them off as best I could. It was best to keep the Jag hidden—bad idea to drive around town when Pryce might be in the neighborhood—so I spent the afternoon watching boring talk shows. It was enough to make me sympathize with Juliet's plight; that egg-scrambler thing really was kind of clever. I had pizza delivered. I peeked out through the drapes to keep tabs on the weather—gray, gray, gray, with on-and-off drizzles. I paced the length of my motel room. A lot. I probably could have walked to Princeton with all the pacing I did.

I tried not to think about Kane.

Butterfly left me alone, even when thoughts of Kane crept past my defenses. Which happened far more often than I cared to admit.

SUNSET WOULD OCCUR AROUND SEVEN, AND MOONRISE forty minutes after that. I needed to be in place well before the moon came up, so at five I stepped out of my motel room to begin the hike back to the chasm. As I zipped up my jacket, I looked at the sky. Low, thick clouds hung there, obscuring the light so that it seemed like dusk already. Misty rain chilled my face. I wondered if the overcast sky would interfere with Pryce's plans. The full moon's effect was felt by werewolves whether the sky was cloudy or clear, but opening a portal to the Darklands required strong magic. Maybe Pryce's wizardry wouldn't work on a night like this.

I could hope. But I couldn't rely on it. I shouldered my duffel bag and set out toward Purgatory Chasm.

Route 146 is not the road to choose if you're in the mood for a stroll in the country. It's a four-lane highway that occasionally slows down as it passes through business and residential areas, like the stretch I was on now. But just because the speed limit was lower didn't mean drivers paid the slightest bit of attention. Cars whizzed by like they were on a practice lap for the Indy 500. There's no sidewalk, so I trudged along the grass beside the breakdown lane, which, in most places, was too narrow for a car to stop if it actually broke down.

As soon as I could, I left 146 for a side street. I'd driven on this street yesterday; from here I could get into the park the back way, which was what I wanted to do.

This road was better. A few yards away from 146, it became a quiet country lane, lined with woods and stretches of tumble-down stone walls. Houses were few and far between. I climbed over a stone wall and walked through the woods, skirting around small ponds and marshy spots. There wasn't much traffic here, but it was better to keep out of sight.

A few hundred yards along, I passed a cemetery set on top of a small rise. It was a desolate, forgotten-looking place, tilted gravestones bristling along the top of the hill. In the dim light, the dark stones were leaden against the gray sky. I shivered and kept walking.

Soon I turned left, following another road that led toward the park. At one point, I heard a car approaching, and I stepped deeper into the woods. It passed, heading north, and kept going. I didn't hear or see anyone else.

In less than half an hour, I stood at my perch on the eastern edge of the chasm. I paused there long enough to check out the Devil's Coffin. It was deserted, but I hadn't expected Pryce yet, anyway. An hour remained until sunset, which meant that the park was still open. It was hard to imagine that anyone would come here for outdoor fun on a miserable day like today, but you never know. Pryce wouldn't want anyone asking questions about what he was doing in the woods. And neither did I. I made my way back to the loop trail, hiked along that for a little way, then went deeper into the woods. When I was far enough off the trail to be out of view in case some stray, masochistic hiker trudged by, I dropped my bag beside a boulder and sat down. I checked my watch. In half an hour, the park should be clear, and I'd return to my perch above the Devil's Coffin.

The drizzle had strengthened to a light rain. I watched it fall, working to clear my mind for tonight's task. Whether I'd finally put an end to Pryce or spend another cold, wet night in the woods, I had to be ready.

A movement on the right caught my eye. As I turned my head, my hand slipped inside my jacket to the grip of the pistol in my shoulder holster. A sharp bark sounded, then two more. A small Jack Russell terrier stood twenty feet away, paws planted and ears cocked, leaning toward me.

I like dogs. But I didn't need this one announcing to the world that I was here. I put a finger over my lips. "Shh!"

Full-scale barking erupted in response.

"Nero? Nero! Here, boy!" A woman's voice came from the direction of the loop trail.

Nero glanced in the direction of the voice, then resumed barking at me. Someone crashed through the woods in our direction.

I stood and grabbed my bag. I started back toward the trail, but Nero followed, barking the whole time. I dropped my bag and sat down again.

A moment later, Nero's owner appeared through the trees. She was medium height, her light-brown hair pulled back in a ponytail. She wore a dark-green jacket and a park ranger's hat. Great. I was busted.

"Thanks for finding my dog," she said, even though it had been the other way around. She bent down and held out a hand. Nero bounded over to her, and she clipped a leash on his collar. "I'm not supposed to let him off the leash, but he's been cooped up in my office all day. I didn't think anyone was here." She patted the dog's back.

"Glad you found him," I said, hoping she'd be on her way.

She straightened and then regarded me, her hands on her hips. Nero, who'd quit barking, sniffed the ground around her feet. "You okay?" the ranger asked me.

"Fine." I kept my face half turned away. With my hood up and the dim light, it would be hard to make out my features.

"No twisted ankle or anything? We get a lot of those here, especially when it's wet like this."

"Nope."

During the long pause that followed, she didn't move. "So

you're sitting out here in the middle of the woods in the rain . . . why?"

I said the first thing that popped into my head. "I had a fight with my boyfriend."

"Ah. Well, you're not going to solve anything by giving yourself pneumonia. Besides, the park's about to close. Come with me, I'll walk you out."

"No, thanks."

She folded her arms and narrowed her eyes. "You know you can't camp here, right?" She nodded at my duffel bag. "I think you'd better come with me. I can give you a lift to wherever you need to be."

I tried to think of a reason to refuse, then shrugged and stood up. I'd already made myself as conspicuous as if I'd asked her to hold my bag while I assembled my sniper rifle. It would be better if she thought I'd left the park. I followed her back to the loop trail. Nero trotted along beside her. He hadn't said so much as "woof" since she'd caught up with him.

Man's best friend. *Hah.* Now what was I going to do?

15

THE RANGER WALKED A FEW PACES AHEAD OF ME ON THE trail. Nero sniffed along one side, then the other, running back and forth as far as the leash allowed. When he stopped to investigate some deeply interesting scent, she paused to let him, glancing back to make sure I still followed.

I came up beside her. "Do you have a cell phone?" I asked.

"Yes. Do you need to make a call?"

"You get reception out here?"

"Of course. We're not that far out in the boonies."

"Then would you mind calling me a cab? When I had that fight with my boyfriend, I got out of the car, and he drove off without me. I do need a ride, but I don't want to inconvenience you."

She considered. "All right. I am a bit short on time—I'm having some friends over for dinner tonight. Can you take Nero's leash for a minute?"

I walked the dog a little way down the trail while she made the call. She put the phone away and caught up with us. "Cab'll be here in a few." I returned Nero's leash to her, and she seemed to relax now that I'd agreed to leave the park. As we walked along the trail, she chattered about her dinner party, telling me who was coming and what she planned to serve.

I smiled and nodded—and thought about how I could get back here to kill Pryce.

When we emerged from the woods, the day was moving past dusk into evening—the time demons could come forth. I peeked into the demon plane, listening for any sign of Pryce's trapped demons. I heard nothing. But moonrise was still over half an hour away. Pryce wouldn't uncloak the cauldron until it was time for his ritual.

The ranger's SUV waited in the parking lot by the Visitors' Center. No cab was in sight. If she left now, I could blow off the cab and return to the gorge.

"I'll just wait with you and make sure the cab shows up." A tiny note of suspicion colored the friendliness in her voice.

"You've got dinner to cook. I'll be fine."

She took a tennis ball from her car and threw it into the woods. Nero raced after it, his legs a blur. The third time the dog brought the ball back, a taxi pulled into the parking lot. I got in, waved to the ranger, and gave the driver the address of a fast-food place near the motel. The ranger's SUV followed us along Purgatory Road, but at 146, where we turned north, she turned south. I let my head drop back against the seat with relief.

The taxi let me off where I'd asked. I paid him and went inside. As soon as the cab pulled away, I left the restaurant and ran south. I stayed well off the road, behind buildings and out of sight of passing cars, until I reached the motel's rear parking lot. I threw my weapons into the Jag, got in, and headed back to the chasm.

It was getting dark now. I checked my watch. The moon would clear the horizon within minutes, and I was a mile away from where I needed to be. I pressed the accelerator, and the Jag surged ahead.

I took the exit for the chasm, rocketed down Purgatory Road, and skidded into the parking lot. I rolled down the window, opened to the demon plane, and listened.

A tsunami of sound slammed my ears. Screams, howls, growls, shrieks, moans—it sounded like the agonized cries of a thousand souls tormented by pain and fear and rage. The voices came from inside the chasm. Pryce must have uncloaked the cauldron, and its imprisoned demons were screaming their throats raw.

Too late for my sniper rifle. Keeping my senses open to the demon plane, I drew my pistol and ran through the woods to the chasm's entrance. The demon plane's filthy gray light was enough to let me pick my way through the boulder-littered obstacle course. Every ounce of my being cringed away from the mind-scrambling cacophony of screeching demons. Still, I pushed myself toward the sound.

At the slope into the chasm, I leapt onto a boulder, then half-slid, half-scrambled down to the next one. The demonic shrieking echoed, bouncing off the rocks, a maelstrom of noise. The din clamored ahead of me, behind me, above me, all around. It felt like arrows piercing my brain. I jumped to a lower boulder and slipped on its wet surface. My feet went out from under me, and I fell on my back.

Huge, outstretched talons zoomed toward me, aiming for my face.

I rolled, and the Harpy slammed into the rock. It crumpled into a mass of feathers and tangled snakes. Its feet kicked, scrabbling for something to hold on to. I aimed my pistol and shot three bronze bullets into its body. Jets of yellow, sulfurous steam hissed from the wounds. Snakes stiffened and struck, their jaws snapping on air.

I fired again.

The Harpy shuddered. It emitted a long, drawn-out croak. Then it lay still. As I watched, its body began to deflate. Dead.

Were there others? I took cover behind a boulder and scanned the sky. The demon racket overpowered all other sounds. I couldn't track any approaching Harpies by their shrieks. But my gut told me this wasn't a solo attack.

There. Two Harpies, incoming. I chose one and held it in my sights, waiting for it to come into range.

Almost . . . almost . . .

Now!

I pulled the trigger. At the same moment, the Harpies wheeled and split up. My shot missed. I locked onto one of the demons and fired again. Steam and feathers spurted from its wing. The Harpy dropped from the sky.

Staying in the shelter of the boulder, I scanned the sky for the third Harpy. Nothing. It was hiding somewhere, waiting for me to step out into the open. I peered along the top of the chasm and into tree branches, squinting through the murk. Where the hell was it?

From the trapped demons' screaming, a new sound emerged. I felt it before I heard it, a low thrumming that vibrated the ground, rising through the soles of my feet. The sound was a rhythmic pulse, like the beating heart of the earth. I glanced at my watch. Less than five minutes until moonrise. Pryce had started his ritual, and I was out of time.

I stood. From out of nowhere, a Harpy plummeted toward me. Bracing myself against the boulder at my back, I raised my pistol and fired off half a dozen shots. I twisted, but not far enough. The Harpy's body sledgehammered into my right shoulder, bounced off, and hit the ground. Pain ripped through me, but I kept the gun on the demon. The Harpy rolled to a stop against a boulder, then lay wedged there, unmoving. Third Harpy down. Already its body was deflating, the stench of decay making me gag.

My shoulder throbbed and burned. I could feel it swelling. I tested my arm; I couldn't raise it more than a few inches. The shoulder was dislocated, no question.

Under my feet, the vibration pulsed, deep and steady.

I looked up. Were there more Harpies? I didn't see any, but that didn't mean they weren't waiting to strike.

A powerful voice rose, chanting, above the demons' cries. With one command, it shattered the night. Wind rushed through the chasm. Thunder rumbled.

Ignoring the pain in my shoulder, I reloaded my pistol, ejecting the magazine and slamming in a new one. I clambered down the slope, slipping and skidding over the rocks, pain jolting down my arm with each bump.

I reached the muck of the chasm floor. Ahead, reddish light glowed. Mud sucked at my boots as I ran, slipping and sliding, toward the Devil's Coffin.

Something hit me from behind, hard. I pitched headlong into the mud. I fell on my right side, agony shattering my shoulder. Swampy water flooded my mouth and nose. As I raised my head, snorting and sputtering, pain knifed my back. I twisted around. Feathers brushed my face as I encountered the spread, drooping wing of the Harpy I'd wounded. I brought up my pistol and fired left-handed into the wing. The Harpy shrieked. Its talons clenched, ripping my back. I ignored the pain and reached back until the gun jammed up against something solid. Three shots, and the Harpy collapsed, a dead weight on my back.

Its talons still gripped me. I fired more bullets into its corpse—extra bronze to hurry the decomposition process. Lightning slashed the sky, the strikes coming fast and furious like strobe lights. The ground trembled. I struggled to push myself up.

The Harpy's talons relaxed, retracted. The dead demon toppled over. As soon as its weight dropped away, I rolled out from under the corpse and pushed myself to my feet. I sprinted toward the Devil's Coffin.

The wind was roaring now. It seemed to blow from every direction, all at once. Ahead, I could see Pryce's silhouette. He stood before a huge cauldron, his arms raised toward the sky.

I fired but, left-handed, my aim was off. The bullet sparked off the cauldron. Pryce didn't even flinch.

For a moment, everything stopped. The wind quit blowing. The thunder and lightning stilled. The cauldron's demonic uproar was choked off. The sudden silence hurt my ears.

I lifted my pistol for another shot.

Pryce's raised arms gestured as though parting curtains. A gash opened in the clouds, revealing a brilliant silver moon. Its light shot through the woods in a beam, striking the cauldron.

I fired.

A thunderclap shook the chasm, knocking chunks of stone from the walls. A rock struck Pryce's head, and he fell. Had my bullet hit, too?

I ran toward him. Inside the Devil's Coffin, the red glow intensified, lighting up the boulder cave. A robed figure stepped out of the glare. Its face was deep inside a hood. I couldn't see whether it was male or female, human or demon—or something else altogether. The figure moved toward the cauldron.

"Stop!" I shouted.

The figure ignored me. It gestured, both arms sweeping upward, and the cauldron rose into the air. Pryce's laugh echoed through the chasm.

I fired. The bullets passed right through the figure, slowing it down as much as they'd slow down a shadow. The figure turned to face the back of the boulder cave, the floating cauldron close behind it, dark shapes against the hellish light.

"Wait!" Pryce shouted. "Take me with you!" Grunting, he crawled up onto the flat slab of rock.

The figure didn't pause. It floated to the back of the cave, then moved to one side. It pointed and the cauldron hurtled through the granite wall. The figure followed, melting into the rock. Pryce dragged himself toward the portal, but before he reached it the red glow blinked out, like someone had turned off a light switch. No trace remained of the figure or the cauldron. They'd disappeared.

Thunder, lightning, wind—all had ceased. The ground was still. I stood in a damp, chilly, overcast, utterly ordinary spring night.

Pryce groaned. I couldn't tell whether it was in disappointment or in pain. I hoped it was both.

He lay on the stone where the cauldron had stood. Blood and mud streaked his face. The skin of his forehead was split where the rock had struck him. I approached him, my gun aimed at his head. He squinted at me, his features twisted in an ugly sneer. Then he smiled, baring blood-smeared teeth.

"Hello, cousin," he rasped. "I knew I should have conjured more Harpies. But I needed all the demons I could get." He gestured with his chin to where the cauldron had disappeared.

"What have you done?"

Pryce giggled. The high-pitched titter was disconcertingly like his father's. "What's done is done," he said. "But the important thing is I've *done* it." Another giggle. "There's nothing you can do about it now."

I kept the pistol pointed at his head. My finger tightened on the trigger. Now. I could end this right now.

From behind me, an amplified voice echoed through the chasm. "This is the police. You are surrounded. Lay down your weapons and raise your hands."

I wasn't surprised the cops had shown up. There were houses not far from the chasm, and I'd fired enough shots to start a small war. Someone must have called 911.

Pryce laughed. "Quite the dilemma, eh, cousin? Blow my head off, and you'll spend the rest of your life in prison. Let me be, and . . . well, you've read the book. You know my plans."

Floodlights lit the chasm. The cop with the bullhorn repeated his warning.

"You're the one who's going to prison," I said. "You'll die there as a mortal."

"I don't think so." In a single motion, he sat up and brought something forward. I nearly pulled the trigger before I saw what it was: a spray can of air freshener. He pointed it at me like a weapon. "Do you know what's in this can? Plague virus."

Plague. The virus that had turned two thousand Bostonians into zombies. It was one hundred percent fatal to humans—for three days, anyway, before they reanimated.

It couldn't hurt me. But there were humans nearby.

"Stay back!" I shouted to the cops. "Plague virus!" Pryce was probably bluffing, but I couldn't take the chance. He'd stolen something from the Old Ones—Juliet had said so—and the Old Ones had engineered the virus.

"Repeat that," commanded the bullhorn.

"Zombie plague!" I screamed.

The bullhorn fell silent.

Pryce was laughing.

"Put that away," I said. "You can't hurt me with it. I'm immune."

"True," Pryce said. "But I'm not." He turned the can toward himself and blasted its spray into his own face. Blood erupted from his eyes and mouth as he fell backward on the Devil's Coffin.

I reached down and felt his neck for a pulse.

There was none. Pryce was dead.

Damn it! I kicked his limp corpse.

"Keep away!" I shouted into the woods. "It's the plague. At the Devil's Coffin."

I'd wanted him dead, yes, but not like this. This was a temporary death. Pryce had wanted to follow the hooded figure into the Darklands, the realm of the dead. When the figure left him behind, Pryce used the stolen virus to get there on his own. The virus was his round-trip ticket into the Darklands. In three days, he'd be back. If he managed to re-create his shadow demon, he wouldn't awaken as a zombie. He'd be a demi-demon again.

"How do you know?" the bullhorn voice boomed out of the dark.

"Because this idiot"—I kicked Pryce's body again—"just killed himself with it. I'm paranormal. That's why I'm still alive.

But don't come any closer—I mean it. You'll be dead in ten seconds. Call in a biohazard team."

Silence. The cops must be conferring.

"Making a false report of this nature is a felony."

Add it to the list. "And when you get a report, you *have* to call in the biohazard guys. I know the law, too. So do your damn job."

Sirens wailed in the distance. Too quick to be the biohazard team. The cops must have sent for backup. The new guys would be thrilled to learn they were walking into a plague zone. Overhead, another sound joined in, the *thwack-thwack-thwack* of helicopter blades. A glaring white floodlight lit up the chasm, roving along the walls and floor. Trees bowed from the force of the downdraft. The wind and light both moved in my direction. I set my pistol down on a rock and moved away from it, raising both hands. I couldn't lift my right arm very high, thanks to my injured shoulder.

The light blinded me a second before the wind made me stagger back a step. I squinted upward, spreading my fingers wide to show my hands were empty. I gestured toward the gun so they could see it, see that it was out of reach. The light moved to illuminate Pryce's prone body. I stayed as still as the chasm's ancient boulders.

An amplified voice boomed downward. "A team is on the way. The park is surrounded. Stay where you are. Do not try to leave. I repeat: Do not attempt to leave the park."

With my good hand, I made a thumbs-up to show I understood.

The helicopter ascended some, and the wind diminished. The floodlight continued to light up the chasm.

I looked at Pryce's slumped-over body, at the solid rock wall through which the figure and cauldron had disappeared. Pryce had escaped me, damn him. He'd gone to a place where I couldn't follow. I wasn't going anywhere; I didn't have anywhere to go.

16

IT TOOK HALF AN HOUR FOR THE BIOHAZARD TEAM TO
arrive. After the first few minutes of waiting, I'd slowly lowered
my arms, then sat down on the edge of the Devil's Coffin stone.
No voice from on high ordered me to resume my former position.
That was a relief. My shoulder was killing me.

The helicopter hovered overhead for about ten minutes, lighting up the chasm like it was noontime, then took off. I sat in
darkness, the sudden silence roaring in my ears. Beside me lay
Pryce's corpse. Dead—for now, anyway. I couldn't believe he'd
pulled this trick. I wanted to kick him again, but what good
would it do? I wanted to use one of my knives to dismember him.
See how he'd like returning from the Darklands to a body that
was chopped up into a dozen pieces.

If he recovered his demonic power, that wouldn't matter. With
a shadow demon, his body would re-form itself, no matter what
I did to it now. And I was already in enough trouble without
mutilating any corpses.

While I waited, I thought about what to tell the police. There
was that outstanding warrant for Pryce's attack on the Paranormal Appreciation Day concert. Given that charge, the authorities
would be ready and willing to believe he'd come here to commit

another terrorist act. Okay, that's what I'd work with. I wouldn't say anything to make the situation more complex than it appeared. Nothing about a cauldron full of demons or a hidden doorway into another realm. No one would believe me, anyway.

I got up to inspect the back of the Devil's Coffin cave. If only I could figure out how to make the portal open.

It was the third time I'd scrutinized the cave's granite walls. As before, I opened my senses to the demon plane. And as before, all was quiet. No red glow, no wails of trapped demons. I moved my hand over the stone, feeling for a crack that might open to a doorway. I rapped with my knuckles, listening for hollow places. But there was nothing. Just solid rock.

Thwack-thwack-thwack! The helicopter was returning. I left the cave and sat down in my former spot. Again, the floodlight lit up the chasm floor. I shielded my eyes against the glare. The downdraft swept toward me, tossing tree branches and ruffling my hair. It whipped Pryce's black hair back from his face. His skin was already turning green.

A voice came over the loudspeaker. "This is the police." Yeah, well, I didn't think it was the Easter Bunny dropping by with some colored eggs. The voice instructed me to lie facedown on the ground in a spread-eagle position. Yay. A faceful of mud was just what I needed to make this the perfect night.

Moving slowly, I complied, because I didn't have a choice. As I dropped to my knees, a ladder unfurled from above. It dangled several feet above the ground.

Cold, gooey mud squished against my cheek. It smelled like rotted leaves. Icy water ran down my neck and inside my collar. Pain screamed through my shoulder as I moved my right arm as far from my body as I could. There was a thump and a splash. More cold, dirty water hit my face as someone jumped from the ladder to the ground.

Hands frisked me, patting lightly and quickly along each limb.

"My right shoulder is dislocated," I said, before whoever was searching me decided to yank that arm into position.

There was a pause. Then the hands moved along that arm where it lay.

The frisker paused again upon discovering the dagger in one of my thigh sheaths. I'd laid my other weapons on the rock next to my pistol, but I kept that one back because it didn't seem like a good idea to be completely unarmed sitting on the Devil's Coffin in the middle of the night. The dagger was removed and handed to someone else.

Hands grasped my left wrist and pulled it behind my back, locking a cuff around it.

"My shoulder!" I shouted, bracing for a jolt of pain.

Instead of yanking my right arm backward, the hands went around my waist and, as gently as possible, lifted me out of the mud.

Once I had my feet under me, I lifted my head to find myself staring at a space-suited alien. Or else, and this was only a little less unlikely, it was a zombie in a biohazard suit. But that's what it was. A greenish face peered through the clear visor.

"Want me to pop that shoulder back into place for you?" a muffled female voice asked.

I peered closer at the face inside the suit. I knew this zombie. Pam McFarren. She was one of the few female zombies on the Goon Squad; I'd run into her before in Deadtown. She was all right for a Goon.

"Okay." I ground my teeth as McFarren felt along my shoulder. She grasped my forearm and bent my elbow at a ninety-degree angle. Slowly, but with steady pressure, she rotated my arm outward, away from my body.

"Make a fist," she said. I did. She held my wrist and kept pushing my arm. The pain intensified, and I bit the inside of my cheek to keep from crying out.

Another gentle push, just a little farther, and the joint snapped into place with a *pop*. A starburst of pain—I tasted blood from biting my cheek—then blessed relief.

"I heard that," McFarren said. "How does it feel?"

"Like new." I moved my arm in big circles. I had the full range of motion back. "Thanks," I said.

"You're welcome. Now I need to finish cuffing you."

I sighed. "Is that necessary?"

"Until we know what the situation is, yes. Please put your hands behind you."

Once she'd locked the cuffs on me, I looked around the chasm. The biohazard team had five members. Three others wore the same kind of suit McFarren had on, so they were probably zombies, too. Judging from the environment suit that made the fifth look like the Michelin Man's chubbier cousin, I'd guess that one was a human. The human seemed to be in charge. He gestured while the others set up lights and bustled around the site.

"Why do you need a hazmat suit?" I asked McFarren. "You've already had the virus."

"That's why they send PDHs on these calls. The suits are to avoid infecting others, in case an outbreak report turns out to be positive. Otherwise, we'd have to go into quarantine."

Like I will, I thought glumly. I'd sit around some boring, secure room while Pryce wreaked havoc in the Darklands.

"But it's always a false alarm," she added.

"This one isn't. Take a look at the corpse." I nodded toward Pryce.

Classic plague victim. The skin color, the blood from the eyes and mouth streaking the skin. The human, awkward in the bulky suit, bent over Pryce, obscuring him.

"Let's give them room to work." McFarren took my arm and led me several yards away. One of the zombies assisted the human with Pryce. The other two stood, arms folded, guarding the site. McFarren kept her hand around my arm. "So what happened here?" she asked.

"Do you know who Pryce Maddox is?" Maybe I should have said *was*, given his current condition.

Behind her visor, McFarren scowled. "Of course I do. He's the guy who launched a demon attack on the Paranormal Appreciation Day concert." Strictly speaking, what Pryce had sicced on the zombies that night wasn't a demon—it was demon essence, a spirit of destruction that materialized in the form of giant crows. Crows with an insatiable hunger for zombie flesh. "Maddox is responsible for a dozen PDH deaths. Every zombie officer on the Squad would like to use his head at our next volleyball tournament."

"String up a net," I said. "That's Pryce over there."

"*Really?* The victim?" Her suit couldn't muffle her evil-sounding cackle. "Oh, man, I hope it's not a false alarm. I would *so* love to be there when his brand-new zombie ass wakes up in custody." She let go of my arm and rubbed her gloved hands together. "All right. You say that's Pryce Maddox. What were the two of you doing out here? How did he come in contact with the plague virus, if it's really the plague?"

Time to trot out my terrorism story. "He was here to set up

an ambush. He planned to spray the virus around to infect hikers."

"How do you know that?"

"I tried to stop him. I've been tracking Pryce."

"Why?"

"For the reward, why else?" After the fiasco on Paranormal Appreciation Day, a $50,000 reward had been offered for information leading to Pryce's arrest. "I got a tip that he was going to be here tonight, so I came to check it out."

"You should've called the cops."

"Maybe." Exactly what Kane had said. "But then there would be another couple of plague victims lying over there. Cop victims. I didn't know Pryce had plague virus. I just heard, from someone who knew someone, that he might show up here. My tip was good."

"When you got here, what happened?"

"Almost as soon as I arrived, three Harpies attacked. Pryce sent them after me. I killed all three—if you want to check out that part of my story, just follow the smell." I swiveled toward the closest dead Harpy and gestured with my chin. "When I got past the Harpies to Pryce, he had a spray can full of plague virus. He showed it to me, told me what it was. While he was waving the can around, some spray shot out. Pryce inhaled it, and that was that."

McFarren watched the team members working by Pryce's body. She looked up and down the chasm. Her visor turned back to me. "It doesn't make sense," she said. "Why here? I mean, this place must be swarming with people in the summer—hikers, picnickers, families. If Maddox's goal was to incite terror, it'd make sense to spray the virus around then. Maximum damage. But right now it's cold. It's wet. There's still ice on the rocks, even. Who the hell climbs around here in mud season?" She lifted one foot to show the thick layer of mud clinging to the sole.

I shrugged. "I don't know what he was thinking. Maybe this was a test site. Maybe he's a rock climber in his spare time. Maybe he liked the place's name."

"Purgatory Chasm. Yeah, maybe." McFarren sounded doubtful. She stood silently for a few seconds. "Okay, here's what bothers me. It's not just the site. It's the timing. The zombie virus is unstable. When it hit downtown Boston, it mutated into something harmless within half an hour. This park is closed from sunset to sunrise. Not a soul around. What's the point of spraying virus here now? If someone shows up and hikes the chasm tomorrow, so what? The worst they'll get is a sneezing fit."

It was true. Pryce had brought the virus here for one reason: to infect himself if the Darklands guardian wouldn't let him through. But what was the point in telling McFarren that? It wasn't like she could follow him into the Darklands and arrest him there.

McFarren spoke again, half to herself this time. "But if the virus keeps changing, maybe it changed into something longer-lasting. Maybe Maddox knew something we didn't." She pounded a fist into her open hand. "I can't wait to question him."

"Be careful," I said. "If the virus has changed, its effects might change, too. Be ready for that when he wakes up. He might have . . . I don't know, the strength of a thousand demons or something." It was the best I could do to warn her. Not even a zombie would believe my story about trapped demons in a cloaked cauldron passing through a secret door into the realm of the dead. What door? Nothing but solid rock here. If I told her the truth, quarantine would be the least of my worries; they'd lock me up in a nice padded room where nice white-coated attendants would take care of me.

"Don't worry," McFarren said, turning toward Pryce. "If that's Pryce Maddox, he'll be very well secured."

There was a commotion over by Pryce's body. The human took several quick steps backward, almost slipping in the mud. One zombie pulled out a cell phone; another leaned over Pryce, peering into his face.

"Positive!" the zombie shouted into his phone. "I repeat: We got a positive here!"

"Good God," breathed McFarren. "You were right."

The helicopter returned and hovered overhead. Something fell from it, smacking the ground. McFarren went over and picked it up. She brought the package to where I stood. Without a word, she unlocked the cuffs around my wrists. "Here," she said, handing me the package. "Put this on."

I took it and shook it out. It was a hazmat suit like the one she was wearing, except front and back alike were marked with a huge red Q.

The scarlet letter. *Q* for *quarantine*. The suit was to identify me as a potential carrier, warning people until I was safely locked away from the world.

I'd known this was coming. I didn't like it, but there was no reason not to cooperate. And it wasn't like I had a whole lot of choices right now.

Over by the Devil's Coffin, one zombie packed up the equipment while the other two zipped Pryce into a body bag. Together they lifted him—his bag was marked with the same red Q—and strapped him into some sort of rescue basket. They stepped back and gestured. The basket was reeled up and swallowed into the helicopter. The ladder returned, and two zombies climbed up, pulling it in behind them. The copter rose. It pivoted in midair and flew east. In a moment, it was out of sight.

I didn't know where they were taking Pryce. Wherever his body went, he was beyond my reach. I looked at the quarantine suit in my hands, then started putting it on.

A SECOND HELICOPTER ARRIVED TO LIFT US OUT. MCFARREN left the cuffs off so I could climb the ladder. It made me feel a little seasick, the way it swayed and bobbed, but I made it. Inside, I took a seat. The hazmat suit was stuffy and smelled dusty. My breath kept steaming up the visor.

McFarren entered the copter and sat beside me. She removed the handcuffs from a bag at her waist, looked at me, then put them away.

"Thanks," I said. A plume of fog blossomed on my visor when I spoke. My voice sounded strangely loud inside the suit.

"I don't think you're a threat," McFarren replied. "But if you resist going into quarantine, I'll have to restrain you again."

I shrugged and looked out the window. What would be the point of resisting? Besides, if they were taking me to the same quarantine facility where they'd taken Pryce, I'd be there when he woke up in three days. I could use those three days to figure out a plan.

Below us, more hazmat-suited workers were setting up barricades around the park. On Purgatory Road, not far from the Visitors' Center, a tanker truck lay on its side.

"What's with the truck?"

"Cover story. We can't let the public panic because one lunatic got his hands on the virus. Officially, the park is closed because of a chemical spill. It'll take at least a week to clean it up." A week was the prescribed quarantine time.

"What about the gunshots? Somebody heard those and reported them."

"Kids playing with firecrackers. That's what distracted the driver and made the truck turn over." Wow. They had all the angles covered. "You'll be expected to sign a witness statement attesting to all this before you're released from quarantine."

"Whatever." I didn't approve of hiding a virus outbreak from the public, but Pryce had only used the virus on himself. It had broken down by now. There was no lingering danger to the public.

The human in the puffy suit climbed into the helicopter and closed the door. With a lurch, we rose into the air. The workers below grew smaller as we moved away from the park.

Wait. We were traveling north. The copter carrying Pryce had gone east.

"Where are we going?"

McFarren glanced at the other zombie officer. "Any reason why we can't tell her?"

The other zombie shook his head. "She'll find out soon enough, anyway."

McFarren turned back to me. "Princeton."

"Princeton?" My visor completely fogged over. I breathed through my nose until it cleared.

"There's a quarantine house in the werewolf retreat."

The steamed-up visor hid how far my jaw dropped. But it made sense. Werewolves were immune to the plague, and no human ventured inside the retreat's borders. It was a secure facility, with sharpshooter posts all around the retreat's fenced perimeter. It was the perfect place to contain a suspected plague carrier.

I almost laughed at the irony. A few hours ago, I'd been wishing I could go to Kane's retreat. Now, I was on my way there. To be locked inside a house on the grounds.

For the rest of the short flight, I kept quiet and watched our progress. We flew over the lights of Worcester, then followed I-190 north; I could see cars traveling on the highway. Then 190 bore right, and we bore left. We flew over dark woods and farmland, broken here and there by the lights of homes. Ahead, bright, stadium-style floodlights ringed a large expanse of forest. I leaned against the window—that must be the retreat.

We set down in a clearing beside a small, concrete-block cottage. McFarren and the other zombie grabbed rifles from a rack. "Silver bullets," she said. "To keep the werewolves back."

One of those werewolves was my boyfriend. I needed to make sure that the biohazard team got out of here before there was any trouble. I jumped out of the helicopter and ran straight through the open door of the quarantine house. It was dark inside. All I could see was McFarren in her suit, lit up by the helicopter's lights, pulling the door shut. "It's only for a week," she said. "Someone will come for you then."

The door shut. A loud *clack!* resounded as the bolt shot home, locking me in. Then another. And then one more. They weren't taking any chances.

Within a minute, the helicopter had lifted off. No shots fired—good. The noise from the whirring blades faded. I stood in darkness and silence, wondering what the hell I was going to do now.

I PULLED OFF THE SUIT'S GLOVES. FEELING ALONG THE WALL by the door, my fingers moved over the cool concrete. I found a light switch and flipped it on, blinking as light flooded the place. I stood in a small living room, twelve by fifteen, with cream-painted cinderblock walls and a cement floor. Small, horizontal windows—barred, I noticed at once—were set high up in the wall where it met the ceiling. Too high for anyone but a bird to peer inside. At the far end was a compact kitchen. The living room's furnishings included a lumpy-looking plaid sofa, a coffee table, and one wooden chair. No phone, no computer, no TV, ensuring people kept in quarantine were completely incommunicado. There were books, though, plenty of books, crammed into an overflowing bookcase near the door. Way more books than I could read in the week they intended to keep me here.

I found the thermostat and cranked up the heat. Then I tore off the ridiculous hazmat suit and threw it into a corner. Nice to be able to breathe without making the world go foggy. There was a short hallway leading past the kitchen. I followed it, taking a few minutes to explore my prison.

Prison—that's exactly what it was. The heavy, triple-locked

security door and barred windows made that clear. At least the place was bigger than a typical prison cell. The hall led to a bathroom and a closet-sized bedroom with a single bed. The cottage was stocked with supplies. The bathroom cabinet held shampoo, soap, toothpaste, and a brand-new toothbrush still in its package. The bed was made with clean sheets, and the dresser drawers were packed with sweats in every size but just one color: gray. And, of course, each item of clothing bore the giant red Q.

I went back to the kitchen and opened some cupboards. They were filled with every kind of food you could imagine—as long as it came in a can. Soup, fruit, Spam, tuna, mushy veggies. And—oh, joy—*instant* coffee. This wasn't just a prison; it was a torture center.

Outside, a wolf howled. Another wolf voice, then two more, joined the first. What was happening? I looked around the living room and spotted the single wooden chair. It might give me enough of a boost to see through a window. I dragged the chair to the nearest window and climbed up on it. Gripping the bars and standing on tiptoe, I managed to see over the sill.

The clouds had dispersed, and the moon washed the land-scape with soft, silvery light. A wolf pack crossed the clearing where the helicopter had landed. The pack was a family group of five, two adults and three young ones. Their eyes glowed in the night. One adult stood watch over the cubs, who romped and tumbled together, while the other ran in small circles, sniffing the ground. The sniffer followed the trail to the front door of my cabin. He trotted back to the others, raised his head, and howled again, alerting the retreat's wolves to a stranger in their midst.

The cubs quit playing to join in, lifting their muzzles and casting out high-pitched howls. Soon, other werewolves slunk from the woods. There was more sniffing, more howling. Glowing eyes fixed on the cabin. Hackles rose. Even from several yards away, I could see the gleam of moonlight on fangs as they snarled.

A chill shivered through me. Suddenly, I was glad about the bars on the windows.

Out of the woods burst a huge silver wolf. Kane. I'd know his wolf form anywhere. Six weeks ago, a bolt of magic had left him stuck in wolf form. But that had been different. Then, Kane had retained his human mind, despite his shape. Now, I was looking at the real thing.

He was magnificent. His silver coat shone like moonlight made solid. Larger than the other wolves, he exuded confidence and grace with each motion. He stood in the clearing—head high, ears forward and alert—and watched the gathered wolves. Then, like the others, he sniffed the ground, following a scent trail right up to the cabin door. I leaned into the window, craning to see him, but the angle was wrong.

But I did see the wolf who followed him. With thick chestnut fur and green eyes, it could only be Simone. She stayed back three or four yards, watching Kane so intently I could almost see his movements reflected in her eyes.

A piercing howl—strong, loud, steady—cracked the night wide open. Simone jumped back, getting out of the way, as Kane charged the other wolves. He ran, snapping and snarling, into the center of the group. Wolves took off in all directions, sprinting for the woods. A few turned and snarled back their own challenge. With bared teeth, Kane lunged at the biggest of them, a gray wolf. Sharp fangs sunk into the gray's shoulder. A smaller white wolf ran in, attacking Kane from the side. Kane leapt up, spinning in midair, and landed with his forepaws on the white wolf's back. A brindled wolf joined the assault, coming at Kane from behind, going in low and aiming for his leg. Kane fell. I screamed as the gray went for his throat. The other two wolves closed in. All I could see was a writhing ball of fur as they tumbled over each other.

No—please no! Not three against one. Werewolves sometimes killed each other on retreat. As long as it happened under the full moon and inside the fence, the government didn't care. I was terrified I'd see this fight break up to reveal Kane's bleeding body on the ground.

A yelp sounded, sharp and full of pain. I gripped the bars, leaning forward, trying to see which wolf had been hurt. The gray broke away and ran for the woods. The other two rolled onto their backs. Kane stood over them, hackles raised, showing his fangs. The smaller wolves lay completely still, except for a nervous, feeble waving of the tip of each tail. Kane backed up a step and issued a series of short, sharp barks. The wolves jumped to their feet and sped off, out of the clearing. Their tails drooped between their legs as they ran.

Kane shook himself and looked around. Only one wolf

remained in the clearing. Simone. She raised one paw tentatively, as if thinking about stepping forward.

Lowering his head, Kane growled. Simone dropped to the ground and showed her belly, her throat, making herself vulnerable. He held his crouch, watching her. Then the tension seeped from his body and he turned away.

He took a few steps toward the cabin, limping. A wound gaped in his back left leg, the one bitten by the brindled wolf. Dark streaks of blood marked his silver fur. He stopped and shook himself again. He turned and licked his injured leg. He sniffed at the wound and licked it more. Then, with a visible effort of will, he walked fluidly to the cabin. Not even a hint of a limp. There was a thump against the door as he lay down in front of it.

I looked back at Simone. She'd rolled over onto her belly, head on her paws, and was staring at the cabin. At Kane. Her muscles twitched. She inched a tiny bit closer, then froze. A minute passed. Her nostrils flared, and she crept forward another centimeter.

Right then, my one wish in the world was to be out there, shifted into wolf form. I wanted to feel my jaws close around that damn chestnut-furred throat. I wanted to snap her neck and watch her blood soak the ground. How dare she look at him that way? Simone's submissive behavior was obvious. She was making Kane her alpha, the leader of her pack. A nice, cozy pack of two.

And Kane was tolerating it.

Of all the wolves gathered in the clearing, he'd allowed her to stay. What did that mean? Why didn't I know more about werewolves?

Even if I shifted into a wolf myself, I still might not understand. As I'd told Kane so many times, I was a shifter, not a werewolf. Taking on a wolf's form didn't mean I'd automatically gain their instincts or understand their ways. Werewolves are neither fully wolf nor fully human; they're something in between. Something I could never be, no matter how many times I changed my shape.

Outside, Simone continued her vigil, her eyes lit up like green fire, watching Kane without a blink. I couldn't see him, but from her gaze I knew he must still be at the cabin door.

Feeling utterly depressed, I stepped down from the chair. I looked at the front door. Kane lay on the other side, inches away and yet unreachable. *Vicky is under my protection,* he'd announced to the werewolves at Creature Comforts. I went to the door and sank down on the floor beside it. I pressed my hand against its cold metal surface, wishing I could feel Kane's warmth on the other side.

There was that other thing he'd said. *The woman I love.* My feelings tangled themselves into an impossible jumble, twisting my heart a million different ways. Had he meant it, or was he merely making a speech for the occasion? I wasn't sure. But one thing was certain. The Kane who'd spoken those words had been a man, talking about a woman. The wolf now lying outside—that was a creature I didn't know.

Weeks ago, when magic had forced Kane into his wolf form, I'd looked into the wolf's eyes and seen Kane. *My* Kane, the man I knew. But the pure wolf that came out in the full moon was . . . something else. Something other, alien, unknown. What would I see if I looked into its eyes? The question scared me.

That was why he'd asked me to come with him on retreat. He wasn't trying to make me into some half-baked, phony werewolf. He wasn't trying to force me into a commitment I wasn't ready for. He wanted me to understand him—*all* of him, not just the part that walked around on two legs, wore tailored suits, and won court cases. He wanted me to understand his beast on its own terms.

I thought I knew Kane so well. But there was this huge part of him, this essential part of him, that I didn't know at all.

17

I DON'T KNOW HOW LONG I STAYED THERE, SITTING ON THE floor, with Kane inches away yet so far out of reach. But I couldn't stay there all night. Eventually I got up and headed for the bedroom.

On my way, I stepped up onto the chair and again looked out the window. Simone was gone. Had she left the clearing—or was she snuggled up against Kane as he guarded my door? Maybe they'd gone off into the woods together to—

Stop it, Vicky.

I didn't know. And that was the problem. I *couldn't* know. I had no understanding of Kane's wolf.

I went through the motions of getting ready for bed. I showered off the mud and found a sweatshirt and pants that more or less fit. I brushed my teeth. The medicine cabinet held a packet of over-the-counter sleeping pills. I took one; maybe it would knock Butterfly out and I could sleep, too.

The whole time, I wondered what Kane was doing, reaching out with my senses as though I could somehow feel him that way. I couldn't. I felt foolish to even imagine that maybe I could.

* * *

AN HOUR LATER, I LAY IN THE HARD, NARROW BED, GUILT gnawing at me. Everything I'd done lately felt like one great big bundle of wrong. *Work, damn you,* I willed the sleeping pill. I tried to follow Tina's advice and find a happy thought, something that made me feel good, but every time I reached for one, I grabbed a disaster instead.

I hadn't stopped Pryce. I hadn't even come close. He'd succeeded in smuggling his cauldron of demons into the Darklands, and then he'd followed it there. For all I knew, he might already have his shadow demon back.

Forget Pryce for now, I told myself. *You can strategize with Mab by dream phone as soon as you're asleep. Mab always knows what to do.*

But how could I forget Pryce when my failure tonight brought the world one step closer to the horrible vision I'd seen?

I didn't bother telling Butterfly to shut up. The thought came from me. Butterfly didn't have to say a word; it could just chomp on the feelings I brought upon myself.

I turned on my side and tried to think of something else. Kane. I'd really screwed things up there. I'd hurt him and left him confused about our relationship, yet he'd still chased the others away from my cabin and guarded the door. But who knew what that meant? Probably that he'd announced I was his responsibility and felt duty-bound to follow through. Kane was big on duty.

And then there was Simone.

All right, so thinking about Kane wasn't helping me relax, either. I rolled onto my back again, searching for something more pleasant to think about.

Family day. Oh, shit. The thought bolted in out of nowhere. Or maybe Butterfly wanted a different flavor to its food.

I was going to miss spending Monday with Gwen's family. And I'd promised Maria I'd be there. To an eleven-year-old, a promise is a promise, even without pinky-swearing. Now I was stuck here for a week with no way to contact her. The police were keeping this whole fiasco under wraps; they'd never acknowledge they knew where I was. Kane might give Gwen a call when he got back from retreat, but he didn't know about family day. Plus, he might be cautious about spreading the word that I was in quarantine until he understood what was going on. And that circled everything right back to the police stonewalling.

I still had the dream phone. I'd get in touch with Maria that way—if I ever managed to fall asleep. But would my reasons even matter? My niece was counting on me, and I'd made a promise I couldn't keep. I could see her face, a scowl line between her brows, her eyes accusing. She'd hang up on me before I could explain. She'd tell Gwen I couldn't be bothered, and then Gwen would be furious, too. And Mom—she wouldn't be furious, but she wouldn't be surprised, either. More expected behavior from the daughter who never called.

These were not happy thoughts.

The hell with thinking; I needed to sleep. Sleep was my only possible refuge. But how can you sleep when your mind won't quit chewing over thoughts of everything you've ever screwed up, while a guilt-demon chews over your guts?

A guilt-demon I couldn't kill because the cops had taken away my weapons.

I made a halfhearted attempt to picture Butterfly in frilly pink underwear, but the image didn't gel. The steady gnawing inside continued without so much as a hiccup.

I got up and swallowed another pill.

Back in bed, I tried to empty my mind. If my thoughts knotted me up with guilt and remorse, I wouldn't think about anything at all. Eyes closed, I imagined my thoughts as soap bubbles. When a thought arose in my mind, I constructed a bubble around it, then gently batted the bubble away. I concentrated on the swirling, iridescent surface of each bubble, refusing to consider what was inside. Not thoughts, just soap bubbles. Colorful soap bubbles drifting on a soft breeze.

I tried to keep things light and easy. Then a thought about Kane arose, an image of his disappointed face, his eyes dark with hurt. I surrounded the image with color, shaping the thought into a bubble, a pretty, glimmering bubble. But when I went to bat the bubble away, I hit it a little too hard, and it popped.

"Pop me like a soap bubble, will you? Isn't that what you said—you'd conjure my ass and pop me like a soap bubble? Well, pop this, sweetheart." Eidolon laughter ricocheted around my mind, scattering and exploding all my carefully constructed soap bubbles. Each time a bubble burst, the guilty thought or regret it masked broadcast itself into my mind, like stadium-sized amplifiers cranked to full volume.

Kane. Pryce. Maria. Gwen. Mom. Dad. Messed up. Broke your promise. Hurt. Betrayed. Failed. The words muddled themselves together in a thick gray fog of self-accusation. *How could you? What were you thinking? Why did you? Why didn't you?* I covered my ears against the babble. Why hadn't McFarren left me one measly bronze dagger?

I squinted through the fog, trying to see the Eidolon that had generated it. It was the only way to reduce the tormenting demon back to something I could handle, back to Butterfly. If I could see the Eidolon, I could confront it. I could talk back to it, belittle it, cut it down to size. Through the fog I was able to make out a silhouette, but it was shaped like a person, not a giant maggot. Then I realized this wasn't gray fog; it was silver mist, shot through with streaks of blue. The silhouette was Mab. She was calling me on the dream phone.

I concentrated on the figure of my aunt, and Mab came into focus. She was in the library at Maenllyd, pacing in front of the fireplace, arms folded tight over her stomach.

"I'm asleep?" Okay, so I was asking for the obvious answer to a dumb question; I wouldn't have gotten the call if I were awake. But I didn't remember falling asleep. It must have happened at some point when I was batting soap bubbles around.

"At last!" Mab stopped pacing and clasped her hands behind her back. "I've been trying for hours to contact you. How are you, child? What happened tonight? Did you stop Pryce?"

My shoulders sagged. "No. I failed." I looked down at my feet. I hated to see disapproval on my aunt's face. She was counting on me, and I'd failed her. Remorse flooded me as my eyes filled with tears. Still, I had to face her.

Feeling sick at heart, I forced myself to look up. Mab was frowning. The sick feeling spread; I knew she'd blame me for screwing up. Mab had high standards, and she never forgave failure.

As I opened my mouth to explain, my aunt pulled out a gun. "Mab, what—?"

She took aim at my stomach and pulled the trigger.

The *bang!* of the report, the impact, the pain—everything happened all at once. I staggered backward, clutching my stomach.

Grim-faced, Mab assessed the hit, holding the gun ready to fire again.

"Mab! You . . . you shot me!"

"No, child, I did not." She dropped her arm, pointing the gun at the floor. "Look and see."

I couldn't, not at first. Eyes closed, I gingerly probed my stomach and abdomen. It had hurt like hell when the bullet hit, but now there was no pain, no ragged flesh. No hot, sticky blood flowed over my fingers.

I looked. My body was intact, but at my feet lay a puddle of goo. As soon as I saw it, I smelled the stink of sulfur and brimstone. In the center of the puddle, melting like a block of ice on a hot summer day, lay the remains of a large maggot. Relief surged through me as I realized that the gnawing feeling in my gut was gone.

"You killed Butterfly?"

Mab blinked twice. "Pardon?"

"The Eidolon that's been bothering me. I call it Butterfly to annoy it." At my feet, the last vestiges of maggot body disappeared into the puddle. "I mean, I did."

"Ah, control through ridicule." She nodded. "No, child, I didn't kill your Eidolon. I killed a Drude that had taken on its shape here in your dreams." Mab rubbed at a spot on the pistol's barrel, then lay the gun on the fireplace mantel. "I assume the Eidolon didn't return to the demon plane after you allowed it to live. It's obviously still on your mind, or else the Drude wouldn't have known to impersonate it."

"You're right." I was still rubbing my belly as though feeling for a wound. I let my hand drop. "I gave it a chance, but it won't leave me alone. I'll have to kill it. That's what I probably should have done in the first place."

Mab pressed her lips together and didn't reply.

"I was going to make the Eidolon materialize and kill it tonight," I added. "But I couldn't, because the cops confiscated my weapons."

With intense interest, Mab leaned forward. "The police are involved? Tell me what's happened, child. Tell me everything since we last spoke."

I filled her in—not on *everything*, just everything that was relevant. I didn't mention the mess with Kane. My aunt was my mentor in many ways, but shoot-first-explain-later Mab would never be my go-to person for relationship advice. I told her about the Harpy attack, the robed figure and disappearing cauldron, and Pryce's zombie-virus suicide. I described the cops' descent on the scene. "And that's how I landed in quarantine," I finished. "I'm stuck here for a week, assuming they remember to come back and let me out. I'm missing family day with Gwen and her kids on Monday."

I paused, wondering whether I should ask Mab to contact Gwen. But that wouldn't work. Bad feelings between Gwen and Mab stretched back twenty years, due to a misunderstanding. Although the tension had eased recently, the two of them still weren't on speaking terms.

Mab nodded absently. Family day wasn't the kind of thing she gave much thought to, anyway. She sat in one of the wing chairs that flanked her library's fireplace. "So Pryce returned the cauldron to the Darklands and then followed it there by infecting himself with the virus."

"Without a shadow demon, he was as vulnerable to the virus as any human. He's making sure that, one way or another, he'll be back in three days." Not many people would choose life as a zombie. Pryce's reasoning, I guessed, was that if he didn't manage to re-create his shadow demon this time, coming back as a zombie would let him try again later. "When the door opened, he yelled, 'Take me with you,' but the robed figure ignored him. Pryce was injured, and the door closed before he could crawl to it."

Mab tapped her chin thoughtfully. "The living may not enter the Darklands without permission from one of its Keepers. And they do not grant permission lightly—that's why they guard the borders. From what you describe, Pryce clearly wanted to disappear into the Darklands, go there physically as well as spiritually, but his request was denied. So he resorted to more desperate measures; the virus was his back-up plan, so to speak." Her tapping finger paused. "I suppose he stole it from the Old Ones."

Mab knew all about the Old Ones and the zombie virus; she'd helped me disrupt their attempt to create a new-and-improved virus to give themselves eternal life. She also knew that their leader, Colwyn, had been captured and Juliet was helping to question him. "Juliet said Colwyn was angry because Pryce had stolen something from them. I'm sure it was the virus."

"Indeed. He expects to make a shadow demon, bind it to himself, and return to his human body, all before that body reanimates. He plans to come back fully restored as a demi-demon, with all of his previous abilities and strengths. He's very sure of himself," she murmured. "Pryce has always been arrogant."

"If he fails," I added, "his spirit gets kicked out of the Darklands after three days. He'll wake up as a zombie, but he won't have been cremated or buried or anything." It was against state law to dispose of the body of a suspected plague victim until permanent death was confirmed.

"When Pryce received his father's life force, he also received Myrddin's store of magical knowledge. That makes him a powerful wizard. If he fails in this attempt, he'll have other plans."

"How long do you think we have?" I asked. "Does Pryce have to stay in the Darklands the full three days—or could he be up and running around right now?" It didn't matter how secure McFarren thought Pryce's body was. If he regained his shadow demon, he could enter Uffern, the demon plane, again. He could pop out of custody, travel through Uffern, and pop into my living room. And the most dangerous weapon I had here was a can opener.

He'd slaughter me within ten seconds. The thought sent a cold wind through my dreamscape.

Mab rubbed her arms, as though she felt it, too. "Don't fret, child. It's as difficult to leave the Darklands as it is to enter. In ancient days, after Arthur stole the cauldron of transformation, Lord Arawn tightened the borders."

"Lord Arawn—he's the ruler of the Darklands?"

"He is. When you and I last spoke, we mentioned *Preiddeu Annwn*, 'The Spoils of Annwn.' Do you recall the poem's refrain?"

" 'Except for seven, none returned.' " Saying the words, I shivered. Must have been that wind.

"Yes. Three shiploads of Arthur's finest warriors, and only seven men made it back. Seven, child. Few return from the Darklands. And none returns unchanged."

I nodded. Pryce had gone in as a human, and there was no coming back as one. He'd return as either a demi-demon or a zombie.

"Pryce was clever to use the zombie virus to guarantee his return," Mab continued, "but I don't think we'll see him before those three days are up. Besides, there are many things that can go wrong between now and then."

I perked up at that. "Like what?"

"The cauldrons, all three of them, draw their power from the special magic of the Darklands. It's not the same as the magic of this world, and that may confuse Pryce. Also, before the cauldron can transform anything, it must be returned to its place at the center of the Darklands, where the magic is strongest. The Keeper you saw will notify Lord Arawn of the cauldron's return, and haste will be made to transport it. It's unlikely, but some accident could prevent or delay its return.

"Besides, Lord Arawn is no fool. He won't simply return the cauldron to service, not after it's been out of his domain for so long. I'm sure he'll purify it in some way first."

"And the purification will reveal the demons."

Mab pursed her lips, then nodded. "Demons are excluded from the Darklands. Annwn is not a realm of tormented and damned souls. Demons have their own, separate region—what they call Uffern, and we call the demon plane. Pryce has bound the demons to the cauldron and cloaked their presence inside it. If those demons are discovered, however, they'll be killed or driven from the realm."

"Then the cauldron would be useless to Pryce, right? No demons, nothing to transform."

"Yes. Pryce is aware of that, I'm sure. I'd wager that he intends to be at the purification ceremony and will make his move then. But that brings up another problem for him. To get to the cauldron, Pryce must find his way through the Darklands to their center. Traveling through that realm may not be easy for him."

I feigned surprise. "Don't tell me his GPS won't pick up a signal in the realm of the dead."

Mab cocked her head. "GPS?"

"Never mind." Never attempt a technology joke—not even a lame one—around my aunt.

Mab stared at me for two or three seconds, then dismissed my comment as irrelevant. "When you killed Cysgod," she said, getting back to the matter at hand, "Pryce lost his animating force. Myrddin restored him by stealing others' life forces and pouring those into Pryce. In this world, the spirits of those Myrddin killed are bound to Pryce. In the Darklands, though, they might escape."

"They can do that?"

"Myrddin bound those murdered souls to Pryce's physical body. Now that body is technically dead and Pryce's spirit is in the Darklands. Annwn is a place of spirits, or shades, as they're called there. For most, it's a temporary way station. Many spirits simply pass through on their way to other realms. Some go into the cauldron of rebirth and return to this world in new bodies. A few—a very few—make the Darklands their permanent home. At any rate, the bonds that hold those other life forces to Pryce are weaker there. They will try to peel themselves away from him, so they can move on to wherever they're meant to be. As they leave him, he'll grow progressively weaker until he's able—*if* he's able—to get his shadow demon back."

That sounded promising. The faster Pryce weakened, the less likely it was that he'd reach the cauldron. "Is there anything we can do to help those spirits leave him? Light a candle or something?"

"That's a good idea. I'll have Jenkins drive me to the village church in the morning. Lighting a candle for each of Myrddin's victims will send them energy and guide them on their way."

Okay, that was something. But it didn't seem like much. "What else can we do?"

Mab folded her hands in her lap. For a long time, she sat motionless, looking into the fire. She didn't turn her head when she spoke. "I'm afraid, child, that I haven't the foggiest."

"But . . ." Mab always knew what to do. Always. I realized my mouth was hanging open, so I closed it. "So, what? We sit around and hope that Pryce's plan blows up in his face?" Although Mab had listed many things that could go wrong for Pryce, I didn't like the idea of counting on his failure.

She turned to look at me then. "I'm afraid I see no alternative." Mab's voice was calm, but there was something strange about her face. It took a moment to realize what it was. Fear colored my aunt's eyes. I'd never seen it there before. She believed Pryce would succeed—and the thought scared her.

My aunt was never, ever scared.

"Can't we go after him? Is there a way into the Darklands from here?" I made a sweeping gesture to encompass my dream-scape. I thought about the red-lit door I'd seen at the Devil's Coffin and began reconstructing it in my mind: a rectangle of misty red light. No, not quite like that. I deepened the shade of red a little and—

"Victory, stop it!" The sharpness in Mab's voice made the image wink out, like she'd yanked the plug on a TV. I blinked and focused on her. "That won't work," she said. "Any portal you create here will lead into another part of your dreamscape. It won't get you into Annwn."

"So how do we get there?"

"We don't. Even if we could cross the border, it would be too dangerous." She clasped her bloodstone pendant. "Victory, I've lived in this body for more than three hundred years, well past my allotted time. If I were to enter the Darklands, I could not take my bloodstone with me. It would be like leaving my strength behind. What's more, Lord Arawn would never allow me to leave. Not without passing through the cauldron of rebirth."

"All right, I'll go." It would be harder without Mab, but I'd faced Pryce before.

"How, child? There's no virus for our kind that will guarantee your return. No." She dropped the bloodstone and shook her head. "I told you, a raid on the Darklands is too dangerous. Remember the poem's refrain, 'namyn seith, ny dyrreith.'"

Namyn seith, ny dyrreith. I wasn't what you'd call fluent in medieval Welsh, but I knew those words: Except for seven, none returned.

Well, there were seven who *did* return. "I'm willing to take the chance."

"I'm not willing to lose you, child." Her voice was firm, but the tone was soft. "Put the idea out of your mind. You're needed here." I was going to ask for what, but she stood and started pacing again. "Our best strategy is to prepare ourselves to battle Pryce if he recovers his shadow demon. What will his first move be? Let us both think about that, and we'll discuss it tomorrow. For now, we'll say good night. Keep this pistol"—she tossed me the gun she'd used to kill my dream-demon—"in case more Drudes appear in your dreamscape tonight. We'll deal with the Eidolon once you're out of quarantine." A faint smile touched her lips. "Butterfly. I like that. It will help keep the demon at bay until we can fight it properly."

"But, Mab—"

Her colors swirled up, fast and thick, obscuring her. Blue and silver filled my dreamscape. I waved my arm in the mist, trying to bring her back, but she was gone.

* * *

I DIDN'T NEED MAB'S GUN—NOT BECAUSE I HAD MY EVER-expanding demon infestation under control, but because I couldn't sleep. As soon as Mab's colors faded, my eyes flew open. I sat up in bed, arms braced, pointing the gun around the room. But there was no gun. Of course not. It existed only in my dreamscape.

I relaxed my empty hands and fell back onto my pillow. Moonlight streamed in through the high windows. In the corner, up near the ceiling, a spider constructed a web, her legs busy as she spiraled inward. She stopped, resting motionless in the exact center of the web. The moonlight washed her out, making her pale gray, a ghost spider hoping to catch fragments of thoughts, memories, and dreams.

She was welcome to mine.

The situation was even worse than I'd thought. Pryce was running around the Darklands, leaving Mab helpless and frightened. *Helpless* and *frightened* were two words that should never, ever be associated with Mab. Yet there they were, thanks to me.

That Eidolon had me, bad. All my thoughts turned to self-blame and regret, going through the familiar, exhausting carousel of hurt and disappointed faces: Kane, Dad, Maria—I hadn't made that dream-phone call to my niece—Mom, Gwen. And now add Mab. Had I *ever* done *anything* right? When you've been infested by an Eidolon, the last thing you need is an entire week alone with your thoughts and nothing to distract you. I'd be a raving lunatic by the time they let me out of here.

"Knock it off, Butterfly," I said out loud.

Moist, smacking sounds of chewing filled the room. Other than that, Butterfly ignored me.

Tina was always eager to fight demons. I should have given her a big-ass sword and told her to cut the damn thing out of me. One way or another, she would have put me out of my misery.

In fact, I'd be doing more good right now if I'd let her disembowel me. An image arose in my mind: Tina standing there, her nose wrinkled with disgust as my intestines spilled to the floor. "Oops," she'd say. But at least she would have sent me to the Darklands, where I could stop Pryce. Here, what good was I to anybody?

Mab said we had to be ready to fight Pryce when he returned;

that was fine as far as it went. But it didn't go far enough. It wasn't action; it was reaction—a loser's plan. And I wasn't ready to give up the battle yet.

Above me, the spider waited, motionless. "Got any ideas?" I asked. If she did, she kept them to herself.

There had to be some way to enter the Darklands. Preferably a way that didn't involve getting skewered by a teenage zombie. I thought back to the old stories. Venturing too deep in the woods, traveling too far north, or sailing too far west—all had led human wanderers into the Darklands. Some found their way out again; others did not.

Except for seven, none returned.

I couldn't wander anywhere beyond the boundaries of this small cabin, so those stories weren't going to help. What else? Pryce had opened a door. But I wasn't a wizard, and I'd be stuck here for the next two nights of the full moon. Still, the Darklands had at least one doorman—that robed figure who'd shut the portal in Pryce's face. Mab had mentioned Keepers, guardians who could grant permission to enter. Who were they? All mythologies station at least one guardian at the border to the otherworld, like Cerberus in Greek mythology, Garmr in Norse, and Nehebkau in Egyptian. Who guarded the border of the Darklands? Who made sure that the living and the dead both stayed where they belonged?

I had it. Not a guard but a psychopomp, a spirit who spent her nights on *this* side of the border, whose job it was to escort departed souls out of this world.

Mallt-y-Nos. The Night Hag.

I remembered the stories. She was said to ride across the sky with her pack of baying hellhounds. Each night, she hunted lost souls, driving them mercilessly across the border and into the Darklands.

Mallt-y-Nos knew the crossing places. Mallt-y-Nos could guide me into the Darklands.

But would she let me in? And, even more important, would she let me out again?

Except for seven, none returned.

I had to try. I threw back the covers and jumped out of bed. My guts twisted as the Eidolon squirmed in protest.

"Get lost, Butterfly," I said. "I've got work to do."

18

CALLING A SPIRIT IS TRICKY BUSINESS. TO DO IT RIGHT, YOU
need a ritual dagger, along with candles, incense, salt, and an
altar loaded up with all kinds of magical paraphernalia. Except
for the kitchen salt shaker, I didn't have any of that. What I had
was my intention.

I stood in the center of the living room, having pushed its few
pieces of furniture against the walls. I took a couple of minutes
to get centered, breathing deeply and going inside myself.
Breathe in . . . breathe out. Breathe in . . . breathe out. No thinking, no guilt, just a steady focus on each breath. When the world
seemed to pulse in time with my heartbeat, I opened my eyes. I
pointed at the cabin floor and moved in a slow, clockwise circle.
I concentrated on my intention: protection. I projected my will
from my brain, my heart, down my arm and through my pointing
finger, creating a sphere of protection around me. Nothing could
enter the circle unless I allowed it.

Let it be so.

Then, I called the Night Hag. I pulled up everything I knew
about her legend. I remembered the terror I'd felt as a child—
lying in bed, sure she was coming for me, pulling my pillow over
my head to block out the sound of galloping hooves. I could see

the pages of a book of Welsh folktales, one from Mab's library, where I'd read her story. I felt the uncanny shiver that had tingled through me when, walking alone at night in a dark Welsh lane, I'd felt *something* pass by. My pulse pounded like those galloping hooves. My whole body trembled with the desire to run, to flee, to stay out of range of the hag and her pack of hellhounds. But I stood my ground.

And I called her to me.

"Mallt-y-Nos!" My voice rang out with a confidence I didn't feel, pushing past the cabin's walls. "Matilda of the Night! Lady of the hunt! Mistress of Hounds! Night Hag, who drives lost souls to the Darklands! I, Victory Vaughn, do invoke thee!"

The words echoed back to me, then faded. My intention cut through the silence, as I held the image of Mallt-y-Nos in my mind. A silhouette on horseback, shadowy against the moon, long hair flying behind her as she rode. She reined in her horse and cocked her head, listening. I called out again: "Mallt-y-Nos, come to me!"

In my imagination, the hag wheeled her horse around. She whistled to her hellhounds. Shrieking a bloodcurdling hunting cry, she raced toward me.

"Come!" I shouted, shrieking too, raising the volume to blot out the horrible sound of the hag's approach. "I command thee!"

Hounds bayed and howled in the distance. The sound grew nearer. The ground shook as thundering hooves pounded closer, closer. I clamped my hands over my ears and kept shouting. I wasn't saying anything now; I was just making noise. Anything to fight the terror of her approach.

An explosion jolted the cabin as the wall collapsed. I staggered back a step, almost falling, covering my face with both arms. A tingle in my shoulder told me I'd bumped into my protective magical barrier, and I jerked forward. I had to stay inside the sphere.

I dropped my arms to see what I'd called.

I stared into the fiery, red eyes of a massive steed. Flames shot from its nostrils, but they broke to the left and right before they reached me. Hounds leapt forward, jaws snapping, but they couldn't get to me. My protection held.

"Quiet!" shouted a woman's voice. The hounds fell back, milling around the cabin. The wall they'd burst through remained intact. The half-dozen hounds that crowded the place didn't look like any dogs I'd ever seen. Each was the size of a small horse.

Their eyes glowed red and orange, lit by inner fire. Saliva dripped from their fangs; it sizzled when it hit the floor.

The horse turned sideways, and Mallt-y-Nos came into view. I blinked. *This* was the Night Hag? The woman astride the horse was young and beautiful, with blue-green eyes and golden blonde hair that flowed, shining, to her waist. She looked nothing like the nightmare hag that had terrorized my childhood imagination. "Why have you summoned me?" she demanded, regarding me imperiously from her demonic steed.

Before I could answer, her face changed. Wrinkles formed around her eyes, on her forehead, between her nose and mouth. Her blonde hair faded to gray, then bleached white. Her skin went from creamy to blotchy red to jaundiced. I gaped, unable to look away, as the beautiful young woman sagged and faded into an ancient crone. Finally, the hair thinned to a few wiry strands. The skin shriveled and peeled away, baring the skull beneath. Flames consumed the eyes, leaving only a red glow.

I looked into the face of death.

The cycle began again. In the course of a few minutes, Mallt-y-Nos flowed from youth to middle age to decrepitude and death. And back again. And then again. I stared, fascinated, almost forgetting the terror of her presence.

In her death's-head form, she pointed a skeletal finger at me. "Why did you call me?" she asked again, her voice impatient. Youthful flesh covered her skull. Her cheeks turned pink; her eyes sparkled. Thick, shining hair cascaded down her back. "Do not suppose, mortal, that you can command me. I came because I was curious. Mortals run from me; they do not request my presence."

That I could believe. Even in her youthful form, she was terrifying.

"I called you to ask you a favor."

Mallt-y-Nos laughed. Wrinkles creased her face as her lips stretched back to reveal the rotted and missing teeth of old age. "Mallt-y-Nos does no favors. All who deal with me must pay a price." Her white hair dropped away in clumps. "Only one thing do I want from mortals, and for that I never have to ask. All mortals must yield to me, like it or no. I live for the hunt, and one day I will chase your soul into the Darklands. You'll have many favors to beg of me then." Her ancient voice cackled with mockery. "'Oh, spare me, spare me, Mallt-y-Nos! I'll give you anything! Just don't drive me into that horrible dark place.' Such laments are sweet music to my ears. Nothing thrills a hunter's heart like bringing the quarry to bay." Her smile beamed from the face of a young woman. "But it is not yet your time, Victory Vaughn. So why have you called me?"

"I seek admission to the Darklands." A hound growled and lunged at me. Its snout bounced off the invisible barrier.

"Down!" Mallt-y-Nos shouted, and the creature dropped to its belly. Her scowl deepened the lines that now etched her face. "Did you not hear what I said? It is not your time."

"I seek temporary admission. Three days. There's a man . . . he used to be a demi-demon, but his shadow demon was destroyed. He's gone into the Darklands to try to revive his demon half. I need to stop him."

The crone snarled. "What do I care what happens in Lord Arawn's realm—or in this one? I care only for the hunt. One day, I will drive you before me. It is not yet your time, but I can wait. Hunters are patient." Again, her features receded into the ghastly grimace of a skull. I shivered at the image of what awaited me. Of what awaits every living creature.

I shook off the feeling. "I know there are doorways into the Darklands. How do I enter?"

"To cross the border, you must pay the price."

"And the price is a person's life. I get that. But there are stories of people who went to the Darklands and returned. What price did they pay?"

"Those mortals made a deal with Lord Arawn. But some betrayed him, and he closed the border to living mortals." Her expression turned crafty. "Still," she muttered to herself, "I can make deals, too." Her face, middle-aged at the moment, took on the stern aspect of a strict teacher. "I can escort you into the Darklands, mortal. But to return to your world, you must bring me three items."

"What are they?"

Her crone's face creased into a grin. "Rhudda's magic arrow; the white falcon of Hellsmoor; and the hunting horn of Lord Arawn himself. Those are things I can use." She raised an aged finger. "But nothing else. The Darklands are shrouded to the living and must remain so."

Mallt-y-Nos was offering me a deal—and bargaining with spirits is a bad idea. I watched as she nodded, cackling to herself, her face altering with each motion of her head. Make that a *very* bad idea. I'd be alone in a strange land, lost, racing against time and who knows what obstacles to stop Pryce. And now the hag wanted to send me on what I suspected would be an impossible scavenger hunt. She was too quick to make her offer, too pleased with herself. She knew she was asking for more than I could deliver.

Except for seven, none returned.

"Your price is too high," I said. "I will bring you one item. Name the one you want."

Her death's-head eyes flared into flame. Anger shot from her like a lightning bolt, shuddering my protective sphere. I cringed. "Three!" she shrieked. "Three or we have no deal."

"And if I fail?"

The young woman tossed her head. "None may cross the border without paying the price." She looked down at me like she'd look at a bug crawling on her shoe. "What is it to me which side you're on?"

Never make a bargain with an otherworldly spirit. I knew that. But the vision of my world in flames, the fear in Mab's eyes—I couldn't stay locked in this cottage and do nothing. I had no choice.

As though they were a single creature, the hellhounds froze. Their heads whipped to the right, nostrils quivering. They lifted their muzzles and howled. The sound, full of rage and hunger, was an echo from a nightmare.

The hag turned her head in the same direction, then looked back at me with the face of a scowling old woman. "Hurry up!" she snapped. "I can't wait all night. Do you agree to my price?"

"I agree." The moment I spoke the words, the air around me shimmered. My sphere of protection imploded, falling around me—on my face, my shoulders, my arms—like a million tiny shards of glass.

The flesh fell away from Mallt-y-Nos's skull as she pointed at me. "Change, shapeshifter," she croaked. A torrent of energy blasted out. It hit me square in the chest and exploded inside me, ripping off my limbs. No, not ripping. Contracting, twisting, changing. Pain—hot, fiery pain—consumed me.

What have you done to me? I tried to scream, but my mouth wouldn't issue the words. My tongue was too long, my teeth too sharp. A howl tore itself from my throat, joining the hellhound chorus. It burned. Every part of me burned.

Oh, God, I'm on fire! It was my last human thought before I shifted.

"RUN!" COMMANDS MISTRESS. HER WILL CUTS ME, A FIERY whip. Pain slices legs, and I move. Wall ahead. I stop, confused. "Run!" Mistress wills it. More pain, worse, pushes me. Other hounds bite. Sharp, sizzling hurt. I snap and snarl back. Too many fangs. They tear me. I run. The wall gives way.

Outside. Cold, but the fire inside me still burns, hurts. Smells: forest, mud, wolf. Many wolves. Ground soft and wet under paws.

"Up!" Mistress's command hurts. The word like fangs in my skull. Must obey, so up I go. No more ground, running in sky. Smells of earth and wolf fade. Smells here: damp, hellhound, horse, fire, mistress. Below, a howl. Wolf. Then no sounds but panting, growls.

"Faster!" Hurts. I yelp, go faster. I swerve, hit another hound. His fangs bite. I rear up. Aim for throat. But "Faster!" comes again and burning cramps torment me. Pain. I run.

Fire inside never stops. *Pain, pain, pain.* I feel its beat, run to it. *Pain, pain, pain.*

We run far, fast. Mistress allows no rest.

Pain, pain, pain.

Hunger rumbles in belly. Where is prey?

Pain, pain, pain.

"Down!" Command hurts. Mistress wills, I obey. Back on earth. Sniff all around. Mud smell, wet rock. Pine trees. Water. Paws squish in cold mud. A strong smell—dead demon. Harpies died here.

"You!" Fiery knives tear through me. Pain howls from my throat. Mistress wants something. Anything, anything—just make this strong hurt stop. I look at Mistress. She points. "Run!"

I run. Another wall ahead. Rock. Hurt drives me toward it. A light in the wall. Red, like fire. Misty, like smoke. Fire hurts. I don't want to run there.

"Run!" Mistress commands. Hounds howl. So much pain. I run where Mistress tells me. I leap into the fire-red wall. Rock melts around me.

Dark.

Empty.

Falling.

19

DARK.

It was dark and I was falling.

I tumbled down a steep slope, somersaulting and rolling and sliding. The baying of the hellhounds assailed my ears from all sides. Sharp stones cut me; smells of grass and dirt and something sharp, electric, rose around me. I scrabbled to grab hold of something, anything, to stop my descent. All I got were fistfuls of torn-up grass.

I came to a stop, sprawled on my face in the mud. That's when I realized something had changed. That raging internal fire—it was gone. I ached all over, but the horrible, burning pain that had driven me was gone. I flexed my fingers; I had hands, not paws. Crossing the border had shifted me back to my human form.

Thank God. Being a hellhound had shown me more flavors of pain than I ever knew existed. I didn't know whether Mallt-y-Nos had forced me to shift because it was the only way to get me out of that cabin and across the border, or whether she was merely a sadistic bitch. But I knew which answer I'd bet on.

Gingerly, I sat up. I tried to open my eyes, then realized they were already open. I couldn't see. Darkness, as thick and solid as black velvet enwrapped me. Panic seized me—that damn Night Hag had blinded me!—until I thought about where I was. The Darklands. Somehow, I hadn't expected them to be *this* dark. A sick feeling of failure lumped in my stomach. I'd lost before I began. I'd never find Pryce or keep my bargain with Mallt-y-Nos if I couldn't see.

A breeze touched my cheek, accompanied by a soft sigh from above. The way the air moved, it felt like something was passing by. A bird gliding close overhead, maybe. But the sigh sounded human. And sad.

"Hello?" I called. "Is anyone there?"

No answer. Whatever it was swept past. But as I listened, more sounds reached my ears: sighs, muted sobs, indistinct murmurings. A fragment of a hymn. All floated down from somewhere above me. As best as I could tell in the disorienting darkness, the sounds were moving. And they all seemed to be moving in the same direction.

Soft, steady crying drifted down from somewhere nearby.

"Are you all right?"

There was no pause in the sobbing, nothing to indicate that whoever was crying had heard me. I tracked the sound. In the distance was a star, a pinpoint of light in the darkness. That tiny, glimmering spot made joy spring up inside me. There was light here.

Overhead, the sobbing flowed toward the light. I stood and went toward it, too.

It was hard going. Unlike the voices wafting over my head, I was earthbound. I tried leaping into the air, reaching to catch a current or grab hold of one of the passing beings, but each time I fell back to the ground, my hands empty. I tried willing myself to fly, and that worked exactly as well as it would back in the human world. So I walked. I was in some sort of forest. There were rocks and trees—how could trees grow in this dark place?—and briars that tore at my arms. I proceeded slowly, feeling in front of me to avoid colliding with boulders and tree trunks, trying to keep my eye on the light. Always I heard sighs and whispers above, moving in the same direction.

The sixth or seventh time I tripped over an invisible root, I tried shifting into a bird so I could fly toward the light. I pictured myself sprouting feathers, imagined air under my wings as I soared toward the light. But nothing happened. The shift wouldn't take hold. Earthbound, I kept stumbling forward.

I must have made better progress than I thought, because the light rapidly grew larger. In ten minutes, it was the size of a doorway. I stood directly under it, still in absolute darkness. Its light didn't reach down here. But above, transparent shapes glowed briefly as they crossed into the light and disappeared. They were people. People flying through the darkness and going into the light. As each one passed through, a note of music sounded. Beautiful. I wanted to go through that doorway, glide into the warm light, become part of that melody. I had to get up there.

All those trees I'd collided with—maybe one of them could finally serve a purpose. If I could climb one, I might get high enough to jump for the bright doorway, or at least peer through it. The light called to me. The more I looked at the doorway, at that lovely, golden, singing light in so much darkness, the more I wanted to go through it.

I stretched out my arms, feeling for a trunk. Something grabbed both my wrists and yanked, hard, pulling me off my feet.

I screamed and tried to pull away, but I was held firmly. I reached for the light, wanting it, calling it to help me, but pressure built around me. I was squeezed by a vise of darkness. I called again to the light, like it could lift me up, carry me into itself. But it didn't. The light grew distant and dimmed.

Darkness tightened around me. I couldn't move. I couldn't breathe; my screams stifled in my throat. Pressure crushed me.

A loud pop sounded, and the pressure let go. I stumbled forward, aware that something still gripped my wrists. There was light here, dim, but I could make out my feet on the forest floor. Another pair of feet faced mine. A man's hands held me. "Let me go!" I shouted, pulling.

"Vic. Victory, look at me."

My name—that voice. In all my life, there was only one person who'd ever called me Vic.

I looked up, into the face of my father.

20

DAD SMILED. HE DROPPED MY WRISTS, AND I THREW MY ARMS around him. He felt solid, warm, like when he was alive. Memories rushed back. When I was a little girl, jolted awake by a nightmare, and my father's arms felt like a fortress against the terrors of the night. How he'd yell, "Come on, Vic!" at softball games when it was my turn at bat. When he'd taught me to drive the Jag, covering his eyes in mock terror as I pulled out into traffic. At my high school graduation, when he'd reached out to offer me a grown-up handshake and then caught me up in a proud hug instead.

Dad. It was Dad. He even smelled the same—spicy cologne laced with a hint of ink.

Dad put his arms around me, lightly at first and then tighter, until he hugged me back as though this one hug, all by itself, needed to make up for ten years of missed opportunities.

I was laughing and crying together, wetting his shoulder with tears. He smoothed a hand over my hair in a gesture so familiar, and so long missed, that I cried even harder.

He let go, stepped back, and took my hand. I hiccupped through my tears. "How did you find me? How did you pull me out of that darkness?"

"Shh," he said, putting a finger on his lips. "This way. Then we can talk."

I nodded, struggling to calm down, to get my crying under control. This weeping mess wasn't the strong, competent demon fighter I wanted my father to see. Wiping my face with my free hand, I laced my fingers tightly in Dad's and let him lead me.

For ten minutes, we moved silently through the dusky forest. I couldn't stop looking at him. My father was exactly as I remembered him. Five foot ten with a thin, wiry build, his shoulders and elbows sharp. Brown, curly hair, a touch of gray at the temples. The face of a scholar: brown eyes, radiating smile lines, behind wire-rimmed glasses; a closely trimmed, salt-and-pepper beard. I remembered how he'd stroke his beard whenever he was thinking. The only thing that was different was his outfit, a medieval-looking tunic with leggings and tall, fawn-colored boots. I noted with surprise that I wore the same thing, only his was black and mine was white.

From time to time, Dad turned to study me, the look of wonder on his face mirroring my own. Each time, he smiled, then again pressed a finger to his lips.

The landscape we walked through was much like the one I'd left behind. The forest consisted of pines, maples, oaks, and poplars, but here the trees were fully leafed out, unlike at home, where they were barely beginning to bud. It was warm, too, pleasantly so, the air soft on my skin. Birds soared overhead and sang from branches. We made our way through the pathless forest, skirting around boulders and fallen trees. The ground sloped upward, gently at first and then more steeply. As we climbed, the terrain became rockier.

We stopped in front of two slabs of rock that leaned against each other, forming a narrow, triangular opening. Dad looked right and left. He twisted around to scan the forest behind us. Then he released my hand and pointed to the ground, indicating I should wait here. He dropped down on all fours and crawled into the cave. A minute later, his head appeared in the opening. He beckoned me inside.

Crawling into a dark underground space is not on my list of favorite things to do, but at that moment I would have followed Dad anywhere. Inside, the narrow passageway opened into a spacious chamber, illuminated by the same soft twilight as the woods. The room was furnished with a bed, a square table with one chair, and a bookcase crammed with books. Of course. Even living in a cave, Dad would need his books around him.

"Welcome to my hideout," he said, grinning. He swept his arm across the space. "Not much to see, but for the moment it's home. Here, sit." He pulled the chair out from the table.

I sat down and ran a hand over the smooth tabletop.

"Would you like some refreshment?" Dad scowled and shook his head as he asked.

"Um," I watched as the shaking grew more insistent. "No, thanks."

"Good." Dad's cheeks puffed out as he heaved a sigh of relief. "If we have food, the magic of the Darklands compels us to ask that of any clay-born person we encounter."

"Clay-born?"

"That's what we call outsiders, those who still possess a physical body."

Outsiders. But I was family. The vast distance that had grown up between my father and me over the past ten years suddenly gaped like the Grand Canyon.

"The old Persephone trick, huh?" I kept my voice light to cover up how much the "outsider" label stung.

"Exactly. I'm not supposed to tell you this, but the hell with it. The food here is made out of magic. Anything you eat or drink in the Darklands extends your stay." His voice resonated with deep seriousness. "Keep that in mind."

"I will."

Dad took a seat on the bed, leaning toward me. We stared at each other. There was so much to say, and neither of us seemed to know where to start. I grabbed the first question that came to mind, the one I'd tried to ask in the woods. "How did you find me in that dark place?"

"The Black. I couldn't let you go up to the light. I just couldn't." His eyes got shiny, and he turned his head away. "Wait, let me back up." He stroked his beard, considering how to explain. "Here, we receive a . . . a knowing when a family member or friend, someone who was important to us in life, crosses the border. The words came into my mind: *Vic's here.* And I thought . . ." He reached over and took my hand. "Vic, I thought you'd been killed." His fingers went to my pulse point, and he shook his head in wonder. "But here you are, both body and soul. How did you—?"

"I'll explain in a minute. How did you get me out of the Black?"

He nodded. "As soon as I knew you'd crossed, I rushed to the edge of the Wood. I swear, Vic, I haven't moved that fast since I played football in school." By football, Dad meant soccer. He'd always loved the game. "To our eyes, the Black is dark, but not impenetrable as it is to yours. I saw you standing there, staring up at the light. That's when I knew you weren't dead—you were on the ground, weighed down by a physical body. Most spirits who travel through the Black never perceive the forest outside it. The Wood is protected by a sort of membrane. I had to tug you through that."

"What if I'd managed to climb up to that lighted doorway?"

He let got of my hand and stroked his beard again. "Then you would have been dead. Your soul would have shed its body in its eagerness to pass through."

A little detail Mallt-y-Nos might have mentioned. I was beginning to think she didn't really care if I found the items in her scavenger hunt. She'd run me through the door and left me to my fate. I never would have found my way out of the Black without Dad's help.

I had a sudden thought. Maybe Pryce hadn't found his way out, either. "Did you get a message that Pryce had come through?"

"Pryce? You mean from the nasty side of the family?" He shook his head. "I know who he is, of course. Demi-demon bastard tried to murder your sister when she was thirteen. But I never met him. There'd be no reason to notify me if he crossed. Is he dead?"

"Sort of." When Dad's forehead wrinkled with confusion, I added, "It's a long story. But here's the condensed version. Pryce was trying to lead a horde of demons out of Uffern to take over the human world. We fought, and I killed Cysgod, his shadow demon."

Dad clapped his hands together. "That's my girl!"

"Now he's trying to re-create it. His shadow demon, I mean. Has there been any news here about the cauldron of transformation?"

"It's been returned. Lord Arawn is very pleased. The cauldron is being transported to its rightful place in Tywyll, our main city."

"It's packed full of demons, Dad. Hidden ones. Pryce is going to use the cauldron to transform a whole bunch of lesser demons into a bigger, more powerful one. I'm here to stop him. Can you show me how to get to Tywyll?

"I . . ." Dad's fingers moved over his beard. His eyes were distant, lost in thought, an expression I'd seen on his face many times. He considered so long I started to get nervous, thinking of how we'd run silently through the woods. And he'd called this cave his "hideout"—was there something he was hiding from?

Before I could ask, he stood abruptly. "I'll do it," he said. "But we don't have much time to prepare. We'll need food for me, and weapons . . ." He eyed my clothes. "I wish I could get you a different outfit."

I looked at my tunic and leggings. Okay, so I looked like someone on her way to a Renaissance faire, but except for the color, they were the same as his. And they beat the hell out of the Q-labeled gray sweats I'd been wearing in quarantine. "What's wrong with my clothes?"

"They're white. White means you don't belong here." It must have been my turn to look confused. "Your clothes are made of magic. Magic is everywhere here. You can even smell it. When I first arrived, I couldn't get that sharp scent out of my nostrils, but I'm used to it now. In the Ordinary, what you call the human plane, only a little magic seeps through, and it's all in the form of energy. Here, magic has substance. It gives a shade like me the appearance of a solid body, and it clothes everyone according to their status. White is for, well, trespassers in the realm. Outsiders."

There it was again. *Outsider* pinched my heart. "I'd rather blend in," I said, shoving the feeling aside. "Do you have a spare suit of clothes in black?"

"No!" Eyes wide, he shook his head vehemently. "Even if I did, it wouldn't do any good. Magic decides your status. If I gave you other clothes, they'd turn white as soon as you put them on. You could roll around in the mud, trying to stain them brown, and they'd be white again by the time you stood up."

"Can I take them back to the Ordinary with me? I'd save a fortune in dry-cleaning bills."

Dad threw back his head and laughed. It was an open, easy, full-throated sound. A sound I hadn't heard in ten years. A pang hit me like a slap, and tears sprang to my eyes.

"Dad, I've missed you so much."

"I've missed you too, Vic." The warmth in his voice erased any chance that I'd ever be an outsider in his world.

DAD PULLED A KNAPSACK FROM A CUPBOARD. HE TOOK down a rolled-up piece of parchment from the top of the bookcase. "A map," he said. "I know the way, but just in case." He packed the map and began filling the knapsack with food. "How's your mother?" he asked.

"She's fine. Looks great." I was glad I'd seen her recently. "She's visiting Gwen's family at the moment."

"Visiting? From where?"

Oh, right. Dad wouldn't know that Mom had moved. Sitting here with him like this, it was hard to remember how long he'd been gone. "Mom lives in Florida now. She bought a condo in a retirement community."

"Retirement?" Dad stopped rummaging in a cupboard and turned to me, frowning. "She's too young for that."

"She's sixty, Dad." A lump leapt into my throat. "You've been gone for ten years."

"Have I? Then it's no wonder . . ." He gazed at the floor, rubbing his beard, and didn't finish the thought. He looked up at me. "Time passes differently here."

That was what the old stories claimed. I could believe it. Dad hadn't aged a day. "Slower?"

"Sometimes slower, sometimes faster. It's just . . . different." He went back to packing. "So does Ann have a boyfriend?" His too-casual tone betrayed his intense interest.

"Mom? I don't think so. She never mentioned anyone." Except those old goats she had to fight off, but I didn't think Dad wanted to hear about that.

"How about you, Vic? You're not dating anyone, are you?" I knew why he phrased the question the way he did—Dad never wanted me to follow Gwen, giving up shapeshifting to take the domestic route of home and family. Although he'd never try to stop me if that's what I wanted, all his hopes and ambitions for me were as a Cerddorion demon fighter.

A pang hit me as I thought how I'd pushed Kane away. I wondered what he was doing right now, and whether Simone was with him. I knew it was right—for both of us—for me to step aside if he was looking for a mate. That didn't make stepping aside easy. Or hurt any less. What was right wasn't necessarily what I wanted, but I couldn't figure it all out now.

"Not at the moment," I said.

Dad nodded. I didn't think he noticed the crack in my voice.

I brought him up to date on the rest of the family. Gwen was much the same as he remembered her, happy and busy in the full-time suburban mom role she'd chosen. He'd lived to see the birth of Maria, but not his two grandsons. When I mentioned that Maria seemed on her way to becoming a shapeshifter, his chest puffed with pride.

"I knew she would!" he exclaimed. "Right at the hospital, the very first time I held that baby in my arms, I knew she'd be Cerddorion!"

"Gwen's not quite as happy about it as you are," I said. "She's worried. Things have changed, Dad. Paranormals of all kinds are out in the open now. And the norms try to regulate us." I filled him in on the zombie plague that had forced the world to acknowledge the existence of the nonhuman among them.

"So that's what that was," he said. "I'd wondered. On this side, there was a huge, sudden influx of spirits into the Black. I received word that a couple of my work colleagues were there. But almost as soon as they got here, they were gone again. They didn't pass through, as most of them do. They didn't wander into the Wood. They just disappeared."

"They went back to their physical bodies. In Boston, they were dead for three days, and then they woke up as zombies. None that I talked to remembered anything about being here. They said coming back was like waking up from a dreamless sleep."

"Well, does that surprise you? You were in the Black. If you'd simply woken up again in your physical body after that, what would you remember?"

"Good point."

Dad rubbed his beard. "The world *has* changed. What about Mab? Surely I can rely on her to stay the same."

I laughed. "You know Mab. If anything, she gets younger." I didn't want to think about what Mab would say if she knew where I was right now.

"Speaking of your illustrious aunt, if she could see us, she'd be scolding me because you've been here all of half an hour and I haven't yet given you a weapon. What do you need?"

"What do you have?"

"Anything you wish. Let's start with a dagger. Sit back, and be amazed."

Dad rubbed his hands together. He spread them apart a little way, and a glowing ball appeared between them. Again he rubbed his hands together and spread them apart, wider this time. The ball grew. When it was a little bigger than a golf ball, he began to shape it, almost like he was working with clay. He pulled it, stretching it out like taffy, into a bar maybe a foot long. He spun the bar, smoothing one end with his hands into a grip. Then he flattened out the rest of the bar into a blade, pinching the edges and running his fingers from one end to the other. A glowing object the size and shape of a dagger hovered in the air.

"Hocus pocus!" Dad said, and snapped his fingers. The dagger clattered onto the floor. At the same time, Dad plopped down heavily on the bed. He bent forward, breathing hard, like a runner who'd just crossed a marathon finish line.

"Are you okay?"

He nodded. "Leaves me a bit winded," he said. "Go on, take a look."

I picked up the dagger. It was solid, warm to the touch, made of metal with a leather grip.

"How did you do that?"

"Magic." He looked up and grinned, reminding me of the time I was five and he pulled a quarter from behind my ear. "I admit the 'hocus-pocus' part was for show."

"I've never seen magic do anything like that."

"Not bad, huh? Although you should see what the royal wizards can do."

"Where does the Darklands magic come from?"

"Some say it comes from Lord Arawn. Some say it flows like water under the land, bubbling up in wondrous springs of pure magic—although no one's ever actually seen a spring like that. Truth is, no one knows. It's like asking where air comes from in the Ordinary."

I tested the dagger's blade; it was as sharp as any in my weapons cupboard at home. A thought struck me, and I smiled. "Hey, can you make me a magic arrow while you're at it? I'll need one to get out of here."

"What do you mean?" The grin vanished from my father's face. I'd been joking, but his dead-serious expression made me nervous. "Vic, how did you enter the Darklands?"

"Mallt-y-Nos. I shifted into one of her hellhounds, and she drove me across the border."

Dad stared at me, his mouth open.

"It wasn't that bad," I lied. It was the worst shift I'd ever experienced. So much pain. The memory made me cringe. "It got me in."

"But to get out," Dad spoke slowly, like he was reluctant to ask, "what did you promise her?"

"I've got to pick up a few things for her while I'm here. I figure the Darklands must have a Walmart, right? They're everywhere now."

No hint of a smile. "What things?"

"Well, a magic arrow, like I said. The one she wants belongs to someone named . . ." I searched my memory for the name. "Someone named Rudy? No, that's not right. Rhudda."

"Rhudda Gawr. The Red Giant. He owns an arrow that never misses its target. It's his second most prized possession."

"What's the first?" At least the Night Hag wasn't expecting me to sneak off with that, whatever it was.

Dad ignored my question. "What else does she want?"

"A white falcon. Have you heard of a place called Hellsmoor?"

Dad stood, pounding a fist into his hand. "*Damn* that hag! She might as well have demanded that you pluck a hair from the beard of Lord Arawn himself—and steal his hunting horn while you're at it." I bit my lip. "Oh, no. She didn't. Vic, you didn't agree to—"

"Let's put it this way: Lord Arawn's beard is safe from me."

Dad sank back down on the bed. His shoulders slumped. He looked tired. And old—older than I remembered my grandfather. He put his head in his hands.

"What is it, Dad?" He didn't answer. I thought again of how we'd snuck through the woods to get here. "Is there some reason you're keeping a low profile? Because you can stay here and be safe. Just point me toward Tywyll and—"

"No." His head snapped up, eyes fierce. "I'm going with you." He looked around the room. "I've shut myself away with my books for too long. I have to tell you, Vic, you're trying to do the impossible. But as long as I'm around, I swear you won't be trying alone."

21

DAD MADE ME ANOTHER WEAPON OUT OF MAGIC, A SHORT sword. But doing so seemed to take a lot out of him. As before, he had to sit down after the weapon assumed its final shape. This time, he leaned back against the wall and fell asleep for a few minutes. I studied him. He seemed thinner than when I'd first seen him, his cheeks sunken. When he awoke with a snort and leapt to his feet, I was sure he was half an inch shorter.

"What's next?" he asked, rubbing his hands together. "How about a battle ax?"

"Dad, when you work magic like that, what does it do to you?"

"Oh, it takes a bit out of me. But I'll be fine." He started to draw his hands apart, a glow already forming between them. I reached out and pressed his hands back together.

"No. No battle ax."

"Vic—"

"I mean it. If you're coming with me, I need you at one hundred percent."

Dad protested, but when he nodded and dropped his hands he looked relieved.

"Besides," I said, "too many weapons weigh a person down. I prefer to travel light." That wasn't exactly what you'd call true.

When I was in unfamiliar, potentially hostile territory, I preferred to travel armed to the teeth. The more blades, the better. But Dad accepted my words.

He armed himself, too, but he didn't need magic to do it. He strapped on weapons he already owned: a dagger, a sword, and a small hatchet. I watched him buckle on his baldric. Yes, he was definitely shorter. Whatever happened, I would not let him work magic around me again.

Within minutes we were ready to go. Dad tossed the knapsack outside the cave and crawled out after it. By the time I'd followed him, he'd put the knapsack on.

"I can carry that," I said.

He looked offended. "Hey, I might be your old man, but I'm not *an* old man. There's a difference, you know." He turned and set off down the slope.

OUR TRIP THROUGH THE WOODS WAS VERY DIFFERENT FROM the previous one. Instead of keeping low and speaking in whispers, Dad stomped along, branches snapping under his feet, whistling a Welsh folk song.

"What's that song? You used to sing it when Gwen and I were little."

"You remember? It's called 'Ar Lan y Môr.'" He cleared his throat, and his voice rang out in a rich baritone: *"Ar lan y môr mae rhosys cochion. Ar lan y môr mae lilis gwynion. Ar lan y môr mae 'nghariad inne, yn cysgu'r nos a chodi'r bore."*

"I do remember—'Beside the Sea,' right? It's the one about roses and lilies."

He chuckled. "You girls always wanted me to sing it in English." He started again, from the beginning: "Beside the sea grow roses red, beside the sea white lilies spread, beside the sea my true love dreams"—I joined him for the next line—"until she's touched by morning's beams."

My voice cracked on the final note. Well, I'd never wanted to be a singer.

Dad laughed and clapped an arm around my shoulders. "Good times, Vic. We did have some good times."

We sang the song all the way through. After the third verse, we came to a wide dirt road and turned left on it.

"Dad, can I ask you something?"

"Shoot."

"When you pulled me out of the Black, we were whispering and sneaking through the woods. Now we're singing at the top of our lungs and acting like we own the place. What changed?"

"I told you, Vic. I've given up my hideout. Now that I'm going to Tywyll, I can be as loud as I please."

"Why?"

Dad smiled. "Why, why, why? You were always brimming over with whys when you were a little girl." For a moment, his eyes went distant with some memory. "Well, here's an answer. My presence is requested in Tywyll, and I didn't wish to go. I wanted to stay in my hideout and read my books. But now we're on the road to Tywyll, so it's no longer an issue."

"Why—?"

"You asked about magic before." Dad was using his lecturer's voice. That meant he'd said all he was going to say about why he'd been hiding at the edges of the Darklands. "As you've noticed, magic is different here. In your world, people use magic. Here, magic uses us. Let me put it another way, one I touched upon before. In the Ordinary, magic is energy, and people manipulate it to achieve their aims. In the Darklands, magic is substance. Everything you see around you—the trees, this path, the rocks, even people's bodies—they're all made of magic. The magic draws on us, on the shades who live here, to animate it."

"So, the magic . . . eats you?"

"That isn't exactly how I'd put it, but I suppose it's not far off. Most of us don't stay here long enough to be fully consumed by the magic. After six months or a year—or what passes for that amount of time here—most shades dive into the cauldron of rebirth for another round of life in the Ordinary."

I was glad my father hadn't done that yet. It was so good to see him, almost like he'd never been gone. "How long have you been here?" I asked. "In Darklands time, I mean."

He shrugged and slid his eyes away. "Oh, well, a while. I'm in no hurry to take a dip in a cauldron. I'm not ready to be reborn. The reincarnation process . . . it wipes your memory clean. Say, for example, that I was reborn as an infant in Florida. And say your mother saw me one day in my baby carriage. She'd stop and coo and fuss over the adorable little baby." He smiled at the image, but there was sadness, too. "And maybe—just maybe— she'd see some spark of something that made her think for a moment of me, of *this* me. But I wouldn't know her at all. My lover, my wife, the mother of my girls. I wouldn't know her."

Dad stopped. He took off his glasses and wiped them with the hem of his tunic, turning away from me as he did. His bent head, his hunched shoulders, the pain I'd heard in his voice . . . A hard fist of remorse squeezed my heart. Everything he'd lost— it was my fault.

I put a hand on his shoulder, but he shook me off. He put his glasses back on and cleared his throat. When we started walking again, he picked up his lecture like there'd been no interruption.

"Magic gets the most out of the newly arrived shades. With time, we become depleted. As magic gets less out of a shade, it becomes harder for that shade to work with magic."

That sounded suspiciously like what I'd witnessed when Dad shaped magic in his cave.

"Mab said there's a cauldron of regeneration. Why can't you—Why can't a shade go into that cauldron?"

"Some can. It's not up to us. The magic chooses. I've seen what happens. We don't know its choice until we're at the cauldrons and it's too late to turn back." He gestured to his outfit. "These black clothes? They show my status. According to the magic that rules this place, that *is* this place, my time is up. That's why I've been staying as far from Tywyll as I can get. In the city, it's hard to resist the cauldrons' pull."

The fist squeezed harder, and I stopped in my tracks. "Dad, go back. I'll do this on my own."

Dad stopped, too, but he acted like he hadn't heard me. "A lot of shades lived long, full lives in the Ordinary. They got bored there, got tired of being old. For them, there was nothing left to do in that lifetime. Those shades don't stay here long; they're more than ready to start from scratch." He shook his head. "But not me, Vic. Not me. I don't feel like I'm done with my life. I don't want to start all over again."

I didn't know what to say. My father had loved his life—his family, his studies—and I'd taken it away from him. All of it. The damn fist in my chest ripped the heart right from my body.

Something—an insect—flew at my head, and I waved it away through the blur of tears.

"Vic . . ."

"Don't say anything, Dad. I know it's my fault. I'm sorry."

"No, Vic, listen to me." My father's voice was low, tense. "There's a demon on your shoulder."

Without turning my head, I glanced toward my shoulder. A black butterfly, with sharp, saw-tooth wings and the face of a demon, rested there.

"Is your dagger bronze?" I whispered. The one he'd made for me wasn't.

"I heard that!" yelled Butterfly. It had a loud voice for such a small incarnation. "If you're going to plot my death, you might as well do it in front of me."

Dad stared at Butterfly, mouth open. He shifted his astonished gaze to me and shook his head. "There's no need to carry bronze weapons here," he said. "Demons are excluded from the Darklands."

"That's why I came out to take a look around, once your precious daughter's guilt made me strong enough. Something to tell the folks back home in Uffern." Butterfly rose and flitted around for a minute, then returned to its perch on my shoulder. "Eh. Nothing special. So, Evan"—my father looked startled at the mention of his name—"are you pissed or what at golden girl here for killing you?"

"Shut up, Butterfly," I hissed.

Dad's eyes grew rounder. "Vic, is that true? Do you think you caused my death?"

I looked at the ground. Butterfly chortled like a buzzsaw in my ear. The damn demon was enjoying this.

My father smacked Butterfly off my shoulder. Then he took my hand. "I've never blamed you, Vic. Never. It wasn't you; it was the Destroyer."

"Yeah, yeah. A technicality." Butterfly hovered in the air, out of range. "Who summoned the Destroyer? Who nearly got her ass roasted and had to be rescued?"

"It doesn't matter," Dad said, speaking to me, not the demon. "My time was up that night. One way or the other, my life would have come to an end. If not the way it happened, then I would have fallen down the stairs and broken my neck, or had a heart attack, or . . . or gotten hit by lightning. Whatever." With his thumb, he wiped the tears that spilled from my eyes. "I was proud to die defending you. I couldn't imagine a better death."

I threw my arms around him.

"Aw, crap," muttered Butterfly. It flew up into the air, and then dived back into my gut. The impact stung. The demon burrowed into my intestines and stayed there, quiet and unmoving.

Dad hugged me back. Then he and I continued along the road. "You can't let anyone see that Eidolon," he said after a bit. "The penalty for bringing a demon into the Darklands is death."

That surprised me. "In the realm of the dead? How can death be a penalty here?"

"Even shades can die. The magic bleeds away, and the spirit disperses. There's nothing left."

"I'll be careful." If I could get my hands on some bronze, I'd finally kill that damn Eidolon. Until then, I'd use Tina's technique to starve it. "It's not much of a demon, anyway. Likes to dress up in frilly pink underwear."

Dad's eyebrows went up at that, then he laughed. Butterfly sulked in my gut.

We walked in silence for several minutes. In my mind, I was reliving the night my father died, trying to understand it as he did. I couldn't see his death as a good thing, but my memories hurt a little less.

And there was one thing I could tell my father. Something I'd been wanting to say, dreaming of saying, for years. But now it was true. "I killed it, Dad. I killed the Destroyer."

"You did?"

"Split its damn head in two."

Dad smiled broadly. "That's my girl. So tell me about it."

As we walked through the Darklands together, I did. I showed him the place on my arm where the Hellion had marked me, explained how the mark had almost gotten the better of me. But despite the demon mark's power, I killed the Hellion that had put it there. Dad's death had not gone unavenged. As I told the story, the guilt inside me shrank and shriveled. It wasn't gone, but it was now tiny, a speck. For the first time in ten years, it almost felt like something I might be able to live with.

WE PASSED A FEW PEOPLE AS WE WALKED ALONG THE ROAD. Some stared at my white clothes. One or two offered me food from bags or baskets they carried. Most averted their eyes.

From what I could tell, most residents of the Darklands wore gray or brown. Dad nodded toward a woman in a long, pearl-gray dress. "Remember I told you that clothing color shows status? Light hues, like that gray, indicate newcomers," he said. "I'd say that woman hasn't been here more than a couple of weeks. The longer she stays here, though, the more her dress will darken."

"What about colors? I saw a man wearing green." He'd been carrying a bow and arrows, and his green tunic made me think of Robin Hood.

"Most shades are simply waiting around until the magic decides it's time for them to move on. Those are the ones dressed in gray and brown. Colors mean the magic has chosen you to do a job in the Darklands. Green is for warriors. Sooner or later—if not on the road, then in Tywyll for sure—you'll see folks wearing red. Red is the color of Keepers, those who tend to various aspects of the realm. There are Forest Keepers, Magic Keepers, Soul Keepers, Cauldron Keepers . . ." He glanced down at his own tunic. "When I first arrived, my clothes were blue. That's for members of Lord Arawn's court."

"You were in the court?"

"For years. Caretaker of the royal library. A dream job for a bookworm like me, except for the fact that I didn't want to be here." He fingered the hem of his sleeve. "This very outfit used to be pale blue. Your mother would've called it robin's-egg. One day, I noticed my tunic had darkened a little. It was like finding my first gray hair. Later, it became more of a slate blue and then, with time, slate turned into navy, which turned into an inky blue so dark it might as well have been black. That's when I left." He glanced at me sidelong. "I may have taken a few books and things along with me."

"What would have happened if you'd stayed? Would Arawn have forced you to be reincarnated?"

"No need. As the colors darken, the pull of the cauldrons grows stronger. I moved to the farthest edge of the Wood, as far away from Tywyll as I could get. It was better there; I barely felt a thing. Had to keep a low profile, though. Soul Keepers patrol the Wood looking for avoiders. When they find one, they escort the shade to Tywyll. Once they get there, the pull of the cauldrons takes over." A shadow crossed his face. Then he shook his head and smiled. "Those bright-red clothes are not very practical for hunting down rogue shades. I could spot a Soul Keeper patrol from half a mile away and slip quietly back to my hideout."

We took a break at midday. Or that's the time Dad said it was. I couldn't tell. The light here never changed. There was no source for it, no shadows cast. The diffuse half-light touched everything the same.

"That's why they call it the Darklands," Dad explained, "even though it's not really dark here. It's more like there's no discernible light source."

We rested under a tree, both of us leaning against the trunk. Dad used his dagger to peel an apple and cut it in slices. I wasn't hungry. I counted that as a good thing, since I didn't know how long I'd have to go without food.

A figure appeared on the road, moving in our direction. This man seemed to be having trouble walking. He staggered along, zig-zagging from one side of the road to the other. I nudged my father, and he craned to see what I was looking at.

The man approached us. In the distance, his tunic had looked gray. Now I could see it was made up of thin stripes: black like Dad's clothes, white like mine. It was like the magic couldn't decide whether he was a trespasser or due for reincarnation. Either way, this man clearly didn't belong here.

He held out his hands, and I thought there was something familiar about his face, the bushy salt-and-pepper eyebrows. "Help me," he said. "I . . . I think I'm lost."

Dad's hand froze halfway to carrying a slice of apple to his mouth. Slowly, like he was fighting the movement, he held out the slice to the man. He pressed his lips together, but the words came out, anyway, each syllable ripped from his throat. "Would you . . . like . . . something . . . to eat?"

The man stared at the apple. I was sure I'd met him before. "I don't . . . I don't feel right," he said. "Maybe some food . . ." He reached out.

"No!" I knocked the piece of apple from Dad's hand. I remembered where I'd seen the man. His name was Ferris Mackey, and he'd been a cab driver in Boston. He was one of the murder victims whose life force had gone into Pryce. "Mack," I said, "you don't belong here."

"I know," Mack said, staring at the apple slice. Ants swarmed to investigate it where it lay in the dirt of the road. "I can't find my cab."

"He's a spirit," I whispered to my father. "One of the spirits that came in with Pryce." Dad nodded his understanding.

"Don't eat anything, all right?" I said. "Not until you, um . . ."

"Not until you find your cab," Dad finished.

Mack looked up sharply, his eyes hopeful under his bushy brows. "Do you know where it is?"

"It's in the Black," Dad said, standing.

"The Black? Never heard of it. You mean Blackstone Street, over by the North End?"

"It's more like the Sumner Tunnel," Dad said, putting an arm around Mack's shoulders and turning him in the direction we'd come. "Kind of dark."

"Why the hell would I leave my cab in the Sumner Tunnel?" Mack was indignant.

"It broke down," I said, getting to my feet. "Don't you remember?"

"I remember a crash, I think, and . . ." Mack shrugged. "I'm not sure. You're right, though," he said to Dad. "It got real dark then."

"Just follow this road," Dad said, pointing, "as far as it goes. Keep going until it's night. Then you'll find where you're supposed to be."

"Follow the road until it's night. Got it, thanks." He peered ahead, judging the distance. Dad clapped him on the back, and he started trudging away.

"And don't eat anything until you get there!" I shouted after him.

He waved a hand in acknowledgment and kept going.

Dad and I turned in the other direction and set out again, too. "Mack was a world-class jerk in life," I said. "He was a bigot and proud of it. I rode in his cab once and was ready to smack him after the first block. But he didn't deserve to die." I turned and looked at Mack's receding figure. "Will he be able to find the Black?"

"If he stays on the road, yes. It goes right to the border. He'll feel its pull as he gets closer. There are Soul Keepers there to help him, too. When he finds his way to the edge of the Wood, his magical body will dissolve and his spirit will fly up into the Black."

"And he'll pass into the light?"

Dad nodded. "We call it the Beyond."

I was glad. Mack wasn't one of my favorite people, but he'd looked so lost and confused wandering through the Darklands, a place he was never meant to be. Even a bigoted jerk should be able to enter that beautiful light and find out what awaited him in the Beyond.

And he'd gotten away from Pryce. "Mab said that the spirits Myrddin bound to Pryce might peel away from him here. So Mack showed us two things: that Pryce has been on this road and that he's weaker than he was when he entered the Darklands."

"This is the main road to Tywyll," Dad said, "so I'm not surprised he came this way."

"I wonder how far ahead of us he is."

"That may not matter." Dad veered into the woods. "I know a shortcut. This way."

Some time later—it may have been an hour, it may have been a whole damn week—I stopped and sat down on a fallen log to catch my breath. "I thought you said 'shortcut,' not 'obstacle course,'" I complained.

Dad, who was several yards ahead, turned around, eyebrows raised. He grinned and came over to sit beside me. "Sorry, Vic. I didn't realize it'd be so hard for you to keep up with your old man."

"I'm a city girl. These woods should come equipped with sidewalks."

Dad laughed. "We're making good time. It's more than a day's walk to Tywyll by the road. We're saving several hours this way. We'll be able to rest for the night and arrive in the city by mid-morning."

"Rest for the night." I looked around at the endless expanse of trees, bushes, and rocks. "I don't suppose you know a hotel around here."

Dad looked surprised. "You used to beg me to take the family camping. Remember that summer in the White Mountains?"

"I was ten, Dad. I've since grown to appreciate the comforts of four walls and a real bed."

He laughed again and patted my knee. "You'll love it," he said, standing. "Come on, we need to make some time."

Groaning, I stood, too. "What the Darklands needs is a subway system," I muttered as I followed him through the forest.

22

SOMETHING WHIZZED PAST MY EYE. I THOUGHT IT WAS AN insect, or maybe Butterfly coming out to play again, until it thwacked into the tree beside me. A quivering shaft protruded from the trunk. An arrow. I ducked and ran for cover, drawing my knife as I kept low. Two more arrows zipped by, each so close I could feel a breeze. The feathers of the third one skimmed my cheek. I dived behind a boulder and scanned the woods.

My father stood still, looking around as though wondering where I'd gone.

"Dad!" I said as loudly as I dared. "Get down!"

He didn't drop. He didn't give any sign he'd heard me. He squinted into the woods ahead of him. "It's all right, Vic," he said at normal volume. "You can come out. The challenge has been issued."

"What challenge?"

Dad cupped his hands around his mouth. "Rhudda Gawr! We acknowledge your challenge! Show yourself so we can discuss terms."

Rhudda Gawr. The Red Giant with the magic arrow.

A chuckle rumbled through the woods, deep and menacing. It seemed to come from all directions, bouncing off the rocks and trees. I stood, my fingers throttling the grip of my dagger, and tried to see who Dad was calling.

The bushes parted, and a man stepped out, carrying a longbow. He was big, with wide shoulders and a large, squarish head, but hardly my idea of a giant. He wasn't even as tall as Axel; maybe six foot five, tops. The "giant's" bushy red beard flowed to his waist, and he wore an odd-looking patchwork cloak in ugly shades of brown, rust, beige, white, and black. Beneath it, his tunic was gray. As he came toward us, a breeze whispered through the forest.

When he was about six feet away from us, Rhudda Gawr stopped. The breeze stopped with him. I could hear it, but I couldn't feel the air move or see the leaves stirring. Strange.

"Put away your dagger, Vic," Dad said. "He won't attack now."

"I'll put away my dagger when he puts down that bow." I could see the feathered ends of arrows sticking up from a quiver he wore on his back. "I'm not going to stand here and play bull's-eye for an almost-giant with lousy fashion sense."

The breeze picked up, but I still couldn't feel it. Rhudda scowled, his face twisting into a hideous pattern of sharp lines. Then he laughed and leaned his bow against a tree.

"'Tis a female!" he exclaimed. "With that shorn head, I thought it was a boy."

He almost got a blade in the gut for that remark. But since he'd put down his bow, I sheathed my knife.

"My hairstyle is none of your business," I said. Okay, it was a lame reply, and I bit my tongue as soon as I said it. But my hair was a touchy subject.

"Just as my—what did you call it?—my 'fashion sense' is none of yours." Rhudda turned to my father. His cape flared with the movement. The sound of the breeze I couldn't feel rose and fell. "The *lady* cares not for my cloak. Perhaps she'll alter her opinion after I've added your beard to it."

As soon as he mentioned Dad's beard, I remembered Rhudda Gawr's story. Back in the days of King Arthur, Rhudda had lived on Mount Snowdon in North Wales. When he was victorious in battle, he took his opponent's beard as a trophy. He won so many beards he had them made into a cloak.

I looked at that garment more closely. It fell from Rhudda's shoulders to his ankles, and it seemed to move and tremble on its own. *Oh, God.* Each beard in the cloak had its mouth attached.

The mouths moved constantly, whispering. It wasn't a breeze I'd heard. It was dozens of detached mouths, all speaking voicelessly.

Rhudda's eyes glowed. "They are compelled to tell and retell the tale of their defeat," he explained. "This garment is not merely a cloak of beards; it is a cloak of stories. Stories of my victories. Wearing it keeps me in mind of my power."

Dad had told me that the magic arrow was Rhudda's second most prized possession. Now I knew what was number one.

"Why did you challenge my daughter? There's no honor in challenging a woman." I shot my father a glare at that, but he made a calming gesture with his hand. In a fast, low voice, he said, "Sorry, Vic. But this guy died back in the Dark Ages. I've got to use arguments he understands." He raised his voice to address the giant. "Even if you mistook her for a boy, she has no beard. Let us be on our way."

"To cross my lands, you must give tribute or answer a challenge. All know that. And I challenge whom I please. Either way, I'll have *your* beard."

"We're in a hurry here," I said. "Name your challenge so I can kick your ass and get on with my business."

Rhudda winced, then turned to my father with a sorrowful expression. "These young ones," he said. "No sense of decorum." The beards of his cloak whispered their agreement. He drew himself up to his full, not-quite-giant height and made a cutting gesture with his right arm. The beards stopped whispering. "Tonight you will accept my hospitality. In the morning, this female will meet me in an archery contest."

My heart sank. The longbow was my all-time worst weapon. I'd been a mediocre student when Mab taught me, but that had been years ago, and I hadn't picked up a bow since. Why would I when a gun was so much more efficient? Not to mention the fact that Rhudda owned a magic arrow—one that never missed its target—and I didn't think he'd let me use it. There was no way I could win.

"Three shots apiece," Rhudda continued. "If she wins, I will grant you safe passage through my lands. *When* she loses, however, I will claim your beard," he pointed at my father, "and a pottle of her blood to fill my mug."

A pottle? What the hell was a pottle? More blood than I could do without, I'd bet.

"So that's why you challenged my daughter and not me." Dad's forehead furrowed with anger.

Rhudda licked his lips. "Clay-born. I could smell her blood a furlong away. Physical blood, not this magic stuff that runs through our veins. Do you know how long it's been since I've tasted clay-born blood?" He leered at me, showing sharp, yellow teeth. Then he returned to my father. "Do you accept my challenge?"

Dad threw back his shoulders. "We accept."

"Wait, hang on. You're challenging me, not my father. I speak for myself." The giant's eyebrow cocked, and again the beards fell silent.

I sized him up, my fingers twitching for my weapons. I could take this guy. Throw the dagger to surprise him, and then run him through with my sword before he even thought to reach for his longbow.

"What if I refuse?" I asked, half a second away from hurling the dagger.

The giant's mouth quirked upward. Six archers stepped forward from the forest, like ghosts materializing from the fog. All were dressed in green, and all had crossbows, aimed and ready to shoot.

One giant I could take. One giant plus six archers with drawn bows—the equation wasn't looking so good anymore.

At least I could try to sweeten the deal. "You offer a poor bargain, giant. If you win, you demand our disfigurement and death. Yet if I win, you promise nothing more than safe passage, which costs you nothing. If I'm to risk everything, for both my father and myself, you must put up more on your side."

Rhudda grinned. The bastard was enjoying this. "And what would you have me wager?"

"One item from your armory. My choice." The odds were against me—*way* against me—but if I had to accept this giant's challenge, there might as well be something in it for me. And there was only one thing I wanted from Rhudda, other than to be left the hell alone: his magic arrow.

An archery contest with a giant who owned a can't-miss arrow. I was so screwed.

Rhudda threw back his head and laughed. The beards of his cloak laughed with him as he clutched his stomach and bent over in mirth. Even the steely-eyed archer aiming his crossbow at my throat cracked a smile. Glad I was so entertaining.

The giant straightened, wiping away the tears of laughter with the back of his hand. "Done!" he shouted. He gestured to two of the archers. "Go to my castle and have chambers prepared for our guests. And make ready the archery range for tomorrow's contest with—" He squinted at me. "What is the name of this strange female who has accepted my challenge?"

"Victory."

This set off another explosion of laughter. Rhudda picked up his longbow and hefted it. When he turned back to me, his face was serious, as hard and cold as marble.

"Victory, eh? Not for long—I promise you that. Not for long."

AFTER I ACCEPTED HIS CHALLENGE, RHUDDA MORPHED INTO a considerate host. Well, if you could overlook the cloak of whispering beards that he never seemed to take off. Those beards served as a constant reminder of the giant's hostile intent as he showed us our comfortable rooms and offered refreshment. I knew enough to turn down the offer of food. Dad wasn't interested, either.

Rhudda's castle was straight out of a fairy tale. Made of shimmering white stone, it boasted more turrets and towers than you could count. Thick walls and a moat enclosed an entire village of thatched-roof shops and houses. My room was high up in a tall, thin tower in the main building. The tiny window overlooked the village. There was a four-poster bed and an elaborately carved wooden chest. A tapestry depicting jousting knights hung on the wall.

"You are free to move about the castle and grounds. Of course, I'm sure I don't have to remind you that if you try to go beyond the outer ramparts, you may expect an arrow between your shoulder blades."

Shoulder blades, whispered all the beards in unison. The eerie half-sound made me shiver.

"There will be a feast in your honor this evening." He eyed my tunic and leggings. "You'll find that chest full of more suitable attire. Is there anything else you require?"

"Yes. I need to see the archery range. And while I'm there I'll need a longbow and a quiver of arrows."

Rhudda inclined his head. "Certainly. I'll have one of my men show you the way." He shouted through the doorway, "Where are my servants? Why is no one attending me?"

Ratlike scurrying sounded in the stairwell, and two men hurried into the room. Both bowed low before Rhudda. "Lazy dolts!" he shouted, and brought down his fists on the backs of their heads. The men sprawled on the floor, facedown. One, then the other, slowly pushed himself onto his hands and knees. Dad offered his hand to help the man nearest to him. The man looked up, and Dad gasped. I followed his gaze. A gasp escaped my lips, too.

The servant had only half a face. Everything below his nose was missing—no skin, no lips, nothing but the yellowed bone of his skull.

The other servant was the same.

"And so you see two of my vanquished foes!" Rhudda chortled. "Both were kings once, weren't you, lads? Both donated their beards to my cloak. Let me see. Here is the beard of Nyniaw." He flicked his finger against a coal-black patch near the cloak's collar. Immediately that beard's whispering rose above the others.

Many years ago in the land of Glywysing lived a king called Nyniaw. None could withstand him when he wielded his sword, or so the arrogant king believed . . .

"And this one"—Rhudda twisted around and brought forward a blondish patch from the back of the cloak—"once adorned the face of Peibiaw."

He pinched the blond beard, and its whispers came forth.

Peibiaw, son of Erb, once ruled the kingdom of Ergyng. Although brave in battle, he was a greedy and foolish man . . .

The two stories twined around each other, tangling their words so that I couldn't make out what either was saying.

The beards' former owners stood silent, hands folded in front of them. A tear traced a line down Nyniaw's upper cheek, then hung from the ridge where his skin ended.

Dad spread a hand protectively over his own beard. Above it, his wide eyes bulged from his ashen face.

Rhudda flung the blond patch back over his shoulder and shook out the cape. Other voices rose up around him in a sibilant cocoon.

"Listen well, Sir Evan," he said to my father. "Soon your voice will join the others, relating step-by-step how your daughter failed you both. After I've won the archery contest, I will drain her blood. Then I will have your beard. And I will hear, over and over, all the delightful details." Rhudda cocked his head and looked at Dad critically. "It is a scrawny beard, but it will do, I think, to patch a worn spot near the hem."

He waved a hand, dismissing us, and turned to his servants. "You, Nyniaw, take our guests to the target range." The first servant bowed low. "Peibiaw, fetch several bows so that Lady . . . Victory"—he rolled his eyes like a bratty teenager—"may choose one to her liking. And an ample supply of arrows as well. Deliver them to the range."

The second servant also bowed. Then he turned and scurried down the spiral stairs.

"It would amuse me to watch you practice, but there are things I must attend to. I'll see you both at supper." He turned abruptly and went out the door. His cape whirled around him, whispers swelling. Then he was gone. My father stared after him, looking like someone who'd just seen the star he was wishing on burn out.

I WAS FURIOUS WITH MY FATHER AS WE FOLLOWED NYNIAW, the beardless former king, to the archery range. "Shortcut? You took us straight through Rhudda's lands. You *knew* he'd challenge us."

Dad sheepishly stroked his beard. "It is a shortcut. I knew you needed the arrow, and I figured we could get it on the way."

"I'm here to stop Pryce. Everything else is secondary."

"We would have had to rest somewhere for the night. If we get out of here tomorrow morning, we'll make it to Tywyll in good time. Don't worry about that." Like I didn't have a million other things to worry about now.

Dad fingered his chin as though making sure his beard was still there. "I expected Rhudda to challenge me. I've gotten pretty good with a longbow."

" 'Pretty good with a longbow' can't beat a magic arrow, Dad." Besides, I'd seen Rhudda's skill when he'd shot at me in the forest. Even without the magic arrow, Rhudda was miles past "pretty good."

"I'm sorry, Vic. But let's not worry about that now. Let's get practicing."

Rhudda's shooting range was in an amphitheater that stood inside the ramparts on the castle grounds' western side. (At least,

Dad said it was the western side. With no sun to orient me, I couldn't tell one direction from another.) I stood on the grass, peering at a target a hundred yards away. One hundred yards. Three hundred feet. That would be the length of a football field. I could barely see the target, let alone aim at it.

Rhudda's servant Peibiaw stood beside me, holding several longbows. The smallest was six feet high and must have weighed forty pounds. "That one," I said. I hefted the bow, took its grip in my bow hand, and pulled back hard on the string. The bow bent slightly under the pressure. I let go of the string, listened to its snap and thwang. Well, I'd give it a try. I took an arrow from the quiver beside me and nocked it in the bow. I drew, feeling the strain in my arm and back as I held the heavy bow as steady as I could.

Aiming was hard. The air was still, so at least there was no wind to blow my arrows off course. Tomorrow, who knew? With my luck, a tornado would snatch up my arrow and drop it in Oz. *Focus, Vicky.* I returned my attention to the target. At this distance, I knew I needed to aim high to account for the arc of the arrow's flight. But how high? I took a guess, and then moved my point of aim slightly to account for shooting right-handed. I drew, double-checked my aim, and loosed the arrow.

It sailed over the target and bounced off the stone wall behind it. Even from a hundred yards away, I could see my shot was a total miss.

Peibiaw stared toward the target with stony eyes. At least he wasn't laughing. Or maybe he was—how would I know? But something told me Rhudda's servants didn't laugh much.

"Here, Vic," said Dad. "Fix your stance. Feet shoulder-width apart, and balance your weight equally between them. You were leaning on the right. Don't line up your body with the target; align with your point of aim." His hands gripped my shoulders as he turned me slightly to the right. "Hold the bow so its balance point presses against the pad at the bottom of your thumb." He adjusted the bow in my hand. "There. Try now. And this time don't aim quite so high."

I drew, then let the arrow go. This one flew over the target, too, although I thought the fletching might have brushed its edge. Maybe. It was hard to tell from this distance.

"Let me try," Dad said. "Just to get a feel for it."

I gave him my bow. He nocked an arrow and let it fly. Peibiaw handed me a spyglass so I could assess the hit. Dad's arrow was in the black, three rings away from the gold at the target's center. His next shot landed in the red, right at its border with the gold. Dad was better than pretty good.

"Okay," he said. "Now I can coach you better. When you aim—"

"Why am I even doing this? You're a way better archer than I'll ever be. You have a chance to win this contest. I'll screw everything up for both of us."

"Rhudda would never accept me as a substitute. He wants to win, and he thinks you're the weaker of the two of us." Dad rested a hand on my shoulder. "He's underestimating you, Vic. Let's show him by how much."

I nodded and nocked another arrow.

I DON'T KNOW HOW LONG I PRACTICED, BUT BY THE TIME I quit, my bow arm was trembling and my shoulder and back ached. Grooves were worn deep into the fingers of my drawing hand. I was managing to hit the target consistently, but out of dozens and dozens of shots, only two arrows had hit the gold.

To have a chance, I needed to hit that gold circle each and every time.

I was in my chamber, getting dressed for Rhudda's stupid banquet. I threw open the chest and pulled out an armful of dresses, then tossed them on the bed. Half the pile slithered to the floor. Long, medieval-style silk gowns in a garden of colors. I didn't want to wear any of them. I didn't want to be here.

There was no way I could win this contest. I might as well open a vein now, fill up Rhudda's mug, and spare myself the humiliation.

"Sure, you could do that. And condemn your father to pain, disfigurement, and an eternity of humiliating, silent servitude." Butterfly buzzed around my head.

"Shut up, Butterfly." I looked around for something I could use as a flyswatter.

"Whatever happens, you'll fail. Your father is counting on you, but you'll let him down. Again."

There, in the chest, was a satin shoe with a jeweled buckle. That could work. I stood, holding the shoe behind my back, and located the Eidolon where it perched, black wings pulsing, on the bed frame.

Slam!

I checked the bottom of the shoe. Nothing. Then a slash of pain as Butterfly's fangs took a chunk out of the back of my neck. I slapped the spot, only to bruise myself with the stupid shoe.

"Butterflies don't move that fast," I griped, dropping the shoe back into the chest. "They flit. They flutter. What they *don't* do is rocket. Anyway, this situation isn't my fault. I didn't challenge Rhudda. He challenged me, and gave me no choice but to accept."

"Of course it's your fault. It's always your fault—haven't you realized that yet? Take a step back. Your father wouldn't even be in the Darklands if it weren't for you."

"Shut up."

"And Pryce wouldn't be here either if you'd gotten it right at the Devil's Coffin."

"I said, shut up."

"And—"

A knock sounded on the door. Butterfly soared up to the ceiling and dive-bombed me, slamming back inside my gut.

Damn, that hurt.

Half bent over and clutching my abdomen, I hobbled to the door. I couldn't get a breath to ask who was there, so I pulled it open.

Dad strode into the room, looking like a medieval nobleman on his way to a banquet. He wore a burgundy velvet tunic and royal blue leggings, along with a short cape made of a rich brocade—but no beards. In the two seconds since I opened the door, the colors darkened. The magic was turning them black.

"You're not dressed yet? Hurry up, Vic, we don't want to keep Rhudda waiting."

"We don't? What I want is to get the hell out of here and keep that damn giant waiting forever." I kicked at the pile of silks by the bed. "I'm not dressing up. I don't see why I should sit at a table loaded with food I can't eat just so that stupid giant can taunt us." I grabbed my father's hand. "Dad, what if I shifted? I've been thinking about it. We could go back to the archery range, where there's room. I'll change into a pterodactyl and carry you over the wall and—"

Dad's expression cut me off, and my hopes of escape faded. "It wouldn't work here. The magic is wrong. Out in the Ordinary, you shift by building up energy until it blasts out and forces the change. Remember what I said about magic being substance here? I could work with that magic to change my form—any shade can—but it's a difficult process and the results are unstable. The magic wants to shape itself to our spiritual energy, our personality, really. That's why shades look like they did in the Ordinary."

Scratch that idea. I hadn't held much hope for it, anyway. In the Black, I'd tried to shift into a bird and failed. No reason it would work deeper inside the Darklands.

"We *need* to be at Rhudda's feast, Vic. Our best chance at surviving is to exploit his arrogance. Think about it. The guy surrounds himself with his vanquished foes. He constantly wears a cloak that never stops telling him how great and powerful and mighty he is. If there's a formula for hubris, that's got to be it."

He picked up a gown from the pile and inspected it. He tossed it aside and chose another. This one was emerald green with gold accents; it had a slim cut and bell sleeves. He held it out to me.

"Humor him, Vic. If Rhudda is going to make a mistake, he'll make it through overconfidence. Our task is to inflate that overconfidence—"

"Until it blows up in his ugly face." It was worth a try, I supposed. Sighing, I took the gown, and Dad went to wait outside while I put it on. His own outfit was completely black now.

Inflate Rhudda's overconfidence. Sharp butterfly wings sawed at my gut as I pictured the arrows that had littered the ground around my target. *Yeah, I was good at that.*

23

RHUDDA'S MASSIVE BANQUET HALL WAS AT LEAST AS BIG AS his archery range, big enough for a couple of pro football teams to start up an impromptu game. The walls were hung with twenty-foot-tall tapestries depicting—what else?—scenes from Rhudda's life. Tables were positioned around the walls, and servants scurried back and forth carrying platters of food and pitchers of ale. In the center, acrobats and jugglers performed, and dogs fought each other for bones tossed by the diners. At the far end of the hall, a long table perched on a platform. Rhudda sat in the middle, parked on a gilded throne. Hubris, definitely. The guy was swimming in it.

"Another pottle of ale!" shouted Rhudda. He waved a huge mug that looked like it held at least half a gallon. So that was a pottle. Tomorrow it would be filled to the rim with my blood.

I made my way across the room, tripping over the hem of my now-white dress. I was required to sit at the high table, but I took the farthest seat from Rhudda. I plopped myself down and propped my chin on my fist, watching everyone else eat. My stomach grumbled, and not from Butterfly's constant irritation. I was hungry, and the food smelled good. Worse, I was thirsty. It felt like my tongue and throat were coated with sand.

I'd steeled myself to make it through this journey without food or drink. But part of me thought, "Why the hell not?" I wasn't going to become an expert archer overnight. After I lost tomorrow, Rhudda would drain my blood into his huge mug, and my physical body would die. I'd be stuck in the Darklands—until it was time for my spirit to be recycled into a new body.

A servant set down a platter of potatoes fried with onions, still sizzling hot, right in front of me. Their scent made my stomach rumble again. No one else reached for the golden-brown morsels. They sat there, smelling like heaven. I pushed the plate away.

Dad, who was sitting beside our host, didn't look like he was having any trouble enjoying himself. His ale mug wasn't as big as Rhudda's, but since I'd come in he'd already drained it twice and was joining Rhudda in calling for a refill. He banged his mug on the table with one hand and threw his other arm around Rhudda's shoulders. When he saw me watching them, he waved me over.

"Hey, Vic, c'mere!" His cap sat crooked on his head, falling over one eye. Never, in all my life, had I ever seen my father drunk. Until now.

That was it. I pushed back my chair and got up to leave. Tonight, of all nights, I did not want to see Dad drunk and sloppy and yukking it up with the giant who wanted to destroy us both. I stepped down from the dais.

"Victory." The edge in my father's voice, as hard and sharp as a sword, made me stop and turn around. Dad had taken off his cockeyed cap, and his eyes burned in a face that was both sober and dead serious. He nodded, a quick, sharp gesture. Then he slapped his squashed cap back on his head and let his face relax back into slackness. He picked up his mug, sloshing ale over the side, and guffawed at something Rhudda had said.

Lifting the hem of my skirt so I wouldn't trip over the damn thing for the fifteenth time, I went over to see what he wanted.

"Ah, here's my little archer!" Dad's words ran together in a blurred stream of sound. "Vic, don't be so glum. Whatever happens tomorrow, happens. Let's enjoy ourselves while we can. Right, Rhudda?"

He slapped the giant on the back. Rhudda and one of the beards of his cloak burped simultaneously.

Rhudda eyed me critically, his look just short of a leer. "I see you found a gown that fits," he said. "It almost makes you look like a proper wench."

Wench? Did he really say "wench"? God, I was trapped in the Renaissance faire from hell.

"Now, *here's* a proper wench." Rhudda grabbed the busty woman who was trying to refill his mug and pulled her onto his lap. Ale sprayed up in a fountain as she squealed and giggled and pushed ineffectually at his arm. In the part of the cloak closest to her, lips pursed and tongues flicked out, trying to touch her. She laughed, but disgust showed in her eyes.

Rhudda let her up and swatted her ass as she bent over to pick up the flagon. She let out a hiss that sounded like pure rage to me, but the giant didn't notice. He called after her as she hurried away, promising her a place in his bed tonight. What more could a wench possibly hope for?

I stepped back to make sure I was out of reach.

"Vic," said Dad, putting a hand on my arm, "our host is in a generous mood tonight."

"Indeed, I am," belched Rhudda. "Your father is an excellent storyteller. Perhaps I'll delay clipping his beard until I've heard all he has to tell."

Was that why Dad had called me over, to let me know he was pulling a Scheherazade, fascinating his enemy with stories to extend his life? If so, he'd given up on me.

Then Rhudda roared with laughter, as though he'd just made the funniest joke ever. "There's only one story I'll be wanting to hear from that beard," he said, wiping spittle from his lips.

For a moment, Dad looked stricken, like Rhudda had punched him hard in the gut. But then he picked up his tankard and joined the giant in his laughter.

"You haven't won yet," I said.

My comment sent Rhudda into fresh fits of laughter. He leaned over, pounding the table, as his beard straggled into his food. For one happy moment, I thought he was choking. But that's not how my luck was running.

"I have, I have," he said. "As surely as Sir Evan here has a beard . . . *now* . . . I've already won." He leaned back. "Two of my archers spied on your practice. They told me what kind of competitor to expect. But even if you were the reincarnation of Robin Hood himself, you could not beat me. None can."

Dad had said that Rhudda's hubris might trip him up. As far as I could tell, it just made him annoying.

"I'm going to bed," I said. "I've got a contest to win in the morning."

"Oho!" shouted Rhudda, shaking my dad's arm. "Did you hear that, Sir Evan? Mark it well, mark it well. I'll want that line in your story of this damsel's defeat."

Laughter roared up and down the high table as I left the hall.

Back in my chamber, I lay in the four-poster bed, eyes wide open and staring at the ceiling. My body was tired—exhausted, really—but I couldn't fall asleep in that Darklands half-light that never seemed to change. I closed my eyes. The moment I did, Butterfly tore its way out of my gut and flitted around my head like a mosquito. Its high-pitched mosquito whine fragmented into words and snatches of phrases.

All your fault.

You're going to lose.

Your father will suffer again.

Your fault.

Disfigurement.

Death.

Failure.

Failure.

Failure.

I buried my head under the pillow to drown out the buzzing, but it was like Butterfly was inside my brain. The sound made me want to scream. I sat up, throwing the pillow across the room.

"Butterfly!"

The air around my head stilled into blessed silence.

Then an aggrieved voice piped up from the foot of the bed. "What?"

"You know what's happening tomorrow, right?" Of course it did. An Eidolon has full access to its host's thoughts.

"Yeah, an archery contest. So what?"

"You keep telling me I'm going to lose. What if I do?"

"That giant gets to drink your blood."

"Right. He'll drain so much blood from my body that I'll die. I'll become a shade in the Darklands, like everyone else here."

"Die? Um, excuse me but did you say *die*? But . . . but what about me?"

"Exactly, Butterfly. What about you?"

"I can't believe it. That is *so* like you. Getting into a situation without thinking about how it will affect anyone else. If you die, I'll fade."

"Yup. Right back into the demonic ether. You'll lose consciousness, your personality—"

"My demonality."

"Whatever. The point is, if I die, you die."

"Well, then, don't die."

"If I don't get some sleep, I won't have a snowball's chance in hell of winning."

"We get snow."

"What?"

"In Hell. Uffern, whatever you want to call it. It's not all lakes of fire and crap like that. It gets cold there. At certain times of the year, a snowball would do just fine in Hell."

"You're missing the point."

"I *get* the point. I'm not stupid, you know. If you weren't so self-centered, you'd realize that." Butterfly took to the air and landed on my stomach. "Okay. I'll let you sleep tonight. But keep in mind that you're forcing me to go without a meal. A poor, hungry demon who—"

"Suck it up, Butterfly. I can't eat while I'm in the Darklands. You can fast for one night. You're looking a little tubby, anyway."

"Tubby," Butterfly muttered. "Talk about adding insult to injury . . . Well, can you at least think about the werewolf for a minute or two? Let me have a little bedtime snack?"

"No." I was not going to feel guilty about Kane. Even though I'd handled it badly, letting him go so he was free to mate with Simone was the right thing to do. My feelings at losing him were my own, a private grief, not a snack for an Eidolon. In my mind, in my heart, I built a wall around them. I'd face those feelings another day—if I managed to make it through tomorrow.

Butterfly grumbled some more, then sank back into me. I felt a couple of twinges in my intestines, and then the Eidolon quieted down.

Peace. Wonderful tranquility.

My aching, exhausted body relinquished its tension, and within a minute I slept.

* * *

IN SLEEP, I TRIED TO CALL MAB ON THE DREAM PHONE. I PIC-
tured her, as clearly as if she sat beside my bed. I brought up
her colors. But the blue and silver rolled endlessly through
my dreamscape. The mists didn't part. My aunt didn't step
through.

I wasn't surprised. For years after Dad's death, I'd attempted
to contact him in my dreams. He never answered. The boundary
between the Ordinary and the Darklands didn't let calls through.
It kept the living and the dead separate, isolated from each other,
each within their own realm.

Mab would be furious that I'd ignored her warning to stay
out of the Darklands. Trapped in a hostile giant's castle, I had
to admit she was probably right. Still, I would have happily
endured the sternest of lectures to hear her thoughts on how to
get out of here, do what I needed to do, and get home.

BAM! BAM! BAM! BAM!

I rolled out of bed and staggered to the door. Some half-faced
servant of Rhudda stood outside. He nodded to me, then turned
and descended the stairs.

I rubbed the sleep from my eyes. I didn't know how long I'd
slept—I still couldn't get used to how time passed in the
Darklands—but now that I was vertical I felt refreshed. Soreness
lingered in my arms and back, but I got out of bed and did some
stretches to loosen up.

As I stretched, got dressed in my tunic, and headed to the
archery range, I actually felt good. Not a peep from Butterfly.
Maybe the demon had snuck away during the night in search of
a new host.

Spectators filled the amphitheater, packing the tiers of seats
so tightly the shades practically sat on top of each other. More
hubris. I'm sure Rhudda thought it would make a better story for
a huge audience to witness my defeat.

But I wasn't going to think in terms of defeat. My father and
I were going to leave this castle together, whole and unharmed.
I'd decided on a plan. As soon as I'd nocked my first arrow, I'd
use it to shoot Rhudda through the eye. Shades could die, too,

and an arrow shot from a longbow at close range should do the trick. Dad and I would escape in the confusion.

Except, I realized with a sinking heart, Rhudda had made escape impossible. He'd stationed his six crossbow archers around the amphitheater. There wasn't a square inch of ground outside their range. If I shot Rhudda, two or three arrows would pierce my heart before his body hit the ground.

Damn. No wonder even Butterfly had abandoned me.

I was the first contestant on the field. I expected to find Dad there to assist me, but he was nowhere in sight. Another abandonment? I didn't think my father would do that to me, but after assessing my dismal archery skills, he obviously figured his best chance was to suck up to Rhudda. I sighed, and picked up my bow.

There was a commotion near one of the entrances, and I saw why Dad hadn't been waiting for me. Four of Rhudda's mutilated servants pulled a wagon into the field. The top of the wagon was a cage of thick iron bars. Inside the cage stood my father.

Anger burned through my blood as they pulled the wagon in a circle around the perimeter of the field, displaying my father to the crowd. Dad gripped the bars but kept his gaze on the ground. Jeers and catcalls followed him. More than ever, I wanted to kill Rhudda. I wanted to put him in that cage and let his cloak of beards chew him down to the skeleton.

The servants stationed the wagon about twenty feet away from me. I waved to Dad, but he didn't look up.

Trumpets blared, and Rhudda came onto the field. The crowd cheered. He stopped, raised both arms over his head, and turned in a slow circle, accepting their adulation. He bowed—once, twice, three times. Then he walked over to me, his hand extended.

I wanted to crush his fingers, force him to his knees, and then stomp on his head. But I accepted his hand and we shook. Up close, Rhudda didn't look so hot. His bloodshot eyes were as red as a zombie's, and his face drooped with tiredness.

Some functionary strode to the middle of the field and raised his hand. This guy had his entire face. When the crowd grew quiet, he read the contest's rules: three arrows apiece, each shot assigned a score according to the ring it hit on the target. After we'd each taken three shots, the archer with the highest score would be the winner. A coin toss would determine who'd go first.

The coin chose me. I hefted my bow. A slight breeze blew

against my arm—good. Yesterday my shots had tended to fly too far to the left. The breeze would help correct that.

I took my stance, darting a look toward my father. He was watching me now, and he gave me a thumbs-up. I chose an arrow and nocked it in the bow. Aim, draw, check—take a deep breath—and loose the bowstring.

The arrow rose in a perfect arc. The breeze pushed it a little. It hit the target, and I grabbed the spyglass to see how I'd done. The arrow jutted from the red ring, inches above the bull's-eye.

"Eight!" declared the scorekeeper.

"That's my girl!" Dad called.

Eight was good. Eight was way better than I'd started out yesterday. But ten was the top score. I'd have to do better.

Scanty applause stuttered around the amphitheater, then dwindled to silence. Rhudda picked up his bow and lifted it over his head. Spectators jumped to their feet, screaming themselves hoarse.

Gee, I wonder who they expected to win.

Rhudda made a big show of selecting an arrow. His quiver held four to my three. Of his arrows, three had black fletching. The feathers of the fourth arrow were bloodred.

Shit. The red one must be his magic arrow. Rhudda expected to win, but he was also prepared to cheat.

Uneasiness stirred in my gut. "Settle down, Butterfly," I hissed. "I need to concentrate." The feeling drained away.

The giant nocked his arrow. The crowd was silent, every person leaning forward. Rhudda aimed, adjusted his stance, and aimed again. What a ham. But when he lowered his bow and roared for a servant to mop his brow, I began to wonder. Rhudda really looked bad. Could shades get sick—or hungover? I glanced at Dad, who gripped the bars of his cage. His mouth was a thin, grim line as he watched the giant.

Rhudda drew his bowstring with a trembling hand. He let the arrow fly. I trained the spyglass on the target to see where it would strike.

Red. Rhudda's arrow had also hit the red, below and to the right of the bull's-eye.

"Eight!" shouted the scorekeeper. The crowd burst into tumultuous applause. My shot had been better, but then I didn't own the castle where they had to live. And all that mattered was the score. Right now, that score was tied.

Rhudda bowed, but I could hear him muttering curses as he

did. He shot me an evil glance that, if it had been an arrow, would have pierced my heart and poisoned me besides. But a look isn't an arrow, and this contest wasn't over yet.

I took my stance and nocked my second arrow. The first had hit above the bull's-eye, so I adjusted my point of aim to compensate. I held my breath as I drew and released.

"Nine!" The score rang across the field before I could focus the spyglass. *There.* The arrow stood in the outer gold, close to the bull's-eye, but not close enough for ten full points.

This time, the applause lasted a few seconds longer. The contest was getting interesting.

Rhudda bent over his quiver. He touched the arrow with red fletching, then picked one of the black-feathered arrows. He stood. Peibiaw wiped a handkerchief across the giant's sweaty forehead; Rhudda shoved him away so hard the servant landed on his ass, handkerchief waving like a white flag.

Rhudda positioned his arrow, aimed, and shot. *Thwack!*

The silence was so absolute, I thought I could hear the arrow vibrating in the target. I pointed the spyglass. Rhudda had hit the border between red and blue.

The scorekeeper's head blocked my view as he bent over the target. I lowered the spyglass and waited for the score.

"Seven." The word was hushed. The resonance had drained from the scorekeeper's voice, replaced by dread. I didn't envy the guy if his master lost.

And Rhudda might lose. The score was seventeen to fifteen; I was up by two points.

No applause. The audience didn't know what to do. A murmur buzzed around the stands. Then a voice shouted, "Hail, Rhudda Gawr!" and others took up the cheer.

Rhudda didn't react. He watched me like he was figuring out how to throw off my aim with his stare.

If only I could get that magic arrow. I'd score a ten, making my final score twenty-seven and putting victory out of the giant's reach. But I was in full view of everyone in the amphitheater, not to mention the guards with crossbows. I couldn't exactly walk over, pluck the red-feathered arrow from Rhudda's quiver, and fit it into my own bow.

Still, if I could score a ten—or even another nine—I could win this.

I prepared my final shot. In my peripheral vision, I saw

Rhudda take several steps toward me. He turned his back to me and waved to the crowd.

Ignore him. I focused on my point of aim and drew.

The moment I released the arrow, Rhudda spread his cape. In unison, its dozens of mouths blew out. It created enough of a breeze to nudge my arrow off its trajectory. The arrow landed in the blue.

"Six!" shouted the overjoyed scorekeeper. A few halfhearted claps sounded from the stands.

My final score was a mere twenty-three. Rhudda now needed only nine points to win.

"Unfair!" shouted a man's voice from a top-level seat.

Rhudda pointed a meaty finger in the direction of the voice. An archer fired, and a man in a brown tunic fell back. He slumped against the stone wall, a crossbow bolt sticking out of his chest. A woman's scream rose, then cut itself off. Rhudda stepped forward and raised his arms. Silence. He lowered his arms and clapped his hands together. Slowly, deliberately: *One, two, three.* He pointed in a wide circle to indicate the audience had better start clapping too, and right this minute. They did, but tepidly. He gestured angrily, and the applause increased. But it didn't crescendo to its previous level.

Rhudda stalked to his equipment. He grabbed his bow and, smirking at me, yanked the red-feathered arrow from his quiver. He nocked the arrow and aimed. He shook his head and blinked. He lowered the bow and wiped a hand across his eyes. Then, in one single fluid motion, he raised his bow and took his shot.

The arrow sped toward the target. Then it turned and—that couldn't be right. I raised the spyglass.

Rhudda's magic arrow had hit the target dead center. A bull's-eye. But not on his target. He'd hit mine.

The scorekeeper fainted.

The crowd went nuts.

"Treachery!" roared Rhudda. He plucked the last remaining arrow from his quiver and aimed his bow at me.

Pain tore through my belly. I thought I'd been hit, but when I looked there was no wound. Rhudda roared again. He was dancing like his feet were on fire, swatting the air around his head. The arrow had fallen from his bow; he stepped on it and broke it in two with a snap.

I ran over and tackled the giant, coming in low and hitting

his knees. He fell like a redwood and landed facedown. I scrambled to my feet. "To your right!" a voice shouted from the stands.

A sword lay on the ground where someone has tossed it onto the field. I snatched it up. Rhudda had rolled over onto his back. Both hands beat the air around his head.

"Stop!" I commanded. I put one foot on his chest and pressed the sword point against his throat. He quit batting the air and lay motionless.

An insect alighted on his nose, wings twitching. It was a black butterfly. One with sharp, oversized teeth.

"Nice work, Butterfly," I said.

"Huh," the demon answered. "*Somebody* had to get your sorry ass out of this mess. And if anyone deserves to feel the bite of guilt, it's this clown." He unhinged his jaw and chomped Rhudda's nose. The giant yelped but didn't move. Then Butterfly took to the air, landed on my tunic, and disappeared.

What a screw-up—you nearly got yourself killed. The thought blasted through my brain of its own accord, and I knew Butterfly had settled back in.

I shoved all self-critical thoughts aside and turned my attention to the groaning giant pinned by my sword. Something was different. Rhudda glared at me with undisguised hatred—nothing new there. Then I realized what had changed. Silence. His cloak had stopped whispering. Each and every bearded mouth was still.

"Attention, please!" Someone—I think it was Nyniaw—had revived the scorekeeper. He stood, leaning on the servant, and called out something unintelligible in a weak voice. He coughed into his hand and tried again.

"The final score," he said, his voice building in strength with each word, "is twenty-three points to Lady Victory, and"—he stopped and cleared his throat—"um, fifteen to Rhudda Gawr. The day goes to Lady Victory!" Applause, whistles, and shouts came from the stands. When they faded, the scorekeeper continued: "According to the agreed-upon terms of the challenge, Rhudda guarantees Lady Victory and Sir Evan safe conduct through his realm." Someone let my father out of the cage. He jumped down from the wagon and ran across the field. I wanted to hug him, but I had both hands on the sword. He put an arm around my shoulders and squeezed.

"Nice shooting, Vic. I knew you could do it."

"In addition, Rhudda grants the winner one item of her choice from his armory."

I needed Rhudda's magic arrow to give to the Night Hag. But was the red-fletched arrow the right one? It couldn't be. The magic arrow never missed. This one had gone out of its way to hit the wrong target.

"I know which arrow you want," said Dad, as though reading my mind. "I'll get it for you." He trotted down the length of the field, pulled the red-fletched arrow from the target, and held it aloft. The audience cheered as he carried it back to me. He waved it over Rhudda's face.

"It's ours now, Rhudda," he said.

"No! You cheated! I know you did!"

"Why, because you tried to cheat, yourself? You lost, Rhudda. Admit it."

"I will never admit it!"

The scorekeeper raised a hand, and everyone stilled. "Lady Victory has won and claimed her prize. I now declare this challenge complete."

Rhudda closed his eyes and groaned.

"You can let him up now," the scorekeeper said, coming over. "His own archers are now sworn to protect you for as long as you're in his realm. If he tries to hurt you, they'll kill him."

"Is that true?"

I lifted the sword from Rhudda's throat, holding the blade ready as I stepped back. But the giant made no move to get up. He rolled over onto his side and covered his head, moaning. "Be quiet!" he sobbed. "Please, please stop."

We stared at the prone giant. There was a change in the air, like a breeze had started up. The beards were whispering. But the sound wasn't the confused mixture of dozens of stories I'd heard when I first encountered Rhudda. All the mouths whispered in unison. *Once there was a cruel and foolish giant named Rhudda Gawr. Rhudda was arrogant, filled with hubris. One day he challenged Lady Victory to an archery contest . . .*

Rhudda groaned again and covered his ears. His cloak of beards had changed its story. Now, every single mouth whispered the tale of his defeat.

24

"I STILL THINK YOU SHOULD HAVE TAKEN HIS BEARD, VIC.
After all, you earned it." Dad stroked his own beard fondly as
we walked. Once again, we were on the main road to Tywyll.
Four of Rhudda's archers had accompanied us to the edge of the
giant's land. I half-expected them to nail us with crossbow bolts
as soon as we crossed the border, but they'd saluted us and then
melted back into the forest.

"Eww, Dad. What would I do with a mangy red beard? Make
a purse out of it?" I shuddered at the thought of sticking my hand
into Rhudda's mouth every time I needed a quarter. *Yuck*.
"Besides, that's one story I don't need to hear again." I'd been
scared. It was a feeling I didn't like, and I saw no need to be
reminded of it.

"It wouldn't tell the right story, anyway. Rhudda has no clue
what happened."

"Neither do I. Care to enlighten me?"

He faked a surprised look. "You just said you didn't want to
hear it."

"Not Rhudda's version. The real story. I did okay in the contest, but what happened at the end?" I pulled the arrow I'd won

from my belt and examined it. It was long and straight and fletched with bloodred feathers. And it had missed its target by a mile. "This *is* Rhudda's magic arrow, right?"

"It is."

"The one that never misses its target?"

"That's right." Dad suppressed a smile as he nodded.

"Okay, so how did the arrow-that-never-misses score a bull's-eye on the wrong target?"

"I know you can figure out that one, Vic."

It was the voice he'd used when I was in high school, quizzing me to help me prepare for a test. The voice that said he wasn't going to tell me the answer until I'd at least tried.

I thought. "It *wasn't* the wrong target."

"That's my girl!" Dad's smile burst into a full-blown grin. "Remember what I said about exploiting his hubris? Worked like a charm. My plan was two-pronged. First, get Rhudda so drunk that he'd still be seeing double in the morning."

"You were pretty deep in your cups yourself."

"You thought so?" He looked pleased. "I wasn't sure how convincing I was. But after Rhudda got drunk enough, that didn't matter so much." He shook his head. "I wasn't drunk, Vic. I had an arrangement with Clarimonde."

"Who?"

"The woman who served the ale." Ah, the proper wench. "She watered mine way down—there was hardly any ale in it at all." Probably tasted like the lite beer I drank at Creature Comforts. I smacked my lips; I was still thirsty. "Poor Clarimonde," Dad said. "When Rhudda was falling-down drunk, she helped him to his chamber, then went inside with him and closed the door. She had a flagon of wine with her, so I hope he passed out before he could assault her." I shuddered and hoped so, too. I hoped the proper wench had given him a proper kick where he'd feel it. "Clarimonde did that so I could slip out to the archery range and accomplish the second part of the plan."

"You switched the targets."

"Rhudda cheats with those, too. Although they look the same from a hundred yards away, the high-scoring rings on his target are slightly wider than the standard, the rings on his opponent's slightly narrower. So equally good shots give Rhudda a higher score."

Oh. Maybe my shots hadn't been as good as I thought. Well, so what? It wasn't like I hoped to make the Olympic archery team. "Go on."

"After I switched the targets, I went back to my room. About two minutes later, some of Rhudda's men burst in. They dragged me off to that damn wagon and locked me in. That's where I spent the night." He grunted. "Damned uncomfortable it was, too. I think Rhudda suspected I might try something, but his men were too late."

I could see now how Dad's plan had played out at the contest. For the first two arrows, the nonmagical ones, Rhudda's aim had been off, thanks to a giant-sized hangover and the target's narrowed rings. In the third round, the magic arrow, aimed by will and not by sight, flew exactly where he intended it to go—striking the precise center of his target. Only "his" target was mine.

"It was a brilliant plan, Dad."

My father looked pleased. "Even if Rhudda realized what happened," he said, "in front of all those people, what could he do? Admit he'd cheated? He was either a loser or a cheater—a choice his ego couldn't stand." He spread his hands. "Hubris, Vic. It gets 'em every time."

"What do you think will happen to him?"

"Rhudda? Those whispering voices will drive him mad. He can't take the cloak off, you know. It's charmed. He had it permanently fastened around his neck centuries ago. He bragged about it to me while he was drunk. Eventually, his madness will cause the magic to mark him for reincarnation. He's lived here for a long time, but magic doesn't like the taste of insanity. So he'll go into the cauldron of rebirth—him and his cloak and probably all those whose beards he took, all together. They'll be washed clean and sent back into the Ordinary." I liked the idea that Rhudda's vanquished foes would finally get a new chance. "As for his castle," Dad continued, "once Rhudda's gone, all that will dissolve. The magic will abandon it, and the place will sink back into the land."

"And the people?"

"They were held by Rhudda's will. That's been shattered, so they're free to move on to their destinies. Most will go to Tywyll—some to reincarnate, some to regenerate—and a few will find their way to the Black and into the Beyond. It all depends on what the magic chooses for them. But all of them will be better off than they were in that place."

"Dad." I stopped and took his arm, making him stop, too. I fingered the black cloth of his sleeve. Black, the color that marked the wearer for reincarnation or regeneration—but wouldn't say which. It was too much of a chance to take. "Turn around and go back to your hideout. I can get to Tywyll from here. Let me go on alone."

"No, Vic." He slowly shook his head. "I won't do that."

"You said you didn't want to be reincarnated! If you enter the city, the cauldron will pull you in, won't it?" He didn't answer. I shook his arm. "Won't it?"

"Maybe. But maybe that's okay." He covered my hand with his. "Yesterday, when that Eidolon was trying to make you feel guilty about my death, I told you my time in that world was up. Maybe my time is up here, too. I hope it's not—not yet. I don't know if I can resist the pull of rebirth. But just like I died the best death I could that night ten years ago, I'm going to squeeze everything I can out of the time I've got left here." His face widened in a grin. "There's no way you're leaving me behind."

FOR AN HOUR (OR WHAT FELT LIKE AN HOUR), WE HAD THE road almost to ourselves. The terrain was hilly, thickly forested on both sides. Here and there, a break in the trees revealed a stone cottage with chickens scratching in a small yard. The Darklands felt like a place where not much had changed in the past dozen or so centuries, and I remarked on that to my father.

"You said time passes differently here. Is that why the Darklands never left the Middle Ages?"

"Partly. But mostly it's due to Lord Arawn. When Arthur and his men raided this realm and stole the cauldron, Arawn closed the border. That was fifteen hundred years ago. Since then, the Darklands and the Ordinary have developed separately."

"So no cars, no computers, no guns?" It would have been nice to have a rifle in my contest with Rhudda. I was good at sharpshooting.

"Shades who arrive here nowadays know about such things, of course. Some even try to create them here. But the magic won't cooperate. It won't shape itself into a television or a car." At the word *car*, his eyes lit up. "How's the Jag? You taking good care of her?"

He didn't even have to ask whether I still owned the car he'd left me in his will. "My prize possession." I hoped the biohazard team hadn't ripped out the upholstery searching for plague virus.

Dad smiled a sad, distant smile. "I miss that car."

More people were joining us now. Shades poured onto the road as the woods gave way to clusters of houses. We were getting near what passed for the suburbs of Tywyll.

A middle-aged woman in a beige dress nodded to us and said, "Good return." I smiled and said "Good return" in reply. She gave me a hard stare, scowling, then ducked her head and moved to the other side of the road.

"What did I do?"

"You wished her a good return. Here, you only say that to people who are wearing black."

Oh. Suddenly I understood the meaning of the phrase. "Good return" was a way to say *bye-bye, so long, bon voyage* to those about to be reincarnated. Maybe the woman was being polite, but I didn't like her saying that to my dad.

Everyone on the road was going in the same direction we were, toward Tywyll. Shades talked and laughed, a few sang or whistled as they walked. The mood was festive, like we were all on our way to a big party.

Two men, both dressed in dusty gray, walked close to my left elbow.

". . . thought I was leaving early enough to get a good seat," one of them was saying. "From the look of things, we'll be lucky to get into the square at all."

"Excuse me," I said, touching his arm. "What's going on?"

His head snapped around. His eyes focused on me, taking in my white clothes, and then went a little glassy. "I packed a picnic," he said, lifting a small sack. "Would you like a sandwich?"

"No, thanks." I ignored my stomach's rumble of protest. "Why are so many people going to Tywyll?"

His eyes refocused, and he smiled, probably relieved I hadn't taken his lunch. "I suppose you haven't heard, seeing as you're a clay-born visitor and all. Well, today is a sort of holiday here in the Darklands. The cauldron of transformation has been returned to us, and we're on our way to witness its purification ceremony. Lord Arawn himself will preside."

It was what I'd been afraid of. Pryce would make his move at the ceremony—I was sure of it. The ever-growing crowd surged around me. All these people. If Pryce's demons escaped, the scene in Tywyll could be as bad as my vision of demon-ravaged Boston.

We were running out of time.

The man's friend leaned forward and spoke around him. "May I offer you a piece of fruit? I've got apples and pears."

"Nope. Not hungry." My stomach called me a liar.

The men nodded and looked at Dad. "Good return," they said in unison. "I hope you'll stay with us long enough to witness the ceremony," said the man with the sandwiches. "I hear it'll be quite the spectacle." They moved ahead into the crowd.

Quite the spectacle. Somehow "spectacle" didn't come close to describing what Pryce was planning.

Dad stumbled, and I caught his arm.

"Are you all right?" He looked exhausted. And shrunken, as though he'd lost another half-inch of height. "Do you want to rest?"

"No, I'm fine." He waved away my concern. "Lack of sleep, that's all."

I studied him. He wasn't just smaller; he seemed somehow less substantial, like if somebody shone a spotlight on him, the beam would pass right through his body.

"Dad—"

He changed the subject, talking over me in his lecturer's voice. He described the city where we were headed. Tywyll, ringed by a high stone wall, was built on a hill, with narrow cobblestone lanes and crowded-together houses. "At its center is Resurrection Square, where the cauldrons are installed." His face paled a degree at the mention of the cauldrons. "Bordering one side of the square is Lord Arawn's palace. It's huge."

Although his voice was strong, our pace had slowed. Dad walked with an old man's gait. Shades passed us on both sides, like water flowing around a rock in the middle of a stream. I didn't know what to do. He wouldn't stop, wouldn't let me speak. He kept trudging along and talking, as though his voice was what made his feet move. But with each step, he looked worse.

By the time we reached Tywyll, there'd be no way he could resist the cauldrons' pull. If I'd understood how this journey would drain him, I never would have let my father come with me.

"Now, Arawn—there's someone you should know about," he

was saying. "Some believe he *is* the Darklands. That as Arawn fares, so fares the realm. He isn't merely another shade who happens to rule this place. He's a god here. He's been here forever, and he's never gone into the cauldron of regeneration. Many believe he's the source of the Darklands' magic. Oh, wait. I told you that before, didn't I?" Dad stopped. He wiped his sleeve across his forehead. "Maybe we could take a rest." He pointed at a low stone wall that bordered the road.

"Sure." I offered him my arm. He shook his head, then changed his mind and took it.

Dad sat on the wall and closed his eyes. Dark circles shadowed the hollows beneath them. His face was wet, covered with an iridescent sheen like oil. His skin was pale, thin, nearly transparent. How could he be changing so much, so fast? The whole time I'd been in the Darklands, I'd had trouble believing my father was really dead. Now, he looked like a ghost, one that would disappear in an eyeblink.

I didn't blink. I sat down beside him and touched his arm. He still felt solid.

He opened watery eyes. "Well, Vic," he said with a rueful smile, "I hate to admit it, but it looks like you get to ditch the old man after all."

"No." For a minute, that one syllable was all I could trust my voice to produce. "I will never, ever ditch you. What's wrong, Dad?" I felt like a fool asking the question. It was obvious what was wrong. My father was dying.

"Remember what I said before? My time here is running out. It's happening faster than I hoped." He wiped his forehead with his hand, then showed me the moisture on his palm: streaks of color, as though a painter had swept watercolors across his hand. "The magic is leaving me. It's sweating itself out. I may have sped up the process. We're close to Tywyll now. The pull is so strong, and I've been resisting it so hard . . ."

I put an arm around him, and he slumped against me. I'd never felt so damn helpless.

"I had a theory," he said, "but it doesn't look like I'll get to test it."

"What theory?" I pulled him closer to me, as though I could hold him here through sheer will.

"About the magic here. There's a legend about springs where pure magic bubbles up from the ground."

I nodded. He'd mentioned that to me when we left his cave.

"It's not just a legend. When I was working in the royal library, I found a map. It showed the location of three such springs. I copied it. I thought if I could get to a spring, it would give me strength to resist the cauldrons, maybe even lighten up these black clothes—that was the theory, Vic. I almost made it. Now, I'll never know."

"Wait. You almost made it?" My pulse picked up at the thought. "Are we near a spring?"

"Not far. But it's too late."

"Which way is it? I'll get you there."

"Forget it. I know the prophecies. I know what will happen, out there in the Ordinary, if Pryce gets his shadow demon back. You can't trade all those lives for mine. I'm already dead." His eyes closed and he paled another degree. "Twice over."

Dad's knapsack—he'd packed a map in it. I jumped up and went through the bag, tossing aside a knife, a cup, some apples. My fingers found a roll of parchment. I pulled it out, opened it. *Yes*. A map.

There was the road we'd been following. There was Tywyll. The clusters of houses were drawn in but not named—how could I figure out where we were? Wait. I'd noticed that crooked dovecote, like a small-scale version of the leaning tower of Pisa. It was in the last village we'd passed. In a minute, I had our location. Dad was right. A spring was close by.

Dad moaned softly. It was a sound I'd heard ten years ago. On that night, my father had died as I watched, unable to help him.

I would not let that happen again.

I scooped up my father into my arms like a child and ran for the spring.

THE WOODS GREW DENSER AS WE WENT DEEPER INTO THEM. I thought we were close to the spring now, but how would I know when we were there? I was afraid I'd run right past it.

Then I heard it.

I stopped. The sound was like water splashing over rocks, but more musical, almost like harp strings. I went toward the sound. It grew louder, and I noticed a sharp, metallic, almost electrical smell. That was how Dad had described the smell of magic. I looked down at him. His eyes were closed. He was so thin, so pale.

Even though I could hear the magic, and smell it—hell, I could almost taste it—I couldn't locate it. I'd follow the sound, only to have it ricochet to another location. Then it would happen again. The spring was hidden somehow. I wanted to weep with frustration. All the time I searched, my father was fading.

A bead of iridescent sweat dropped from Dad's forehead. It fell to the ground with a soft *plink*, like a note on a toy piano. The tiny sphere didn't flatten or sink into the ground. It rolled. Another drop of sweat followed it.

Dad had said he was sweating out the magic that made up his body. Maybe these small drops of magic were returning to their source.

I followed the rolling spheres. They went up a small rise, curved around a tree, and disappeared into a pile of leaves on the forest floor. The music of the spring seemed to be coming from behind me now, but I focused on the beads of magic. Another fell from Dad and rolled into the leaf pile. I walked around the pile. The drop didn't emerge from the other side.

I gently set Dad on the forest floor. Then I reached out to clear away the pile of leaves. My hand passed through something solid. It felt like a thin sheet of ice, except it wasn't cold. There was a loud crack, like a mirror breaking, and the illusion fell away. A small pool, perfectly round and no bigger than two feet across, glimmered at my feet. I'd found the spring. Magic, like liquid gems in a million brilliant colors, flowed and shimmered at my feet. The pool sparkled with an internal light, brighter than any I'd seen in the Darklands. It was beautiful, mesmerizing. I could watch those shifting colors forever.

I tore my gaze away and went back to my father. The magic was leaving him even faster now, returning to the spring. Somehow I had to reverse the flow. But how? Did he drink the magic? Bathe in it?

"Dad," I said. He opened his eyes. Even that small effort seemed to cost him. "We're at the spring. What do I do now?"

A shadow loomed over us. "You die," boomed a man's voice.

My instinct was to look up, toward the voice. But I ducked instead. A sword blade swished over my head.

I somersaulted and scrambled to my feet, drawing my sword.

A blur of red came at me. I parried his blow. I could see my attacker now: he had dark hair and a coal-black mustache; a tall, broad-shouldered man in a red tunic. He kept coming at me. I backed away from the spring, concentrating on fending off his hailstorm of blows.

"Stop it!" I shouted. "I don't want to fight you. I'm trying to save my father's life."

"I am a Keeper of the magic. You have uncovered the hidden spring. You must die."

There's no reasoning with some people. I charged him.

The Keeper laughed. He blocked my thrust with his sword, as I'd expected. I slid my blade along the edge of his and moved it in a wide circle, like swinging a lasso, bringing it around and aiming for the side of his throat. Again he parried the blow.

I brought my arm up and twisted slightly, coming at him with a backhanded stroke. He blocked, but took a step back, his eyes wide with surprise.

"Leave us alone," I said, "and I won't kill you."

The Keeper snarled and came at me. I wasn't going on the defensive again. I met his attack and countered, pushing him back.

My ears strained to catch the sound of a splash behind me, to pick up some sign that Dad was using the spring. All I could hear was the harplike music of the flowing magic and my own harsh breathing.

The Keeper backed up another step, and I pressed my advantage, moving forward and aiming low. My blade slashed his left thigh. I raised it again and attacked from the right. He stopped the thrust and raised his arm, lifting my blade and forcing it to the side. At once, he sliced straight across, aiming for my head. I ducked.

The sweep of his stroke left his body wide open, and as I came up I sliced him deeply across the stomach. Rainbow-colored blood spilled from the gash.

The Keeper dropped his sword. Clutching the wound, he crumpled to his knees, then fell facedown on the forest floor.

I snatched up his sword and ran back to the spring.

My father wasn't there.

Surely I'd laid him down right here, beside the spring. But the ground was empty.

Even shades can die, my father had told me. *The magic bleeds away, and the spirit disperses. There's nothing left.*

Nothing left.

No. I wouldn't accept that. He must have dragged himself away from the fight. I circled through the forest, searching, calling. Nothing.

I went back to the spring and stood beside it. I cupped my hands around my mouth and poured everything I had into my voice.

"Dad? Dad, where are you?"

I shouted until my voice was a mere croak, and even that didn't stop me. I called and called, but the only answer was the lush music of magic bubbling in the spring.

25

DAD WAS GONE. I COULD STAND HERE CALLING FOREVER, BUT no answer would come. Yet how could I leave? I sank to the ground, my head in my hands.

You failed him again, buzzed a voice inside my head.

I couldn't rouse myself to tell Butterfly to shut up. The Eidolon was right, anyway.

And this time, you took two lives. That Keeper was only trying to do his job. And you're letting the poor schmuck bleed to death on the ground. You cut him down, then you didn't even bother to see if you could help him, did you?

"Letting" him bleed to death—was the Keeper still alive? I lifted my head. I got up and went over to where he had fallen.

The man hadn't moved. He lay on his face, and his tunic had darkened to a deep burgundy. For a moment I thought it was blood, but shades' blood was rainbow-colored, like the spring. As I watched, burgundy deepened to black. The Keeper wasn't dead yet, but if he didn't get to the cauldrons, he'd die in this clearing.

I rolled him onto his back. His eyes were closed; his pores sweated out magic. The wound in his stomach gaped like a huge, shocked mouth. This guy wouldn't make it to the cauldrons or anywhere else.

What could I do? The spring's musical bubbling filled the woods. Dad had hoped the magic would revive him. Could it help this dying Keeper? It was worth a try.

I went to the spring and, cupping my hands, dipped them into the pool. A sharp, electric tingle pricked along my forearms like needles. My fingertips buzzed with an odd, sizzling sensation. Walking quickly and trying not to spill any, I carried the liquid magic back to the fallen Keeper. I knelt beside him and let the magic drip from my hands into the gash.

The Keeper cried out, although his eyes stayed closed. The magic bubbled and steamed. Was it helping or hurting him? I stood, watching. The steam rising from the Keeper's body expanded, surging up in colorful billows. Some got into my nose and throat and I backed away, coughing. If eating magical food was a bad idea for the clay-born, breathing magic was probably worse.

I couldn't see the Keeper anymore; fog filled the woods. It was beautiful, like an abstract painting of the most exquisite colors you could imagine, but set in motion. I watched the hypnotic dance of colors. They took away a little of the pain that seared my heart.

Until that whiny voice started up again. *Oh, so now you're an art lover? You can mope around here and look at the pretty colors all you want. But if you don't haul ass to Tywyll and stop that Pryce, you'll feel a hell of a lot worse. You think two deaths feel bad? Wait until millions die—and it's all your fault.* A cackle. *I'll be the fattest Eidolon in the history of demonkind.*

"Since when did you become my conscience?"

Oh. Silence. *Is that what I'm doing? Never mind.*

Yet Butterfly was right. For all I knew, Pryce may have already succeeded. But if there was anything I could do to stop him, I had to try. Millions of lives *did* depend on me.

I gazed into the beautiful fog of magic, listened to the music that filled the forest. There was no other sound. "Good-bye, Dad," I whispered. Then I turned around and headed back to the road that led to Tywyll.

THE CAPITAL CITY OF THE DARKLANDS WAS EXACTLY AS DAD had described it: a maze of narrow cobblestone streets that wound past squeezed-together shops and houses. Some of the buildings were stone; others were half-timbered, with overhanging upper stories that looked ready to tumble into the street.

I'd entered Tywyll through the southern gate. My sense of direction hadn't improved; I'd seen the word *Southgate* carved in ornate letters over the entrance. Shades were still pouring into town for the ceremony. The crowd flowed like a river of bodies through the streets, carrying me with it.

"Where's the ceremony being held?" I asked a young woman in a charcoal-gray tunic.

"Resurrection Square, where else?" Her tone implied it was the stupidest question she'd heard in a while. She gave me a sidelong glance. "By the way, would you like—?" She fumbled in her pocket.

"Not hungry, thanks." I cut her off before she could show me the roll or the orange or whatever she'd brought to eat. I didn't need to see any food right now.

The crowd was moving steadily uphill, along a lane that gradually got steeper. My heart pumped harder with the effort of climbing. At the very top of the hill, the street widened into Resurrection Square. Going through the tight, narrow lanes of Tywyll, I'd expected the square to be small, nothing like the vast space that opened before me now. The place was larger than Rhudda's archery range and banquet hall put together. In its center, three huge cauldrons clustered together in a triangular formation. Each of them looked to be ten or twelve feet high. I recognized the one that had been stolen from the Peabody, although it had grown so large that Pryce would need a crane to lift the thing now. The cauldron of transformation had been spiffed up, its dents repaired and its bronze polished so that it seemed to shine with an inner glow.

Bleachers stretched along three sides of the square. Shades climbed the steps and jostled each other for seats. More shades thronged the square at ground level. My group turned right, heading for a set of bleachers. I stepped out of the flow to take a better look around.

Along the stone wall beside me, a set of steps led up to a second-story balcony. That looked like a good vantage point; from up there, I could check out the square and maybe spot Pryce in the crowd. No one appeared to be on the balcony, although I couldn't be sure from this angle. Keeping low, so I couldn't be seen from the ground, I started climbing.

About halfway up, I paused. Kneeling on the steps, so I could just peer over the railing, I scanned the square again. A high platform with three golden chairs, the middle one distinctly regal-looking, had been erected in the space between the cauldrons. No one stood there yet, but the platform was obviously the spot where Lord Arawn would preside over the ceremony. The square was filling up fast, shades pouring in through all four entrances. So many people. Was Pryce among them? It was impossible to tell.

I looked up, checking the rooftops. Silhouetted against the sky stood a tall man; a crossbow dangled from his hand. Eight archers were stationed around the square; two on each side. Good. The cauldrons were well guarded. It would be hard for Pryce to approach them.

"Come up." A voice drifted down from the top of the stairs like a warm spring breeze. "Don't be afraid."

Whenever I hear a disembodied voice urging me not to be afraid, I figure it's a good time to have a weapon in my hand. I drew my sword. Holding it ready, I went up a few more steps.

"Come," breathed the voice.

A woman came into view on the balcony. She had long, straight, white-blonde hair, and she wore a welcoming smile and a scarlet cape. A Keeper. She held out her hands to me, then her mouth rounded with surprise.

"You're clay-born!" she exclaimed.

"That's right. Don't offer me any food, please."

"But only shades may climb the stone stairs! You must descend at once!"

"Why?

"Because . . . because . . ." The woman sputtered, too shocked to get the words out. Then something caught her eye across the square. "Look—over there! You'll *see* why."

The Keeper pointed to a balcony like ours on the other side of the square. I ran up the last few stairs to see what was happening. A man—a shade—stood on the opposite balcony, looking out over the crowd.

"I see a guy standing on a balcony. So?"

"Shh! Watch."

I stepped back so I stood between the Keeper and the wall. I could see what was happening, but anyone looking up from ground-level wouldn't notice me.

On the other balcony, the shade raised both arms above his head in a gesture that seemed more resigned than triumphant—a surrender, not a victory. He tilted his head back. After a moment, thin tendrils began to rise from his fingers. The tendrils looked like smoke, except they weren't gray but rather multicolored, like the fog that had filled the spring's clearing. The rising tendrils joined together into a swirling rainbow of vivid, glorious colors: red, blue, green, yellow, purple, gold, and myriad shades in between. The magic was so lovely. The rainbow grew, arcing, and stretched from the man to one of the cauldrons. It looked like a path made of glittering jewels.

The man dropped his arms. A red-cloaked Keeper stepped forward and helped him climb onto the path. I realized now that the shade's outfit was midnight black. He bowed to the Keeper and then walked—no, *glided*—along the rainbow. His feet didn't move. At the end of the path, he stopped. He looked around once, twisting to the left and right, and then he raised his arms again. In a graceful swan dive, he plunged into the cauldron.

"Good return," whispered the Keeper in front of me.

The rainbow exploded in a blast of light. Colors burst and flared and sparkled like fireworks. Then they subsided—fading, drifting, and finally disappearing.

Whoa. That was strange. But even stranger was the fact that no one in the square paid the slightest bit of attention to the spectacle. Shades milled around, talking to each other and pushing their way through the crowds. No one had glanced up at the shade walking on a rainbow above their heads. No one had flinched at the boom or *ooh*ed and *ahh*ed over the display.

The last of the colors faded out. The shade who'd dived into the cauldron didn't reemerge.

The Keeper turned, searching my face for a reaction. "That was a reincarnation, wasn't it?" I asked.

"Yes. The time had arrived for that spirit to leave the Darklands and be clay-born into a new body."

I eyed the cauldron he'd jumped into. "What happened to his magical body?"

"You saw—the colors, the lights. That was the magic dispersing."

Talk about going out with a bang. "How come no one in the square noticed all the fireworks?"

"The 'fireworks,' as you call them, are not visible from the ground. They would be a distraction to those whose time has not come, so the magic shields them." The Keeper fixed me with a schoolmarm glare. "I am a Cauldron Keeper," she said. "The same as that Keeper across the square. We help shades make their returns. *Now* do you understand why you cannot—?"

"Look," I interrupted, "there's another one."

To our right, a black-clad woman stood on a different balcony. Next to her stood yet another Keeper.

The woman on the other balcony was shaking her head vigorously. The Cauldron Keeper there touched her arm, and she yanked away. She pushed past the Keeper and started down the stairs, but the Keeper caught her and lifted her back onto the balcony.

"She doesn't want to do it," I said.

"It's not her choice."

My fingers tightened around the grip of my sword. I judged how long it would take to run down these stairs, push my way through the crowd, and mount the other stairs to rescue her. Too long.

"You cannot rescue her," said the Keeper, as though she'd read my thoughts. "There's nothing to rescue her from. Put away your sword. That Keeper isn't forcing her; he's merely assisting. Some shades do resist, yes, but sooner or later the magic must be obeyed. It is Law. And it is our job to help shades accept what must be."

Dad. An image of him—dressed in black, ghostly, sweating out magic—flashed through my mind.

Across the square, the Keeper stood behind the woman, a hand on each forearm. Slowly, the Keeper raised the woman's arms. Even from this distance, I could see her shaking. She let her head drop back onto the Keeper's shoulder, and the rainbow colors rose from her hands. This time, the rainbow bridge stretched to a different cauldron.

"Ah," said the Keeper who stood with me. "A regeneration. I suspect she'll be pleased."

The far Keeper spoke to the trembling woman and pointed at the cauldrons. Her head snapped forward, and she dropped her arms. She leapt onto the rainbow and ran along it. At the height of the arc, she sat down and slid feet-first, her hair streaming behind her, like a kid on a playground slide.

This time, there was no explosion, no burst of colors. The woman disappeared into the cauldron, then floated up again, carried on a shining cloud. Colors gleamed around her head like a halo, and her black dress had lightened to a silvery gray. She stepped from her cloud onto the bridge and glided back to the balcony she'd started from. When she stepped off the rainbow, she turned around, facing the cauldrons, and held her arms out straight in front of her. The bridge dissolved into a spectrum of colored light and flowed into her fingers and up her arms. She glowed with it as the light filled her body. The woman hugged the Keeper and skipped down the stairs.

"Now, that *was* a good return." The blonde Keeper smiled.

"Why was she so afraid?" I asked, sheathing my sword.

"When a shade is called to the cauldrons, we don't know whether it's to be regenerated, as she was, or reborn, like the first shade you saw. Some don't wish to leave our realm. Usually, it's because they're waiting for a loved one from their previous life to arrive here. But there are many reasons a shade may wish to remain in the Darklands. And there are equally as many reasons why a shade may wish to return to the Ordinary as quickly as possible. But it's not our choice. The magic always decides."

If Dad had come to Resurrection Square and climbed these stairs, he might have been regenerated. But he wasn't willing to take the chance that he'd be reincarnated instead. Once the rainbow emerged and attached itself to a cauldron, it was too late to go back.

"There's no way to influence which cauldron the magic chooses?"

The Keeper looked slightly shocked, as if I'd made a fart joke instead of asking a question. "There are false priests who claim to understand and control the ways of magic," she said. "They grow rich defrauding those who wish to choose their fate in this square. But those . . . those *charlatans* have no power over the magic. It is Law here, just as gravity is Law in your world."

"What if a shade tries to resist the magic's pull?"

"Some do, for a time." Her scarlet shoulders shrugged. "But as the pull of the magic grows stronger, the physical body grows weaker. Eventually, all must succumb. It is Law."

She really liked that phrase. I wondered if she had it embroidered on a pillowcase at home.

I was still thinking about Dad. "But what if someone is *really* strong willed and does resist the pull—say, for years? What happens then?"

"For years?" She squinted skeptically. "Impossible. As I said, a shade might try. But that's why we have Soul Keepers, to assist anyone so deluded in coming here, where we Cauldron Keepers assist them further."

"But what if a shade evaded the Keepers', um, 'assistance' and hid out from the magic for a long, long time? What would happen to him?"

She considered, her hands flat on the balcony's edge. In the square, another rainbow exploded as a shade was reborn. "It is not good for a shade to resist the magic's pull. There is a reason we trust the magic."

"It is Law?" I said the word with a capital L, the way she did.

"Yes." She tilted her head, considering. "But more than that, the magic knows when renewal is needed. Here, magic draws from spirit, but everything is carefully balanced. Magic will not take more from spirit than spirit can bear. That is why the pull grows stronger as the shade grows weaker. If a shade were to resist the pull for too long a time, the spirit would become too thin to hold the magical body together. The body would disintegrate, and the shade would die."

"So there's no . . ." My throat was so dry it was hard to talk around the lump in it. "No chance of regeneration?"

"It would be too late."

"And that's Law, too, huh?"

"It is." If she wondered at the bitterness in my voice, she didn't show it. "Now . . ." Her featherlight touch nudged me toward the stairs.

I didn't move. I was trying to figure out how to ask about the hidden spring.

"Go!" she said more insistently. "A shade waits to climb the stairs. It pains them to wait when they are so close. If you don't go now, he'll have to wait until after the purification ceremony. Let him up!"

A man in a black tunic and leggings stood at the bottom of the staircase, one foot on the first step. He'd twisted around to look at something behind him, and all I could see was curly brown hair. My heart jolted. *Dad.* But then he turned my way, peering anxiously up the stairs, and I saw he was clean-shaven and had a crooked nose. Not my father.

Still, my legs shook as I made my way down the stone steps. The man watched me descend, his mouth tight. A kaleidoscope of emotions—fear, hope, worry, anticipation, regret—chased each other across his face.

What would I say right now, I wondered, if this shade had been my father?

The man stepped aside to let me pass. "Good return," I said.

He replied with an uncertain smile. Then he took a long, deep breath and started up the stairs.

I watched him go. About halfway up the staircase, he disappeared—passing, I guessed, through the magic shield. From here, there were no rainbows, no colors, no fireworks or shining clouds. But a few minutes later the man trotted back down the stairs. His clothes were now pale yellow, and his dubious smile had been replaced by a broad grin.

He waved to me and then called to someone in the crowd. A woman in a tan dress ran to him. When they hugged, he lifted her off her feet and spun her around. Then, arm in arm, they went to find seats for the ceremony.

I wished the waiting shade had been my father. Regeneration, reincarnation—why had that even mattered? All that mattered was the survival of his spirit. I thought of the woods near the spring, how utterly empty they'd felt as I called Dad's name. After so many years, I'd finally found my father. Now I'd lost him again—this time beyond any place I could search.

26

I TRIED TO WARN ARAWN. I LOCATED THE ENTRANCE TO HIS palace—Dad had said the building bordered Resurrection Square—and was surprised to find it unguarded. That is, until I attempted to approach the door. It was warded; I couldn't get closer than ten feet away. It wasn't like hitting an invisible wall. At a certain distance, I simply couldn't move any closer. I could walk and walk all day, and the door would always remain ten feet ahead of me. There was no way to reach the palace, no one to carry a message to the king. I gave up and went back to the square.

There, I stayed on ground level, keeping close to the walls. The bleachers might offer a better view, but if something happened and I needed to move fast, I didn't want to waste time climbing over people. I made a circuit of the square, checking faces in the stands, watching the throngs on the ground. A couple of times, I thought I saw Pryce. But when I approached, a hand on my sword hilt, it always turned out to be someone else.

Maybe Pryce hadn't made it here. Maybe Ferris Mackey wasn't the only murder victim whose spirit had escaped him. Maybe Pryce had weakened and faded into nothing somewhere on the road to Tywyll. And maybe I'd look up and see pigs dancing an aerial ballet overhead. Anything was possible, but I knew where I'd place my bets.

Trumpets blared. The crowd hushed as everyone craned toward the central platform. A man appeared there, waving, and the spectators cheered. A woman emerged beside him. Both wore blue— members of the court—but with gold capes. Wizards? Had to be; their magic was needed to purify the cauldron.

There must be a tunnel from the palace to the cauldrons. The wizards had arrived that way, then climbed up to make a grand entrance on the platform through a trapdoor.

The third person on the platform must be Arawn himself. He was considered both king and god here, and he looked the part. The lord of the Darklands stood tall and straight, soaking in the crowd's adoration. He was muscular and dark-bearded and moved with an easy grace. His clothes were regal purple, and a gold crown glittered on his head.

Arawn stepped forward, and the crowd stilled. I almost wished I had a pin, so I could drop it to hear the clatter.

"My friends and subjects," he said, his deep voice carrying through the square. "Today we come together to restore a treasure that, long ago, was stolen from our realm. Today, the three cauldrons of Arawn are reunited: the cauldron of rebirth, the cauldron of regeneration, and—once again in its proper place— the cauldron of transformation.

"You all know the cauldrons of rebirth and regeneration. One cleanses the spirit so it may be clay-born anew. The other strengthens the spirit and its magical body, fortifying their bond. Yet, few of you have dwelled in our realm long enough to know the power of the lost cauldron."

A murmur went through the crowd.

"Transformation—what does it mean? Turning one thing into something else. Centuries ago, foolish Arthur believed this cauldron would turn cowards into brave men. Other clay-born fools thought it would turn dead bodies into living ones or transmute lead into gold. In the Ordinary, the cauldron could do no such things. At best, it could transform raw meat into cooked—and then only with the help of a fire."

He waited, smiling, as dutiful laughter rippled around the square.

"Here, in the Darklands, the cauldron draws upon our magic to transform what is lesser into what is greater. It can take disparate things and join them together into a greater whole. Not physical things—not lead into gold or shards of glass into a mirror. Spiritual things, magical things. Wisps of spirit that have strayed. Bits of magic that have peeled away. In this cauldron, such things can come together in a new whole." He swept his arm to indicate the crowd. "If you feel diminished—tired, somehow smaller—and the magic calls you, this cauldron will build you up again. But it won't simply restore you; it will find your essence and magnify it. It will transform you into something greater than you were before."

Excitement buzzed through the stands. I thought of Dad. If only I had something of him—some wisp of his spirit, as Arawn had said—perhaps this cauldron could give him back to me. But he was gone, and I had nothing.

Arawn lowered his arm, and the crowd quieted. "Our realm has been deprived of this cauldron for far too long. Now, my royal wizards shall perform the ritual to purify it. And then your king, Lord Arawn—yes, I myself—shall be the first to be transformed. You will see a king greater than any you have known before."

Not if that king jumped into a cauldron full of demons. What would happen if the lord of the Darklands, the source of its magic, combined spiritually with the essence of hundreds of demons? *As Arawn fares, so fares the realm.* Arawn wouldn't become greater; he'd be defiled, and with him the magic of his kingdom, sickening the land, corrupting the bodies of the shades. The Darklands would become an extension of Hell.

I had to stop him.

"Wait!" I tried to shout, but my parched throat wouldn't emit more than a croak. I started pushing my way through the packed square. If I could warn Arawn, his wizards would know what they were dealing with.

The king didn't even notice my attempt to reach him.

"Let the purification begin!" he proclaimed. As the crowd cheered, he took his seat and the two wizards stood. They went to the side of the platform nearest the cauldron of transformation. The wizards flipped their gold capes back over their shoulders, making the garments flare like wings. Silence fell upon the square as they raised their arms. Glowing prisms of light emanated from their fingertips, then grew and brightened. Fingers began to move as, working together, the wizards summoned magic and wove it into a complex pattern above the cauldron.

Where was Pryce? I scanned the square. Everyone was focused on the ceremony. On the rooftops, Arawn's archers stood sentry. Only one had his crossbow raised—aimed at me. I stopped trying to push my way to the platform. He held the bow steady a moment longer, then lowered it. But his stare stayed fastened on me.

The wizards continued to weave the magic. Their spell hung in the air, shining, an intricate piece of shimmering, colored lace. Music emanated from it, soft at first but growing as the spell developed. The sound was like the music of the spring, but more complex. Instead of random notes, this was a composition, with melody and harmony and counterpoint. Spectators listened and watched, rapt. No one moved.

If Pryce tried to rush the platform, the archers would spot him immediately.

Together, the wizards slowly brought their arms down. The glimmering spell followed, drifting toward the cauldron. Its music filled the square, mystical, like music half-heard in a dream and more beautiful than anything earthly instruments could produce. The spell touched the cauldron's rim, and the vessel glowed with prismatic light. The light reached through the square, its colors bathing shades' faces. Everyone was transfixed. The light washed over all with its caressing magic.

I felt it, too. Where the light touched my face, I felt lighter, cleansed, uplifted somehow. Purified. The ritual was working.

Maybe it would work to get rid of the demons.

The wizards guided their spell inside the cauldron. Its metal resonated with the music, adding deep bass notes, like a huge bell tolling. The sound reverberated through the square. I felt it all the way to my toes.

Then the cauldron struck an off note, shattering that perfect harmony.

The crowd gasped. Arawn gripped the arms of his chair and leaned forward. The wizards glanced at each other, uncertain.

Another jarring note sounded, a sledgehammer blow that threw the spell's music off-key. The notes jangled and slid away from each other. Now, the cauldron spewed out the discordant sounds of a haunted carousel in a child's nightmare.

The royal wizards gestured frantically, trying to repair their spell. Arawn was on his feet, a hand on his sword hilt.

The music stopped. A scream emerged from the cauldron, a

chilling, desperate sound, rising in pitch and volume. People covered their ears. Some turned and moved toward the exits. A window shattered in the palace, then another.

A demon screaming—just one—like I'd heard that night in Purgatory Chasm.

Shit. The spell wasn't purging demons from the cauldron. It was releasing them.

Pryce—or Myrddin, more likely—had rigged the cauldron to make the purification spell a trigger. And now that the trigger had been pulled, there was no way to stop it. The demons would emerge. As what, I couldn't guess.

Where was Pryce, damn it? If I couldn't hold back the demons, maybe I could prevent him from turning them into a shiny new shadow demon for himself.

More screams joined the first. The cauldron glowed crimson, like a devil costume, like the hottest flames of Hell.

In an explosion of sulfur and smoke, a fury of demons burst from the cauldron.

There were hundreds of them, more. Huge, hideous things with scaly bodies, leathery wings, and ugly boars' heads. Some soared into the air. Others jumped to the ground, snatching shades who tried to flee. The square was a madman's vision of Hell. Ash and burning embers rained down from the sky. Demons dived into the crowd, leaping on spectators, slashing them with their claws, ripping off limbs. One demon perched on the edge of the cauldron of rebirth, chewing on the shoulder end of an arm. Others snatched people, flew high in the air, and dropped them on the crowd.

On the platform, a demon tore off the female wizard's head and tossed it into the square. The other wizard lay broken over his golden chair. Four demons held the struggling Arawn, looking like they intended to play tug-of-war with the Darklands' king.

No! If Arawn died, the land died with him. Demons would overrun the place, gobbling up the remnants of its magic. With that power, they'd invade the Ordinary—and my terrifying vision of devastation would become reality.

Frantic, I pushed toward the platform. I couldn't fight all these demons, but I'd do what I could to protect Arawn.

The crowd stampeded in the opposite direction, away from the platform and toward the exits. "Let me through!" I yelled. I struggled to move forward, but I was trying to dog-paddle against a tsunami.

A sound boomed through the air, like a hundred cannons firing at once. "Silence!"

The demons paused in their attack. The shades quit screaming. Everyone looked up. On a rooftop stood Pryce. He wore a tunic and leggings of the palest gray. Beside him, demons held the limp, dangling bodies of Arawn's archers.

Two demons dropped the archers and picked up Pryce. They carried him through the air and set him down on the platform, where other demons still held the king. Facing Pryce, Arawn raised his chin defiantly. Pryce drew his sword. He lifted it high, so all could see it. Arawn spat in his face.

The crowd held its breath.

Pryce glared as spittle slid down his cheek and dripped from his jaw. He wiped his face. Then, with a roar, he ran the lord of the Darklands through.

Pryce withdrew his sword, and the demons let Arawn go. As the king collapsed on the platform, the ground shuddered. The sky darkened. Around me, shades cried out and clutched their stomachs as though they'd also been stabbed.

"I am your king now!" shrieked Pryce. He brandished his bloody sword. "I annex this realm as a territory of Uffern." His eyes swept the crowd. "Hail me."

Silence.

Pryce reached down and took the golden crown from Arawn's head. He set it on his own. "Hail me!"

A sound arose, but it was nothing more than a groan. All around me, shades grew thinner, rainbow-colored rivulets running down their faces. They were sweating out magic, as Dad had earlier. With the loss of Arawn, the magic was leaving them. Again shades moved, backing away from the platform, some turning and breaking into a run.

"Idiots," Pryce snarled, the crown crooked on his black hair. "I'll make you wish you'd obeyed me." Again, he lifted his sword.

From his raised arm, a shadow stretched upward. No, not a shadow; more like a bodiless spirit. The figure was transparent; it had depth and dimension. It was rooted in Pryce but stretched above him. Myrddin.

"Now, Father!" Pryce shouted.

The spirit of Myrddin gestured, and every demon froze. The wizard began to gather demons together, making motions like he was casting a huge net and drawing it in. The demons, some struggling, were slowly reeled back toward the cauldron.

Pryce was going to do something—use the cauldrons in some way—to combine those demons into a single entity, and then bind that entity to him. He'd become a newly restored demi-demon.

Or something worse.

I had to stop him. Seeing him up there on the platform, I knew how. I had a magic arrow that never missed its target.

Shades pushed toward the exits, trampling each other, moving me away from the platform. The crush of bodies was so tight I couldn't get my hand near the arrow in my belt. I hoped I didn't need a bow. I'd never be able to aim in this throng. If I could get the arrow free, I'd focus on my target—the exact center of Pryce's black heart—and throw. I moved my hand. My fingertips brushed the fletching. Then a shade tried to duck under my arm, pushing my hand away from the arrow. Another stamped hard on my foot, and I yelled with frustration and pain.

On the platform, Pryce's head snapped around. His gaze locked onto me for a moment before he looked up and spoke to his father. Myrddin paused. The demons he was dragging back to the cauldron stilled. Some strained against the pull, but they couldn't break away.

Myrddin pointed at me. Immediately two demons dropped from the sky. Shades screamed and scrambled away, knocking me to the ground. The demons grabbed my arms. Their bat wings beat as they lifted me into the air. I yelled and kicked, expecting to be ripped in two. But they didn't tear me apart. They flew me over to the platform and set me down in front of Pryce. The demons found my sword and dagger and tossed them aside.

Myrddin resumed hauling in his net of demons. Some tumbled into the cauldron of transformation.

Transformation. Pryce was going to fuse them all into some sort of super-demon. He stared at me, his lip curled in an ugly sneer.

"Cousin." He spat the word. "I thought I'd have to kill you to get you here. But I needn't have wasted my effort. All I had to do was make sure you knew I was going to the Darklands, and you followed me here like a puppy."

"I followed you here to stop you."

"And a marvelous job you're doing of it, aren't you?" His sneer got even uglier. "*I* brought you here. I played you like a violin. Father said I might need your life force. As it turns out, I do. Some of the souls that came with me into this place have gotten away." Like Mack, wandering along the road in search of his taxi. "My human side has grown thin, and I need to build it up to balance my soon-to-be-restored shadow demon. Otherwise, the demon will have too much power. And I must *always* be in control."

"You never had a human side, Pryce."

Myrddin dumped the last of the netted demons into the cauldron.

Pryce glanced upward. "Ready, Father?"

The wizard nodded and shrank back into Pryce's body. Behind Pryce, Arawn moaned. *Moaned?* The lord of the Darklands wasn't dead. He was trying to crawl toward the cauldron of regeneration.

Pryce turned and kicked Arawn savagely in the ribs. Another kick snapped the king's head back, breaking his neck. Arawn lay on the platform like a doll dropped by a careless child. The demons that held me chortled with malicious glee.

Pryce plucked Rhudda's arrow from my belt. "You won't be needing this," he said. He snapped it in two, then tossed the pieces on the fallen king. He grabbed my waist and tried to lift me off my feet, but the two demons still had my arms.

"Let go, you morons!" he snapped. "Return to Uffern and prepare my place—unless you'd rather accompany me now." He pointed into the cauldron.

In a flash, the demons released their grips and took to the sky. They shot like rockets toward the north.

Pryce grabbed me around the waist. He half-carried, half-dragged me to the edge of the platform. I struggled and kicked. I dug in my heels but couldn't hold my ground.

"Now, cousin," his voice buzzed in my ear, "we transform what is lesser into something far greater."

Before I could reply, Pryce toppled into the cauldron of transformation, dragging me with him.

27

MY ARMS FLAILED, REACHING FOR SOMETHING, ANYTHING. Pain nearly split my arm in two as our fall jerked to a stop. I'd managed to hook my right elbow over the cauldron's edge. I reached up with my left hand and gripped the rim, struggling to pull myself up.

Pryce clung to my waist as we dangled inside the cauldron. My instinct was to try to knock him off—kick at him, bang him against the wall—but I resisted the urge. I didn't want him to fall into the cauldron and merge with all those demons. I needed to drag him out with me.

I looked down. Whoa, big mistake. From outside, this cauldron appeared maybe twelve feet deep. Inside, though, it was bottomless. At least, I couldn't see any end to the space that yawned below us.

Getting out of here would definitely be a good thing. I braced my feet against the wall and pushed out and up. If I could just hook my other arm over the rim . . .

"Let go, damn you!" shouted Pryce. He grabbed my belt with one hand and tugged at my arm with the other, trying to loosen my grip. I ignored him and concentrated on hauling us out. My feet slipped on the wall, and I scrabbled to regain a toehold. My arms trembled with the strain. Pryce's fist pounded at me—my arm, my back, my kidneys.

Abruptly, he stopped hitting me. His laugh echoed hollowly through the cauldron.

I didn't like the sound of that laugh. I chanced another look down. Pryce was drawing a knife from a sheath in his belt.

I twisted sideways, pushing out with my feet, and slammed us both into the wall. Pryce grunted and tightened his grip on my belt. He cursed, and I looked down to see the knife tumbling end over end as it fell.

Score one for the shapeshifter.

But my victory was short-lived. More blows battered me. I let go of the rim with my left hand and reached down to grab Pryce's face. My thumb found an eye and pressed. He swore and grabbed my wrist, yanking my hand away. I jerked upward, breaking his grip, and drove my fist back down. His nose cracked under the blow. Again, I got my hand around the cauldron's rim and tried to pull us up.

Somewhere far below, a rumbling sounded. The cauldron shook.

Pulling harder, I managed to hook my left arm over the cauldron's rim. Almost there. I heaved, and got one leg up. Now I lay on the rim, but Pryce still hung from my belt. The weight felt like it was cutting me in half.

The rumbling intensified, hurting my ears. The pressure threatened to crush my head.

I reached down to grab Pryce by the hair and haul him up. As my fingers brushed his scalp, he suddenly wasn't there. Whether he'd lost his grip or purposely let go, Pryce plummeted into the cauldron's depths.

The rumbling stopped, like some angry volcano god appeased by a sacrifice.

I hoisted myself onto the platform, then spun around and peered into the cauldron. The interior was dark, smoky. I couldn't see anything through the murk. Pryce had disappeared.

The city, too, was overrun with smoke. I got to my feet. All around me, Tywyll was burning. Bodies littered the ground. Demons that had evaded Myrddin's net swooped through the sky or rampaged through the square. Screams rose over the terrified babble. An airborne demon—fangs bared, hideous face twisted, claws outstretched—dived at me. I somersaulted out of the way. There, a little to my right, lay my dagger where the other demons had dropped it. I snatched it up and got to my feet. I turned, knife poised, ready to attack.

But the demon stood there, staring stupidly at a blade that protruded from its chest. Someone had stabbed it from behind. As I watched, flames—not bright, but dark as shadows—flared from the blade. The demon howled. It touched the sword, and its hand caught fire. The shadowy flames spread up its arm. The howl became a scream as the demon batted at the flames. They spread to its other hand. Soon dark fire flared from every part of its body. The blade withdrew with a slick, sliding sound. The burning demon danced and writhed, its furious, agonized screeches rending the air. Its body shimmered. The shimmers turned black, like embers winking out, and the demon collapsed into a pile of black dust.

Above the pile, holding a black-flaming sword, stood Arawn, lord of the Darklands. He was alive.

Arawn kicked the ashes, scattering them across the platform. His face was streaked with filth and soot. So were his robes. Under the dirt, they were no longer purple but lavender.

Lord Arawn had been regenerated. He must have gone into that cauldron while I was struggling to get out of the other. Or maybe it was harder to kill a god than Pryce thought.

Two more demons landed with heavy thuds. They charged Arawn, coming at him from both sides. I hurled my knife at one, getting a solid hit between the wings. The demon roared and whirled around. As it turned, it lost its balance. It teetered on the edge of the platform, wings flapping crazily, then plunged into the cauldron I'd climbed out of.

Arawn drove his flaming sword into the other demon's stomach and held it there. Black flames sprouted from the wound, and the king yanked out his sword. As before, the demon was consumed by fire, burning until it was nothing but ashes.

Chest heaving, Arawn held his sword ready as he surveyed the square. Most of the fighting had moved to my left, on the square's north side. Shades pressed toward the exit, shouting and trying to escape. Demons scythed through crowd, tossing bodies left and right. Some demons stomped through the exit and into the street. Others took to the sky. All were heading north.

Lord Arawn squinted at them through the smoke.

"They're making their way to the border," he said.

"Which border?"

"With Uffern. They're trying to get back to Hell." He turned to me, his eyes mirroring the dark flames that still burned along his sword. "You are a stranger in my realm. Who are you?"

"My name is—"

An explosion rocked the platform, knocking both of us to its floor. Fire rained down from the sky. I threw up my right arm to protect my face; red-hot pain seared my forearm. I brushed at the spot, but there was nothing there.

Nothing but the place where I'd been marked by a Hellion.

A roar, primal and vicious, shook the city. I looked up. A massive demon, fifty feet tall, shot up from the cauldron of transformation. Its blue skin, the color of moldering bruise, flickered with hellflame. More flames shot from its eyes. A building on the edge of the square burst into flame.

It was Difethwr. Pryce hadn't created a new shadow demon. He'd resurrected the Destroyer.

Fear sliced through me with a blade of flaming ice. Difethwr. My worst enemy. Chief demon of Hell. My father's murderer. Destruction personified. I'd killed this Hellion once. But the Destroyer I'd killed had been nothing—a baby, a toy—compared to the nightmare that now rose from the cauldron.

Pryce dangled from the Hellion's chest as though he'd been glued there. His head and limbs hung limply. Was he dead? Difethwr raised its arms. Pryce's head snapped up, eyes open, and his arms moved skyward in the same gesture. His expression was pure terror. Pryce had been right; without more human spirit in him, he couldn't control the Destroyer. Without my spirit, he was the weaker half of his new demi-demon whole.

Difethwr roared again, torching another building. With Pryce drooping from its chest like a rag doll, the Hellion jumped from the cauldron and bolted through the south gate. Explosions and flaming buildings marked its path.

I couldn't believe it. I didn't want to believe it. But the Destroyer was back.

I had to stop the demon before it completely ravaged the Darklands. Before it found its way to the Ordinary. If Difethwr entered my world, I had no doubt my vision of destruction—flames, death, ashes everywhere—would come true.

My foot was on the ladder when a hand fell heavily on my shoulder, fingers clamping hard enough to bruise. I turned to see

Lord Arawn scowling at me. His sword no longer burned, but the same dark flames still flickered in his eyes.

"You will speak to me in my palace." His words were not a request.

AS FOUR ARMED GUARDS MARCHED ME THROUGH THE TUNnel to Arawn's palace, I wondered whether our destination would be an interrogation room or a cell. It was neither. Instead, they left me in a small, well-furnished sitting room deep inside the palace. A fire—one with normal, yellow-and-orange flames—burned in a stone fireplace. Crossed swords were mounted over the mantel. Tapestries hung on the walls, and a mahogany bookcase held leather-bound volumes. Ornately carved wooden chairs, with brocaded cushions on their seats, were positioned around the room.

Guards stood outside the door—I'd pulled it open to look—but they'd let me keep my knife and Rhudda's arrow (I'd picked up the pieces before I left the platform). Not that a broken arrow was much of a threat, but the guards didn't seem bothered by my weapons. Until someone demonstrated otherwise, I'd consider myself Arawn's guest. A guest with a knife at the ready.

I paced, feeling restless and irritated. My demon mark was hot and sore, like a hornet's sting. I was wasting time, waiting in this cozy room while the Destroyer was out there torching the Darklands. My best chance for killing the Hellion was *now*, when it was newly resurrected, disoriented, and unsure of itself. But I couldn't kill it without decent weapons. And that was one of the reasons I needed to talk to Arawn.

I plopped down in a chair and lay the broken arrow on the floor. Where was Arawn? If he didn't show up soon, I'd leave. I'd kill any guards who tried to stop me. I'd smash down the door and—

Deep breaths, Vicky. For ten years, the Destroyer's rage had burned in me through the mark I bore. I'd fought to control it then. I wouldn't let it control me now.

Anyway, I didn't have long to wait. The door opened, and Arawn strode into the room. His face was still streaked with blood, grime, and soot, although his robes had cleaned themselves, their pure, pale lavender practically glowing. His sword was sheathed at his side.

"Don't bother offering me anything to eat or drink," I said, before he could speak. "I'm not interested." My chances for leaving the realm weren't looking good, thanks to the broken arrow lying beside my chair. But until I knew for sure that I was stuck here, I'd resist any and all offers of Darklands-style hospitality.

Besides, I was so hungry and thirsty by now, I was almost afraid I'd say yes.

Arawn stared at me for a long moment. He wasn't a handsome man, but power radiated from him the way light radiates from the sun. His power, though, was dark. Death power. His craggy face, all sharp angles partially softened by a well-trimmed black beard, seemed half-veiled by shadow. His eyes burned darkly under thick black brows.

The lord of the Darklands inclined his head. "As you prefer. Although personally, I could use some wine to steady my nerves." He motioned to a servant, who scurried from the room and then reappeared almost immediately, carrying a golden tray with a crystal decanter and one goblet. The servant filled the goblet with deep ruby wine and handed it to Arawn. The king took a sip, closed his eyes, and drained the glass. His Adam's apple bobbed. When the servant had refilled the goblet and withdrawn, Arawn spoke.

"As I recall, you were on the point of telling me your name."

"Victory Vaughn. But I answer to Vicky."

His eyes narrowed. "You're Evan Vaughn's daughter?"

I nodded, swallowing the lump that sprang to my throat.

"Your father ran from my court trying to avoid his fate. That was foolish of him. One day, like it or not, his name will appear in my book."

"What book?"

"*The Register of the Cauldrons.* When a shade comes to Resurrection Square for a return, magic records his or her name in the current volume. That's why I was delayed. I was consulting the court archivist about what happened. An entire volume filled itself with names—ugly, demonic names—for the cauldron of transformation. Your name appeared but, the archivist tells me, it was soon erased, presumably when you climbed out. And there were two others—"

"Pryce Maddox and Difethwr."

Arawn nodded. "So tell me, Victory-Vaughn-who-answers-to-Vicky, why did disaster strike my realm today?"

"Pryce was the one who left the cauldron on your doorstep at the Devil's Coffin."

"Laden with hidden demons."

I nodded. "He's a demi-demon."

A thunderstorm of anger swept across Arawn's face. "How can that be? A demi-demon would never gain admittance to my realm. His garments were gray. He entered as any other shade whose time in the Ordinary has ended."

I explained how I'd killed Pryce's shadow demon and how Myrddin had brought his son back. "Without his shadow demon, Pryce was the same as any human. Do you remember a sudden influx of human spirits into the Black?"

"Spirits that didn't pass through to here or the Beyond but returned to the Ordinary? Yes, I do."

"They were victims of a plague, a disease that made them dead for three days and then brought them back to life. Pryce purposely infected himself with it."

"So he could enter my realm with the guarantee of a quick return to the Ordinary." Arawn stroked his beard. The gesture reminded me of Dad. "You say Pryce carries the spirit of Myrddin Wyllt. The wizard must have guided him out of the Black and across the Darklands to Tywyll." His gaze snapped to me. "And you. How did you come to be here, Victory? From your refusal of refreshment, I take it you don't intend to stay."

"No. I made a deal with Mallt-y-Nos."

"Ah." He sat back in his chair and steepled his fingers. Firelight glinted off an onyx ring. "The Night Hag does not enter into any deal, as you call it, without being certain that she'll benefit. Preferably while doing harm to the other. Let me guess. She requires you to smuggle something out of the Darklands before she'll allow you back into the Ordinary."

"Yes, she wants—"

"It doesn't matter what she wants. She could ask for . . ." He looked around the room, then gestured at the fireplace. "She could ask for a speck of dust from my hearth, and the prohibition would be the same. Those who enter may bring nothing in, and those who leave may take nothing out. It's been my principal rule ever since Arthur raided the Darklands and stole my cauldron." Arawn chuckled, but his face remained hard. "It cost him, though. It did cost him. Many of his men became my subjects.

Your world has a poem about it, I believe. Do you know the refrain, 'except for seven, none returned'?"

I nodded, my mouth even drier than before.

The satisfaction faded from Arawn's expression, and he sighed. "I thought I was getting it back—the cauldron, I mean. But obviously I got more than I expected. Many souls have been lost. My city is in ruins. And all because Pryce smuggled in something that doesn't belong here."

"The hidden demons."

Arawn nodded. "Nothing comes in; nothing goes out. It's a good rule, as you must agree after today's events. So you'll understand, I trust, why I cannot allow you to break it for the sake of a foolish bargain."

"What if I can do something for you—would you make an exception then?"

Arawn looked me up and down. Not with a leer, but as one warrior sizes up another. "And what service are you offering?"

"I can kill the Destroyer."

Arawn gripped the chair's armrests and leaned forward. "What did you say?"

"I can kill the Hellion. I did it before."

Arawn's eyebrow went up. "You said you killed a shadow demon. Those can be vicious, I grant you, but this is Difethwr, the Destroyer. The chief commander of the legions of Hell."

Irritation surged again. "I *know* what the Destroyer is." I had no time and no need for a Demonology 101 lecture. I rubbed at my demon mark, trying to calm it, as irritation flared to anger. "And I *did* kill it. I killed them both. On the same night." I'd damn near died doing it, but I wasn't going to admit that to Arawn. Not when I needed weapons and assistance from him. Not when I wasn't willing to admit to myself that I didn't know if I could do it again.

Arawn sat back in his chair. In one hand, he held his crystal goblet of wine. With the other, he stroked his beard, regarding me. Dark flames flickered in his eyes as he sized me up. "You believe you can kill the Destroyer now?"

"Let me put it this way—I can't let it live. Ten years ago the Destroyer marked me." I rubbed the demon mark some more, then noticed Arawn staring. I made myself stop. "As long as the Hellion lives, I'll never be free of its influence."

Even now, as we sat here in Arawn's private chambers, anger and frustration kept growing, a pressure building behind my eyes. My demon mark ached and burned; my fingers itched for a weapon. The only way, a voice inside me whispered, *the only way* to relieve the feeling would be to smash something. To take Arawn's crystal goblet and shatter it, then drive the shards into that smug face . . .

Stop, Vicky. Breathe. Arawn had done nothing to earn my anger. A deep breath shuddered its way into, then out of my lungs. That feeling of rage wasn't me; it was my demon mark. I couldn't let the Destroyer take control.

Arawn watched me, his intelligent gaze taking in my struggle as I fought down the rage. I pushed away the image of his face, slashed and bleeding, of myself laughing as I struck again and again. *No.* That was Difethwr's laughter, not mine. Not me. I closed my eyes and focused on my breathing. When the violent image faded and all I could see was darkness, I opened them again. Arawn still watched me with hawklike eyes.

When I spoke, my voice was steady. "As I said, I can't afford to let the Hellion live. The Destroyer is bigger and more powerful than before, thanks to all those demons Pryce packed into the cauldron. Pryce is bound to it, but he can't control it. I don't think the Hellion can even control itself, not right now. It's confused and enraged and disoriented." A bad combination for a Hellion.

Arawn nodded. "I have much to attend to here, and—do not tell anyone this—my injuries are not fully healed. I am not at my full strength." He set down his goblet. "I cannot interfere in the bargain you struck with Mallt-y-Nos beyond my borders. What price does she demand?"

Was he going to help me, or did he just want me to get the hell out of his realm? He'd watched my struggle; banishing me would banish one little piece of the Destroyer.

"I can't return to the Ordinary with the Destroyer on the loose."

"I understand. But you haven't answered my question."

"The Night Hag asked for three things." I reached down and retrieved the pieces of Rhudda's magic arrow. "This."

"A broken arrow?"

"It belonged to Rhudda Gawr. I won it from him in an archery contest. It wasn't broken then."

"You?" His voice betrayed surprise. "You beat Rhudda Gawr at archery?"

"I won his magic arrow," I repeated. "Pryce broke it. I was hoping it could be fixed."

Arawn took the pieces and examined them. "I'll see what my armorers can do. What else?"

"A white falcon that nests in Hellsmoor."

Arawn's stonelike face gave nothing away. "And the third item?"

"Well, um, apparently Mallt-y-Nos has a great admiration for . . ."

"For my hunting horn, yes?" When I nodded, he sighed. "She's desired it for centuries. I use it to call the wild hunt." He steepled his fingers again, chewing his lip as he thought. He reached a decision and folded his hands. "You say you can kill the Destroyer. I want it out of the Darklands. Rid me of the Destroyer, and I will give you my hunting horn."

My heart thumped with hope. I was getting somewhere. "I'll need better weapons."

"Of course. I'll send for my armorer to assist you." He called over the servant who stood by the door and spoke to him. The servant nodded and left the room. "My armory is at your disposal. But there is only one weapon in my kingdom that I believe is capable of defeating a Hellion." He stood, drawing his sword from its scabbard. The steel-gray blade, engraved with mystical symbols, didn't reflect the firelight; instead, it seemed to absorb it. "Darkblaze. It is the symbol of my power. You saw its flames?"

I nodded.

"When its blade burns, Darkblaze can kill anything. Shades. Demons. Even me, and I am a god." His gaze caught mine and held it. "But a weapon this powerful may be used only in pursuit of a just cause. If wielded for the wrong reasons, the flames extinguish."

"What are the wrong reasons?"

"Greed. Envy. Hatred. Lust. Choose your favorite among the seven deadly sins."

He was giving me a warning. "In other words, anger is on the list."

"Understand this, Victory: *Darkblaze will not strike an angry blow.*"

Fine. I couldn't think of any cause more just than destroying the Destroyer. Pryce's goal was to expand the demon plane into other realms, turning them into hells for him to rule. If he managed to harness the Destroyer's power, there'd be no stopping him. Multitudes would suffer. That sobbing child in my vision—and millions like her—would die. I was angry, yes, but it was a just anger. As long as I kept my focus on protecting the innocent, Darkblaze and I would get along fine.

Watching Difethwr disintegrate into a big heap of demon ash—and Pryce with him—that would be a bonus.

Arawn held out his sword hilt first, offering it to me. I stood and reached for the weapon. As I curled my fingers around the grip, a vibration, subtle but unmistakable, trembled along my arm. It felt like the sword was taking my measure. The vibration buzzed around my demon mark, lingering there. The mark burned and bubbled under the skin. Then the sensations faded. I raised the sword, moving it, trying its weight, its balance.

"What makes it flame?" I asked.

"A deserving opponent. As with so much else here, magic makes the determination."

Good. No incantations to learn. Darkblaze itself would guide me in knowing when to strike. I set the sword on the mantel and buckled on Arawn's sword belt.

There was something I needed to ask him before I set out. "Speaking of the magic, you mentioned a magical book."

"*The Register of the Cauldrons.* Yes, what of it?"

"It lists the names of those who've taken a swan dive into one of your cauldrons?"

A slight scowl darkened the king's face, as though he thought I was being disrespectful, but he nodded.

"What about . . . what if a shade doesn't make it into a cauldron?"

"Such as those who perished in my city today?"

"Yes," I said, even though I was thinking about Dad.

"Those names are not recorded. When a shade perishes in the Darklands, its spirit ceases to exist. What does not exist has no name to record."

Evan Vaughn, I thought. *My father's name is Evan Vaughn.* There was comfort in the very syllables, as though the fact that I knew my father's name kept him from slipping away.

There was no way Dad could have made it to Resurrection Square before hell broke loose. But maybe that spring, with its flow of life-giving magic, was like an extension of the cauldrons. I was about to ask when Arawn's servant appeared in the doorway. "My lord—" he began.

"Ah, my armorer is here."

"No, my lord. A man is demanding admittance. He says it's about . . ." He nodded at me. "Our guest."

Dad? Hope coursed through me. Who else would look for me here?

Sounds of scuffling came from the hallway. A muffled half-shout rose, then was cut off. Someone snarled.

Arawn snatched Darkblaze from the mantel.

Another snarl. That didn't sound like my father. It sounded like—

A figure appeared in the doorway, dragging two of Arawn's guards in a double headlock. It was Kane.

Kane—in the land of the dead?

Oh, God, no.

His eyes snapped with fury as he scanned the room.

"Kane, are you—? What's happened?"

His gaze softened when it lit on me. "Vicky." He saw Arawn, and the softness turned to steel. "I've come to take you home."

28

NO FLAMES FLARED FROM DARKBLAZE. ARAWN STARED AT Kane, then set the sword back on the mantel. "You are welcome in my kingdom. Please release my guards."

Kane dropped the men on the floor and straightened, opening his arms to me. Relief rushed through me as I realized his clothes were white, like mine.

"You're not dead," I whispered as he folded me in his arms.

He pulled me close, covering my hair and face with kisses. Like he could never get enough of touching me. His warm woodland scent surrounded me, blotting out the sharp smell of magic. Then he pulled back, holding me at arm's length, studying my face.

"And you?" he asked.

"I'm not dead, either. You can tell by the clothes. The living wear white."

"Thank God." Again he pulled me to him. Over my head, he spoke to Arawn. "She doesn't belong here. You will release her to me."

Arawn chuckled. "I believe your friend has come to play Orpheus, Victory. I'll leave you to explain our arrangement."

His footsteps crossed to the door, then paused. "And you are welcome, sir, to help yourself to some wine."

"No," I whispered.

"It's all right," he murmured against my hair. "I know not to accept."

Holding Kane's hands in mine, I stepped back. "Lord Arawn, could you do me a favor?"

Arawn turned. His expression suggested he thought he'd already granted me a favor or two too many.

"Could you ask your archivist whether my father's name has appeared in the *Register*?"

His eyebrows went up, but he inclined his head. Then he swept from the room, his guards casting angry scowls at us as they scrambled to their feet to follow him.

When the door closed, I stood on my tiptoes to kiss Kane. He groaned and pressed me into him. The kiss—warm and deep and delicious—tasted of everything I could ever want, of every single reason I had to return to the world of the living.

I looked into his gray eyes, heavy-lidded with desire. "Kane," I said, although I already knew the truth, "please don't tell me you came here to rescue me."

There. A flash of disappointment. He covered it quickly, but some part of him had hoped I'd swoon with gratitude at his feet so he could sweep me up and carry me off into the sunset. Or whatever passes for a sunset in this world.

"I don't need rescuing." As I said the words, my demon mark twinged, urging me toward anger. I ignored it. I didn't want to be angry with Kane.

"My mistake. I thought you did." The sharpness in his voice suggested anger was perfectly okay with him. He broke away from me and walked to the other side of the room. At the wall, he wheeled around, his face tight. Then his shoulders sagged and he sighed. "So much happened so fast. First a helicopter landed in Princeton. Then the wolves all started freaking out because there was a stranger in the compound. I picked up your scent, but also the smell of plague. All my instincts screamed to protect you, and I fought any wolf who got too curious. And *then* the Huntress came charging in and went straight to your cabin."

"You know about the Night Hag?"

"All werewolves do. We call her the Huntress, or the Mistress of Hounds. When she shows up, it's never good news."

All right. I could see why he'd been worried. Kane knew I was immune to the original zombie virus, but he also knew that the Old Ones, in their quest to give themselves truly eternal life, had attempted to create a super-version that would affect paranormals. When Kane scented plague virus and saw the arrival of a spirit whose task is to drive souls into the next world, he jumped to the obvious conclusion.

"You know what it's like after a shift," he continued. "The next morning, I had my human brain back, but my memories from the night before were flashes of sensation: images, scents, the sound of your voice, galloping hooves, the baying of hellhounds. No big picture, no overarching meaning. All I had was the unshakable feeling that something terrible had happened to you."

He strode back to me and took me in his arms. His hands roved over my back, like he had to keep touching me to believe I was real. I felt the same way about him.

"I tried everything I could think of," he said in my ear. "I went to the cabin and shouted through the door. I climbed up to peer through those damn tiny windows. Nothing. Except I could smell you. I could smell the plague. And I could smell death. The Huntress carries the smell of death with her, but I couldn't tell if it had come from her or from . . . from another source. It was just death." With a squeeze, he let me go, but he caught my hand and held it. "I even tried to talk to the Princeton guards. They're not allowed to socialize with us, of course, but I was going crazy from not knowing. I got nothing from them, either. If they'd been briefed about the helicopter, they weren't talking."

"So you summoned the Night Hag." Mallt-y-Nos must feel like Miss Popularity, getting called twice in two nights. "Wait, how could you call her? It was a full-moon night—weren't you in wolf form?"

"Like I said, one of her names is Mistress of Hounds. She can communicate with wolves. But that wasn't necessary. Moonrise was after midnight, and I called her as soon as it was dark. I was still in this form." His human form. The moon that shines on the Ordinary is absent from the Darklands, so he wouldn't change here. "The Huntress—the Night Hag—confirmed you'd crossed the border 'with body and soul still together,' which I took to mean you hadn't died. Hoped, anyway. But then she said, 'Many enter, but few return.' She was in her death's-head form, and her laugh . . . Vicky, it sent chills through me."

"You made a deal with her so she'd let you in to find me." What price had she demanded of Kane? How many more impossible items would we have to collect before we could leave? Arawn knew what Mallt-y-Nos was up to—what if he refused to let anything else leave his realm? Kane, who'd come to rescue me, would be stuck here himself. "Kane, you shouldn't have bargained with her. You're a great negotiator, but the Night Hag is in a different league. You could have your whole staff of lawyers go over any deal she offered, and she'd still win in the end." Never mind that I'd made a deal with her myself.

He called me on that one. "No bargains? How did you get in?"

"I, um, said I'd bring back a few souvenirs, that's all."

"Like what—'I let a shapeshifter into the Darklands and all I got was this lousy T-shirt'?" Exasperation colored his voice.

"Lord Arawn is helping me. I'll be fine." Fine and dandy. Just as soon as I found some duct tape for Rhudda's arrow, did a little birding on the outskirts of Hell, and brought Arawn the head of the new-and-definitely-not-improved Destroyer.

"Vicky." He put both hands on my shoulders and stared into my eyes. "What did you promise her?"

"A magic arrow—already got it." Both pieces. "A white falcon. Arawn's hunting horn." I ticked off each item on my fingers as if it were no big deal. One, two, three, and I'd be home. "Arawn has already promised me the horn."

"Another bargain?"

"He'll give it to me after I've killed the Destroyer."

"The Destroyer—you mean the Hellion? I thought you already killed that thing."

"I did. Pryce brought it back." Kane gaped at me in disbelief. "Remember I told you that Pryce was trying to revive his shadow demon? That cauldron he used to trap demons was the cauldron of transformation, stolen from Arawn centuries ago. Pryce cloaked the demons and returned the cauldron to the Darklands. Arawn tried to purify it so it could be returned to use, but the cauldron was rigged so that the purification spell released the demons. Pryce jumped into the cauldron. All those demons transformed into the Destroyer, bound to Pryce." I hesitated. "He, um, tried to pull me in with him, but I climbed out. And then—"

"Wait, he tried to transform you, too? That's it, Vicky. I'm not going to let you run around this place chasing after him. Pryce alone is bad enough. Pryce plus the Destroyer—no."

"'*Let* me'?" I squeezed his hand so hard that, if he'd been anything besides a werewolf, the bones would have cracked. He jerked away. "Since when did I ever ask your permission to do anything?" If this was the result of taking our relationship to the next level, maybe it was time to take one giant step backward.

"Okay, that came out wrong. Sorry." He didn't sound sorry. He sounded mad as hell. "But it's the same as always. You go rushing in alone, determined to save the world all by yourself. No help from anyone. No thought for those who care about you."

My own anger was seething, too, but again I pushed it aside. *Count to ten. One . . . two . . . three . . .* I made myself stay calm. *Eight . . . nine . . . ten.*

"You want to help me? Okay. We'll do this together. We'll defeat the Destroyer, and then we'll both go home."

He pulled me to him again. "The Destroyer is Arawn's problem. Come home with me now."

"It's *my* problem, Kane." In so many ways I didn't even want to try to count them. "And the only way I can leave here is to give the Night Hag what I promised her."

"I can get you out."

"This isn't like persuading a jury with a brilliant closing argument. Mallt-y-Nos will never budge on her terms."

"Let me try. I talked her into letting me in. If she won't listen to me, we'll go after the Destroyer together."

I stepped away. "We don't have the time to waste." He looked hurt at "waste," but too bad. It *would* be a waste of time, and he needed to understand that. "You saw what the Destroyer did to this city. I've got to stop it before the whole realm goes up in flames." And after that, the human world.

Kane opened his mouth like he was going to argue. But he didn't. His face softened, and he reached out to brush my cheek with his fingertips. "I just want you to be safe," he said, his voice husky. "And with me."

Anger melted. I reached up and held his hand against my cheek, then turned and kissed the palm. He put his other arm around my shoulders and we stood there, close and warm, holding each other. How could I ever want anything else, when this felt so good? After a few, way-too-short moments, I placed his hand on my right forearm, where he could feel the angry, pulsing heat of the demon mark. His eyes widened at the strength of it.

"I'll never be safe while the Destroyer lives."

He nodded. And then he kissed me.

I kissed him back, and warmth spread through me. Something deep inside reached toward this man who'd laughed with me, made love to me, argued with me, fought beside me—and ventured into the realm of the dead to find me.

A brisk knock rapped on the door, bringing me back to the here and now. A shade dressed in blue stuck his head inside. "Lord Arawn's armorer, at your service."

"We'll be right with you," I said. He bowed and shut the door. I turned to Kane. Back to the business at hand. "Arawn wasn't happy about my deal with the Night Hag. We'd better negotiate with him now, so he'll let you take out whatever you promised her."

He shook his head. "Not necessary. She didn't ask me for anything like that."

"Then what was her price?"

"Nothing I can't pay." He put his arm around me and steered me toward the door. "But never mind that now. Let's go kill the Destroyer so you can come home."

29

ARAWN'S VAST ARMORY FILLED A STONE-WALLED ROOM THE size of a small warehouse. I picked out three bronze-bladed throwing knives. They were enough. I had Darkblaze and didn't want to be weighed down as we chased the Destroyer. Kane is no swordsman, but he chose a couple of knives and a wicked-looking bronze ax. Ax fighting doesn't take a lot of finesse, and he had the strength to make each blow count.

Arawn waited for us at a table near the armory's doorway. The king seemed tense, angry, but that wasn't surprising with an out-of-control Hellion ravaging his kingdom. He'd spread out a map of his realm, Difethwr's path of destruction marked in red. The line zigzagged across the map like a jagged scar. From Tywyll, the Hellion had gone south, and most recently was reported west of the city.

"Where's the border with Uffern?" I asked.

"Here." Arawn pointed to the section marked Hellsmoor. "In the north. Most of the region is swampland, but a steep mountain range marks the border itself." He traced a finger along the edge of the map. Beyond the mountain range was a sea of flames.

That was where I wanted Difethwr. At the edge of the

Darklands, far from the Ordinary. If I couldn't kill the Hellion, I'd do my best to drive it back to Hell.

But I had every intention of killing it.

Once I'd traveled to Hellsmoor, my demon mark would call the Destroyer to me. Like it or not, I was bound to the Hellion. But I could use that bond to my advantage.

"What's the quickest way to get to the border?" I asked.

"I'll lend you two steeds from my stables. They can travel anywhere in my kingdom in an hour, whatever the distance." He watched me from the corner of his eye. "They are the same breed Mallt-y-Nos rides."

Great, flying horses that breathed fire. The last time I rode a horse, I was eight, and my steed had been hand-carved and fixed to a carousel. Something told me this ride would be more than a little wilder. But if it would get me into position in an hour, I was all for it.

I told Arawn my plan. He agreed to evacuate a corridor between Difethwr's current position and Hellsmoor, and sent messengers to begin that work. We couldn't stop the Destroyer from torching everything in its path, but we could minimize the loss of life.

"All right," I said, heading for the door. "Let's do this."

We followed a blue-clad servant down a stone hallway. Arawn walked beside me, Kane a few steps behind.

"Lord Arawn," I said, a flutter of worry in my chest, "did you ask your archivist about the register?"

He nodded, his lips tight. "Evan Vaughn has not passed through any of the cauldrons."

What should I feel—relief or despair? I didn't know. I decided to press for more information. "Outside of your city, there's a spring . . ."

"It is forbidden."

Yeah, I'd kind of gotten that idea when the Keeper tried to lop off my head. "Okay, fine, but if someone did happen to . . . um, say someone stepped in that spring, accidentally. What would happen?"

He stopped so abruptly Kane walked into him. Arawn glared at me. " 'Accidentally'? When the spring's Keeper was viciously cut down?"

Somehow, I didn't think Arawn would want to hear about

self-defense. "I just want to know what effect the magic would have on a shade who was . . ." I couldn't say *dying*. ". . . who was fading."

Arawn's hawklike eyes fixed me with a hard stare. He seemed to weigh the Keeper's death against my offer to kill the Destroyer.

"Go to the stables, Victory, and choose a steed. If you do not leave at once, I shall have you arrested for defiling the spring and murdering its Keeper." He wheeled around and strode away, his footsteps echoing on the stones.

"What was that about?" Kane asked.

I didn't answer. I was thinking about Arawn's words: *murdering its Keeper.* So the spring's guardian had died. I hadn't meant to kill him. I'd even tried to save him. But the magic had failed him.

That meant it had failed Dad, too. My heart clenched as I forced myself to admit it: He was gone, his spirit already dissolved into wisps of nothing.

It was the Destroyer's fault. The Hellion had sent my father here. Dad had only tried to hold on, for too long, to remnants of the life he'd loved. The life the Destroyer had taken away from him.

And Difethwr would continue to destroy, leaving nothing behind but death and pain and misery, until I stopped it. Kane put a hand on my arm, but I shook him off. I couldn't speak. Hatred, hot and bitter, choked me. Hatred for the Destroyer, for Pryce. For their war on my family. For their vision of a future consumed by flames.

My demon mark burned. Somewhere, a roar of hatred answered my own. It echoed through me, setting my blood on fire. I'd called the Destroyer, and the Hellion had heard me. Now to send it back to Hell.

DESPITE THEIR FEARSOME APPEARANCE, ARAWN'S STEEDS WERE easy to ride. The horses obeyed the rider's intentions. Just mount, set your mind on where you want to go, and hang on. Within an hour, we were in Hellsmoor. The description of Hellsmoor as a "swamp" was too kind. "A fetid quagmire of quicksand and filthy water" would have been more accurate. The air was heavy with the stink of marsh gas; columns of flame shot upward, then extinguished. Snakes as thick as my arm whiplashed through the water.

I hated this place. And I poured my hatred into my demon mark. *Hear that, Difethwr? Come and find me.*

Our horses had landed on a small hummock, beside a cluster of twisted, skeletal trees. About a mile away, sawtooth mountains rose like a fortress wall. I'd wanted to land there, as close to Uffern as possible, but the horses wouldn't go any closer. Even here, they seemed nervous, pawing the ground and snorting. Flames shot from their nostrils in short blasts. I tried to urge my horse back into the air, choosing a mountain and setting my intention there. He shuddered and whinnied but didn't budge.

Stupid horse. I'd *make* him do what I wanted. I drew back my arm, my fingers in a tight fist. A hand caught my wrist and held it lightly but firmly. The demon mark on my forearm pulsed and burned, like someone was rhythmically zapping it with electric shocks.

"Vicky, what are you doing?"

Yeah, what are you doing? echoed a voice inside my head. *Solving a problem with violence, as usual, I see.*

Oh, great. The Eidolon was back. It had been so quiet in Tywyll, hiding like a coward in my gut from Pryce, that I'd almost forgotten about it. It hadn't complained about violence there, when I'd kept its demon ass out of that cauldron.

You don't care about my ass. You were saving your own shapeshifter ass.

"Shut up, Butterfly," I muttered.

Kane looked startled. "What did you call me?"

"Nothing." I opened my hand to show I wasn't going to hit anything, and Kane released my arm.

"So how are we going to get up there?" I pointed at the mountains.

"Perhaps I can help," said a voice from the swamp.

I turned around so fast I almost fell off my horse. Behind us stood a man in a boat. He'd poled up silently, not even a splash to announce his approach. I didn't like being snuck up on. This guy was lucky he hadn't gotten a knife hurled into his eye.

"I'd offer you refreshment," he said, "but I have nothing in the boat." The man was blond, with blue eyes and a thick beard. He wore a red tunic and a sword belt.

"You're a Keeper?"

"A Border Keeper. My task is to prevent demons from crossing into our realm. Quite a few have left the realm today, with my . . . ah, assistance." He grinned and patted the sword at his side. Then he reached into the bottom of his boat and lifted the corner of a tarp that lay there. Beneath it lay the severed, grimacing heads of half a dozen demons. "There's a reward for each one I bring in."

"We need to get to the top of those mountains," I said, "but our horses won't go any closer."

"That's because they can't. There is a spell on that range that prevents creatures from flying over them. Only the white falcon is immune."

The white falcon of Hellsmoor—the final prize in the Night Hag's scavenger hunt. "Why is that?"

The Keeper shrugged. "Perhaps its magic is stronger. It's well known that the white falcon has the power to go where others cannot. At any rate, the spell's purpose is to prevent demons from flying over the mountains and into our realm, and it serves that purpose well." His eyes narrowed. "Why do you want to go there?"

"To kill a Hellion that's coming this way. Can you take us?"

He considered. "I can. For a price."

"A price?" Anger leapt up inside me. "There's no time to haggle, damn it. The Hellion that's coming will snap your puny sword like a toothpick and turn you into Border Keeper flambé."

He regarded me without blinking.

"What's your price?" Kane asked, his voice neutral.

"What can you pay?" the Keeper countered.

Goddamn deal-making spirits! I jumped down from my horse and bounded into the boat. By the time my feet hit the deck, my sword was in my hand.

The Keeper's eyes went wide, and he stepped back. The boat rocked precariously. "You wield Darkblaze."

"That's right." I advanced, pressing the sword's point into his chest. "And unless you want me to wield it on you, you'll take us to those mountains right now."

"Vicky," Kane said above me. "Put away the sword."

Suddenly I saw myself from the outside. Wild-eyed, scowling, brandishing a sword whose bite meant certain death. My demon mark didn't merely burn or sting; it glowed like a beacon. It was drawing Difethwr to me. I could feel the Hellion's approach. With each earthshaking step Difethwr took, my anger grew hotter, the urge to destroy more overpowering.

The Keeper crouched before me, shaking. My arms ached to strike, to feel the blade whoosh through the air, to meet the resistance of flesh and bone, and then keep slicing. I wanted the smell of hot blood, the melody of an anguished cry.

Look at the sword, said Butterfly's voice in my head.

Darkblaze gleamed dully in the light.

It's not flaming, is it? Remember what that means? This guy isn't an enemy. For cripe's sake, put the sword away.

The Eidolon was right. With effort, I sheathed the sword. I avoided looking at Kane.

Listen, I've got more than enough chow for now. So don't do anything stupid that'll get us both killed, okay? Butterfly's voice faded. Other than a slight gnawing when I thought about how close I'd just come—twice—to unnecessary violence, I barely knew the Eidolon was there.

The Keeper rubbed his chest. "Here's my offer," I said. "You get us to the mountains. If I kill the Hellion, Lord Arawn has promised me his hunting horn." I gestured at the tarp that covered the severed demon heads. "Any reward beyond that is yours."

"Agreed." The Keeper sounded so shaky that I think he would've accepted a cup of swamp water as payment to avoid making me angry again. He may have been a whiz at killing stranded demons, but fighting a crazy woman with a magic sword and a werewolf with a battle ax—weighing those odds, who wouldn't decide to cooperate?

Still, I thought I'd offered a decent price.

Kane dismounted and looped our horses' reins around a tree branch. I moved over to make room, taking a seat, and he stepped into the boat.

"Are you all right?" He took my hand as he settled beside me. The demon mark glowed through my sleeve.

"Calling the Destroyer is . . . hard. This new version of the Hellion feels more powerful than before." *Way* more powerful—I didn't want to admit how much. If my demon mark had previously felt like a bonfire, now it felt like a nuclear reactor in meltdown mode. "I can handle it."

"Are you sure?"

I yanked away. "It's not like I have a choice." What was I doing? Kane wanted to help, and I responded by turning into a seething ball of fury. I reached for his hand and gentled my voice.

"Please be patient with me. To do this, I have to push down everything in me that isn't the Destroyer's essence. That leaves anger, violence, rage . . . Those feelings call out to the Destroyer. I have to bring them forward, and the demon mark magnifies them." I swallowed. "But the real me is still in there somewhere, too."

"I understand." But his eyes made me wonder. He patted my hand and let it go.

I clenched my hand into a fist and then opened it again, stretching the fingers. *Clench, release. Clench, release.* It cooled the fire in my forearm by a few degrees.

The Keeper dug his pole into the water and pushed, propelling the boat forward. We glided silently through the water toward the stark stone mountains.

Clench, release. Clench, release. The movement distracted me from the simmering anger that felt ready at every moment to boil over into rage. The anger was there, calling the Destroyer, but it didn't possess me. *Clench, release.* I watched my hand open and close, focusing only on that, noticing how my fingers bent, feeling their nails dig into my palms, then unfurling them again.

"Look!" Kane's exclamation made me jump. A throwing knife was in my hand before I realized I'd moved.

"What?" I turned back and forth, scanning the swamp for a huge, ugly Hellion. "The Destroyer?" We'd be sitting ducks in this boat.

"No, sorry, it's the falcon. In that tree."

I squinted along the line of his arm to see a large bird perched on a dead branch. It was snow white, with a powerful chest and a hooked, cruel-looking beak. As we passed, the falcon turned its head, following us with dark eyes. Then it took to the sky, rising slowly as it flapped its massive wings. Its wing span must have been four feet. The bird climbed into the air and soared toward the mountains.

Nice if we could do that.

"Its nest is on that mountain," remarked the Keeper. "On a cliff a thousand feet up."

Of course. If I survived my encounter with the Destroyer, my next job would be to scale a thousand-foot cliff and coax the bird to hop onto my shoulder. *One thing at a time, Vicky.* At least now I knew where to look for the falcon. I'd figure out how to catch it later.

The Keeper steered the boat to a narrow strip of beach at the base of a cliff. Dark granite stretched up and up as far as I could see. There was no way we could climb the steep face. I couldn't fight here, with a mountain at my back and the swamp at my feet. I'd kill the damn Keeper for wasting my time. *Clench, release.* I sat on my hands, keeping them away from my weapons.

"This won't do," I said. "I have to be up there. If I can't kill the Hellion, I need to drive it back into the demon plane."

"I surmised as much. Above us is a lookout station. The ground is level, there's room to fight, and it overlooks Uffern."

"And it's thousands of feet straight up!" My fingers clenched into fists, and this time I didn't release. I really wanted to smash this guy's face. "Even if I had wings, I couldn't get up there, so what good is it?"

"Vicky." Kane's calm voice washed away some of my anger. "If it's a lookout station, there must be a way up."

"Indeed." The Keeper nodded. "Arawn's wizards created this range as a border defense. Some of the mountains, such as this one, are hollow. The path is inside." He muttered a few words and made a sweeping gesture, like drawing aside a curtain. An opening appeared in the cliff.

"I'll check it out," Kane said.

"Be careful," I called. I drew a knife and stood between him and the Keeper. I wasn't going to let this guy corner us in some sort of trap. The Keeper folded his arms across his chest in a casual, nonaggressive posture, but he kept his eyes on me.

Kane reappeared. "It's like he said. The mountain is hollow, and there's a path, a ramp, that spirals up to the top."

I put away my knife. The Keeper gave me a slight nod. "I will show you the way," he said. Kane helped him drag the boat into the cave. I surveyed the swamp. A shadow glided over the stagnant water as the white falcon soared overhead. Other than that, the place was still, though I could feel the Destroyer's approach.

It was coming. Would I be ready? My demon mark burned, craving violence. Did I want to fight the Destroyer—or join it?

Clench, release.

I followed the others through a narrow opening in the granite, wide enough at the bottom for the boat to clear, then tapering upward to a height a few inches above my head.

The cavelike entryway widened into a hollow mountain, just as Kane had described. The same dim, even light that suffused the Darklands illuminated the inside. A ramp, complete with railing, spiraled steeply upward.

"What's your name?" Kane asked the Keeper as I approached.

"Edern ap Nudd." He bowed. "A knight of King Arthur." *Except for seven, none returned.* Suddenly I felt a twinge of sympathy for the guy. Like me, he'd been clay-born when he entered the Darklands. What would it feel like to come here as a living person and never be able to leave? A chill ran icy fingers along my spine. I didn't intend to find out.

"I spent centuries as Lord Arawn's prisoner," Edern continued. "Then more centuries in his court until I persuaded him I could be trusted. Now I patrol the border."

Kane told him our names, but I was too impatient for formalities. "How long does it take to climb to the top?" I asked, peering upward.

"You don't climb. You ride. I'll show you." Edern walked to the base of the ramp. He gripped the railing as he stepped onto the incline. When he let go, he began to glide up the ramp. He went about ten feet, then grabbed the railing and hoisted himself over the edge, landing lightly on his feet in front of us.

"The magical current carries you, like a fast-flowing river. It takes perhaps ten minutes to reach the top."

Ten minutes. Better than the hours-long climb I'd imagined. "It works for clay-born, too?" I asked. "Not just shades?"

"Aye. It carries whatever steps into its flow."

Kane looked up, craning as he followed the spiral that seemed to go on forever. "How do we get back down?"

"When we reach the top, I'll reverse the flow. It prevents enemies from following us."

"Let's go." I started toward the ramp.

"Wait, Lady Victory." Edern put a hand on my shoulder, lightly, as though he feared my reaction. "Riding the flow takes a . . ." He searched for the right word. "A lightness of touch. Hold the railing until you feel yourself floating on the current. Then let go. Don't try to propel yourself. Focus on keeping your balance."

"Balance. Right." How hard could it be? Like one of those moving sidewalks at an airport.

"Take care. If you fall, the magic presses you down. It can drown the clay-born."

Drowned by magic. Wonderful. Why couldn't anything be

easy here? Maybe the Destroyer had the right idea—raze every-thing, burn it all to ashes. Obliterate the Darklands, and let souls find their way to some other realm. I pictured the mountain in flames, this ramp a river of fire, and I laughed. The sound that echoed through the hollow mountain didn't sound like me. It was deep and many-voiced, like a chorus of demons. Like the voice of the Destroyer. The burning ache in my arm forced me to come back to myself.

Edern's sword was drawn, ready. "There are some among the clay-born," he said in a low, tight voice, "who are half-demon."

"Not her." Kane held his battle ax. "You touch her and I'll kill you."

Edern's eyes went back and forth between us.

"You think I'm a demi-demon?" Moving slowly, I held out my left arm, the one not marked by the Hellion. "Your blade is bronze, right?"

I pulled up my sleeve, baring my forearm. "Nick my arm. See if bronze affects my flesh."

Edern came forward. Kane growled a warning. "It's okay, Kane," I said.

Edern flicked the blade against my arm, so quickly I didn't feel its sting. He watched as the blood welled up. No sulfurous steam emerged. The flesh didn't bubble or melt. He stepped back, satisfied. Both he and Kane put their weapons away.

I pulled down my sleeve. The shallow cut had already stopped bleeding.

"I didn't think you were an enemy," Edern said. "Darkblaze didn't flame when you drew it. But the sword could have been counterfeit, and I had to be sure." He extended his hand. "You could have killed me then. I could have let you drown in the ramp's magic. Let us acknowledge that we may trust each other."

"Go on, Vicky," Kane said at my ear. "We could use an ally."

I shook. A grin widened Edern's face. He gestured at the ramp. "Try riding the flow for a little way. When you let go of the railing, keep your hand near it. Go up a few feet, then grab the railing again and lift your feet to stop yourself. See how it feels."

I grasped the railing and stepped onto the ramp's base. It was like stepping into water with an undertow. I couldn't see the magic, but I could feel the current that lapped at my feet, then moved upward, swirling around my ankles, sucking gently, urging me forward. The pull didn't feel too strong. I looked up. I couldn't see the peak from here. "This will take us all the way to the top?"

"Don't underestimate the flow. It's more powerful than you imagine. Careful, now."

I let go. At once the current yanked my feet forward. My body tilted backward, and I nearly landed on my ass. I lunged forward to compensate, and my feet almost went out from under me. Trying to steady myself, I grabbed the railing. Immediately the pull lessened, flowing softly around my ankles. I looked back. In a couple of seconds, jerking around like a mannequin, I'd traveled twenty feet along the ramp.

I looked over the railing. I was about eight feet above the cave's floor. As Edern had done, I vaulted the railing and jumped down.

Kane and I took turns riding the flow a little way, then grabbing the railing and jumping off. Edern shouted instructions: "Bend your knees!" "Use your arms!" "Keep your eyes up!" After a few tries, we could each stay reasonably steady as we glided up the ramp.

Edern nodded his satisfaction. "I think you're ready. I'll cloak the entrance, and we can go up." He gestured, and the entrance disappeared. "It's still there," he said. "But anyone looking would have to feel along the wall to find it." He gestured toward the ramp. "Ladies first?"

Oh, please. Okay, so Edern had last walked the human plane during the age of chivalry. But that didn't mean I had to go first, toward whatever waited at the top of the mountain. We'd agreed to trust each other, yes, but what was that old saying? Trust, but verify. In this case, it was going to be, Trust, but don't show 'em your back. I didn't like the idea of an armed man behind me. And anything could be waiting at the top of the ramp. For all I knew, it could dump us out a side door into Uffern, like Pryce pushing me out that window in my client's dreamscape.

"You go ahead," I said. "We'll follow."

"As you prefer." He didn't look bothered to be first in line. Maybe I was being too cautious.

Edern stepped onto the ramp and looked back at me. "Remember," he said, "balance and lightness of touch." He let go and moved upward.

Kane went next. He wobbled a bit at the start—and nearly

fell over when he looked back to see if I was on my way—but within a few yards was gliding nearly as smoothly as Edern.

My turn. Clutching the railing, I stepped onto the ramp. Warm, tingly magic wrapped itself around my ankles and licked at my calves. When I felt a lift, like I was a leaf floating on a stream, I let go.

Holding my arms out for balance and keeping my left hand near the railing, I let the current carry me forward. The stiffer I stood, the harder it was to stay upright, so I kept my knees soft and my back slightly rounded. Half-crouched, I felt like a sumo wrestler ready to take on an opponent.

The current shifted and rippled under my feet, and once—just once—I made the mistake of looking down to see what carried me. The moment I tilted my head, my legs shot out from under me. I fell forward and sideways, banging my head on the wall before I managed to grab the railing. I gripped it with both hands and lifted my feet until they were out of the flow. Bent over the railing, I could see down, way down, to the bottom of the mountain. Another mistake. I closed my eyes until the vertigo passed. Okay. So now I knew why Edern kept shouting about keeping our eyes up.

Holding on to the railing, I got my feet back under me and bent my knees. Eyes up. I let go. For the rest of the journey I kept my chin lifted, watching the rock wall ahead as I spiraled up the inside of the mountain, moving toward whatever awaited me at the top.

30

LEAVING THE CURRENT WAS AS SIMPLE AS STEPPING OFF AN escalator. As I neared the top, Kane held out his arms to me. I reached out and grasped both his hands. One step and I left the current behind. We stood on a platform of rock inside the mountain, the peak doming over our heads, surrounded by granite walls—and higher up than I wanted to think about.

Edern stood at Kane's shoulder. As soon as I left the current, he went to the top of the ramp. He said some words in a language I didn't recognize, making a counterclockwise spiral motion with his hand. "I've reversed the flow," he said. "Now it will take us down when we've finished here."

Assuming we survived.

"This way," Edern said, and walked straight through the wall. My heart lurched, certain he'd tricked us, leaving us trapped on the platform.

Then Kane followed him, disappearing into the solid rock. Immediately he stuck his head back through. It looked odd, like a trophy hanging on a wall.

"The doorway's here," he said. "It's still cloaked, that's all." A hand appeared below the head. I took it, closed my eyes, and stepped through. It felt like walking through a cool mist.

When I opened my eyes, I stood in a large, flat arena, oval in shape and ringed by a waist-high stone wall. At my back was a cliff that jutted up another twenty feet, coming to a peak that capped the hollow part of the mountain. Otherwise, we stood at the top. The arena was empty except for the three of us.

"As I told you below, this place is a lookout station for the Border Keepers," Edern said. "To the south, the Darklands. To the north"—he gestured to our right—"Uffern."

I walked to the side overlooking the Darklands. Arawn's realm stretched before me for miles, the swamp of Hellsmoor giving way to forests and rolling hills beyond. From up here, it looked quiet, peaceful, a place for shades to rest after they'd worked long and hard in their clay-born lives. There was no sign yet of Difethwr's approach, but I knew the Hellion was on its way. I could feel each footstep in the pulsing of my demon mark.

As soon as I focused on the mark, pain shot through my arm, and the scene before me changed. Flames burned everywhere, consuming the landscape. The swamp boiled, the rocks melted, creatures shrieked with pain and terror as their flesh charred. It felt *right*. Another demonic laugh bubbled up in me, and I had to fight it down. *No.* This was Difethwr's vision, not mine. But calling the Hellion to me made it harder and harder to find the line where I ended and the Destroyer began.

I closed my eyes and pulled back until I could feel that the mark I bore wasn't me. It was the Destroyer in me, yes. But I was stronger. I had to be.

Something brushed my arm, lightly, and I opened my eyes to see Kane's concerned face.

"Just making sure you're still with us," he said.

I smiled. "Yeah, I'm still here." Barely hanging on, but here. He put his arm around me, and I rested my head against his shoulder. It helped. The burning inside me calmed a little.

Edern came up beside us. He carried a spyglass, like the one I'd used on Rhudda's archery field, but bigger. "I have done the service I promised you, bringing you to the mountains. Now, tell me more about why you're here. You said a Hellion approaches. What is its name? From which direction does it come?" He jerked his thumb over his shoulder, toward the demon plane. "Not from Uffern, I suspect. Occasionally a demon attempts to scale the mountains and enter our realm, but today a dozen demons or more approached the border from our side.

That's never happened before. Tell me, Lady Victory, what is happening?"

"The Hellion is Difethwr, the Destroyer. Right now, it's rampaging through your land." Edern's expression turned grim. It got grimmer as I brought him up to speed on how Pryce had used the cauldron of transformation to change hundreds of personal demons into a far bigger, far nastier demon. "The cauldron spat out the Destroyer. Pryce is bound to it, but the Destroyer is in control. I'm trying to draw them here."

"How do you call the Hellion?" His eyes strayed to my right arm, where the demon mark glowed through my sleeve. "Are you a sorcerer?"

"No, I'm not. Pryce isn't the only one with a bond to the Destroyer. Ten years ago, it marked me. I'm using that mark to draw the Destroyer this way. I can't command the Hellion, but I can call it. When it gets here, I'll kill it."

"With Darkblaze."

"That's the plan. I killed the Destroyer once before. Lord Arawn believes I can do it again, so he loaned me his sword." When Difethwr arrived, I'd have to wield Darkblaze left-handed. My demon-marked arm refused to raise itself against the Hellion. But I'd trained myself to fight with either hand.

Edern searched the Darklands through his spyglass. When he lowered it, he looked as though he'd come to some decision. "I will help you," he said. "My own sword, Demonsbane, has dispatched a Hellion or two in its time." He patted the hilt. "Never one as powerful as the Destroyer, of course, but we'll give that demon some trouble so you can move in for the kill."

I tilted my head, skeptical. "For what price? Don't even think about asking for Darkblaze. It's not mine to give."

"Dark—?" Edern threw back his head and roared with laughter. "I see you're catching on to our ways. We do like to bargain here." He chuckled. "But it would never occur to me to bargain for Lord Arawn's own sword. What a notion. No, Lady Victory, I ask no price beyond our original agreement. I wish only to help." He placed a hand over his heart and bowed his head.

"Thank you." I bowed in return, then glanced to the right. "I want to check the north side, to see whether any demons are massing in Uffern." Hellions have a way of knowing when trouble is brewing. Disasters attract them like a rose garden attracts bees. Difethwr would be hard enough to deal with; we didn't need demonic reinforcements.

Edern nodded. "I'll keep watch here."

I turned to Kane. "Want to take a peek at Hell?"

"Not particularly." He looked down at his white tunic and leggings, so different from the expensive suits he normally wore. "But I think I've already proved I'll follow you anywhere."

Together we crossed to the northern border. Kane held my hand, but I pulled away, folding my arms across my stomach. Too much of the warm fuzzies would dim the signal I was sending to Difethwr. And every minute that the Destroyer wasn't here was a minute of destruction in the Darklands.

At the wall, we looked into Uffern. The air there was dim and dirty, thick with smoke from fires that blackened the landscape. Even the lakes burned. The ground was scarred and pitted. Everything was dead. Even at this distance, you couldn't avoid the stench of sulfur and brimstone on the scorched wind.

This was how I'd seen the Darklands earlier—a ruined land of pain and death and desolation. This was what the Destroyer would do to every place it passed through, everything it touched.

In the distance, two or three demons flew with batlike wings. But no Hellions gathered below the mountains.

"Ugh," said Kane. "Scratch Uffern from our list of vacation spots." He glanced at me, but I couldn't smile.

"Fine with me." We went back to stand beside Edern.

"There's some smoke in the distance, but it reaches across the horizon," he said, handing me the spyglass. "I can't pinpoint the Destroyer's location."

I looked through the spyglass. Hazy smoke stretched along the horizon. So much destruction. My demon mark flared, excited, but the rest of me felt sick.

A blur of white sailed through the circle of my vision. I adjusted the spyglass to focus on the falcon that soared over Hellsmoor. It felt strange to observe the beautiful bird from above. Suddenly, it folded its wings and dived. I followed it with the spyglass. A jet of water plumed, and the falcon rose again, wings flapping. A snake twisted in its talons. The falcon gained altitude, carrying its prey back to its nest.

A good hunter. And one that could go where others could not.

No wonder the Night Hag wanted the falcon. She'd have a blast watching it dive-bomb the souls she chased.

The nest was on a ledge that jutted out from the sheer rock face, far below where I stood now. It was inaccessible, unless . . . "I don't suppose your magic escalator has an exit at the falcon's nest."

Eyebrows raised, Edern shook his head.

I set the spyglass on the wall. The white falcon was a distraction—one that let me avoid what I was almost afraid to do. Difethwr's approach was too slow. I had to strengthen my call.

The Hellion was coming. I could see the smoke in the distance. Even more, though, I could *feel* it. The heat from my demon mark spread up my arm. Instead of trying to hold the feeling back, I let it grow. I opened my heart to anger, to rage, to the blind urge to destroy. The fiery feeling burning through me—agonizing, like my soul was on fire, blazing inside and out.

"Over there!" Edern said.

I scanned the horizon. To the right, a column of smoke rose, denser and thicker than the general haze. It was red at the bottom, lit by flames, and sooty black at the top. "It's the Destroyer," I said. "Give me some room—I'm going to reel it in."

Edern clapped my shoulder, then moved away. Kane stood in front of me, a warm glow lighting his eyes. "I know this isn't the time or the place, but the hell with all that." He pulled me to him, folding me in his arms and pressing his mouth against mine. For a moment, my demon mark fought him, urging me to pull away. Then I thought "the hell with it," too. I kissed him back, drinking in his strength, his goodness and loyalty—things I'd need if I was going to survive this encounter.

"I love you," he said. "Whatever happens, remember that."

"I . . ." My feelings tangled in a jumble of confusion. The anger I'd called up wanted to take over, claiming me, obliterating all other emotions and burning them to ashes. But somewhere inside me, the other feelings hung on. Loyalty, honor, the desire to do what's right . . . and love? Could a fragile thing like love survive the Destroyer's wrath?

"Shh." He touched a finger to my lips. "It's all right. You don't have to say anything." He kissed my forehead, a gesture so tender that tears welled in my eyes. Then he moved away.

I blinked rapidly and wiped my face. My heart thumped as I

watched him go. I let myself feel its rapid beating. Then I turned back to the job I had to do.

The column of smoke had veered farther right. I rolled up my sleeve, exposing my demon mark, and focused my full attention on the Destroyer. I dropped all defenses I held against the Hellion. No pushing down, no holding back. I threw away thoughts of Kane and love and anything else I'd ever cared about. I craved only destruction. Only pain, burning, rubble. An explosion rocked Hellsmoor. My arm exploded, too. That's what it felt like as hellfire erupted from the demon mark.

I held up my arm like a beacon, a demonic Statue of Liberty lighting the way for utter destruction.

The Hellion roared in response. It was too far away to hear, but I heard it anyway. The sound reverberated inside my head. It shook me down to my toes.

The hellfire spouting from my arm burned brighter.

Something tore itself from my gut and fell at my feet.

"Whoa, it's *ugly* in there." That damn Eidolon. "Hey, how come I can't fly?" Its black wings fluttered, but the demon stayed on the ground.

Stupid annoyance. I don't know why I hadn't killed it before. But now I had bronze. I pulled a throwing knife and hurtled it at the Eidolon.

It jumped away a nanosecond before the knife struck the dirt.

I stomped my foot—once, again, again—trying to squash it like the bug it was. Damn, it was fast. It took off running for the north wall, all six of its legs flashing.

I checked Difethwr's progress. The Hellion had veered off course again. I didn't have time to mess around with Butterfly.

I scooped up my knife and returned it to its sheath. "Edern!" I called. "There's a demon trying to go over the north wall!" I returned to my station and raised my arm, renewing my call to Difethwr.

"Where? I don't—Wait, you mean that insect?"

"It's not an insect; it's an Eidolon."

"Oh. Well, it's scurried back to Uffern now. Too small for much of a reward, anyway."

Damn thing didn't even say good-bye.

I turned back to Hellsmoor. The Destroyer was coming fast now. I snatched up the spyglass. *There.* I could see it now: the warty blue skin, shimmering with hellfire, and the dull glow of the flames behind its eyes. Pryce no longer hung from its chest. He ran behind it, stumbling, like he was being dragged along. He'd bound himself to the Hellion, physically and spiritually. As the Hellion moved, so did he.

Difethwr rushed through the swamp, leaping from one hummock of grass to the next. Wherever it stepped, the grass withered or the water boiled. A fish hurtled from the water. Flames shot from the Hellion's eyes and blasted it to ashes.

I didn't see the white falcon. I hoped Difethwr wouldn't, either. The demon was barbecuing anything that moved.

At the foot of the cliff, the Hellion didn't pause. It sprang into the air, caught a handhold, and—moving incredibly fast—began climbing straight up. Pryce clung to its back like a baby monkey.

I stepped back. I tried to extinguish the flame that spurted from my demon mark, but it wouldn't go out. I shook my arm, I spat on it. I tried to break my connection to the Destroyer. Nothing worked. The demon mark burned like a welder's torch.

And then my right arm fell to my side, as useless as a burning log hanging from my shoulder. Difethwr was almost here.

I drew Darkblaze with my left hand and stood ready, trembling with eagerness for this fight.

With a whoosh and a roar, the sword burst into shadowy flame.

Difethwr leapt over the wall, dragging Pryce behind.

Now. I raised Darkblaze.

With a will of its own, my right arm came to life, clamping its hand around my left wrist and forcing the sword downward.

I looked down in confusion. My right hand grasped my left, holding it firmly against my thigh. I tried to make my right-hand fingers let go. I couldn't move them. I twisted, yanking with my left arm, but I couldn't get loose. Darkblaze pointed futilely at the ground. It wasn't just that my demon-marked arm wouldn't fight. It was worse. This new, stronger version of the Destroyer had control of that arm.

"Difethwr!" Pryce's voice made me look up. "Behind us!"

Edern charged, his sword ready to run the Hellion through. Flames gushed from Difethwr's eyes, stopping Edern and wrapping him in a fiery cocoon. Yellow, stinking smoke rolled across the arena. Demonsbane clattered to the ground. The Keeper did not burn, but his agonized screams sliced the air like jagged shards of glass.

I struggled against myself, trying to lift Darkblaze.

Flames pouring from its eyes, Difethwr raised its head, hoisting Edern into the air. The Keeper's clothing went from red to black as magic gushed from his body. The Hellion turned north, toward Uffern. Edern moved that way, too. Difethwr reeled in its eye-flames, bringing the dangling Keeper close enough to hug.

As my right arm tried to hold me in place, I hobbled toward them.

Edern screamed again. With a fiery blast, Difethwr shot the flames across the arena and past the far wall, over Uffern. Wrapped in fire, Edern flew with them.

The stream of fire held him there, in thin air, thousands of feet above the ground.

Difethwr cut off the flames, and Edern fell into Uffern. His screams echoed, then grew thin. After a moment, I couldn't hear him at all.

Fury exploded inside me. A good man had died as I stood by helplessly.

Difethwr turned as though I'd called its name. Flames flickered behind its eyes.

Darkblaze's own flames licked at the dust, the toes of my boots. I wrestled with myself, trying to raise the sword, but my right arm was like iron.

The Hellion couldn't seem to decide what to make of me. Was I its enemy—or was I part of it?

Pryce seized on Difethwr's indecision to grab control. He picked up Edern's dropped sword and walked over to me. The Destroyer followed him.

I watched them come, the wall at my back. Maybe, if they got close enough, I could swing my whole torso around and catch the Destroyer in the calf. With Darkblaze, it might be enough.

Pryce stopped just beyond my range. His sneer was uglier than ever.

"You've lost. With Difethwr as my shadow demon, nothing can stop me."

"You think the Destroyer is your shadow demon? Looks more to me like you're the Hellion's puppet."

Come closer, damn you. Just two steps. We'll see what happens to that sneer when Darkblaze bites your flesh.

Pryce stayed put. "Insults from a dead woman don't have much sting, I must say. Right now, Difethwr is confused. But as it comes back to itself, it will remember our previous alliance. It will remember the prophecies. Together, the Destroyer and I will unite the three realms—Uffern, the Darklands, and the Ordinary—under my rule." He studied me, then laughed. "For a while, I worried that perhaps you were the Cerddorion champion some prophecies foretell. But look at you. You can't fight. You can't even hold a sword." He spat at me, as Arawn had spat at him in Tywyll. The gob hit Darkblaze and sizzled. "I don't believe there is a Cerddorion champion. But, to be sure, I'll annihilate your kind. First you, then that horrible old bitch you call your aunt. After Mab, your niece Maria. And that's just the start. I won't rest until I've wiped every last drop of Cerddorion blood out of existence."

He laughed again. Never had I hated anyone more.

Pryce raised Demonsbane to strike me.

Behind him, the Destroyer roared and spun around. The Hellion's movement lifted Pryce from his feet, and he dropped the sword in surprise.

My right hand let go of my wrist as the demon-marked arm fell to my side. With a shout of triumph, I raised Darkblaze. Dusky flames ran along its blade. Eagerly, I ran at Pryce, angling the sword upward, aiming to drive its blade through his heart.

The point touched his chest. *Finally. Finally I'd kill the god-damn son of a bitch.* With all my strength, I thrust.

And Darkblaze shattered.

31

DARKBLAZE'S FLAMES SPUTTERED AND EXTINGUISHED AS THE shards of its blade fell to the ground. I stared at the hilt in my hand. *Darkblaze will not strike an angry blow.* That's what Arawn had said. I'd given my connection with Difethwr too much power over me. I'd hated Pryce too strongly. There was too much of the Destroyer in me when I attacked.

The sword had destroyed itself rather than be used that way. I let the hilt fall and drew a bronze-bladed knife.

The Destroyer bellowed and spun, whipping Pryce around as it moved. To my surprise, the Hellion's back was a mass of wounds. Black demon blood poured from numerous gashes, whose edges bubbled and melted, a sure sign they'd been inflicted by a bronze weapon.

Difethwr roared and turned again. That's when I saw Kane.

He darted out from a solid rock wall and hacked into Difethwr's back with his battle ax. When the demon spun around to smash its attacker, Kane faded back into the rock.

The ramp's exit—it was cloaked, so Difethwr couldn't see it. Kane was timing his strikes—rushing out from camouflage when the Hellion's back was turned, then ducking back into the doorway—to make the attacker seem invisible.

I snatched up Demonsbane. Edern's sword had a good, solid bronze blade, like the sword of Saint Michael, the sword I'd used to kill the Destroyer before. I whispered the invocation, then held my breath.

No flames appeared.

Too much to hope for. Still, the Destroyer would feel the bite of Demonsbane's bronze, as the wounds on its back showed.

Difethwr blasted its eye-flames toward the rock wall. *Shit.* The flames would go right through the hidden door. I stabbed Demonsbane into the Hellion's thigh, then ducked and ran around behind it as it turned.

"Over there!" Pryce shouted, pointing. With a blast of flame, Difethwr turned, but I dropped and rolled out of the way.

Kane emerged again and, aiming low, smashed his ax into the Destroyer's Achilles tendon. He must have severed it, because suddenly that leg wouldn't support the demon's weight. I struck a blow from the other side, and the Destroyer staggered, nearly falling.

Difethwr pulled in its eye-flames and hobbled toward Uffern, dragging its injured leg. It was running from us. Demons can regenerate, but they need to be in the demon plane to do it. From here, though, the demon plane was several thousand feet straight down.

Pryce stumbled beside the Hellion, bound to it, pulled along by its greater strength and will.

At the edge of the arena, they stopped. Difethwr looked over the wall. As the Hellion leaned forward, so did Pryce. He screamed at the sheer drop. Difethwr sat on the wall and swung its injured leg over the edge. Was that far enough into the demon plane for it to regenerate?

I wasn't going to wait to find out. With Demonsbane raised, I ran across the arena.

Pryce shouted a warning, and Difethwr turned its head. Flames flickered behind its eyes, then dimmed. The Hellion was weakening.

Kane ran beside me, his ax at the ready. We could do this, even without Darkblaze. Together, we could finish off the Destroyer.

We never got the chance. Difethwr pitched itself over the wall. Its bellows joined with Pryce's screams in an unholy duet.

Smoke hung over the spot where they'd fallen.

I ran to the wall and looked down. Below, Pryce and the Hellion tumbled through the air, limbs flailing. Their bodies grew smaller. Then the screaming stopped, like someone had hit a switch.

They disappeared. Pryce and the Destroyer simply vanished in midair.

Kane looked at me. Black demon blood smeared his cheek. "What happened?"

"I don't know." I gripped my sword, half-expecting the Destroyer to reappear. My right arm felt different. The burn of my demon mark had faded to an itch, and when I tried, I could move my arm again. I flexed my fingers and transferred Demonsbane to my right hand.

Whatever had happened to them, Pryce and the Destroyer were gone. Vanished into Uffern.

I slid Edern's sword into Darkblaze's sheath and turned to Kane. He stared at me with an expression I couldn't read.

"Why . . ." His voice died. He swallowed and tried again. "Why did Arawn's sword break?"

How was I supposed to answer? Because I let my anger overwhelm me? Because I hated Pryce more than I cared about my promise to Arawn? Because it felt good to give in to rage, to kill what I despised, whatever the consequences?

I chose the answer that rolled all those reasons into one: "Because there's too much of the Destroyer in me, Kane."

I walked away, going over to gather up what was left of Darkblaze. I cut a square from my tunic and lay the fragments on it. Tears blurred my vision, and I wiped them away impatiently. I didn't want to miss any pieces. Broken as it was, I would return Arawn's sword to him. Maybe his wizards could fix it.

Maybe my fairy godmother would show up with a magic wand and a happily ever after.

Kane helped me search for shards. He didn't speak. I knew what he was thinking, though. He was reconsidering that whole "I love you, whatever happens" thing. What else could it be? How could he love someone who, deep in her soul, would always be driven by the urge to destroy?

The norms thought monsters filled the streets and alleyways of Deadtown. But nothing there was more monstrous than me.

When we'd gathered up all the fragments we could find, I knotted the corners of the cloth, securing them inside.

Kane went to the stone wall and leaned against it, looking out over the Darklands. I joined him. A haze of smoke still hung over parts of the landscape, but it was dispersing. The Darklands would recover. Magic would help rebuild what was lost. I wished there was some magic that could fix what was wrong inside me. Edern had mistaken me for a demi-demon. Maybe he was more right than he'd known.

"There's the white falcon," Kane said, picking up the spyglass. The bird seemed to hover in the air, wings outstretched. Beautiful. "I've been thinking about how to trap it . . ."

Below us, the falcon jerked. It tilted, its wings splayed oddly, then plummeted from the sky. It dropped into the swamp and didn't rise.

I caught my breath. "What happened?"

"Someone shot it! I saw—I think it was an arrow. Come on."

Kane ran for the entrance to the ramp and disappeared through the cloaked doorway. I followed. Thank God Edern had switched the current. All we had to do was step into the flow.

On the trip down, I kept picturing the falcon's fall, how in a second it went from serene beauty to a crumpled ball of bloody feathers dropping awkwardly to the ground. It felt like my fault, even without Butterfly telling me so. Maybe it was. Maybe my bond to the Destroyer meant that whatever I admired, whatever I cared about, would be destroyed.

At the ramp's bottom, Kane felt along the rock wall until he found the cloaked doorway, and together we dragged Edern's boat through it.

Why the big hurry? I wondered. The falcon was dead. I walled off the part of me that cared about such things. It was too dangerous.

"I know where it fell," Kane said. "Near where we left the horses." He stood in the back of the boat and started poling us in that direction.

I looked around the swamp, not letting myself think about the white falcon. But I couldn't ignore the consequences of its death. I'd failed to fulfill my bargain with the Night Hag; she'd never accept the bird's corpse. I couldn't leave the Darklands. Like Edern, I'd be one of the many who didn't return. Maybe Arawn would let me take Edern's place here as a Border Keeper.

Kane grunted, pushing the boat forward. I could see the hummock where we'd left the horses. Only one stood there now. The other must have broken away in fear when the Destroyer passed by.

"It was right around here," Kane said, stopping the boat. He used the pole to probe the swamp.

Something floated beside the boat—a white feather. I plucked it from the water. It was spattered with drops and smears of rainbow colors—magical blood. More blood pooled on the water's surface, shimmering like an oil slick.

I showed the feather to Kane. "It's dead, Kane. The falcon is dead. Whoever shot it took the carcass away. He's probably roasting it right now."

Kane took the feather. He scanned our surroundings as though looking for smoke from a cooking fire.

"I was joking about roasting it."

"There's nothing to joke about, Vicky. This is a disaster. Without the falcon—" He sighed and handed the feather back to me. "Maybe the Night Hag will accept this as a token of your effort."

"I wouldn't count on that." I tucked the feather inside my tunic, anyway.

"Neither would I. But it's worth a try. And it's not our only bargaining chip."

"What are you talking about?"

He shook his head and pushed off with the pole. He steered the boat to the hummock and our remaining horse. "I'm sure I tied both sets of reins the same way," he said, undoing the knots.

"It doesn't matter." It didn't. The horse had probably gone home. Or else the Destroyer had blasted it into ashes that had blown away. There was nothing I could do about it. I was tired of struggling to fix things when I couldn't change them.

Kane climbed up onto the horse; I mounted behind him. I put my arms around him and leaned my cheek against his muscled back. *Ah.* For a moment I let myself enjoy his strength, his solidity. Home, I realized. His body felt like home.

But the white falcon was dead. Home? For me, the Darklands was home now. I loosened my grip on Kane and sat back. And then we were in the air, flying toward Arawn's palace.

THIS TIME, WE DIDN'T MEET ARAWN IN HIS SITTING ROOM. We were escorted to a small, bare room off the main corridor.

There was a table against one wall, but no chairs. The fireplace was cold and swept clean.

We didn't have to wait long. The door opened and Arawn strode in. "I'm very busy," he said, holding out his hand. His features were like granite. "Give me the remains of my sword."

"You know about that?" I handed him the parcel. He laid it on the table and opened it. Then he swept the whole thing onto the floor. I winced as pieces of Darkblaze skittered across the stone tiles.

"I know everything that happened. My sentries reported to me before you arrived here."

"You sent men after us?" My voice rose in anger. "Instead of spying, they could have helped us."

He whirled around, his face a picture of fury. "And ended up like Edern ap Nudd, one of my oldest and most trusted Keepers?"

Kane stepped between us. "If your men watched us," he said, using his reasonable negotiator's voice, "they know Vicky achieved her purpose. The Destroyer is gone from the Darklands."

"Yes." Arawn took a step back. "That is why I upheld my side of the bargain. It's already done. I summoned the Night Hag and gave her my hunting horn on your behalf. I also gave her Rhudda's magic arrow." An unpleasant smile touched his lips. "She was not pleased."

"Why not?" I asked.

"The arrow, as you recall, was broken. But she never said it had to be whole. She had no choice but to accept it. As for my hunting horn, when I learned of your deal, I acquired a new one. She did not specify which horn she wanted, so she could not refuse the one I offered. It was mine, it was a hunting horn, and it fulfilled the deal." He shook his head. "Mallt-y-Nos was very sloppy in her bargaining with you. Obviously, she thought you'd fail."

I touched the white feather inside my tunic. I *had* failed. Not that it mattered now.

"She had her amusement," Arawn continued. "She drove you into the Darklands and then left you here to become my problem." His face darkened into another scowl. "And look at the trouble you've caused me. Rhudda is an ass, but he's also my vassal. You humiliated him, and in doing so you undermined my authority. He kept order in a section of my realm that is now in disarray." He held up a hand and counted my sins on his fingers. "You killed my Magic Keeper and defiled the spring he guarded. Edern is dead because he tried to help you. You shattered the sword that has protected this realm for more than a thousand years." He kicked the hilt like it was a piece of trash. It spun across the room. "Inside your very body, you brought a demon here."

"Just a small one." Butterfly hadn't hurt anything. Well, except when it took a chunk out of Rhudda's nose—and the giant deserved that. The Eidolon had spent most of our trip through the Darklands lodged deep in my gut.

"That's not what I meant. Bringing in a guilt-demon is a serious offense in itself, but you did something worse. You came here marked by the Destroyer. My wizards tell me that it was *your* presence in the cauldron of transformation that resurrected Difethwr. If you and your damn demon mark hadn't gone into the cauldron, a far weaker demon would have emerged. In a very real sense, I blame you for the destruction of my lands."

Arawn had run out of counting fingers. He made a fist and pounded the table.

"Everything you say is true." The enormity of all those screwups made me want to look at the floor. But I met Arawn's gaze and held it. "But it's also true that I never acted with malice. I killed the Magic Keeper in self-defense. I even tried to help him after he fell. I defended you from demons in Resurrection Square. And I did send Pryce and the Destroyer—and even that guilt-demon—back to Uffern." I took a deep breath. "So in light of my service, I have one more favor to ask."

"A favor?" Arawn's expression suggested "favor" was the dirtiest word he'd ever heard. "And what is this *favor*?"

"I want to take Edern's place at the border."

"Vicky, no!" Kane moved forward like he could block the words I'd spoken.

I stepped around him. "I'm an experienced demon fighter. I can—"

"A Border Keeper? When your demon mark will constantly call the Destroyer back to this realm? No!" Arawn pounded the table again, making it shake. "I told you—I want you gone!" He pointed at me. "You are banished from my realm. If you are still in the Darklands by this time tomorrow, you will be executed.

Your body—its physical and magical manifestations alike—will be burned and the ashes thrown into Uffern, so I can rest assured that no trace of that Hellion remains here."

Banished. My head was spinning with Arawn's accusations and pronouncements, but that one word came through. Banished. And on penalty of death. What the hell was I going to do now?

"Mallt-y-Nos won't let me leave," I said. "The white falcon she wanted, the one that nested in Hellsmoor . . . it's dead." I pulled the white feather from my tunic.

Arawn stared at it. "More trouble you've caused me."

"If you'd order the Night Hag to let her leave—" Kane began.

"She *can* leave! She can leap off a cliff into Uffern for all I care." He waved the suggestion away and narrowed his eyes at me. "I told you, I will not interfere in your bargain. I have nothing to do with deals made beyond my borders. You have one day. Then your life is forfeit."

"Vicky." Kane put his arm around me and pulled me close against him. "I came here to bring you home. That's what I intend to do. Let's go. I'll talk to the Night Hag."

"You?" Arawn snorted. "Do you truly believe you have anything left to bargain with? Mallt-y-Nos owns you."

Dread made me go cold. "Kane, what did you offer her?"

"You don't know? Oh, that's rich. He pledged—" A far-off note sounded. Arawn looked sharply toward the door. So did Kane. A low, nasty laugh came from Arawn's throat. "Do you hear that, hound? Your mistress calls you."

Oh, no. The dread turned my heart to ice. The Night Hag—what names did the werewolves have for her? Huntress. Mistress of Hounds.

That's what Arawn called him—hound.

The note sounded again. "It's not the horn she wanted, but it's clear enough, is it not? Your time here is finished—go!"

Kane shuddered. He bent over as though someone had punched him, hard, in the stomach.

"It's only for a year and a day, Vicky. For you, I would have—" His words turned into a strangled groan as he began to change. Fire sizzled over him. A memory of that pain seared through me. His skin blistered and bubbled. Smoke rose, and the skin split and shredded to accommodate a huge body covered in black fur. His arms grew and his back twisted, forcing him onto all fours. A howl of anguish escaped his throat. Fangs sprouted and grew to terrifying size as his nose and chin stretched into a muzzle. The fire consumed his eyes, then glowed from the sockets. More flames shot from his nostrils. The pain of that inner burning—I reached out to touch him and he nearly snapped my hand off. The hellhound backed away, growling, acid dripping from his fangs.

In the distance, a long, clear note rang out.

Kane's head snapped around, tracking the sound. Another blast, and he bounded toward the door. He leapt into the air and passed through the solid door. Drops of acid sizzled on the stone floor after he'd gone.

I stared at the door. "A year and a day."

"Yes." Arawn sounded unaffected by the horrifying change we'd witnessed. "He agreed to serve the Night Hag as her hellhound for that length of time. She told me all about it. Tonight, and each night of the next thirteen full moons, he will run with her pack."

Kane couldn't have known, couldn't have understood, what he was getting into. It was the worst bargain he could make. That excruciating pain, the humiliation of being driven by the Night Hag. The running and running until his paws bled. For thirteen full moons, each of them three nights long. Including tonight, that made forty times he'd endure such agony.

He thought he was doing it for me. God, after tonight he'd despise me for the rest of his life.

"My men will escort you to the place where you entered my realm," Arawn said. "They will remain with you until you have managed to leave or, alternatively, until they have carried out your execution."

He pulled a bell cord. Immediately the door opened and four guards, dressed in green, marched in. All were heavily armed with swords and knives, with bows and arrows. One of them, a tall man with a coal-black mustache, looked familiar. Except the last time I'd seen him, he was wearing red.

"That's the Magic Keeper!" I peered at the man's face. He looked back at me without emotion. Yes, it was him—no doubt. The only difference was his eyes. The irises were rainbow-colored, like the spring he'd guarded. I turned back to Arawn. "You said I killed him."

"You did. Fortunately for him, the magic of the spring restored his life."

I'd poured that magic into his wounds. "So—"

"The fact that his life was restored is immaterial. He died, and you were the cause of his death."

But I wasn't thinking about the legal technicalities. I was thinking that the magic had cured him. If it did that for the Keeper, it could have cured Dad, as well.

I had twenty-four hours, time enough to find Dad. After we got to the border, I'd slip away from the guards and find Dad's hideout in the woods. He must have gone back to his cave. He'd hidden there from the Soul Keepers for a long time. Together, we'd elude Arawn's enforcers and live in the woods.

I moved toward the door, eager to get going.

"Victory," said Arawn, his voice softer, "I know you think me a tyrant, but I am a reasonable man. Despite the trouble you've caused, I bear you no personal grudge. I am merely trying to protect my people."

I wasn't so sure I believed that. *Sorry about the execution— it's nothing personal.* Uh-huh.

"Since demons attacked the realm, shades have poured into Resurrection Square to be restored or reborn. My Keepers can barely handle the flow. Still, I requested to be informed if a certain name appeared in *The Register of the Cauldrons*." He paused, watching my face. "That name, Evan Vaughn, was written into the book an hour ago. Your father has made his return."

The few hopes I'd managed to scrape up for the future crashed to the floor.

But wait—maybe he was still here. Maybe he'd been regenerated.

"Which cauldron did he pass through?"

"The book doesn't record that information. However, I spoke with the Cauldron Keeper who helped your father with his return. She knew him from his days at court."

"What did she say?"

"Resurrection Square is very busy right now, you understand. The cauldrons are working at full capacity. Shades who have been hurt in demon attacks are lined up along each set of steps and across the square. The Keepers have had trouble maintaining order, so many of our wounded are desperate for help. But because she knew your father, this Keeper was curious about his return. She's quite certain that his bridge stretched to the cauldron of rebirth."

Rebirth. The fate Dad had wanted to avoid. What was left of my heart cracked in two. Yet there was consolation in knowing his spirit had survived. Somewhere, a proud mother and father were fussing over a newborn animated by the spirit of my father. I hoped they'd take good care of him.

But he was lost to me.

And losing him a second time hurt every bit as much as the first.

32

NONE OF THE GUARDS SPOKE TO ME DURING THE HOUR IT took Arawn's flying horses to reach the border. Not a good idea to get too chummy with someone when tomorrow's to-do list includes killing her, burning her body, and scattering the ashes in Hell.

The Night Hag was already waiting for us at our destination. As we dismounted, she came out of the woods in her middle-aged aspect. As she greeted me, her skin sagged and wrinkled into old age.

She snapped her fingers, and her pack of hellhounds ran to her side. They sniffed the air and snarled, baring their teeth at me and my escorts. All were huge and fierce-looking. Was Kane among them? He must be, but I couldn't tell which one was him. They were all the same—angry and vicious and, I knew, in constant, terrible pain. Mallt-y-Nos pointed at the ground and shouted a command. The hounds crouched, quivering and growling, ready to spring up and attack.

A bony finger poked my arm, and I looked into the face of death. "I hope you have something for me," the voice of Mallt-y-Nos spoke from the bare skull. "Our bargain has rewarded me poorly so far."

"You got what you asked for."

"I didn't ask for a broken arrow. I didn't ask for a third-rate hunting horn." The young woman pouted. "Still, if you've brought me the white falcon, I'll consider our bargain fulfilled."

Without a word, I pulled the feather from my tunic and held it out to her.

"That's all?" Mallt-y-Nos knocked the feather from my hand. The hounds shifted, tense. "Where's the rest of it?"

"I can make you a better offer." I'd thought about this on the ride here.

Mallt-y-Nos was middle-aged again. She cocked her head. "What?" The question held guarded interest.

"Let me pass, and I'll take Kane's place among your hellhounds."

"Pfft." She batted my suggestion away. "A substitution of one for another gains me nothing."

"Then grant me the same terms you granted him—I'll join your pack for a year and a day."

The crone scowled. "I have enough hounds. I want a falcon."

"The falcon is dead. I can't help that. But if you let me cross the border, I'll . . . I'll owe you a favor. I'll be in your debt." An open-ended obligation on the hag's own terms—a terrible idea, but my very last resort.

"You're in my debt now, and you cannot pay. I'll not extend bad credit." She was silent as her appearance passed from old woman to corpse to skeleton. When she was young and beautiful again, she turned to the guards, smiling flirtatiously. "There's no sense in delaying the execution. Without the falcon, I'll never allow her to cross." She tossed back her hair and smoothed her hands along her sides. The guards watched with interest. "Let me kill her now. I'll have my hounds tear her to pieces. You'll find it good sport, I'm certain."

The hounds growled and lifted their heads, sniffing in my direction. Kane was among them. If the Night Hag gave the order, he'd have to obey. Would he understand what he was doing? Would he remember? The thought hurt worse than fangs and flames ever could.

The former Magic Keeper shook his head. "Arawn's orders were clear. She has one day."

The hag pouted again. "But one day will spoil my fun. Now, her lover is among my hounds. Tomorrow, the full moon will have passed and he'll leave my pack for a month."

"That's not my concern."

Mallt-y-Nos batted her eyelashes, but she was aging now and her attempts at persuasion were losing their power. Her voice went from sexy to shrill. "She's in default. I will have satisfaction!"

As they argued, a piercing cry sounded overhead. We all looked up. A large white bird circled in the sky.

"My falcon!" Mallt-y-Nos exclaimed. She squinted at me accusingly. "You said it was dead."

"I—Maybe I was wrong." But I'd watched it fall. I'd picked up the feather, seen the blood in the water. How had it survived?

The falcon circled downward, drifting near us. The aged Night Hag reached for it with gnarled hands, but it evaded her grasp and flew to me. I held out my arm, and the falcon landed on it. Its talons gripped me, but gently. The Night Hag watched it greedily.

"You said if I give you this falcon, you'll consider our bargain fulfilled."

She stretched out a hand, then hesitated. "How do I know it's the right one?"

"There's only one white falcon in the Darklands," said a guard. The others nodded in agreement.

Mallt-y-Nos bit her lip. As her face passed through death and back to youth, she stared at the bird.

"In front of these witnesses," I said, "will you let me cross the border if I give you this falcon?"

She nodded.

"Say it."

"Yes. Yes, I will."

Before I could move, the falcon hopped from my arm to the hag's shoulder. She quickly looped a leather thong around its leg. "Go, go." She waved toward the woods. "You may pass."

The hounds growled as I stepped forward, but they didn't move to stop me. I took one last look at the pack. Seven pairs of glowing, hostile eyes watched me. I searched them all, but I didn't see any trace of Kane. He was utterly changed, trapped inside his hellish form.

"I'm sorry," I whispered, hoping he'd understand. Then I walked forward without looking back.

THE FOREST AROUND ME DISSOLVED INTO DARKNESS. I HEARD the sighs and whispers of souls passing overhead. Instead of moving with them, I walked away from the light. This time there were no trees or roots to trip me. I walked confidently, until the blackness around me turned to gray, until a beam of silver moonlight struck my face. I blinked. I stood at the bottom of Purgatory Chasm, in front of the Devil's Coffin.

The night was cold and damp. I didn't have a coat—just gray sweats marked with large, red Qs. Damn. I was still under quarantine. And I was about twenty-five miles away from the quarantine site. If I wasn't there when the authorities came to let me out, I'd have some explaining to do. Probably from solitary confinement.

I had to get back to the Princeton retreat. I glanced up at the sky. I wouldn't go back tonight. You'd have to be insane to try to sneak into a werewolf enclosure during the full moon.

I wasn't crazy. I was cold. And hungry.

Purgatory Chasm was closed to the public—that chemical spill story. No one would come here for several days. I'd stay here tonight, then figure out how to get back to Princeton tomorrow.

Glad for the bright moonlight that lit the way, I climbed out of the chasm. I broke into the ranger station and turned on the heat, then rummaged through the staff kitchen and found some stale cookies and a peanut butter sandwich. I was pretty sure peanut butter doesn't go bad, so I ate it. I drank about a gallon of water, then lay down on a sofa to sleep.

I hadn't slept since Rhudda's castle.

Right before I drifted off, I thought I heard galloping hooves. Dogs baying. An old woman's cackle. And above it all, the high, thin cry of a falcon.

"VICTORY? VICTORY, ARE YOU THERE, CHILD?"

I heard Mab's voice even before I saw the blue-and-silver swirls that meant she was calling me. They billowed up now in my dreamscape.

"I'm here."

Mab didn't wait for me to picture her. She stepped out of the mist, waving it away with both hands. "Thank all the heavens," she said, a hand on her heart. "You didn't answer when I tried to contact you last night. But that's not what concerned me. I couldn't feel you at all. You were *absent*." She peered at me, as though making sure I was really there. "You went to the Darklands, didn't you?"

"They'll have to change that 'Spoils of Annwn' poem now: Except for *eight*, none returned." Nine, if you counted Kane. But after being a hellhound, would the man who returned be recognizable as Kane?

"You're nothing to boast about, child. It was a foolish, dangerous thing to do." Mab tried to set her features in her stern look, but relief washed the sternness away. "Tell me what happened."

"I saw Dad. He was hiding out to avoid reincarnation." The word *reincarnation* sat like a stone on my heart.

Mab smiled. "That does sound like Evan. But start at the beginning, child. How did you cross the border?"

No printing out images and dropping them into my subconscious this time. I didn't want to relive it all. So I told her the story, starting with Mallt-y-Nos and the bargain we'd made. Mab pulled a chair out of the mist and sat down, leaning toward me as she listened.

"You didn't see Pryce and the Destroyer fall all the way to the ground?" she asked, when I got to that part.

"They disappeared in midair. What do you think happened?"

"Myrddin somehow took control. That would be my best guess. His magic is strongest in the demon plane." Through her blouse, she clasped her bloodstone pendant. "Myrddin, Pryce, and the Destroyer as a single entity will be a powerful enemy—unless they tear each other apart."

"We can always hope." Not an approach that ever seemed to do much for me.

"We can do more than that, child, and most likely we shall have to. Now, tell me the rest. How did you manage to fulfill your bargain with Mallt-y-Nos?"

"Arawn gave her the broken arrow and a spare hunting horn, not the one he uses for the wild hunt. Because of the bargain's wording, she had to take them. All I had of the falcon was a white feather. I thought the bird was dead, but it flew in as I was trying to talk Mallt-y-Nos into letting me back into the Ordinary. Some coincidence, huh?"

"Not a coincidence, I think. A white falcon appears in the prophecies." She passed a hand across her brow. "Time grows short, child. You must return to your studies of *The Book of Utter Darkness* at once."

"It'll be a few days. I have to go back into quarantine. If I'm not in that cabin when they come to let me out, the Goons will be knocking on my door within the hour."

"As soon as you can, then. The book may be ready to show us new things."

"I'm not sure I want to see them." Not after what it had showed us last time.

She nodded, shuddering. "I'm afraid you must, though. That vision we both saw—remember, it is not carved in stone. Pryce hasn't won yet."

And neither had we. I'd never felt so far from winning in my life. I'd never felt so strongly that "Victory" was just a name. "Mab?"

"Yes, child?

"A while back, you said you wondered if you were right about me. What did you mean?"

"I said that? I'm sure I don't recall now." She brought up her colors, preparing to go. "Put it from your thoughts, child. You need rest after the journey you've had."

She was right. Already my mind was reaching for sleep again.

"And Victory . . ." Did she add a slight emphasis to my name? I was too tired to know for sure. "I'm glad you're one of the few who returned."

33

BY MORNING, I HAD MY PLAN. I USED THE RANGERS' COMPUTER
to email Juliet: Do you know a vampire who can drive? I need
a ride from Sutton to Princeton tonight.

While I waited for her reply, I checked the headlines (nothing
about plague virus) and played about two dozen games of Soli-
taire. It was the only game on the computer.

Juliet was still up. Her email came back: Yes. What trouble
are you in now? Don't tell me in an email, but I'll want all the
details later. Where, exactly, do you need to be picked up, and
at what time?

Once all the arrangements were made, I thought about sending a quick email to Gwen, explaining about family day. But it
was too risky. Gwen's nice, normal family didn't need to get
tangled up in my problems. I cleared the Web browser's history.
I turned off the computer and went to the kitchen to finish off
the stale cookies. Then I waited for nightfall.

WHEN THE HUGE BLACK PICKUP TRUCK SKIDDED TO A STOP
at the meeting point, I waited for the tinted window to roll down

before I stepped out of the woods. When it did, I was astonished to see Juliet's face peering out at me.

"Surprise!" She grinned, fangs gleaming.

"Juliet, you don't know how to drive."

"I'm a fast learner. Honestly, it's not as hard as it looks." The truck lurched forward. "Oops."

"Put it in Park. I'll drive."

"Put it in what?"

I stepped up on the running board, reached through the window, and shifted to Park.

"Now it won't roll."

Juliet stared at me. "Did you know your sweats are inside out?"

"That's to hide the big, red Qs on them."

"Oh, you *do* have a story." She grinned again. "Me, too."

She slid over to the passenger's side, and I got in. We settled into our seats, and then I pulled into the street. "You first. How did you get out of our apartment?"

Juliet leaned back in her seat and waved her leg in the air. "Look! No ankle bracelet! I'm a free woman." She sat forward again. "Thanks to an eyewitness to that judge's murder. The guy recorded the whole thing on his cell phone. It's taken him this long to get the courage to come forward."

I couldn't blame him. Seeing an Old One rip someone's throat out would make most people think twice.

"All charges against me have been dropped. I'm still helping with the interrogation, but they're paying me, not coercing me. And I'm dating that cute Goon, Brad. This is his truck."

"Nice." I was glad the last couple of days had been good to somebody. And maybe now the constant delivery of "as seen on TV" products would stop.

"Your turn," Juliet said. "Why are you wearing an inside-out fashion disaster and driving me to Princeton the night after all the werewolves have left?"

Her question reminded me I'd missed family day, and for a moment I wished I'd risked getting a message to Gwen. Too late now. I'd try to make it up to Maria when I got out of quarantine—if anyone in my family was still speaking to me.

"It's a long story," I said. "Remember that Harpy attack? Well, Pryce really was trying to kill me . . ." *Here we go again,* I thought. It took the entire drive to Princeton for me to explain everything that happened.

WHEN THE WOLVES LEAVE A RETREAT, SO DO THE GUARDS. Most of them, anyway. They keep a skeleton staff on hand to prevent teenagers and thrill-seekers from sneaking in. But Juliet and I had no trouble getting inside. I climbed onto her back, closed my eyes, and got a super-vampire-speed piggyback ride through the front gate and to the door of the quarantine cottage. The guard may have felt a breeze as we went by, but he never saw us.

The tricky part, and the reason I needed a vampire, was getting into the locked cottage. We stood in front of it now, inspecting the door. It was secured by three deadbolts, each with a different key. I'd watched from the helicopter as three Goons stepped forward, each opening one lock. The keys belonged to the authorities who'd stuck me here—I doubted they kept duplicates at the retreat.

"So," I said, putting a hand on the door, "this is my temporary home, and I'd like to invite you inside."

Juliet grinned. Her fangs glowed a little in the moonlight. She pointed at the locks—one, two, three—and each clicked open.

"The door is open," she said, bowing low with a flourish. "There lies your way."

Everyone knows that if you invite a vampire into your dwelling, nothing, not even a locked door, can keep that vampire out.

" 'There lies your way'? That sounds like Shakespeare."

"*The Taming of the Shrew*. I hope you don't mind if I don't come inside. Tonight, it's the taming of the Goon for me." She winked and disappeared.

I went inside and closed the door. When the locks clicked back into place, it was like I'd never left.

AN HOUR LATER, I WAS LYING ON THE LUMPY PLAID SOFA reading a copy of *A Midsummer Night's Dream* that I'd found in the bookcase, hoping to pick up a couple of new Shakespeare quotes I could use in conversation with Juliet. A weird way to say thanks, but she'd love it. The going was slow, though, and my eyelids kept drooping.

A mosquito buzzed around my head. I waved it off, but it was back in a minute, whining in my ear. Wait—this was April. April is too early for mosquitoes.

"That better not be you, Butterfly."

The whine turned into words. "Now, I could say how badly you screwed things up in the Darklands. Or I could say how disappointed your niece was when you blew off family day. But notice I'm not saying those things. So don't kill me. Like, I might add, you tried to do very brutally on top of that mountain."

"Go away." I put the book over my face.

"Wow, what a welcome. And when I'm here to keep a promise."

"What promise?"

"News from the demon plane. Boy, do you have a short memory. But never mind. I'll go. I'm sure you're not interested in knowing what happened after the Hellion and the demi-demon went over that cliff."

I sat up. The book dropped in my lap. "Tell me."

"Oh, *now* she wants to know. Well, maybe I don't want to tell you anymore. Not after you hurt my feelings."

"You're not making me feel guilty, Butterfly. Just annoyed."

"I don't like annoyance. Tastes bitter." That annoyed me even more. "Okay, okay. They both survived. Winked out halfway to the ground, then winked back in elsewhere in Uffern. Magic— the demi-demon's got a wizard who's helping him." So Mab was right about Myrddin. "But they're not exactly getting along," Butterfly continued. "They're fighting each other for control. Difethwr is powerful, even more than before, and it doesn't like being bound, but the demi-demon has the wizard on his side. It's a toss-up who'll win."

Neither, I hoped. Best-case scenario: They'd both perish in a battle to their mutual deaths. I knew the worst-case scenario, that they'd start cooperating and Pryce would push forward with his goal of expanding Hell, was far more likely. But with the Destroyer's rage and Pryce's arrogance, cooperation wouldn't happen any time soon.

Mab was right that time was short, but it hadn't run out yet. A small blessing, but I'd take it.

"Thanks, Butterfly." I couldn't believe I was saying thank you to a guilt-demon.

"*No problemo.* See you around."

"Don't count on it!" But the demon had gone. Really gone, it seemed, from the lack of gnawing in my gut. Make that two small blessings.

I gave up on Shakespeare and went to bed. Usually I was awake at this time of night, but my trip to the Darklands had thrown me off schedule. Otherworldly jet lag.

Clearing my mind, I let myself drift off. Butterfly stayed away. Either Tina's trick had finally worked, or else the rage and violence I'd felt on that mountaintop had been too much for it. *Hah*. There was a new trick for Tina: Get rid of your demons by scaring them away. I'd have to tell her about that one. I let the thought fade and settled into sleep.

In my dreamscape, I drifted through a blue sky, riding on a fluffy pink cloud. Wait—pink cloud? Not exactly typical in my dreamscape. Then I recognized the colors: Pink and blue meant Maria. My niece was calling me on the dream phone.

I imagined her sitting beside me on the cloud, her legs folded, her pale blonde hair pulled back in a ponytail. A minute later, there she was.

"Sorry about missing family day," I said.

She shrugged. "It's okay. Aunt Mab called. She said you couldn't make it."

Mab had called Maria on the dream phone? Gwen would freak. Thanks to the old enmity between her and Mab, she'd forbidden contact. "You know you're only allowed to talk to your mom and me on the dream phone."

"Grandma, too. Mom said." She tucked a stray wisp of hair behind her ear. "Anyway, Aunt Mab didn't call on the dream phone. She called on the *phone* phone. Grandma talked to her. She told us you were sick and couldn't go out. Are you feeling better?"

Mab must have gone into the village to call from the phone at the pub. And I'd thought she didn't pay attention to things like family day.

"I'm fine. I'll be good as new in a few days."

"Good, because we decided to wait on family day until next Saturday so you could be there."

"Really?" The lump in my throat surprised me.

Another shrug. "It wouldn't be any fun without you."

It took a minute to get the lump down to a manageable size. "So how are things going?" I asked.

"Okay. Mom and I aren't fighting as much. And I like having

Grandma here. But I miss you." Her smile was almost shy. "You really think you can come this weekend?"

"I'll be there."

"Cool. I won't make you promise this time, 'cause I know that sometimes, you know, things happen."

"Yes, things do happen." And all you could do was try and be ready for them.

Maria yawned, and I suggested she get some rest. The same thing Mab had said to me. For some reason, that made me smile.

THE WORST THING ABOUT QUARANTINE WAS THE BOREDOM. One day blurred into the next as I slept, read, and ate food out of cans. Over and over I did those things, all the while trying not to think about Kane.

I wasn't very good at that last part—not thinking about him.

All day long, I imagined where he was and what he was doing. I didn't understand the details of his work as a lawyer, but I could picture him in his office, surrounded by books and papers, or standing in the hallway talking to Iris or one of the younger partners. I could see him sitting in his favorite lunch spot, hamburger in hand, eyes on his laptop screen. I knew so well how he looked sitting on his sofa, holding the remote, loosening his tie by maybe half an inch as he watched the news. How he slept on his right side, face pressed into the pillow.

And I could see him as a wolf—graceful, strong, majestic. His fur silver, his alert gray eyes glowing like moonlight.

So many times, he'd come for me. He'd traveled to Wales to tell me I was important to him. He'd gone up against Myrddin to save me. He'd attacked the Destroyer when I couldn't raise my sword. And he'd traded his freedom for the chance to bring me back from the dead.

Mallt-y-Nos would try to break him. He'd resist—of course he would—but all that burning pain, all the humiliation and bending to a hostile will—it would take a terrible toll. What would he lose? His confidence? His easy smile? His belief in justice and higher ideals?

I didn't want him to lose *anything*.

And so the days passed, and Kane was always in my thoughts. The Kane I'd had. The Kane I'd lost. And the giant question mark of what he would become.

* * *

THE SUN HAD BARELY SET ON MY LAST NIGHT IN THE COTTAGE when I heard a howling in the distance. I looked up from my book. Wolves? I listened. No, not wolves. Baying hounds.

Two minutes later, when the fiery steed of Mallt-y-Nos burst through the wall, I stood in a hastily-made sphere of magical protection, ready to confront her.

Hellhounds surged into the room. They snapped and lunged, held back by the magic. I counted them. Six. Kane wasn't part of the pack. Of course he wasn't—the next full moon was three weeks away.

The horse pawed the floor, its iron hooves striking sparks. A skull peered around its neck. Mallt-y-Nos pointed a bony finger at me. As her youth returned, her face twisted in fury.

"I will not be cheated!" she shrieked. "Where is it?"

"I don't know what you're talking about." It took an effort to keep my voice steady as I looked into her shifting, terrifying face.

"My falcon! It's gone."

"I don't have it." But inwardly I cheered the falcon's escape. I'd rather picture it soaring over Hellsmoor than kept captive by this hag. "Maybe it's returned to the Darklands, back to its nest."

"No! I'd know if it crossed the border." Her middle-aged face frowned. "The bird flew to you before—it alighted on your arm. It's come back to you now."

"Look around," I said. "You won't find it here."

At their hag's command, the hounds tore through the cottage. On the hunt, they sniffed and searched everywhere. It didn't take long. The cottage was small, and I hadn't seen the falcon since I left the Darklands. The hounds returned to their mistress, heads low with shame at their failure, and cringed at her feet. She waved a hand and they yelped in pain.

Sick at heart, I looked away.

"I will make you a deal," said Mallt-y-Nos, squinting at me through aged, cloudy eyes.

"I don't think so. Our last deal didn't work out so well."

"Bring me the falcon, and I will release the werewolf from his servitude."

My heartbeat sped up. "You won't force Kane to be a hell-hound?"

"Not if you return the falcon to me. Alive."

I watched her face as it moved through death and back to youth. I had no clue where the falcon could be, but maybe I could locate it. Maybe it would come back to me, as the hag assumed. Still, something about this deal—something beyond the fact that the Night Hag was proposing it—felt wrong to me. My gut didn't like it.

Then I remembered. Mab said the white falcon was mentioned in the prophecies. Whatever was coming in the battle with Pryce and his demons, the falcon was involved. As much as I wanted Kane's freedom, I could not risk interfering with destiny. I would not trade away the lives of millions of people. Kane wouldn't want me to.

Slowly, I shook my head. "The falcon is not mine to give you."

The Night Hag screamed with rage. Her horse reared, her hellhounds cowered. When she spoke, it was from the blank face of a skull with fire burning in its eye sockets.

"Know this, Victory Vaughn. I am on the hunt for you. I and *all* my hounds. We will not rest until we run you down. Beware the next full moon."

She wheeled her horse around and left the way she came. Her hounds followed. And then I was alone in an empty room.

ON FRIDAY AFTERNOON THE GOONS HAD A FEW QUESTIONS before they let me out of quarantine. The big one: Pryce's body had disappeared—did I know anything about it? Sure. His connection with the Destroyer had allowed him to travel into the demon plane, but how could I explain that? Instead, I reminded them I'd been in quarantine for a week and didn't know a thing beyond the triple-locked door of this cabin.

We went over my official cover story what felt like a million times: I'd hit my head in a fall, been in the hospital as Jane Doe for a week, and had regained consciousness this morning. The hospital in question had all the records, as well as staff who'd swear I'd been there. Reminding me of the dire penalties I faced if I told anyone the truth about Pryce's plague attack—penalties like disappearing into Goon Squad custody for a whole hell of a lot longer than a week—they finally let me go.

They'd brought the Jag for me and parked it out front. When I walked through the gate, a man leaned on my car. Kane.

I didn't run to him. He didn't throw open his arms. He stood there with his arms folded, looking . . . haunted. But he'd come.

Looking around the parking lot, I didn't see his car. "How did you get here?" So many questions tumbling through my mind, so many things I wanted to say, and that's what came out of my mouth.

"Taxi," he said, then shrugged like a sixty-mile cab ride from Boston to the middle of nowhere was something he did every day. "Juliet told me you'd be getting out today. And I thought . . ." His voice trailed off, and a pained look flickered behind his eyes. "I thought I'd like to be here, maybe keep you company on the ride back to town. That okay?"

I nodded, not trusting my voice.

We rode in silence. More than once I started to speak, but it felt like talking would break something fragile. He reached over and laid his hand on my leg. I covered it with my own. For the moment, it was enough to have him beside me.

It was getting dark as we passed through the checkpoints into Deadtown. Zombies were beginning to venture out for the night. I pulled over in front of Kane's building and cut the engine. He put his hand on the door handle but didn't open it.

"I resigned from Simone's campaign," he said. "It's going to be a tough year."

I nodded. I wanted to tell him I knew how much of a sacrifice he'd made for me, but I couldn't find the words.

The silence stretched.

"Vicky, what I said on top of that mountain—"

"Don't." I wanted to spare him the awkwardness of taking it back. "It's all right."

His eyes sparked. "No, it's not. And I'm not going to leave this unsaid. I meant it, Vicky. I meant it then and I mean it now. There will be times when you don't believe that—when you *can't* believe that—but I swear it's the truth." He got out of the car and closed the door. He strode up the steps, but before he made it to the front door, I was out of the car and running up beside him.

"Kane."

He turned around. His eyes held pain and misery and more suffering than I could bear to see. But there was something else there, too. Love. After he'd seen the Destroyer in me, after he'd endured the anguish of running with the Night Hag, he still loved me.

Of all the times he'd come for me—running into danger, crossing the ocean or between the worlds—the short trip to Princeton and back meant the most.

"I . . . I feel the same way," I said, and the love in his eyes grew stronger than the pain. "Whatever happens."

We met in a kiss that said everything we'd struggled to express. And more, far more.

Kane was right. It was going to be a tough year. But we'd get through it. When the Night Hag tried to break him, I'd build him up again. Whatever happened. Because Kane was right about something else, too. Together, we were unbeatable.

THE WEATHER TURNED BEAUTIFUL FOR FAMILY DAY. IT WAS the kind of spring day—soft air, warm sunshine, scents of grass and flowers—that made people believe the long New England winter might finally be over. After lunch in the park, I sat at the picnic table, talking with Mom and Gwen, watching Nick and the kids kick around a soccer ball. Zack showed off for his baby brother, as Justin stood on the sidelines and watched, his thumb in his mouth. Maria, with her long legs, ran like a gazelle. And it wouldn't be much longer before she could run *as* a gazelle, if she wanted to.

"Maria had another false-face episode this morning." Gwen actually smiled as she said it.

"She told me. A walrus, right?"

Gwen nodded. "It was so different from last time. She took a picture of herself right away, so she knew not to be scared. Then she started playing around."

"She was so funny." Mom laughed. "She stood in front of the mirror making walrus faces. She got Justin and Zack making them, too. Then suddenly she said, 'My tusks are gone!' and asked what was for breakfast."

"Well," Gwen said, "it's hard to eat cereal with tusks, after all."

I was glad Mom was here. Gwen and Maria were both more relaxed, and I didn't feel like I was tiptoeing through some minefield between them.

"Look," said Mom, pointing. "There's that bird."

I twisted around to see, then caught my breath. In a tree at the edge of the park perched a large white falcon.

"You've seen it before?" I asked.

"It's been around the neighborhood for the past week or so," Gwen said. "We thought maybe it was migrating."

The falcon sat statue-still. It seemed to fix its stare on me.

Could it be the Hellsmoor falcon? Huge white birds of prey aren't exactly common in the suburbs. Maybe I could buy Kane's freedom after all.

If only I knew how this bird fit with the prophecies. So far, the book had been silent about that.

"Aunt Vicky!" called Maria. "Come and play. You can be on my team."

"Okay." As I stood, the falcon took wing. It circled once over the park, then flew away. The soccer ball rolled my way, and I joined in the game.

FAMILY DAY LASTED THROUGH SUPPER AND INTO THE EVE-ning. When the kids had gone to bed, I said my good-byes, promising to visit again in a few days. Out in the driveway, I was opening the door of the Jag when a voice said, "That engine is sounding a bit chuggy. When's the last time she had a tune-up?"

It was my father's voice. And it was coming from overhead.

I looked up. The white falcon perched on the garage roof. "Hi, Vic," it said.

I should have been speechless. But I managed one syllable: "Dad?"

The falcon flew down and landed beside me on the ground. He hopped through the open car door and perched behind the steering wheel. Then the bird that sat in the driver's seat of my car opened his beak and laughed my father's laugh. "I never thought I'd be sitting here again. Too bad I can't reach the ped-als." He looked at me with rainbow-colored eyes. Like the eyes of the Keeper who'd been brought back to life by magic. "Let's go for a ride," he said. "Just a quick spin around the block."

The falcon—Dad—hopped over to the passenger seat. I got behind the wheel and started the car. "How . . .?" I couldn't even begin to put words to my question.

"Drive, and I'll explain. I don't want the family coming out to see why you haven't left yet."

I backed the Jag into the street. "Does Mom know?"

"Not yet. Don't tell her. I want to let her know in my own time." He shook his head. "I don't know why you told me she'd gotten old. She's still a beautiful woman."

Even to a shapeshifter, this was weird. During a shift, the animal takes over. It has an animal brain; it follows impulses and instincts. It doesn't hold conversations and try to drive a car.

I steered down the street. "Okay, Dad, we're driving. Explain."

"You knew how much I wanted out of that place, Vic. But on my own terms, not as a whitewashed soul poured into some brand-new infant body."

"A falcon's body is better?"

"Yes, because I'm still me—my personality, my mind, my memories. I changed bodies, but I kept everything that was important. That's what I wanted, ever since I landed in the Darklands. So on that first day, when you told me about the Night Hag's demands, I thought maybe I had a chance. With the cauldron of transformation returned to Tywyll, maybe I could transform myself and hitch a ride out on the white falcon."

So that was Dad's theory. It was why he'd insisted on coming with me. He was grasping at a straw that might return him to the Ordinary.

"Why didn't you tell me?"

Rainbow-colored eyes regarded me, then blinked. "I wasn't sure it would work. And I didn't want you to worry."

"Not worry? You left the spring, Dad! I thought you'd died." Again.

The falcon ducked his head. "Sorry about that. I knew that sooner or later you'd be headed to Hellsmoor, and I had to get there first."

A realization hit me. "You killed the falcon."

"Only temporarily. Oh, and I borrowed one of your horses to get back to Tywyll."

Things were beginning to fall into place. "Arawn told me you made your return. But he said you went into the cauldron of rebirth."

"That's where my bridge led to, it's true. But it's like I told you, Vic, I had no intention of being reborn. When I went to Resurrection Square, I had the falcon—this body—under my cloak. There was such chaos there, no one noticed. I'd been chosen for rebirth, but the falcon hadn't. So even though the cauldron pulled me strongly, at the same time it repulsed the bird. The conflict was enough to keep me from sliding into the rebirth cauldron."

"So your bridge went there, but you didn't."

"Exactly. When I reached the end of the bridge, I waited until the Keeper looked the other way. Then I hopped down onto the platform—the one they'd erected for the ceremony—and jumped into the cauldron of transformation. I don't know exactly how it happened—it was kind of hazy in there—but my spirit was bound to this bird's body. The falcon flew out of the cauldron, but its spirit was mine." We drove in silence for a minute as I processed what he'd said. "After that," he continued, "you know the rest. I followed you to your meeting with Mallt-y-Nos and handed myself over. And you and I both got out of the Darklands."

The falcon that was my father preened his feathers.

"Mallt-y-Nos is looking for you," I said.

"Let her look. I'm faster than she is."

"She's not going to give up, Dad. She's a hunter."

"So am I, now. This body has amazing instincts. And don't forget—the white falcon of Hellsmoor can go where others can't. It's a useful skill, although I'm still figuring out how it works. The hag won't get me."

We'd gone around the block several times by now. I pulled over. "Will I see you again?"

"You bet, Vic. Remember what I said? You can't get rid of your old man that easily."

My old man who happened to be a bird.

I got out of the car and opened the passenger door. The falcon flew out, flapping his wings as he climbed. Then he soared like a white shadow across the night sky.

I watched until I couldn't see him anymore. I was glad for his freedom. Yet the words of the Night Hag were lodged like a knife in my gut: *Bring me the falcon, and I will release the werewolf from his servitude.*

My father, or the man I loved.

How could I possibly choose?

ABOUT THE AUTHOR

Nancy Holzner grew up in western Massachusetts with her nose stuck in a book. This meant that she tended to walk into things, wore glasses before she was out of elementary school, and forced her parents to institute a "no reading at the dinner table" rule. It was probably inevitable that she majored in English in college and then, because there were still a lot of books she wanted to read, continued her studies long enough to earn a master's degree and a PhD.

She began her career as a medievalist, then jumped off the tenure track to try some other things. Besides teaching English and philosophy, she's worked as a technical writer, freelance editor, instructional designer, college admissions counselor, and corporate trainer.

Nancy lives in upstate New York with her husband, Steve, where they both work from home without getting on each other's nerves. She enjoys visiting local wineries and listening obsessively to opera. There are still a lot of books she wants to read.

Visit Nancy's Web site at www.nancyholzner.com.